Reviews for *Candi, or the optimist*

"This book [*Candi*] represents everything that is
reprobate in modern society today. It illustrates,
perhaps more clearly than any recent novel,
the unfortunate moral and intellectual decay of
American literature."

–*The Southern Baptist Review*

"Degrading to women…
Candi is the most misogynistic novel I have ever
read."

-Dr. Deborah Gill- editor, *The Womanist Weekly*

"Those who appreciate good writing and good taste
will no doubt join me in hoping and praying that
Jay Michael Arnold will never again write another
novel."

-Susanna Joy, *Family Values Coalition*

Candi
or, the optimist

a picaresque novel by
Jay Michael Arnold

ISBN: 0615745474
ISBN-13: 9780615745473

dedication: 4444

The author would like to acknowledge all of the following for their unfailing support and constant inspiration; and without whom, the writing of this novel simply would not have been possible: caffeine, nicotine, amphetamines, alcohol, and the absurd fucking paradox that is human existence.

"Persons attempting to find a motive in this narrative will be prosecuted; Persons attempting to find a moral in it will be banished; persons attempting to find a plot in it will be shot." –Mark Twain

"The novel is not the author's confession; it is an investigation of human life in the trap that the world has become." -Milan Kundera

"A cowboy realized himself on a horse, and a man might be broke, impotent, and a poor shot and still hold up his head if he could ride."–Larry McMurtry

Chapter 1

Baytown, Texas; How Candi offered Mike a blowjob;
And how they crossed The Baytown Bridge and began their little odyssey

It wasn't the best of times or the worst of times, and that was the whole fucking problem...

These words, like a famous first line from a classic American novel, stoked the scullery campfire of Mike Curd's mind as he dandled his hard-on through his green corduroy pants.

His ride was a rental car. About fifteen minutes earlier he'd pulled into the Baytown Valley Truck-Stop. He'd parked near the air-pumps and left the car running to keep it cool. Mike noticed a beautiful young woman walking around the parking lot. She moved from pickup to pickup with deliberate yet casual ease. Eventually she stopped at a blue Ford pickup.

The greasy roughneck sitting behind the wheel of the blue pickup rolled down his window as she leaned inside. Mike watched her bend over. She leaned into the roughneck's rusty old ride and swayed her ass back and forth like a pendulum.

Later that same day, in a Pasadena beer-joint, that same roughneck would describe her to his buddies this way: "She was a damn whore," he'd tell them. "And here's what she looked like. Let's just say fellas. She wasn't wearin a damn yella ribbon if ya know what I mean?"

He'd take a swig off his Lone Star beer and say, "She was wearin these damn blue jean cut-off shorts. And dammit fellas! Them shorts hugged her tight ass in all the right ways. I'm tellin ya. Them were the kinda blue jean cut-offs that ride up in the back. Showed like half her damn ass cheeks. And they was frayed at the bottom. Ya know. With them little white strings just a danglin down on her damn thighs. Ya fellas know what I'm a talkin bout."

The roughneck would swill down the last of his Lone Star beer. He would order another and say, "And this whore had this damn threadbare white t-shirt on too. And boy do I mean threadbare, fellas! Sweet little baby Jesus in the damn manger suckin on Mary's titty! She had this damn threadbare white t-shirt that was one of them damn mid-driffs. Ya know the kind I'm talkin bout. Showed off her damn pierced belly button. And hugged her damn tits just the right way. In fact fellas. Her damn t-shirt was ripped right down the front. Right along the damn neck. And boy howdy! Did this damn whore have some damn nice tits! I mean this was some bone-if-eyed," the roughneck would adjust his hard-on through his jeans, "God created that shit on the seventh damn day cleavage, fellas!" All of them would laugh.

"And to top it all off," the roughneck would say, "This whore's damn t-shirt had a damn picture of Hank Williams Jr. on it. Yep. She was a country girl. Now it don't git no hotter than that, fellas." He would take another swig off his beer. "Dammit fellas! All that whore wanted for a damn blowjob was a damn ride across the Baytown Bridge too! Ya know what I woulda done to her? I woulda grabbed me a hand-full of that damn dark hair of hers. And then I woulda pushed her damn mouth down hard on my dick. I woulda pushed her mouth down so damn hard she woulda been tastin my damn cum for three damn weeks." The roughneck would raise his beer bottle in a toast. "Life just ain't worth a livin iffin ya can't make a damn whore choke on your dick ever now and then!"

Mike dandled his hard-on even harder through his green corduroy pants. Her ass teetered back and forth like a metronome atop her long legs and high heels. Mike believed she had the longest, sexiest legs he'd ever seen in his life.

Not far from Mike's car was a tall sign which read:

BAYTOWN
VALLEY

CHECKS
CASHED

Cruisin'
Fried Chicken

FRESH TACO S
SERVE HERE

WE CASH PAYROL
CHEK I

SHOWERS
RESTROOM
RESTAURANT
REST AREA

Keeping one hand dandling his hard-on, Mike reached with the other hand into his pocket. He opened up an orange prescription bottle and popped more amphetamines.

"So why didn't ya let that damn whore suck your dick?" one of the roughneck's buddies would later ask him.

"Well shit," the roughneck said. "The damn cops showed up and that whore scurried off like a coon in my headlights. And I figured. I was on my way home from a two week shift off the coast on a rig. And my old lady wouldn't like it if I ended up in the Harris County Hotel. Instead of showin up back at home tonight for my kid's birthday party."

The young woman hurried away from the pickup as the cops pulled into the parking lot. She sat down on the curb over near the air pumps. She quickly pulled a lollipop from her small purple purse. She unwrapped the wrapper and tossed it into the nearby bushes. She began sucking on the green lollipop and watching the cop car.

She was unusually good-looking for a whore, Mike observed. Of course, admittedly, he hadn't seen that many of them. Here's what he meant. She wasn't the kind of stereotypical Holocaust-victim-thin, heroin junkie whore that he imagined usually frequented truck stops and sleazy motels. She must be new to the business, he thought. I wonder if she charges more because she's still so young and good-looking.

She glanced up across the parking lot and their eyes met. She was now staring him down. As she sat there on the curb, her long legs opened and closed like the gaping mouth of a dying copperhead.

Mike's mouth went suddenly dry. He stopped dandling his hard-on and placed both hands on the steering wheel. He realized that she was definitely staring him down. Another pickup passed by her slowly, either uncaring or unawares of the cops. However, she didn't respond. She stared Mike down. Five minutes later, with beef jerky, a six-pack of beer and cigarettes in hand, the cops drove away.

Somehow she gracefully rose from the curb onto her long sexy legs. As before, Mike noticed that her steps were practiced; each one a deliberate and skillful balance between aimless meandering and predation. And yet, it seemed to Mike that she walked with more purpose this time. As if resolved somehow...

When she reached his car she leaned over and knocked on the passenger's side window. Her breasts pressed up against the glass. Her nipples were visible through her sweaty threadbare white t-shirt. It was your typical hot, humid summer day in Houston, Texas. On her t-shirt, in big letters right under the picture of the bearded cowboy with huge sunglasses, read the word: BOCEPHUS. She winked at Mike with beautiful baby blue eyes. The kind of baby blue eyes that reminded you of a George Strait song. And yet, Mike noticed, they seemed almost too blue to be real.

She smiled a cinematic, demur Southern-belle kind of smile. And then she knocked on the window again. Mike pressed the window button. His heart raced. As the window lowered she closed her eyes and drew in a long breath of cold air-conditioning. When she opened her eyes again she looked right into his and said, "Hey there, pardner. Tell ya what. I'll give you a blowjob if you fucking drive me across that there fucking bridge."

"Excuse me?" Mike said.

"You got cotton in your ears?" she said.

"What?"

"You fucking heard me. Oh, come on pardner. It's a heck of a fucking deal if you ask me. Get it? Fucking deal? Get it? Fucking deal? Get it? Get it?"

"Uh, I don't know"

"Oh come on now! You been fucking checkin me out for like twenty minutes. From all the way across this fucking parking lot. Yep. I fucking spotted you even before I chatted up that fucking roughneck in the blue pickup. You must be workin on a pretty solid hard-on by now." She stared down between his legs. She grinned. "Yep. I was right. Nobody knows pricks better than this girl."

"I don't know"

"Well, pilgrim," she said, feigning a Western twang and swaggering like John Wayne. "You fuckin better make up your pretty little mind pretty fuckin quick. Or else Old Marshall Dillon is gonna get wind of our little negotiations here. And then me and you are gonna be spendin the night in the Harris County Hotel. If you know what I fucking mean?" She smiled.

Mike panicked. He felt like everyone at the truck stop was suddenly staring at them. Without really thinking he unlocked the doors of the car. She didn't wait for an invitation. She opened the door, hopped in the passenger's seat and said, "Let's blow this joint, pardner. Get it?"

Mike was too nervous to get the joke, and too nervous to shift the car into drive.

"Well come on, pardner," she said, "Let's ride!"

✳ ✳ ✳

As Mike pulled the car onto the road she leaned forward and adjusted an ankle bracelet. On the back of her t-shirt underneath the confederate flag it read: HERITAGE NOT HATE. The words puzzled Mike. But his eyes quickly averted downwards. Leaning forward, her shorts tugged down revealing a dark-blue thong. She had a really nice ass, Mike observed again. And then, as if from propriety, he averted his eyes quickly away. Even though she hadn't noticed him and nobody was looking.

She sat up, turned to face him and said, "You seem pretty nervous there, pardner. How about I," she held up her hands and made quotation marks with her fingers, *break the ice*, by tellin you a joke. I mean would that help?"

Mike shrugged.

"Here's one of the best fucking jokes. Ever told by anybody anywhere," she said, "Ever! I'm actually fucking famous all over H-town for tellin this joke. Yep. It's true! Ask anyone in fucking Houston about this joke. And they'll point right to me and laugh their fucking ass off. You know, pardner. My Uncle Tom always used to say- The best jokes are always stories... You think that's true?"

Mike just shrugged.

"Ok. Well. Here's the joke. So there's this young teenage guy hitchhikin along Highway 59. Right here in Houston. South on 59 towards Sugarland. Anyways. After a little while an eighteen wheeler truck pulls over. And the trucker invites him to get on up in the cab. So the young guy crawls into the truck and thanks the trucker."

"So they get goin down the highway. Well the young guy notices a fucking monkey just sittin on the fucking dashboard. Right there in the cab of the truck. And he's really fucking puzzled about this monkey. You know? So anyways. The young guy finally asks the trucker- Why's there a monkey on the fucking dash?"

"And then the fucking trucker says to him- I'll fucking show you why. So then the trucker just fucking reaches over and slaps the ever livin fucking shit outta that fucking monkey. I mean he just slaps that fucking monkey as hard as he fucking can. And then right on cue. That monkey fucking jumps down off the fucking dash right onto the trucker's lap. Then that monkey fucking unzips his pants. Whips out his dick. And starts givin the trucker a blowjob." She paused and chuckled as if imagining the scenario.

"Anyways. The monkey finishes off the trucker. Cleans him up. Puts his dick back in his pants. Zips him up. And then fucking jumps right back up on the fucking dashboard. So of course the young guy is fucking shocked all to the bad place. Then the trucker turns to the young guy and asks him- You wanna try it?"

"And then the young guy. He's scared shitless, right? He says to the fucking trucker- Ok... Just don't hit me that hard..." She slapped her knees and laughed out loud. "Get it?? Just don't hit me that hard... You know?? Like how hard the trucker hit the monkey... Get it?"

Mike didn't laugh.

"Oh well," she said, "That's still the best fucking joke ever!"

Mike thought her joke was funny but he was too nervous to laugh. His mouth and throat were too dry and his stomach ached a little.

"Well," she said, "Now that the fucking ice is all broken. I reckon we'd better get down to business. I mean your dick ain't gonna suck itself, pardner. Am I right?" She popped the lollipop from her lips and set it on the dashboard. "Let get to it..."

It was weird, Mike thought. He'd always imagined a whore being more callous about the sex act. Somehow more resentful of what she was being forced by society to do. Oddly enough, he mused, she almost seemed eager.

She climbed over towards him and leaned her head down into his lap. Even though she was sweaty she still smelled good. Not like perfume. More like raspberries. She glanced up at him and smiled. "By the time we get to where we're goin, pardner," she said, "I'll have you whistlin fucking Dixie." She chuckled at herself and said, "And I don't even fucking know what the fuck that means!" She laughed out loud. "I just made that shit up. Just now"

As the car ascended the steep bridge her body leaned against his. She unzipped his pants and massaged his hard-on with one hand. And then, she deftly nudged her other hand down around his balls.

Mike took a deep breath. He felt like he was on a roller coaster slowly clicking its way upwards towards the big drop. The Baytown Bridge was six lanes wide. The sunshine blistered and glared off the asphalt. He tried not to swerve. He paid as much attention as possible to the other cars making their ascent alongside them.

She licked the hard shaft of his dick up and down. She sucked on the head of his dick. And then she made that same popping noise with her lips that she'd made a few minutes before with her lollipop. Normally Mike liked to watch while getting a blowjob. But all he could do was lean back and count the bridge's steel cables and stone columns.

***

The Fred Hartman Bridge, or as the locals call it, the Baytown Bridge, was built in 1997. It arches gracefully for nearly three miles across the massive Houston ship channel. At the apex of its arched underbelly its cable-stayed columns appear pert against the industrial jungle of petroleum refineries stretching all the way to the nearby Gulf of Mexico It replaced the Baytown Tunnel, a two lane underground tunnel built in 1953, facilitating traffic between the small cities of Baytown and La Porte, just east of Houston.

Way back in 1903, the famous Goose Creek Oil Field was discovered in Baytown. It's amazing when you think that the Texas Oil Boom and the evolution of Houston into the busiest port and fourth largest city in the United States all started with some bubbles in a swampy bayou. Today, the Baytown Refinery is the largest oil refinery in the United States. It employs over half the city. It sprawls over 2,400 acres of land along the ship channel, processing about half a million barrels a day and glowing at night like a city unto itself.

***

She snapped the elastic of his underwear against his waist. Her head was still in his lap. Mike breathed in deeply. He felt relaxed now. He slowed the car down as they neared the foot of the bridge. She deftly zipped him up but left his belt unbuckled. It was the absolute best blowjob ever, Mike thought. And there was something about the altitude of the bridge and the descending motion of their ride which heightened the experience. Of course it had been quite a while since Mike had done more than just beat off. Plus, she'd probably had a lot of practice.

She sat up and reclined back in her seat. She reached over and retrieved her lollipop from the dashboard. She dusted it off and stuck it back in her mouth. She turned to look him up and down, smiling kindly as if she'd just given a lost and starving puppy some food.

Mike didn't know what to say to her. He wished she would say something first. But she only stared him down, still smiling that charitable smile of hers. In addition to the relief provided by the blowjob, Mike felt surprised by his performance on the bridge. One of the things he promised himself when he left Connecticut for this road trip was that he was going to pick up a whore. He knew it was a classic literary motif- very Salingeresque. And he thought for sure that he could get an entire chapter for his novel from the experience.

And yet, in the past, every time he pondered being with a whore, Mike always worried that he wouldn't be able to perform sexually. There was something about paying for sex that unsettled him. Something about the desperation behind whoring which made him think he'd be incapable of strictly enjoying the carnal experience itself.

It was the same story for him at strip-clubs. Granted, Mike had only been to two strip clubs in his lifetime. But he'd hated both experiences. He enjoyed the naked women. And he definitely got a boner both times. But there was always a measure of sympathy he felt for the strippers.

Mike saw strippers and whores as essentially victims. And in a way, he'd always felt that to pay someone for sex was kind of like rape. Of course, he mused, that could just be his feminist ex-girlfriend Lisa talking. Nevertheless. Mike was pleasantly surprised that he'd remained hard and then cum so forcefully in her mouth. He thought to himself- Take that Holden Caulfield!

As their ride reached the bottom of the bridge Mike turned to her. He wondered if she could sense his pride. "So," she said, finally breaking their awkward silence, "What's a dazzling urbanite like you, doin in a rustic setting like this?"

"What?"

"You got cotton in your ears, pardner? Ok, listen up. I'm gonna say it just one more fucking time. For the dumbass sittin right next to me." She spoke slowly this time. "So... What's a dazzling urbanite like you, doin in a rustic setting like this?" She moved her hand in the air slowly as if coaxing him.

Mike just looked puzzled.

"Come on, pardner! What fucking flick is that line from?"

"I have no idea"

"What do you mean you have no fucking idea?"

"You mean it's from a film?"

"Yep"

"I don't know"

"It's from *Blazing Saddles*! Come on, pardner! Don't you fucking remember that scene? *Blazing Saddles*!" You remember! Gene Wilder plays the fucking Waco Kid. And he says to Clevon Little, who plays Bart the black sheriff- So what's a dazzling urbanite like you, doin in a rustic setting like this? That's one of my three favorite fucking flicks of all fucking time!"

"I've heard of it," Mike said, "but I've never seen it."

"Oh my fucking God! You gotta be fucking kiddin me?" She sucked on her green lollipop, smacking it between her lips, making that popping sound again. "You know what, pardner? *Blazing Saddles* just might even be better than my blowjobs!" She laughed. "And that's really sayin somethin too!"

✳✳✳

They rode down off the bridge onto 146 South into the city of La Porte and then exited on Barbours Cut Boulevard. "Take the first left right up here," she said, "and then pull into that Exxon."

The sign read:

EXXON

PORT AUTO
TRUCK STOP

ROOMS EEKLY
$189

FISHING BAIT

"Just pull in here," she said. "Well, pardner. It sure was a pleasure doin business with you. Even if I did have to fucking suck your sweaty dick. And swallow your fucking cum." She laughed and punched his shoulder playfully.

Mike pulled the car into the station and parked near the sign. As she grabbed for the door handle, Mike reached over to touch her arm, to stop her. But he stopped himself. "Do you need anything?" Mike said. "Let me buy you something before you go. Do you need anything else?"

"Now why the fuck would you wanna do that? I mean you already fucking busted your nut in my fucking mouth. Am I right?"

"I don't know," Mike said, looking down. "I guess I just feel like a ride across the bridge isn't enough..." Mike searched for the appropriate word, and then said, "...compensation..."

"Listen up, pardner. They don't let anybody walk across that bridge. So you actually did me a big favor here. I mean, honestly, I'd rather suck the strange dick of somebody like you than have some roughneck fuck me in the ass with a corncob in a truckstop bathroom." Again she grabbed for the door handle.

"Wait," Mike said. "What do you mean *somebody like me?*" He realized how awkward his concern sounded. And yet he felt somehow compelled to ask her. "You don't even know me. For all you know I could've been an undercover policeman."

She burst out laughing. "Oh my fucking God! That's almost as fucking funny as the trucker with the monkey joke!" She bit down into her lollipop. She crunched the candy shell and then chewed the pink bubble gum inside. "I mean fucking get real, pardner! You got," she raised her hands and made quotation marks with her fingers again, "*nice guy,* written all over you. Wait! Let me guess." She looked him up and down and scratched her chin deliberately to feign contemplation. "I'll bet you were worried about whether you'd be able to cum in my mouth or not. Weren't you? Am I right?"

Mike realized his face betrayed the accuracy of her guess. "Hey," he said, "For Chrissakes, you don't have to insult me."

"Insult you? How the fuck did I insult you? I mean was it the whole," she made quotation marks again, "*nice guy,* comment? Or the whole you worryin about bein able to cum in my mouth comment?"

Mike didn't know exactly which one it was, or for that matter, why he was so annoyed. All he knew was that all his life, every time he heard the words *nice guy,* he translated it *smuck.* "Never mind, for Chrissakes," he said. "Like you said before- Nice doin business with you."

"Goddammit," she said, "Lighten the fuck up, will you? I mean. You're actin like a fucking housewife surfin the crimson cuntwave." She gently put her hand on his arm. "Listen up, pardner. Believe me. There's nothin wrong with bein a nice guy. This world is a fucked up place. And us women we need more nice guys. And as for you worryin about bein able to cum," she said, and then swallowed her gum. She licked her lips and smacked loudly with a smile. "Trust me, that wasn't a problem. You did *real* good, pardner. Just like a *real* man."

She slid her hand off his arm and leaned back against the seat. She savored the air conditioning once again. "Now," she said, "Get your fucking nice-guy ass into that fucking store. And buy me some more fucking lollipops. Charms Blowpops... Sour apple... You know. The bright green ones." She fiddled with the radio knobs. "And get me a few lottery tickets too. I'm feelin fucky today."

"Fucky?"

"Yep. I'm feelin fucky. It's short for fucking lucky."

'Where did you hear that?"

"Hear that? Fuck you. I fucking made that shit up, just now!"

"I'll have to remember that"

"And oh yeah. When you're in that fucking store. Grab me a copy of *The Houston Press*. It's fucking free. And it's usually on a rack near the front fucking door of the place."

As Mike reached for the door handle she hit him on the shoulder with the back of her hand. He turned to face her. She spit on her palm and then stuck her hand out offering him a handshake. "By the way, pardner," she said smiling, "Call me Candi- with an *i*."

Chapter 2

La Porte, Texas; An etymology of the word cunt;
The Ballad of Lisa Bulldyker;
And how Candi made Mike use the word cunt and what
happened afterwards

Candi ripped the wrapper off her green blowpop and stuck it in her mouth. "Can we turn up the air conditioner, please?" she said. "Yep, it's another hot and humid fucking day! Welcome to fucking Houston, Texas. The greatest city in the fucking world!"

"Are you being facetious?"

"Am I bein what?"

"Are you being facetious?" Mike said. "It means, sarcastic? Are you being sarcastic when you say Houston is the greatest city in the world?"

"Absolutely fucking not! Houston *is* the greatest city in the world."

"Clearly," Mike said, shaking his head, "You've never been to New York City."

"Hey pardner. Fuck New York City. I mean fuck New York City in the fucking ear with a broken beer bottle. New York City is old fucking news. I mean it's been fucking done. Just you wait and see. You're gonna absofuckinglutely love Houston. I tried to leave this city once upon a time. Didn't work out for me. And I'll damn sure never ever ever try to leave it ever again." She folded the lottery tickets and stuck them in her back pocket.

"Here's your *Houston Press,*" Mike said, handing her the magazine. "And I picked up a copy of *Texas Monthly* too. It seemed like a cool magazine. I thought it might give me some insight into Texas…for my novel."

"Oh my fucking God," she said. She snatched the *Texas Monthly* from his hand, nearly ripping its glossy pages. "What a fucking waste of money! You'll never get that $5.99 back!"

"This kind of condescension," Mike said, "coming from the woman who just asked me to buy her lottery tickets? Talk about a waste of money."

"Seriously, pardner. Let me tell you. *Texas Monthly* is the biggest rich-asshole circle jerk of all fucking time. I mean it's just a bunch of rich assholes writin about their rich-asshole lifestyles. That only them and their rich-asshole friends are rich enough to actually fucking afford."

"For Chrissakes," Mike said, smiling, "Why don't you tell me how you *really* feel?"

"You know what really gets my fucking goose? It's that this great state of Texas is actually a really fucking great place to live. In fact. It's probably the best fucking place to live in the whole goddamn fucking world. And Texas is a huge fucking state too! I mean there's lots to fucking do here. Lots of history. And lots of interesting fucking people and places!"

"So," Candi said. "You'd think since all that shit's true about Texas. That a fucking magazine called *Texas Monthly* would have somethin interesting to fucking write about. Am I right?" Candi flipped through the glossy pages. "Hold up a second. As soon as I fucking wade my way through all the million dollar jewelry and designer clothes ads. I'll fucking show you what I fucking mean."

Mike was amused by Candi's patriotism for the state of Texas. And yet, he didn't find it at all inspiring or endearing. He had once read an essay in *The New Yorker* which argued that all forms of patriotism, whether on the national or state level, betrayed a kind of intellectual and emotional naiveté. Candi's childish fervor for her home state of Texas, Mike reminded himself from the essay, was fueled by typical middle-American, Norman Rockwell sentimentality, and Christian moral values.

And Mike expected nothing less from this whore. In fact, he was hoping she would keep it up. This is perfect fodder for my novel, Mike thought, recalling yet another essay on the art of the novel, describing this experience as a literary goldmine of plebian predilection.

"Here we go, pardner!" Candi said. She opened up the pages of *Texas Monthly*, "I finally fucking found an article. Goddammit.

There's a fuck ton of fucking advertisements for million dollar ranches and boutique clothes in here. I guess these rich pricks who publish this piece of shit just don't realize that there just might be a few fucking poor people left in the great state of Texas. Either that or they just don't fucking give a shit."

"So what's the article about?" Mike said, hoping to interrupt her proletarian rant.

"Oh my fucking God! You're gonna fucking love this shit. Wow! This is sooo fucking perfect. And sooo fucking typical. This is exactly what I'm fucking talkin about. This article here is called *Do I Dare To Eat a Peach?* Listen to this shit." Candi read the beginning of the article aloud, laughing as she read.

Mike wasn't surprised that the Prufrock reference in the title of the article was lost on this whore.

After reading about half the article, Candi laughed her ass off. "Wow! Can you fucking believe this fucking guy?"

"I have to agree with you," Mike said. "That does seem pretty masturbatory."

"Do I wanna eat a fucking peach?" Candi said, feigning a snobby accent that sounded more British than anything. "Or do I wanna eat a cheeseburger? Or how about some fucking oatmeal? Yep! A whole fucking article where this self-important rich-asshole douche-bag asks himself why he's such a picky eater!"

Mike chuckled.

"I'll tell you what I'm askin," Candi said. "I'm askin why the fuck anybody else but this rich-asshole fucking cares! Talk about investigative fucking journalism, huh? See what I mean? Fuck *Texas Monthly* right in the ear with a prickly pear cactus."

Mike couldn't help but laugh along with Candi at the absurd narcissism of the article. And he couldn't agree with her more. Recently Mike realized that he'd grown anesthetized to the special kind of bourgeois conceit published in the predictable pompous pages of magazines like *The New Yorker* or *The Atlantic*.

In fact, a few years ago, Mike had written a letter to *The New Yorker* but never mailed it. In it he'd claimed that, "Elitist intellectuals, academics, journalists and socialites pump this historic publication full of their privileged spunk; making it more and more difficult to turn its hallowed, albeit sticky pages." Mike enjoyed being clever.

But Mike was surprised that this common whore could've come to such a similar conclusion. Namely, that *Texas Monthly* much like *The New Yorker*, serve only the purpose of fashionably decorating the coffee tables of the American aristocracy.

"Who is this fucking shithead who wrote this, anyways?" Candi said. "I mean who does he think he fucking is? And how arrogant of an asshole do you have to be? I mean to actually think anybody besides you and your fucking rich-asshole friends and family gives two shits about you bein a picky eater when you were a fucking kid?"

"What's his name?" Mike said.

"John *Splooge* or somethin like that"

They both laughed together.

"Wow! I mean how the fuck do you even get the chance to write an article like this? I mean who the fuck sits down and thinks. Yeah, that sounds like a great idea for an article! What the fuck?"

"He's probably an editor," Mike said. "That's how it works."

"What do you mean?"

"He's probably an editor. So *he's* probably the one who sat down and thought it was a great idea. That's how he got to write it. He's probably one of the editors. Maybe even the chief editor. Look in the front of the magazine for his name." Mike was genuinely curious now. And honestly still surprised by the fact that he and Candi could share the same sentiment.

Candi thumbed through the front of the magazine. "Oh my fucking God," she said. "You're absolutely fucking right! Here's his fucking name! John Splooge! You're fucking right, pardner! He's one of the fucking senior editors! What a fucking stuck-up prick asshole!"

"It happens all the time," Mike said. "Literary nepotism. It's a kind of masturbatory journalistic incest."

"Ok, honestly, pardner," Candi said. "I didn't understand one fucking word you just said. But I think I fucking agree with you!" She laughed. "I'll tell you this, pardner! I would love an opportunity to meet John Splooge. I really would! Just so I could kick him in the fucking nuts. And tell him to stop wastin everybody's fucking time."

Mike and Candi both laughed their asses off. "I'd tell him," Candi said, "that if he wants to whack-off to pictures of himself holding a fork and knife," she held up the picture in the magazine. "Then do that shit in private like everybody else! I mean have some fucking decency for fuck's sake!" Candi rolled down the window and tossed out the magazine.

This was one of those rare moments in life, Mike mused, making sure to remember the exact wording for his novel, when two people who are nothing alike, laugh together about the same damned thing, for nearly ten minutes straight.

"Now," Candi said, "*The Houston Press*! That's a different fucking story!"

"Oh yeah, why is that?"

"Well, for starters. It's fucking free. So anybody can fucking get a copy and read it if they want. It's not just for rich-assholes. And it's fucking awesome. Let's not forget that part! I mean *The Houston Press* has got shit for everybody to do on the weekend. Rich or poor or whatever. It's got fucking investigative journalism. It's even a little fucking raunchy sometimes! Holy fuck! I fucking love *The Houston Press*."

"You like it?" Mike said, smiling, "Really? I couldn't tell."

"Seriously though, pardner. You know what I wish?" She rolled up the magazine with both hands. "I wish I could fucking roll up each week's copy of *The Houston Press*, just like this. And then stick it in my pussy and fuck myself with it. I mean it's that fucking great!" She pounded the rolled up magazine against her crotch and moaned and screamed. "I would fucking cum all over that shit!"

Mike winced a little but couldn't help laughing.

"I pick up *The Houston Press* every fucking Thursday. And then I plan my whole fucking weekend with it. Seriously. I live my fucking life by *The Houston Press*. It's kinda like the Bible. It'll never steer you wrong."

Candi was unbelievable, Mike thought. He wished he could record her every word. She was a Rabelaisian goddess in the guise of a common whore. She seemed more like a character out of a classic American novel than a real life common truckstop whore. Candi was quite the raconteur, Mike observed. Nobody could just make up dialogue like this. And dialogue like this was just what he needed for his novel. It was literary gold. This common whore, Mike realized, was beginning to look like the perfect muse.

The only problem, Mike thought, was that he had planned to just *start* his journey in Houston. He was planning on heading out of town immediately. He would take Interstate 10 going west and drive all the way to California, very Steinbeckesque.

His novel would be the ultimate roadtrip-odyssey-journey novel. Mike envisioned the caption in the *New York Times Book Review*- BESTSELLING AUTHOR REVITALIZES THE PICARESQUE NOVEL GENRE. His novel would be a satirical homage to classic American literature, especially southwestern literature. In it he would lampoon the venerable works of that wild bunch of American writers: Twain, Melville, Hemingway, Salinger, McCarthy, McMurtry and many others.

"So," Mike said, "How far is it from here to downtown Houston?"

"Well, pardner. We're actually in La Porte, Texas right now. But downtown Houston's not too far from here."

"Hey, I've got an idea," Mike said. "I'm writing a novel."

"Oh yeah?"

"Yeah"

"That's pretty fucking cool. I guess."

"Thanks"

"What's it about?"

"I don't know yet. But it's going to be about a journey."

"You mean like a road trip?"

"Sure"

"To where?"

"Well, I don't know yet."

"How about to nowhere special?"

"What?"

"Never mind"

Mike was too excited about his new idea to ask her to explain. "So," he said, "I'm writing this novel. And I want to put the city of Houston in it. I want to start my journey right here in Houston, Texas."

"Ok"

"So here's my idea. Why don't I give you a ride downtown? And you can show me around Houston?" Mike decided he was going to milk Candi for all the local flavor, culture and character dialogue he could get out of her, and then get back on the road.

Or put another way. Mike would prospect for this whore's literary gold for as long as possible.

"You mean like me be your tour guide?"

"Exactly"

"You mean like this?" Candi said. "Way back in 1836 the Battle of San Jacinto was fought right over yonder." She made a dramatic pointing gesture. "It's the battle where Texas won her independence from fucking Mexico. Let's just say. Sam Houston and the rest of them Texians kicked some fucking Mexican ass that day! It's La Porte's claim to fame, you know?"

"Which reminds me of a joke," Candi said. "How do they know there were six thousand Mexicans at the Alamo?"

Mike shrugged.

"There were six pickup trucks...Get it? Six pickup trucks? Get it?"

"No"

Candi frowned. She moved her hands like a stewardess giving instructions before a flight and said, "Over there is the San Jacinto Battleground State Historic Site. In that park we've got the San Jacinto Monument. It's the world's tallest stone monument. Even taller than the fucking Washington Monument in D.C"

"So it's an obelisk, then?"

"If that means it fucking looks like a big concrete dick with a hard-on, then yessir"

Mike chuckled.

"But please sir," Candi said in a deep, very official sounding voice. "Please hold all you're your fucking questions until the end of our fucking tour. Thank you very much. Anyways. Like I was sayin. You can even take an elevator ride to the very top of the San Jacinto Monument. And from there you can see the Battleship Texas docked nearby. And the Houston skyline about ten miles away." She leaned towards him and whispered, "Just wait till you see that beautiful Houston skyline. It's fucking amazin."

"You know, Candi. I think you really missed your calling in life. You really should've been a tour guide."

"Shut the fuck up," she said. "Are you fucking kiddin me? Fuck bein a fucking tour guide. I mean. I'd be bored to fucking death doin that shit. At least with suckin strange dicks. It's never a dull fucking moment!"

"Well, how about this," Mike said. "You be my tour guide for the rest of the day. And I'll buy you dinner and then drop you off wherever you want."

"Some grub sounds good," Candi said.

"Dinner, anywhere you want," Mike said. "I'll even take you out to the nicest restaurant in Houston."

"Well I could really use a margarita right about now. And some fucking chips and queso too." She smacked her blowpop between her lips. "Ok, you got it, pardner." She spit in her palm and extended her hand to him again. "Shake on it?"

Again with the hand-shaking, Mike thought. Shake on it? Who says that? And for that matter, who shakes hands anymore? Candi was definitely a goldmine. Or he wondered, planning the wording of his novel- was a diamond in the rough a better metaphor? Mike shook Candi's hand and said, "You got it."

"Just remember pardner," Candi said. "Don't you get any big ideas. I mean it's gonna take a whole lot fucking more than a few margaritas to get into *this* girl's pants!"

✳ ✳ ✳

Mike and Candi left La Porte and drove west on Highway 225 towards downtown Houston. Almost immediately off to the right they could see The San Jacinto Monument, all by itself in a distant field.

A little ways down the road, Candi rolled down the passenger window of the car. She leaned halfway out, flicked off a woman drifting into their lane of traffic and yelled, "Learn how to fucking drive you stupid fucking cunt!"

Mike grimaced. Candi settled back into her seat and rolled up the window.

"Don't you find *that word* degrading?" Mike said.

Candi had to think for a second. "You mean, cunt?"

"Yes"

"Sure I fucking find it degradin. That's why I fucking called that cunt a fucking cunt. I was fucking pissed off at her."

Mike decided to play a little Socrates with Candi. "How would you feel if I called *you* a cunt?"

"Depends, I guess"

"Depends on what?"

"Well sometimes I deserve to be called a cunt."

"Oh really? When is that?"

"When I'm actin like a cunt"

Mike chuckled, and then felt a little guilty.

"Wow. If you think that shit's funny," Candi said, "then you just *gotta* fucking hear this joke. It's fucking hilarious! And it's a joke that's a story too. Like I said before. Jokes that are stories are the always the fucking best!"

"Are you sure it isn't the other way around?" Mike said. "Maybe the best stories are always jokes."

Candi frowned at him. "Are you gonna shut the fuck up and let me tell this joke? Or what?"

Mike wished he hadn't chuckled. "Actually," he said, "If it has *that word* in it, then I don't want you to tell me the joke. I don't want to hear it."s

"Oh no fucking way, pardner! You just gotta hear this. This is a fucking good joke. No, I take it back! This is a fucking great joke!"

"So," Candi said, "One day Little Johnny asks his daddy- What's the difference between a pussy and a cunt? Well, his daddy thinks for a minute and then says to him- "Come with me, Little Johnny."

'Oh, for Chrissakes," Mike said.

"So his daddy takes Little Johnny into the bedroom where his mama is sleepin in the nude. I mean she's naked as a jaybird. Sleepin right there on the bed. So his daddy whispers to Little Johnny- You see that soft furry patch of hair between your mama's legs, right there? That's a pussy..."

"So, then Little Johnny asks his daddy- Can I touch it and see how soft and furry it is? And then... his daddy says- No way! And then his daddy says- Hush up, goddammit! You might wake up the cunt!" Candi slapped her knees and laughed out loud.

Mike couldn't help but chuckle again, but he felt worse this time. "That's not cool, Candi," he said, "I shouldn't be laughing."

Candi ignored him and laughed her ass off. Once she regained her composure she said, "Come on, pardner. You mean you never called a woman a cunt before?"

✳ ✳ ✳

CUNT –noun Slang: Vulgar
1. vulva or vagina.

2. disparaging and offensive
    a. a woman.
    b. a contemptible person.

3. sexual intercourse with a woman.

Origin:
1275–1325; Middle English *cunte*; cognate with Old Norse *kunta*,
Old Frisian, Middle Low German, Middle Dutch *kunte*

    In the Middle Ages there was a street in London known as Gropecunt Lane. It was a popular hub of prostitution in the city. Apparently it was commonplace in medieval times to name a street based on its economic function within society.

    Throughout the years the word cunt has been defined in many ways. Arguably, the most entertaining definition of the word cunt comes from an English antiquarian who authored a book in 1785 called, *A Classical Dictionary of the Vulgar Tongue.* Coincidentally, this collector of vulgar words and phrases was himself named Francis Grose. And in his dictionary, Grose defined cunt as "a nasty name for a nasty thing". It is perhaps no coincidence that this particular definition of cunt appears in a dictionary of the vulgar *tongue.*

***

    "You mean to tell me," Candi said, "You never called a woman a cunt before?"

    "No, absolutely not"

    "But you've wanted to, right?"

    "No, I haven't. *That word* is just not in my dictionary. It's just not a part of my vocabulary."

    "Well why the fuck not?"

    "Like I said before. It's a degrading word. It degrades women."

Mike thought back to when he saw *The Vagina Monologues* performed at Yale Divinity School. After the performance, to support the Women's Studies Department, he'd bought a black t-shirt which read: GOD LOVES VAGINAS. He never wore it.

"*That word*, Candi," Mike said, "It objectifies women."

"It fucking does what to women?"

Mike recalled the words of the feminist scholar Andrea Dworkin. He said, "It reduces a woman to nothing more than her sexual organ."

"No shit that's what it fucking does, you fucking dick!" Candi grinned.

"Oh, ha-ha very funny," Mike said. He shook his head. "I'm serious, Candi. Think about how degrading it is to reduce someone, male or female, to nothing more than their sexual organ."

"You know what, pardner? All I can think about right now is that you just used the words, sexual organ. What the fuck is this? High school biology class? I think you meant to say that it reduces a woman to nothin but her clit. Didn't you?"

"Yes," Mike said, "That's exactly what I meant. Thank you once again for your tasteful clarification of terms." How ironic, Mike thought, that this common whore was making comments about high school, especially considering she probably never even graduated from it.

"Well, pardner," Candi said, "You oughta try it sometime. I mean it feels fucking great."

"Try what?"

"Callin a woman a cunt"

"I don't think so"

"You really mean to tell me that you never ever ever ever ever ever wanted to call a woman a cunt?"

"No. No I haven't..."

✳✳✳

Mike thought back to his ex-girlfriend at Yale. Her name was Lisa Bulldyker. They met in a Feminist Studies class. They'd shared research for a paper on Estelle Freedman. Mike remembered there being only one other man in that Feminist Studies Class. And of course, he was gay.

Before Mike and Lisa ever had sex, Lisa had insisted on first giving him five blowjobs. She'd told him it was her personal policy for establishing a more equal gender dynamic in dating. Lisa Bulldyker didn't seem to mind giving blowjobs. In fact, she seemed to actually prefer it to sex. Her only stipulation was that Mike never touch her head while she was blowing him. She felt it was degrading. Lisa even refused his offers to give her oral sex.

After the fifth blowjob, which she gave Mike at the Beineke Rare Books Library over behind the copy of the Gutenberg Bible, Lisa finally explained her policy to him. She explained that a blowjob reversed the phallic paradigm by shifting the power traditionally associated with the man to the woman. It had to do with being actively penetrated in the mouth versus what she labeled being passively penetrated in the vagina or anus during intercourse.

Mike remembered that after the blowjob, as Lisa explained this theory to him, he'd noticed she still had a little smidgeon of his cum on the corner of her mouth. He recalled not being able to take his eyes off it as she explained, "I'm going to write a paper on this theory," Lisa said, inadvertently licking his cum from the corner of her mouth, "I know this scholarly journal that specializes in feminist sexuality and-"

Mike and Lisa dated for a while. In fact, Lisa had performed the 'Reclaiming Cunt' portion of *The Vagina Monologues* which he had dutifully attended. And she'd bought the exact same t-shirt. Or rather, he'd bought it for her. However, it wasn't long into their relationship that Lisa began to really annoy him.

Mike had recently concluded that much of what annoyed him about Lisa also annoyed him about himself. Mike had decided that everyone in academia, including him, was pretentious. It was simply sort of the nature of the academic beast. Mike had come to the painful conclusion that academics are collectors and keepers of specialized knowledge. And for the price of tuition they sell this specialized knowledge to other people. Academics are nothing more than petty trivia peddlers.

The ancient Greek philosopher Socrates condemned the Sophists for making a profit off teaching philosophy. It was immoral, Socrates claimed, to sell truth. And yet, philosophy professors venerate Socrates as the Father of Philosophy while, like the Sophists, drawing a paycheck at the very same time. Shortly before fleeing New Haven, much to his chagrin, Mike had recently realized that he was participating in one of the greatest hypocrisies of all time- academic philosophy.

Academics spend their entire lives pouring over books only a few dozen other people in the world have read; or, for that matter, even give a shit about. And once that particular tome is sufficiently highlighted, academics triumphantly write a paper with a plethora of footnotes. This paper will in turn be published in a scholarly journal only a few dozen other people in the world will read; or, for that matter, even give a shit about.

And yet, Lisa Bulldyker took academic pretension to what Mike felt like was a whole new level. Lisa had been the kind of aspiring academic who, after attending a lecture by Judith Butler, started referring to the Holocaust as The Shoa, even though she wasn't Jewish.

Lisa was the kind of academic who listened to NPR and browsed the *New York Times* in the morning so she could begin sentences with- "This morning I heard on NPR," or "Yesterday I read in the *New York Times...*"

And perhaps worst of all- Lisa Bulldyker was the kind of academic feminist who could no longer simply enjoy a bottle of wine and the movie *Casablanca* without some bitter, intellectualized commentary she had picked up in a Gender Studies or Feminist Criticism class. If Mike or any other walking-talking phallus ever said anything even half-romantic, Lisa chimed in with an angry, predictable rant about the cult of domesticity or *The Feminine Mystique.*

In one of her many angry, predictable feminist rants, Lisa had single-handedly ruined the romance and nostalgia of *Casablanca* for Mike. And even Humphrey Bogart wouldn't have gotten a word in edgewise. Of course, as Mike's friend Sonny Quillan had once said- Bogie would never have wasted his fucking time getting a word in edgewise; he would've just slapped that bitch and then kissed her as both the music and his phallus swelled.

In Mike's experience, academic feminists like Lisa conveniently allowed themselves to use the word bitch or cunt in what they saw as the proper context; but never allowed men to use it in any context. Mike remembered Lisa using the word cunt once, in what she deemed a proper context; when a female student received a better grade than Lisa on a presentation covering 'Maternalism in the Americas' in their Feminist Studies class.

And sex with Lisa, well Mike could only describe it as definitely a Joycean experience. Mike recalled how Lisa had difficulty getting wet. And this made fucking her pussy hazardous. And this meant that Mike didn't get to fuck her pussy as often as he would've liked. Incidentally, Lisa never seemed to mind.

Mike remembered how Lisa's explanation for why her pussy was dangerously dry turned into yet another painful, never-ending presentation of a chapter from her forthcoming doctoral dissertation. Mike concluded that Lisa Bulldyker had simply taken too many feminist classes. And the unfortunate byproduct was that romantic movies like *Casablanca*, novels like *Jane Eyre* and *Moby Dick*, and sex had been ruined for her, and him, once and for all.

There was one sure way, Mike recalled, to make Lisa's pussy wet and ready for fucking. All Mike had to do was buy her a few micro-brewed beers, preferably from some obscure brewery in Canada, and then discuss the novelist Jonathan Franzen. It was that easy.

Anytime Jonathan Franzen was mentioned, Lisa's pussy would salivate like a Pavlovian dog. She loved hearing about how Franzen demanded that his novel be removed from Oprah's book club list. She adored how Franzen refused to grant an interview with some prestigious journal or newspaper. Mike concluded that it was not Franzen's books women like Lisa loved so much; but his cocky attitude and over-inflated literary ego. Then again, Mike thought, he was probably just jealous of the Franzen phenomenon.

Nonetheless, a few micro-brewed beers and a discussion of the Lambert family later, and Lisa's cunt was wet and ready for some good old fashioned, cult of domesticity-style fucking. I guess, Mike thought to himself, when it came to feminist cunts like Lisa, Franzen should have titled his book, *The Erections*.

Candi interrupted Mike's ballad when she said, "Hey, pardner, I've got an idea."

"Do I really want to hear this?"

"You can call *me* a cunt, if you want to."

"No thanks"

"Come on, pardner! It'll be good practice for you!"

"No thanks"

"Come on! You know you wanna. Just fucking say it already!"

"I said- no thanks"

"I won't fucking get mad. In fact, I'll bet callin me a cunt would make you feel a whole lot fucking better. I'll bet you've always wanted to say it out loud."

"I haven't, actually"

"Bullshit," Candi said, turning to face him. "I'm gonna fucking make you use the word cunt. In fact, I'm gonna make you call *me* a cunt."

✳✳✳

Words like cunt and fuck have the Latin designation, *mutatis mutandis*, meaning they can be used as nouns, adjectives, pronouns or even participles; not necessarily your standard Sesame Street-style grammar lesson.

If you read carefully or at all for that matter, you will notice some of the most illustrious fictional characters in the literary canon use the word cunt. Thus, Mike and Candi join the ranks of Leopold Bloom, Hamlet, the Wife of Bath and Mellors to name only a few.

✳✳✳

"I fucking mean it, pardner," Candi said. "I'm gonna *make* you call me a cunt."

"You're going to *make* me?" Mike said, shaking his head in disbelief.

"Come on you little pussy," she said, "Call me a cunt." Candi grinned, and then reached over with both hands and tickled his ribs. "Say it! Cuuuuuuuuuuuuunt"

"For Chrissakes, Candi! Cut it out. I'm driving here."

"Say cunt! Say cunt! Say cuuuuuuuuunt!" Candi yelled. She leaned over and whispered into his ear. "Here's what I want you to say. I want you to say- Stop sayin cunt you dirty fucking cunt!"

Mike felt Candi's lips and hot breath on his ear. He said, "You're not funny. And I'm not going to say it."

"Ok, pardner," Candi said, sitting back in her seat, "I fucking tried askin nicely."

Mike was surprised she'd given up so easily. And he really wished her lips and hot breath was still tickling his ear.

Candi punched Mike in the groin. "Call me a cunt!" she yelled.

Mike winced. "Ouch! What the hell was that about?" He rubbed his groin. "I'm driving for Chrissakes! You're going to get us-"

Candi punched him in the groin again and again and again. "Call me a cunt!" She punched him harder. "Call me a fucking cunt! Say- Stop sayin cunt you dirty fucking cunt!"

The car swerved towards the highway guardrail. "Hey goddammit," Mike said, "Stop!"

Candi laughed and said, "I'm not gonna stop punchin you in the nuts until you call me a fucking cunt!"

The car swerved into the other lane this time. Another car swerved to miss them and the driver honked angrily and gestured. Mike said, "Stop hitting me, bitch!"

"Wrong word, pardner!" Candi punched him again and again and again.

"I'm serious! That really hurts!"

"Say it! Call me a cunt!" Candi punched him again and again and again.

The car swerved and grazed the guardrail. "OK! Stop it!" Mike shouted, "Stop it you fucking *cunt*!"

Mike pulled the car onto the shoulder of the highway as traffic whizzed by them. He rubbed his groin and stared out the window at the gargantuan petroleum storage tanks along Highway 225. Each tank was painted with a massive mural of the legendary battle of San Jacinto.

Candi sat back in her seat, smiling. She pulled out another blowpop, smacked it between her lips, exhaled deeply and said, "Oh baby! Was that as good for you as it was for me?"

Mike still rubbed his groin, wincing in pain. He still looked out the window, away from Candi. Finally he whispered to her, "You...fucking...*cunt*."

"Feels fucking great, don't it?" Candi said. "I mean to actually *say* the word out loud like that? To actually fucking say what you're really fucking thinkin. Feels fucking great, don't it?"

Candi leaned over towards Mike slowly. For a brief moment Mike felt like she was going to kiss him. "Oh, and just so we're fucking crystal clear, from now on," she whispered softly in his ear, and then punched him as hard as she could in the groin one more time. "Don't you ever fucking call me *that word* ever again!"

Chapter 3

Mike's box of books and what Candi found inside;
The Ballad of the Only Book Candi ever Read;
How Candi and Mike dined at Ninfa's;
What they said about theodicy and Candi's bright idea

"So what's with the fucking box of books in the fucking backseat?" Candi said.

"Just some books I thought might help inspire my novel."

She reached into the backseat and tugged the small cardboard box forward into her lap. "Are you gonna read *all* of these?"

"I've already read them all, many times," Mike said, smiling. "They're all classics of American literature."

"So, if you already fucking read them, then why are you gonna fucking read them again?"

Mike was puzzled by her question. "Because, uh, well," he said, "They're classics of American literature." Mike was starting to hate it when Candi asked stupid questions. It was really annoying.

"I'm just sayin, pardner. Maybe you should try readin some *new* fucking books. You ever fucking think of that?"

"Why no," Mike said, "I never thought of that, actually. What a brilliant idea! Got any more sage advice for me?"

"*Sage* advice? Well I don't know what that fucking word means. But I think I know what you fucking meant *by it.* So yeah," Candi said, "Here's some sage advice for you. Go dick yourself!"

Candi pulled a large binder from Mike's box. "Wow, pardner. There must be like over two hundred fucking typed pages in here. What the fuck is this, your novel?"

"No," Mike sighed, "It's my doctoral dissertation. I'm ABD."

"You're fucking what?" Candi said. "A-B-D? What the fuck is that? Is that some kinda fucking disease?"

ABD certainly seemed like a disease sometimes, Mike thought to himself. Wow, out of the mouths of whores. Mike could think of a lot of academics suffering from this disease for years, and in some cases it was a terminal illness.

"No," he said, "It's not a disease. ABD is academic short-hand for- All But Dissertation. It means I've finished all my classes. And all I need to do in order to graduate with my PhD is write my dissertation."

"What's a fucking dissertation?"

"It's like a really, really long research paper."

"Well, thank fucking God for that!" Candi said. "For a minute there all I could think was that you had ABD, and I just fucking swallowed your cum." She wiped her brow dramatically and added, "That was a fucking close one!"

Mike couldn't tell if Candi was being serious or not.

Candi thumbed through the binder. "So, how long did it take you to write all this?"

"Two years"

"Holy fucking shit! Two fucking years? Wow! I'll bet you're glad to finally be done?"

"Actually- I'm not done. It's not finished yet."

"No shit? How much longer until you're done with it?"

"I don't know"

"What do you mean you don't know?"

"I mean, a dissertation takes time. You have to research, document your sources and outline the chapters and-"

"Wait a goddamn fucking minute, pardner. You mean to tell me, that all you have to do in order to graduate from college and get a job is finish writing a fucking paper? That's all?"

"It's not that simple."

"Oh, really? Well, actually- it sounds just that fucking simple to me. Holy fuck! You've already got like two hundred pages here! Listen, pardner. Just go ahead and fucking say-whatever you gotta fucking say already- about whatever you wanna fucking say it about- and then fucking finish it already."

"Hey, Candi," Mike said, "You really don't know what you're talking about so just don't-"

"And! If all you need to do to graduate is write a fucking paper, then what the fuck are you doin here? I mean what the fuck are you doin sittin in some rental car in Houston, Texas, poppin prescription pills and writin some fucking novel?"

"*You're* judging me about graduating college? Oh, for Chrissakes! You've got to be kidding!"

"Oh sure, go ahead," Candi said, "Draw your pistol and fire the," she raised her hands into the air and made quotation marks with her fingers, "*I'm Better than the Ignorant Whore Silver Bullet.* Yep, sure it's predictable, but it'll always be a fucking classic. Stops them whores dead in their tracks every fucking time!"

Candi closed his binder gently. "Believe me, pardner. I've gotten pretty goddamn good at dodgin that bullet."

Mike was too annoyed with her to feel any real remorse. He said, "Why do you even give a shit about my dissertation anyway? It's not your problem."

"Don't worry, pardner. I don't really give a shit." Candi sucked on her blowpop, smacking it loudly. She paused for about a minute, and then said, "It's just, I mean, there are sooo many fucking people who'd like to go to college and better their lives, ya know? And if you told them that all they had to fucking do in order to graduate from college and draw a steady fucking pay-check was write a fucking paper- I *guaran-goddamn-tee* they'd get it done. That's all I'm sayin."

Mike couldn't help but feel like Candi's righteous indignation was somehow personal, that she was really talking about herself. Or, he thought, maybe just somebody she knew. It was impossible for Mike to imagine Candi attending college; or for that matter, even wanting to go to college in the first place. "Listen," Mike said, "At this point, I don't even know if I'm going to finish my dissertation. You see, something happened to me recently and I've been-"

"I told you already- I *really*, really don't give a shit."

"But"

"I really don't," she said. "I'm a fucking whore, pardner, not a fucking therapist."

There was silence between them for a few minutes.

"Take 610 West right up here," Candi finally said. They took the ramp on the left side of the highway and merged onto 610. "There's GulfGate Plaza over there on the right. Keep goin for a few miles. And then when you see Reliant Stadium off in the distance. Home of the Houston Texans! The best fucking football team ever! Turn off onto 288 and head downtown." Mike merged through the massive flow of Houston traffic. "So, pardner, tell me. How in the bad place did you end up in Baytown, Texas?"

"Well, I flew into Hobby Airport from LaGuardia this morning. I rented a car, took a few wrong turns, and then got lost. After I crossed that bridge I took the first exit, turned around, and then ended up at that truck stop."

"You were fucking lost alright."

Mike didn't know exactly what Candi meant by that. He said, "So, how did *you* end up in Baytown, Texas?"

"You wouldn't ever fucking believe me if I told you."

"Try me"

"No fucking way. I fucking mean it. It's a really, really unfucking-believable story."

"Well, now you have to tell me."

"Maybe later, pardner"

Candi glanced back over her shoulder and then pointed to the backseat. "And what the fuck is up with that old-ass, antique typewriter back there?"

"It's an Olivetti Lettera 32," Mike said, "Just like the one Cormac McCarthy wrote his novel *Blood Meridian* on."

"Never fucking heard of him."

"McCarthy supposedly bought his typewriter for like fifty dollars in a pawn shop in 1963. I read that he wrote over five million words on it before selling it at auction a few years ago for about a quarter of a million dollars."

"So you went and got a typewriter just like this famous writer-guy?"

"Yeah"

"Because you wanna be a famous writer-guy too?"

"Well, uh. I got it because I respect McCarthy as a novelist. And having a similar typewriter would be-"

"Hold it right there, pardner. Which one is it? Is it a *similar* fucking typewriter? Or the *exact same* fucking typewriter?"

"The exact same one. But it's-"

"So let me get this straight. You bought an old-ass fucking typewriter. Just like somebody else's old-ass fucking typewriter.

So you could write a novel just like his. And then get famous just like him?"

"Oh for Chrissakes, Candi. I bought it to inspire me. I respect McCarthy as a writer and-"

"Sounds to me like you've got more of a hard-on for this McCarthy guy. Than you do for his fucking books."

"Why are you turning this shit around on me?"

"Sounds to me like you wanna write a famous fucking novel. So you can sell this fucking typewriter you wrote it on. For a quarter of a million bucks. Am I right?"

"Listen, Candi. You don't know what the hell you're talking about here. I just-"

"You don't have to get sooo fucking defensive about it. I mean. I'd fucking sell a typewriter I wrote a famous book on. For a quarter of a million bucks. In a fucking heartbeat!"

"McCarthy sold it for charity."

"Look, pardner. If I'm gonna be your fucking tour guide for the afternoon. Then you're gonna have to fucking lighten up a little. And not be so fucking defensive about every goddamn thing I fucking say."

"Ok," Mike said. "It's just that every time I say something. It seems like all you do is-"

Candi interrupted him, "Let's take a look-see at these books here, pardner. See what you got here." Candi lifted the books one at a time from the box, admiring the covers of each and reading the titles aloud: *Catcher in the Rye*, *Blood Meridian*, *The Adventures of Huckleberry Finn*, *Collected Short Stories of Earnest Hemingway*, *Lonesome Dove*, *On the Road*," she stopped reading suddenly and stared at one of the books. "Oh my fucking God! No fucking way!"

"What is it?" Mike said.

"Oh... my... fucking... God!" Candi moved her hand slowly, gently over the cover of the book as if the title was engraved in velvet gold. "I've only read one book in my entire fucking life. And this is fucking it, right here."

Only one book in her whole life? Mike didn't know which was harder to believe. That Candi had actually read a book, or that the one book she'd actually read was one of *these* books, one of *his* books. "Well," Mike said, "which book is it?"

Candi moved her fingers over the words on the cover of the hardbound book again, savoring the sensation. She said, "*Moby Dick*."

"You've read that?"

"Yep! Every cocksucking word of it," Candi said. "It's the only book I ever read. Yessir! Once upon a time me and Herman fucking Melville right here, we spent some time together in a Greyhound Bus Station. Right here in good ol Houston, Texas."

"I'd really love to hear *this* story."

"Sure," Candi said. "Where should I start? Oh yeah, I was taking a Greyhound Bus as fast as I fucking could outta Texas."

"Where were you going?"

"Not important"

"How old were you?"

"Not important," Candi said. "Listen up, pardner. Do you wanna hear this fucking story or not?" Mike nodded. "Then fucking zip it. Ok? So, me and my boyfriend were headed the fuck outta Dodge, if you know what I mean. We'd been ridin together for a spell. We met right here in Houston, at the Livestock Show and Rodeo. He was a *real* cowboy."

"You mean he rode bulls or something like that in the rodeo?"

"Hey, pardner. Trust me. A lot of assholes ride bulls and rope steers at the rodeo. That don't make a man a cowboy." She smacked her blowpop between her lips.

"Oh really?" Mike said, "What do you mean by cowboy, then?"

"Anyways. Me and him were sittin at the Greyhound Bus Station here in H-Town. On the corner of Main Street and Webster downtown. So he gets up and goes to the bathroom." Candi paused, as if remembering something fondly. "That man looked sooo good in a cowboy hat. He wore this white Stetson. Not many men can pull off a cowboy hat, ya know." Candi smiled, and then seemed to return to the present. "Anyways. Only problem was, he was gone to the bathroom for a really, really long time."

"So finally I go check the men's bathroom and he ain't there. I'm like, what the fuck? Where is he? Where the fuck did he go? So I check everywhere. But he ain't anywhere. After a while I go back to our seats and just wait for him. I sit there and wait a really, really long time. I mean I'm just sittin right there on that fucking seat, waitin for him to come back from the fucking bathroom."

"Hey," Mike said, chuckling, "was your boyfriend's name, Godot?"

"Huh?"

"Was his name, Godot?" Mike said again, laughing this time.

"What the fuck kinda name is that?" Candi said. "No. His name was Kris, with a *k*."

"Never mind," Mike said.

"Anyways. At some point," Candi said, continuing her ballad, "I fucking find a copy of *Moby Dick* somebody left on a seat nearby. Honestly, when I read the title, I fucking thought it was porn." She laughed out loud. "Anyways. I sat in that fucking bus station for twelve straight days and read that whole fucking book. And I don't even fucking like reading! In fact, I fucking hate it! I reckon I just needed somethin to take my fucking mind off Kris bein gone."

"How long was Kris gone?"

"I never fucking saw him again."

"What? You mean he just never came back?"

"Yep. I haven't seen him since..."

"Why?"

"Why what?"

"Why did Kris leave?"

"The bad place if I fucking know," Candi said. "People just run away sometimes." Candi smiled and poked Mike in the ribs, "Kinda like you, pardner."

✳✳✳

"I offer to take you to the nicest restaurant in Houston, Texas," Mike said, "and you want to go here?"

Mike and Candi had taken 288 towards downtown and then merged onto Highway 59. They exited Polk Street and then took a right on Runnels.

"I know it doesn't look fancy," Candi said, "but Ninfa's Mexican Restaurant is fucking amazin. Trust me! It's the best fucking Mexican food east of the Pecos River. Plus! It's a Houston landmark. In fact! It's a *national* fucking landmark."

"Hey, Candi. Did anyone ever bother to explain the concept of *hyperbole* to you?"

"I don't know what the fuck you just said to me. But. I'm not bullshittin you about this place bein a national fucking landmark. Do you like fajitas?"

"Sure"

"Well, way back in the good ol days. Mama Ninfa was the very first person to take sliced beef, put that shit in a fucking homemade tortilla, and call it fucking fajitas."

"Is that really what they're called on the menu?" Mike said, grinning. "Did she really call them, *fucking* fajitas?"

"Ha-Ha-Ha-Ha! Shut the fuck up, smart-ass." Candi said. "I'm not shittin you, pardner. Fajitas were invented right here in Houston fucking Texas. And *this* place here is the original Ninfa's Restaurant!"

The sign outside read:

THE ORIGINAL
Ninfa's
on Navigation

Desde 1973

THERE'S ONLY ONE ORIGINAL NINFA'S
AND THIS IS IT.

Mike and Candi were seated outside on the back patio at a green table with a white umbrella. There was a bubbling Roman fountain nearby.

"Since you're payin, pardner," Candi said, "Shut the fuck up and let me order for the both of us. Trust me. You won't be disappointed!"

Their waiter's name was Genaro.

"We'll start with some chips and queso, of course," Candi said to him. "And we'll both have a Platinum Margarita. That's made with *Patron* tequila, right?" The waiter nodded. "And we'll have the guacamole for an appetizer. And the Mixta Campesino to split."

"I'm not really that hungry," Mike said.

"Oh, trust me pardner. You'll be hungry once you smell this fucking food! You're in for a real fucking treat."

✳ ✳ ✳

"So," Candi said, "What's your really, really, really long research paper about? You know, the one you just can't seem to finish?"

"You mean my doctoral dissertation?"

"Yep, that's the one"

Mike guessed that Candi remembered the correct word, but simply chose not to use it. "Well, it's about the philosophical problem of evil." Mike wondered how in the hell he was going to explain the philosophical problem of evil to someone like Candi.

As he watched her slurp her margarita, Mike concluded that Candi was a near-extinct species. She was that rare animal which combines lack of education with natural intelligence. She wasn't book-smart. However, she wasn't dumb either. Explaining his dissertation to her would simply be a matter of figuring out how to dumb-down his language. After all, Mike thought, the philosophical problem of evil is very sophisticated philosophy. "Well," he said to her, "it basically questions the existence of God. I investigate the question- Why would God allow so much pointless pain and suffering in the world?"

"Ok," Candi said, dipping a corn chip into the queso, "So the fuck what?"

"What do you mean, so what?"

"I mean. Ok, you ask the fucking question. So what's your fucking answer?"

"Well, it doesn't boil down to just one simple answer. It's actually more complicated than that."

"Oh yeah?"

"You see, there is a longstanding philosophical dialogue between theists and atheists-"

"Oh for God's sake," Candi said, smiling, "And pun abso-fucking-lutely intended right there." She nudged him with her elbow, "Get it? Get it?

Mike frowned.

"You know," Candi said. "For somebody who knows sooo fucking much. You sure have trouble givin a simple fucking answer to a simple fucking question."

"That's just it, Candi. It's *not* a simple question. I guess for some people who never really think it through, it can seem like a simple question with a simple answer. But actually it's a very sophisticated philosophical question."

"Ok, Mr. Smarty-Pants. So just gimme a fucking example then. I mean, tell me a fucking story so I can understand. And it better not take you two hundred fucking pages either!"

That was it, Mike resolved, that was the last straw. He was sick and tired of Candi's catty comments about his dissertation. He decided to put her in her place once and for all. He decided to make Candi realize, and then admit to him, that she was way out of her intellectual league. Mike realized that in doing so, he would probably make Candi feel like the uneducated whore that she was. However, he thought, she was asking for it...

"Well," Mike said, "In my dissertation I examine logically possible worlds..."

"Huh?" Candi said, right on the ignorant cue Mike had anticipated, much to his satisfaction.

"When discussing the philosophical problem of evil," Mike said, shifting his vocabulary into intellectual gear, pretending he was back in a graduate philosophy seminar at Yale. "It is helpful to consider logically possible worlds. One must consider that-"

Candi interrupted him. "You do that a-fucking-lot, ya know?"

"I do what?"

"Whenever you start to talk all smart. You always start your sentences by sayin- *one* does this. Or *one* must consider. Or *one* does that. It's kinda weird. Why the fuck do you talk that way?"

At some point in his academic pilgrimage towards tenure, Mike began faithfully using the impersonal pronoun *one* when discussing intellectual topics. He didn't know the reason, only that it was commonplace academic jargon. "I'm not going to let you change the subject, Candi."

"I was just curious," she said, grinning, "That's all."

"And how can you say I do that *a lot*, anyway?" Mike said. "We've haven't even been together that long."

"Trust me, pardner. We are *not* fucking together."

"You know what I meant." Mike sighed. "Listen, Candi. I'm not going to let you change the subject. Do you want me to tell you about my dissertation or not?"

"Sure I do, pardner. Shoot!"

"Alright then," Mike said, mustering his graduate seminar vocabulary once more. "One must consider," he said. He paused to wince at his rote use of that word again. "That there are other possible worlds besides ours. Wherein there might be less pain and suffering, or no pain and suffering at all. However, one must also consider the logical possibility that *this* is the best of all possible worlds."

"Holy fucking shit, pardner," Candi said. "I didn't understand a goddamn fucking word you just said."

Mike grinned at his success in making her feel stupid. "I told you! It's not a simple question, or a simple answer."

"Wow! You sure said a fucking mouthful, pardner. And all this time I thought I was the only one with a mouthful!" She nudged his arm. She chuckled and said, "Get it? Mouthful? Get it? I was the only one with a mouthful? Of your cum? Get it? A mouthful of your cum? The blowjob on the bridge? Get it?"

"For Chrissakes," Mike fired off at her, "I get it!"

Candi laughed. "Simmer down there, pardner," she said. "You're awful touchy, aren't ya? Must be those fucking prescription pills you're always poppin."

"I guess so," Mike said, fumbling for the right words this time. "I guess I just don't understand why you're always joking about... I mean, why you always have to bring up..."

Candi interrupted him. "Listen up, pardner. I didn't understand everything you said a minute ago. But! I did hear what you said right at the end though." Candi smiled. "And all I have to say about that is. If *this* is the best of all possible fucking worlds, then I'd hate to fucking see the other ones. Am I right?"

Mike was glad Candi changed the subject. Even though *she* seemed fine with joking about what happened on the bridge, he was glad neither of them wanted to talk about it.

Mike then decided he wasn't done putting Candi in her intellectual place. He said, "It may be *unlikely* that our world is the best of all possible worlds. And we may not *like* the idea that it is. However. I think it is logically *possible* that this *is* the best of all possible worlds."

"Damn," Candi said, "That seems like a real fucking downer to me."

Even though Mike had originally planned to humiliate Candi by putting her in her intellectual place it pleased him that she was at-least-partially engaging the topic with some seriousness. It actually felt good, Mike thought, to be talking to someone about his theory; and not having to worry about getting every nuanced point correct, or using impressive philosophical terms.

Mike then decided to forget about putting Candi in her place, for now. He decided instead to really try to explain his theory to her. If he could make *her* understand his theory, if he could explain it where Candi could understand it, then maybe he could finally write it into a publishable paper. "I have this theory," Mike said, "It's actually a *theodicy*."

"What the fuck is that?"

"A theodicy is a story that attempts to explain why God would allow pain and suffering in the world. A theodicy tries to give a good reason why God would allow so much pain and suffering."

"I do like stories."

"Good. I call my theodicy, The Dumb Luck Theodicy. At least that's what I'm going to name the paper when I publish it."

"Cool fucking name you got there," Candi said. She dipped another corn chip into the guacamole. "I like it so far. Go on..."

"Thanks," Mike said. In five years of graduate school nobody had ever complimented him on the name of his theodicy, which he felt was very creative and intriguing. "I named it that because I think that God could only have produced a world without pain and suffering by dumb luck. Or to say it another way, it's logically impossible for God to *deliberately* create a world without pain and suffering."

"So you're tellin me," Candi said, smiling, "that God plays the Lotto after all? So I'm not the only one scratchin off lottery tickets, hopin for the best, huh?" She laughed out loud.

"Come on, Candi, this is serious."

"I am bein serious, pardner. It seems to me like what you're sayin is that the creation of the world was just God scratchin off a fucking lottery ticket. Is that what you're sayin?"

"For Chrissakes, Candi. I'm really trying to explain this to you."

"Ok, ok! Fine! I'm just sayin." She slurped down the last of her margarita and ordered another.

"Here," Mike said, pulling a pen from his pocket. "I'll write down my logical argument for you." He grabbed a Ninfa's napkin, unfolded it, pushed it into the middle of the table in between the chips and queso, and then wrote this down:

(P1) God is perfectly knowing and perfectly free
(P2) If God is perfectly knowing and perfectly free, then God is perfectly good.
(P3) God is perfectly good (from 1&2)
(P4) If God is perfectly good, then God must create the best of all possible worlds.
(P5) God must create the best of all possible worlds (from 3&4)
(P6) The best possible world is a world of free agents
(P7) Free agents cannot (of logical necessity) be perfectly knowing or perfectly free
(P8) If free agents cannot be perfectly knowing and perfectly free, they cannot be perfectly good. (negation of 1&2)
(P9) Free agents cannot be perfectly good (from 8)
(P10) If free agents cannot be perfectly good, then God cannot create a possible world of free agents who must choose right action
(P11) If God cannot create a possible world of free agents who must choose right action, then the best possible world that God could create would be a world of free agents who always choose right action by dumb luck
(P12) God cannot create a possible world where free agents always choose right action (from 9&10)
Therefore, the best possible world that God could create would be a world of free agents who always choose right action by dumb luck

"So," Candi said, "*That's* what a logical fucking argument looks like, huh? Damn. And I thought logic was supposed to clear things up. Not fucking confuse them even more."

"Let me explain how the conclusion logically follows from the-"

"No fucking way, pardner. You can take your logical arguments. And your fancy-schmancy words. And your bullshit conclusions. And you can shove em right up your ass. In fact. You can take this napkin and go wipe your ass with it for all I care.

Cuz that's all it's fucking good for." She shoved the napkin onto the floor.

"But, this argument is the only-"

"Can't you just fucking explain it to me?" Candi said. "I mean. I thought this was supposed to be a story explainin why God allows so much fucked up shit to happen in the world? Where's the fucking story? Trust me, pardner. Your napkin ain't helpin out me or God one goddamned bit." She laughed. "So. Just tell me a fucking story already. I mean what did you call it again?"

"a theodicy"

"Yeah. Just tell me one of those…"

Mike looked down at his argument on the napkin on the floor. He sighed. Outlining the argument into premises and a logical conclusion, he realized, was the only progress he'd made on writing his dissertation. Maybe, he wondered, that was his problem.

"Come on, pardner. You can fucking do it. Just turn your little argument into a little story. And then fucking tell it to me like that."

"Ok, I'll try it."

"Can you start the story with- *once upon a time?*"

"No, I can't"

"Dammit"

"Ok, let me think for a minute," Mike said. "Well, first of all. Let's agree that God creating humans with free will is a good thing."

"What the fuck is free will?"

"Free will is the ability to make free choices. Free will infuses our choices with moral significance. You can either choose to do the right thing or the wrong thing."

"Sorry, pardner. I don't understand. You're gonna have to give me a fucking example. Come on! Tell me a story…"

"It's like when a lion kills a zebra. Nobody calls that murder, right?"

"Right"

"It's not murder because animals are different from humans. Animals act on instinct. They don't make real choices like we do."

"Ok, I'm with ya"

"And yet. When a human kills another human we hold her morally responsible. Because we believe she could have acted otherwise. She made a real choice. She has free will."

"Ok," Candi said. "So it's like this. God wants us people to have free will. Cuz if we didn't we'd just be actin on instinct just like the fucking animals. Am I right?"

"Exactly!" Mike said. "And one may suppose that if God exists, then God desires a real relationship with humans. That is, God would want humans to freely choose to do the right thing. And, even choose freely to do wrong."

"Ok, I'm following you now."

"Free will gives all our choices, our good and our bad choices, real significance."

"Ok, that makes sense. I'm on board with the fucking free will thing. Go on."

Mike was encouraged. "So if free will is a good thing, then *ergo*, that means that any world that has-"

"Hold up there, pardner. What the fuck did you just say? I mean, what was that fucking word you just said?"

Mike thought for a second and then said, "You mean, *ergo?*"

'Yep. That's it. What's that fucking mean anyways?"

"It's Latin. It means, *therefore.*"

"Then why the fuck didn't you just say, therefore?"

Mike was so accustomed to using the word *ergo*, and *ergo* so accustomed to his peers and colleagues being accustomed to his use of the word *ergo*, that he couldn't *ergo* think of a response to Candi's inquiry.

"You also do *that* a fucking lot, ya know?"

"Do what?"

"You use a fancy-schmancy fucking word. When you could just as easy use a regular old fucking word instead. Why the fuck do you do that?"

"Again, I wouldn't say I do it a lot."

"You sure fucking do, pardner. You just don't notice it, that's all. I mean. It's like you said before. We haven't been ridin together very long. But I already noticed you usin weird words like that a bunch of fucking times. I just never asked you what they meant before."

"Ok. So what other words have I used?"

"Well. Earlier you kept sayin something like," she raised her hands and made quotation marks with her fingers in the air, "*qua*. I mean, what the fuck is that about?"

"Oh yeah," Mike said, nodding, "*qua* is another Latin word. It means, *as*."

"Oh my fucking God," Candi said. "You see? This is exactly what I'm fucking talkin about! I mean. It's one thing to use a fancy-schmancy word when you actually need one. But you're usin fancy-schmancy words for regular old words like there-fore and as! It's like you're tryin your fucking hardest *not* to be understood!"

"Actually," Mike said, "I'm trying to be more precise."

"More fucking pretentious, ya mean?"

"It's simply a way to nuance your-"

"I mean. It's like you're talkin in fucking code or somethin," Candi said. "It's like you're goin outta your way to use words that only your smarty-pants college friends can understand." She grinned. "And I'll bet that makes you feel awful special now, don't it?"

"Oh for Chrissakes, Candi"

"And," Candi said, grinning even wider this time, "I'll bet it makes your smarty-pants college friends feel awful special too? It's like a fancy-schmancy, smarty-pants circle-jerk!" She laughed out loud.

Mike fumed and gulped down the rest of his margarita. He ordered another and said, "Can we *please*, get back to my theodicy?"

"Tell you what there, pardner. You can only fucking explain your theodicy to me on one condition. You gotta speak fucking English. I ain't one of your smarty-pants college friends. So that means I don't cum in my pants when you talk in Latin. Got it?"

"Fine"

"Ok, pardner," Candi said. "Now let's hear this story about how God likes to play the black-jack tables in the casino all night long." She laughed.

Mike snarled at the waiter, asking about his margarita. He sighed, collected his thoughts once again, and then said, "Ok" He paused for a moment, frowning and thinking.

"Well?"

"Oh for Chrissakes, Candi. Where was I?"

"You were tellin me about how free will gives my good and bad choices real significance."

"Right," Mike said. "Ok. So if free will is a good thing, just *a* good thing among many other goods, then *erg*..." He stopped himself, "then, *therefore*..."

Candi grinned.

"If free will is *a* good thing, then therefore, any world that lacks free will is lacking a good thing."

"Come again?" Candi said, and then chuckled, "which ain't somethin I usually say to a man." She winked at him.

Mike thought of how to reword his point, missing hers entirely. He repeated himself, "If free will is *a* good, then any world that doesn't have free will is lacking a good thing."

"Ok. I think I'm back with you. But can you make it a story?"

Mike decided to play Socrates with her instead. "Let me ask you a question, Candi. If God is perfectly good, then God would create the best of all possible worlds, right?"

"Sure"

"But. Any world which lacks free will *cannot* be the best possible world. Because it lacks a good thing, namely, free will. Right?"

"Ok, I gotcha now," Candi said. "So you're tellin me that God's gotta create the best possible world that he can. Because after all, he's God and he's the best. Because God is always the fucking best at everything he does."

"Exactly"

"Basically," Candi said, "God's gonna make damn sure he puts free will into any world he creates. Because if the world didn't have free will we'd be minus a good thing. Am I right?"

"Exactly!"

"And *ergo*," Candi said, grinning, "If we're minus free will, we might as well be animals. Or even fucking robots, right? So if we're minus free will, we're just shit outta luck. And God wouldn't create the world and just leave us shit outta luck? Am I right?"

"Yes!" Mike said, "Yes! That's it!"

Mike had successfully played Socrates, he thought, and some-body like Candi was actually able to understand his theory. If I can explain this theodicy to an uneducated whore like Candi, Mike thought, surely I can sufficiently explain and defend it in a scholarly paper.

"Ok," Candi said, "I'm with you so far. See, pardner? Aren't you glad we ditched that fucking logical argument? It's a worthless piece of shit. I'm just sayin."

"Therefore," Mike said, ignoring her comment, consumed instead with their progress. "If God creates a world, then that world *must* include free will."

"I said I'm right there with you, pardner. Now drive on down the trail!"

"Ok. So God *must* create a world with free will. But, if a world includes free will, then that means God can't interfere with free will. God *can't* interfere with human choices."

"I don't get it."

"God cannot create a world with free will and then just turn around and suspend free will. Here's what I mean. God cannot give us free choices and then just interfere with our choices when we make the wrong ones."

"Why the fuck not? It seems like God could do whatever the fuck God wants, right?"

"No, that's just it. If we have free will," Mike said, "And remember, free will means we have the ability to make genuinely free choices. If we have free will then God can't just stop a murderer from murdering, or a rapist from raping."

"So," Candi said, "You're tellin me that if God decides to give people free will, then basically, from then on God's hands are tied. God can't do shit. Even when people make bad choices?"

"Yes"

"And that's why it seems like God doesn't give a fuck about us when bad shit happens to us?"

"Yes!"

"And that's why God ain't wearin a white Stetson cowboy hat and never comes ridin to our rescue?"

"Exactly! Yes! You've got it!" Mike said, and then frowned. He thought about the way Candi had just worded her interpretation. "Well, yes…in a manner of speaking. God *must* allow the murderer or rapist to make a free choice. Even if it causes pain and suffering to others."

"Hold your horses there, pardner." Candi said. "It seems to me that. If a woman is about to get raped. And if God could stop the rapist. Then God would fucking do it."

"No, Candi, that's just it." Mike said. "God *must* choose. Either God gives us free will which means letting us make our own choices, even if those choices cause pain and suffering. Or God can interfere with our choices, which you're right, would prevent pain and suffering. But God would deny us the good of free will by doing it."

Candi snatched Mike's pen from his hand and grabbed another napkin. "So," she said, "What you're tellin me is this..." Candi wrote this down on a napkin:

God really doesn't have a fucking choice

God's gotta make the best world possible, so-

God's gotta make a world with free will, so-

God's gotta honor free will, so-

God's gotta not interfere with people's choices, so-

Therefore, God's gotta let a rapist rape

Mike glanced at his pen in Candi's hand, and then down at her argument on the napkin. "Actually," he said, "You got it! That's it, Candi. Wow."

"So that's it, huh?" Candi said. "That's the story you're fucking tellin me?"

"Exactly"

"Well, pardner, then I gotta tell ya. That's the holiest load of horseshit I've ever heard in my fucking life."

"What?"

"Let me ask *you* a question."

"Ok"

"Would *you* stop a rapist if you could?"

"That's not the point, Candi."

"Wouldn't you at least *try* to stop a rapist? I mean, if you could try?"

"Oh for Chrissakes," Mike said, "Goddammit."

"Goddammit is right," Candi said.

"And I really thought we were making some progress." Mike said. "For Chrissakes, Candi, you missed the whole point. God created the rapist with free will. And in order to preserve free will God cannot interfere. It would be like God going back on God's original agreement."

"I don't know about you, pardner. But I didn't sign any fucking agreement."

"Ok" Mike said, "Forget about signing any agreement. That's not what I really meant anyway. I meant. If God interferes with human free will. If God suspends human free will for even *one* bad choice, then God has actually *prevented* a good. And logically speaking, it is impossible for God to prevent a good."

"Wow" Candi said. "Even if preventing the good of free will would prevent the pain and suffering of a rape, you're sayin God still wouldn't do it?"

"It's not that God *wouldn't* do it. It's that God *couldn't* do it. That's the whole point."

"Even if it's rape?"

"Yes. Even in the case of rape," Mike said, wincing a little as he said it. "Don't think about it as rape. Think about it as the good of free will giving our good choices *and* our bad choices *real* moral significance."

"So you're tellin me a story about how God would just stand right there and do absolutely fucking nothing. And just watch while some outlaw raped a woman?"

"I know," Mike said, "It sounds really bad when you say it like that. But, if you-"

"So then God allows rape all to preserve the good of free will?"

"Again, yes. But, like you said before. God has *no* choice in the matter. Logically speaking, God *cannot* interfere with human free will once it's been established."

"Ok, pardner," Candi said, "I completely fucking understand what you're tellin me."

"Really?"

"And you're right. It's definitely fucking logical."

Mike sighed with relief.

"But," Candi said, "It's also kinda fucked up."

"It's not sooo fucked up," Mike said, "when you think about it this way. Think about it like this. God's done the best that God could do in creating our world. God couldn't have done it any better. Because God is the best, right? You see. That's where *dumb luck* figures into all this. The best that God can do is to create a world containing free will. And at the point of creation, whenever that was, when the world contained free will, *that world* was the best of all possible worlds. And it still is."

Mike watched Candi's response. She seemed to be soaking it in.

"In fact," Mike said, "Any and every world God creates which contains free will, is the best of all possible worlds. And it always ends up being the best of all possible worlds."

"So," Candi said finally, "*at the moment* God creates a world with free will, that world is the best possible world. And that's because at least God *made it possible* for us to live in a world where everybody always chooses to do right. But if we don't choose right then God's off the fucking hook. Because God *can't* interfere with our choices, right?"

"Yes! Absolutely"

"So," Candi said, "The story you're tellin me is this. There could only be a world without any pain and suffering and murder and rape if that world just *happened* to turn out that way. And it would just happen to turn out that way by dumb luck, right?"

"Yes, goddammit!" Mike said, "Goddammit, that's right!"

"Because," Candi said, "If God like programmed a world with no pain and suffering, then it would be a less-than-perfect-world because it lacked the good of free will, right?"

"Yes!"

"Oh, I get it," Candi said, "Seems pretty logical to me. Still pretty fucked up, but logical."

"It's like I said before," Mike said, "We may not like it. It may seem a little fucked up. But that doesn't mean it's not the case. That doesn't mean it's not true."

"Yep"

"In fact," Mike said, "Logically speaking, our world *must* be the case. If God created this world we live in, then this *is* the best of all possible worlds." Mike wanted to celebrate so he ordered them another margarita.

He'd done the impossible, Mike thought. Not only had he successfully explained his theodicy to Candi, of all people. But also, he'd convinced her to agree with him too. Mike envisioned his paper published in such scholarly journals as *The Philosophical Review* or *Faith & Philosophy*. He imagined packed rooms at philosophy conferences. Jealous colleagues paying him *faux* accolades. And the possibility of tenure.

"But," Candi said, interrupting his academic reverie. "I don't fucking buy it, ya know."

"What?"

"I just don't fucking buy it. I mean. Sure it's logical and all. Sure. But I just don't buy it for a fucking second."

"But if you agree that it's logical, then you must agree-"

"I've got my own," she raised her hands and made quotation marks with her fingers, "*theodicy*, ya know." Candi smiled. "Yep. I've got my own little theodicy. And I just might write my own really, really, really, really long-research-paper about it too."

"Oh, for Chrissakes, Candi! I really thought we were having a serious discussion here. I was really starting to appreciate your honest and serious feedback."

"I am serious," she said, "You stuck-up sonuvvabitch. What? You think you and your smarty-pants philosophy friends are the only people who ever gave any fucking thought to why this world is such a fucked up place? Believe me, pardner. I've given it a lot of fucking thought."

Mike guessed that Candi was actually serious. And for just a moment, he felt a little chagrined. And yet, Mike reminded himself, he was sure that whatever common, middle-class American Sunday-school answer to the problem of evil that Candi was going to try to pass off as her own, would certainly be something he'd heard before. So he decided to humor her. "Ok, fine," Mike said, "Let's hear *your* theodicy."

"Well," Candi said, "First off. I call it, The Cockroach Theodicy. Pretty cool fucking name, huh?"

Mike shook his head.

"Hey! I fucking liked the name of yours!"

"Ok," Mike said, "It's a cool name."

"Right. Ok. It goes like this. Let me ask *you* a question now. You ever step on a cockroach?"

"Sure, lots of times."

"Ever call an exterminator?"

"Yes"

"And did you ever feel bad about it?"

There were beginning to be moments, albeit brief moments, when Mike was impressed by Candi. Like now. She was using the Socratic Method and didn't even know it.

"Well?" Candi said, "Did you ever fucking feel bad about it?"

"No"

"Well why the fuck not? I mean. A cockroach is a livin thing that can feel pain, right?"

"Yes, cockroaches can feel pain."

"So didn't you ever feel fucking bad about the pain and suffering of a poor little cockroach?"

"No, I didn't," Mike said. "What's your point?"

"Well why the fuck not? Shouldn't you feel bad? Shouldn't you be concerned about preventing the pain and suffering of another livin thing? Even if it's just a fucking cockroach?"

"Cockroaches are not sentient, Candi. That means that cockroaches don't experience the same kind of pain and suffering as you and me."

"I'm not sayin it's the same. You're right. It's fucking *not* the same. But! Cockroaches can still feel pain. And they can still suffer a painful death, right? I mean just because you can't do math or logic don't mean you can't feel pain and suffer from it, right?"

"Ok, you're right."

"So why the fuck don't you feel bad about it?"

"Well, I *could* feel bad about it. And I suppose I could *prefer* that the cockroach not feel pain and suffer. But honestly, I don't."

"Exactly," Candi said. "But! Even while you're *preferrin* that the cockroach not feel pain and suffering, does that mean you're gonna actually give a shit enough about the cockroach to actually do somethin about it?"

Mike was a little puzzled. So far, Candi's theodicy was not turning out to be the standard middle-American answer every faithful lemming learns in Sunday school.

"I mean," Candi said, "Just because you *could* do somethin about the cockroach's pain and suffering. And just because you *could* prefer that the little guy not be in pain and suffering. That doesn't fucking mean you're actually gonna step in and try to stop it. Am I right?"

"I suppose"

"And suck on this dick for a second," Candi said. "Let's say you're not even the one steppin on the cockroach. Let's say it's somebody else doin the stompin. Are you gonna give a shit enough to try to stop them?"

"Well"

"Come on now," Candi said, "Honestly? Really? Are you ever gonna feel bad enough to run over there and stop somebody from stompin a cockroach?"

"Ok. No, I wouldn't"

"Thank you. Me neither. Nobody fucking would. So the question is still on the table. Right here on the fucking table between the chips and queso. Why wouldn't you try to prevent the cockroach's pain and suffering?"

"I guess," Mike said, "It's difficult for me to feel *that much* sympathy for a cockroach."

"Thank you! Me too! You know somethin pardner. You're not as fucking out-of-touch as I thought."

"Thanks a lot"

"So why is it sooo fucking difficult for you and me, or for anybody, to feel enough fucking sympathy for a cockroach to actually try to prevent the little guy's pain and suffering?"

Mike didn't like where this Socratic line of questioning was going. "I guess," he said, "Cockroaches are pretty low on the food chain. There's a big difference between me and a cockroach. Too big of a difference. If a fellow human were suffering, or even a dog or cat, I would step in and try to stop the-"

"Exactly! Thank you! You said it motherfucker. There's *too big* a difference between me and a cockroach. There's just *too big* of a difference for me to give *enough of a shit* to try and prevent its pain and suffering."

"So what's your point, Candi?"

"My point is this. I think God must be a lot like you and me."

"Oh for Chrissakes"

"No, no, now. Hear me out here. The way I figure it is this. There's a *way* bigger difference between me and God, then there is between me and a fucking cockroach. So if I could prevent a cockroach's sufferin, but I just can't seem muster up enough sympathy to *actually* interfere and stop it, then why would I expect God to do any different for little ol me?"

"What?"

"I mean. You don't think I'm immoral or evil or even callous for not helpin out that little cockroach, right?"

"You're right, Candi. I wouldn't morally condemn you for refusing to help a cockroach. But there is another-"

"Thank you," Candi said. "So why should we expect God to be any different? Why should me or you think less of God for not helpin us out?"

"Actually," Mike said, "I expect God to be very, very different from you or me."

"Why?"

"Because," Mike said, "If God does in fact exist, then God is a perfect being. And that means God is perfectly good. And if God is perfectly good then God would try to prevent all pointless pain and suffering."

"I agree, goddammit," Candi said. "God *is* perfectly fucking good. But! If you can't morally condemn me for not bein able to give a shit about a cockroach's pain and suffering. Then how can you morally condemn God for the same damn thing? I mean. Me and you are off the hook for not givin enough of a shit about a cockroach. So God should be off the hook for not givin enough of a shit about me and you. That's all I'm fucking sayin, pardner."

"Oh, for Chrissakes, Candi," Mike said. "I can't think of the world or God that way."

"Oh, but wait a second there, pardner. You fucking *can* think of the world and God that way! You just don't *want* to think of them that way." Candi smiled and said, "About five fucking minutes ago you yourself said- we may not like it but that doesn't mean it's not the case. Remember?"

Mike shook his head.

"Looks to me, pardner," Candi said, "Like we're ridin the exact same fucking horse into the exact same fucking town. Doesn't it now?"

✳ ✳ ✳

Mike and Candi stood in the parking lot of Ninfa's after dinner. She pulled out a blowpop and said, "Hey I gotta bright fucking idea for your novel."

"Oh really?" Mike said, "Well then, by all means Gertrude Stein, let's hear it."

Candi didn't seem to give a shit what Mike's archaic literary reference meant. "You want your novel to be about a road trip, right?"

"A journey," Mike said, "Actually, a kind of odyssey."

"You mean like a quest?"

"Sure"

"You mean where you look for somethin valuable? Like in *Monty Python's Quest for the Holy Grail?*"

Mike sighed and said, "Yeah, something like that."

"Or like a cattle drive up north like back in the Old West?"

"Let's just call it an odyssey, ok?"

"Well, pardner. I've got the brightest fucking idea for your novel. You're gonna just fucking love it. I mean you're just gonna fucking cum in your pants when you hear this."

"Ok, ok. What's your bright idea?"

"What if me and you took a little," Candi made her quotation marks, *"odyssey,* together? What if tomorrow me and you went on a drive about three hours north of Houston? I know this little Texas town where somethin real valuable is buried. Kinda like buried treasure. Anyways, the way I figure it is. I need to pick up this buried treasure and fucking pawn it. And you need a great fucking idea for your novel. So I reckon we both fucking win, right?"

"What exactly is buried out there?"

"I know you're suspicious, pardner," Candi said. "And if you had just half the fucking brains your college degree says you do. Then you'd probably never agree to just drive out northwards into the Texas countryside with a whore you just met this afternoon. But! At the same time. If I told you what the buried treasure was it would fucking ruin the suspense of our little story here, right?"

"Can you at least tell me the name of the town?"

"Like you would fucking know it if I told you. Believe me, pardner. It's nowhere special."

"I don't know, Candi. I should probably stick to my original plan. You know. Driving to California tomorrow. My novel is supposed to be about an odyssey from Houston to California. I envision it being very Steinbeckesque."

"Shit, pardner. Fuck California! Fuck California right in their liberal earthquakin asshole. I'm tellin ya. California is just like fucking New York City. It's already been fucking done. I'm tellin ya. That fucking odyssey has been done. It's like spurrin a dead horse if you ask me."

"I don't know, Candi."

"Listen up pardner. I guaran-goddamn-tee you that nobody. And I mean fucking nobody ever wrote a fucking novel about an odyssey to *this* fucking place! That's what makes my bright idea sooo fucking bright!"

"Uh, I really don't-"

"And me and you could have some real adventures along the way. Just like they did on them cattle drives back in the Old West. Come on, pardner! Haven't you always wanted to have some real fucking adventures?"

"Well"

"Believe you me, pardner. I'll see to it that you've got so many fucking adventures you're gonna be able to write five fucking novels after it's all said and done."

Mike sensed desperation in Candi's voice; and yet, he couldn't be certain. Is this bright idea of hers, Mike wondered, just a clever ruse? Was Candi just trying to get him to drive her somewhere she needed to be? And what's going to happen to me, Mike thought, when, or even if, I get there? He felt a little sick at his stomach.

But even if it were just a clever ruse, Mike reasoned, as long as he didn't end up dead, taking a drive with Candi would definitely inspire his novel or at least a few chapters.

"Don't worry, pardner," Candi said, patting him on the shoulder, "I'm not gonna take you out on some lonely fucking Texas highway. And then go all Aileen Wuornos on your ass if that's what you're thinkin."

"Aileen who?"

"Oh you know. Aileen Wuornos. That fucking famous whore. You remember? She was that whore who became a serial killer. They made that fucking movie *Monster* about her."

"Oh yeah. I remember that. I didn't see the movie though."

"I just wish I looked as good as Charleze Theron!"

You're hotter than her, Mike thought to himself.

"They fucking executed her ass for that shit, you know?"

"I know," Mike said, shaking his head. "Just another shameful example of how capital punishment inevitably-"

"You know what I think?" Candi said. "I think. The only thing that pisses men off even more than when their woman gets an abortion without them knowin it, is when a fucking whore cuts off their dick, and then sticks it in their mouth instead of suckin it."

Mike winced.

"I'm tellin you, pardner. That Aileen Wuornos was one pissed-off fucking whore."

"I think," Mike said, "She was mentally unstable. It's really sad that our society has-"

"Oh come on!" Candi said, smacking her blowpop between her lips. "That's fucking bleedin-heart liberal bullshit and you know it!"

"What?"

"Every fucking time somebody commits a fucking crime that nobody can believe they committed people call them crazy."

"Why is that bullshit?"

"Oh, it's bullshit alright. I mean fucking Hitler killed millions of fucking Jews so everybody calls him crazy. Charlie fucking Manson orders a bunch of dumb cunts to murder some rich Hollywood pricks and of course he must be crazy too. You ever consider for just a fucking minute that these kinda people might *not* be crazy? Maybe they're just really, really, really, really fucking pissed off?"

"I think it's safe to say," Mike said, "That both Hitler and Manson were more than just pissed off. In fact, I think that-"

"And look at what they called that fucking flick about Eileen Wuornos. They called it, *Monster*. Just the title of that flick should tell you what people really think. That people really think a whore like Aileen Wuornos must have been a fucking monster to do the shit she did. That people think she was just a monster. Like she wasn't even fucking human."

"I don't think that's what people actually mean when they-"

"What a fucking slap in her fucking face! You know what I bet? I bet every time she executed one of those nasty motherfuckers. I bet she felt perfectly fucking justified for what she'd done. And I bet it felt sooo fucking good to her too. Nope! I don't reckon Aileen Wuornos was a monster. I think she was just fucking pissed off at the goddamned fucking world."

"Oh, for Chrissakes, Candi," Mike said, feeling a little nauseous now. "What do you mean she was just pissed off? Why?"

"Why? Why? Who the fuck knows why! All I know is. People do some fucked up shit when they're pissed off. It's like when animals go crazy from bein locked up in a fucking zoo. Or some circus elephant just one day decides to trample all the fucking kiddos who are waitin for a ride."

"I'd like to believe we're better than the animals," Mike said. "After all, unlike the animals in the zoo, we humans *can be* rational."

"And we can be irrational, pissed-off sons of fucking bitches too! And that's all I'm fucking sayin about that shit."

Mike wondered why Candi would offer an apologetic justifying the execution of nasty motherfuckers by a pissed-off whore, while at the same time trying to convince him to go with her on a drive into rural Texas in search of buried treasure. Of course, Mike reasoned, if Candi wanted to cut off his dick and stick it in his mouth, she didn't need to take him into the countryside to do it. He was certain Candi was familiar enough with plenty of dark alleys in Houston which would do just fine.

Candi's apologetics and soliloquies, Mike was beginning to think, seemed more for the sake of argument than a genuine expression of her feelings. He was reminded of something his grandfather used to say about people like Candi- that she would argue with a fence post.

"Oh, come on now! Don't worry pardner," Candi said. "And don't get your panties all up in a fucking bunch either. I'm not gonna cut off your dick and then stick it in your mouth." She laughed out loud. "Now! I might cut off your dick. That part's true. But! After all we've fucking been through together I'd never go and stick it in your mouth."

Mike didn't laugh. "So this town," Mike said, "It's only three hours from Houston?"

"Yep. Just about a three hour drive northwards. This little town's kinda right in the middle of nowhere. But! Along the way. I'll show you some sites and a few other fantastic little Texas towns. And I'll spin you a few Texas tall tales. How's that sound to you, pardner?"

Mike's stomach began to settle back down.

"You really gotta get off the interstate," Candi said, "If you really wanna see Texas. Great shit for your novel. I'm telling you. I fucking promise."

"So you're not going to tell me anything else about this town or the buried treasure?"

"Nope. Sorry, pardner. It's gotta be a fucking surprise or no fucking deal."

"This buried treasure of yours," Mike said, "It doesn't involve anything illegal does it? I don't want to find myself in the middle of a drug deal or-"

"Hey! Just because I'm a whore doesn't mean I fucking do drugs. You fucking asshole! And just for the fucking record. I don't ever do drugs. Ever! And I try to never hang out with people who do."

"That's not what I meant."

"Don't get me wrong," Candi said. "I'm not judgmental. Believe me! I just don't wanna be in the wrong place at the wrong time. With the wrong fucking people. My daddy used to say- A companion of fools suffers harm. And I fucking believe that shit."

That someone like Candi could so effortlessly take the moral high-ground never ceased to amaze and puzzle Mike. Still, he reasoned, for the sake of needing Candi around for his novel, he decided to make amends. "I'm sorry, Candi."

"And by the by, pardner," Candi said. "Those prescription pills you been poppin all day long. I'll bet you didn't buy them at a fucking pharmacy, right? Am I right?" She smiled and winked at him.

"That's my business"

"Whatever you fucking say, pardner. You know me. God fucking knows I don't fucking judge. But I gotta tell you. Those fucking amphetamines are bad news. Especially the way you been poppin em. I mean that shit will kill you faster than a bullet from a motherfucking .45."

"Well, doctor," Mike said, "Thank you sooo much for your expert medical advice."

"Why do you pop that shit anyways?"

"It helps me be creative and write."

"Well then I reckon you didn't take enough of it while you were writin your dissertation, huh?"

"It picks me up, ok? It puts me in a better mood."

"Yeah, I reckon it does. But it's such a phony kind of mood don't you think? I mean. It ain't really real life when you take that shit all the time."

"Listen, Candi," Mike said, "You don't know the first goddamn thing about my life. I know you don't think I have any real problems but you're dead wrong. Everybody, rich or poor, has their own problems. And everybody, rich or poor, has their own solutions to those problems. Mine just happen to come in prescription bottles."

"Fair enough," Candi said. "Simmer down there, pardner. I said I wasn't judgin you. I'm just tryin to give you some friendly fucking advice. That's all."

"You don't ever do any drugs, huh?" Mike said. "Somehow I find that really hard to believe."

"Why is that sooo fucking hard to believe?"

"I guess, well. I guess because of what you do for a living. I would think that being a whore would be a really, well, a really difficult life. I guess I just wonder how you cope."

Candi smiled and said, "How do I cope? What a fucking question!" She laughed out loud. "How do I cope?"

"What's so funny?"

"Listen up pardner. I do my best *never* to cope."

"What do you mean?"

"Copin ain't livin."

"Come on, Candi. Everybody copes. Whether they know it or not. Whether they'll admit it or not. Everybody copes."

"Not me," Candi fired back at him. "I'm too busy grabbin life by the dick and fondlin and suckin and fucking it till it cums."

Mike thought it was extremely ironic that Candi chose that metaphor.

"Anyways," Candi said, "copin is for pussies."

"Oh really?"

"Yep. At some point in life you just gotta say to yourself- I'm here. I didn't ask to be here. I don't know why I'm here. But! I'm fucking here. And I'm not gonna fucking be here for very long. So I better fucking make the best of it."

Mike recalled a quote by the French existential philosopher, Albert Camus- *At a certain point in life, every man is responsible for his own face.*

Mike studied Candi's face in the pale mélange of moonbeams and city streetlights. There was courage in the way she sucked blowpops and fortitude in the way she described grabbing life by the dick. There was an authenticity in her baby blue eyes which suggested the paucity of any pretense. And yet, Mike observed, there was a recondite sadness in the way her smile curled upwards across her young face. It didn't seem to be a sadness about her present circumstances; but instead, a longing for something which permeated both her past and future.

"Well, pardner," Candi said, "You ready to see if you got what it takes to be a cowboy?" She tossed her spent blowpop stick on the ground. "Are we goin on a drive up north?"

Mike took a deep, timorous breath. He looked her body up and down, glancing at her tits and ass. For a brief moment, he wondered if their odyssey would include them fucking. Candi was absolutely gorgeous, and absolutely fuckable. And yet, Mike realized that when he first met her, he would have actually preferred a blow job. It seemed somehow less personal and exploitive. But ever since their series of conversations, especially her presentation of her Cockroach Theodicy, Mike desperately wanted to actually fuck Candi's pussy.

In addition to actually fucking Candi's pussy, Mike wanted adventure. He wanted ideas for his novel and wanted more than anything to go on a good old fashioned Homeric odyssey. After all, that's why I fled from Connecticut, he told himself. And with Candi along for the drive it was guaranteed to never be a dull moment. Her bright idea seemed to be the perfect plotline for a novel...

There are certain choices you make in life which, intrinsi-cally, are neither good nor bad because the consequences of these choices are impossible to predict. Only once the choice is made and time brings to fruition its consequences, can you either cel-ebrate or regret your choice. And yet, there remain some choices which, even in the clarity of hindsight, you cannot decide whether to celebrate or regret. Perhaps this is because the consequences of these choices prevail upon you both the heights of pleasure *and* the depths of pain.

Mike was about to make just such a choice.

"Let's do it." Mike said. "Let's go on a drive."

"Yes!" Candi exclaimed, "Let's ride!"

Chapter 4

*The Ballad of Pierre Cagniart; The Magnificent Magnolia Hotel;
An Etymology of the word Rape; What Mike and Candi revealed when
they played the 'Who Would You Fuck Game';
How Mike and Candi drank all night and what Mike confessed*

"So," Mike said, "Where should we stay tonight?" They drove down Navigation Boulevard towards downtown Houston. "I'd like to take you to a really nice hotel."

"Bear left up here," Candi said, "and then down through that tunnel under that street. And then bear right onto Franklin Street and go under 59."

"So where should we stay?"

"Well according to *The Houston Press*," Candi said, "There's only one place to stay when you're in Houston, Texas. And that's downtown. In the magnificent Magnolia Hotel! It's on the corner of Texas and Fannin."

The historic skyscraper building which houses the modern-day Magnolia Hotel was at one time the headquarters for Shell Oil Company and later the Houston Post-Dispatch Newspaper. It was the tallest building in Houston for only one year, way back in 1926. Today it's one of Houston's finest luxury hotels.

"It's even gotta rooftop fucking pool *and* a hot tub!" Candi said. "Holy fucking shit! Can you imagine the fucking view of the Houston skyline from up there?"

"Sounds good to me"

"Holy fucking shit. This is gonna be amazin! I'll bet you they've got a heck of a fucking bar up there too. Nothin but top-shelf liquor. And you're buyin motherfucker!"

"But of course," Mike said.

"Oh, yeah," Candi said. "Can I carry your copy of *Moby Dick* around with me?" She cradled the book to her chest like a young girl with a baby doll. "I'd kinda like to thumb through it. It's been a while."

"Sure," Mike said. It was still disconcerting for him to think of somebody like Candi reading *Moby Dick*. Mike doubted that she really appreciated the text, or even had the ability to appreciate it. He doubted that she ever realized that the novel was about so much more than Captain Ahab's search for the white whale.

"I thumbed through a first edition of this book once," Candi said.

"This story," Mike said, "I've got to hear."

Candi smirked at him and then began her ballad. "Well, I was fucking this prick who went to Texas State University. And so I found myself in San Marcos for the weekend. Actually. You really should fucking go to San Marcos someday. It's a fucking beautiful campus. And the San Marcos River is crystal fucking clear and seventy-two fucking degrees all year round and-"

"Wait a second," Mike said. "You said, Texas State University, right?"

"Yep"

"Wow. What a coincidence. My friend back at Yale. His name was Sonny Quillan. He graduated from Texas State University."

"I'm surprised anybody from Texas State ever went to your fancy-schmancy college."

"Well," Mike said, "Sonny wasn't just anybody."

"Anyways," Candi said. "Like I was sayin. This prick I was fucking took some class called intellectual history or some stupid shit like that. Anyways. The professor who taught that class was this Frenchman named Pierre Cagniart. How a Frenchman ended up in fucking San Marcos, Texas, I'll never fucking figure out."

"Anyways. One night this Pierre Cagniart hosted a dinner party for his students at his house. And my then-fuck-buddy took me along for some free food and booze. Let me tell you. It was the coolest fucking party ever. Cagniart served wines and cheeses. It was a real classy spread! I mean I fucking felt like I was in, gay Pair-eee! If you know what I mean?"

"Cagniart must've been in his sixties. He chain smoked. And back then, I did too. So I think he really liked that about me. Anyways. He smoked these nasty-ass French coffin-nails that John Lennon smoked too. I forget what they're called."

"Gauloises," Mike said, "They're called Gauloises ciga-rettes. One of my favorite French philosophers, Jean-Paul Sartre, smoked them too."

"Wow," Candi said, "Thanks for the info, worthless-trivia boy! Am I tellin you a fucking story or are you a contestant on a fucking quiz show?"

"Sorry! For Chrissakes"

"So," Candi said, "Cagniart even wore a cute little silk hand-kerchief wrapped around his neck and tucked into his collar."

"It's called a *cravat*," Mike said with a French accent.

"It's called- *shut the fuck up* while I'm tellin you a story!"

"Sorry"

"So Cagniart lived in this big old house near campus. He was makin two of the rooms in the house into a big fucking library. With wooden shelves and slidin ladders and everythin. Just like in that fucking flick, *My Fair Lady*. It was fucking awe-some. Anyways. While my then-fuck-buddy was gulpin down red wine and gettin shit-faced, I wandered into this unfinished library. And in this big glass bookcase there were a lot of old books. I mean really fucking old antique books. And inside I fucking saw a copy of *Moby Dick*."

"That's a first edition, Cagniart said to me. I turned around and he was holdin two glasses of wine. He handed one of them to me and smiled. I told him about how *Moby Dick* was the only book I'd ever read. I can still remember his face. And for some weird reason he didn't seem shocked by that at all."

"Anyways. He asked me if I'd like to hold the book. And I said- fuck yeah I would." He opened up the bookcase and handed it to me. It was totally fucking awesome. So we lit up our coffin nails. Drank our wine. And talked about *Moby Dick* almost the whole fucking night."

"What about your date?"

"He got drunk off his ass and drove off early with some of his buddies. I think Gary P. Nunn was playin in town that night. Anyways. Me and Cagniart smoked a shit-ton of coffin nails. And drank more than a few bottles of wine. It was fucking awesome. It was the only time I ever talked about a book with anybody. And let me tell you, pardner. He was the smartest man I ever fucking met."

"I hope you realize," Mike said, "That he probably just wanted to fuck you."

Candi looked down. She pressed her lips together and breathed deeply. "I reckon I'd like to think he just enjoyed talkin to me about the book."

"So you're telling me that you *didn't* fuck him?"

"No, pardner. I didn't fucking fuck him. But you know what? Fuck you! Fuck you very much for askin."

"Sorry. I didn't mean to-"

"Anyways. Me and Cagniart sat there until dawn. I still remember his accent. His French accent gave him the cutest little lisp. As long as I live I'll never fucking forget his cute little lisp."

"Candi, I really am sorry you know...."

"And you know what?" Candi said, "He was fucking obsessed with Wyoming. I mean he had pictures of cowboys ropin cattle. Buffalo and Indians and all that western shit. For some fucking reason all he wanted was to move out West to Wyoming. And be a cowboy. Can you imagine? A man as smart and as cultured as him? Just wantin to be a cowboy? So I told him. Listen up, Pierre. You'd look really good in a cowboy hat. He fucking loved that."

"Anyways. We talked all fucking night. Mostly about *Moby Dick*. I told him I thought Ishmael totally had a hard-on for Queequeg."

"You said what?"

"You fucking heard me. Come on! Read that fucking book. Read *Moby Dick*. It's gotta be the gayest book ever fucking written. I mean think about it for a fucking second. It's a story about a bunch of men on a ship together for a few years. No women on board, pardner. And they're all lookin for a *sperm* whale called Moby *Dick*! It doesn't get any fucking gayer than that!" Candi laughed.

"It's fucking obvious," Candi said, "Ishmael wanted Queequeg to fuck his brains out. He totally had jungle fucking fever. Ishmael wanted Queequeg to put his harpoon somewhere... And it wasn't in the whale, if you know what I mean?" Candi nudged Mike with her elbow and winked at him. "Get it? Get it?"

"Trust me. Ishmael was on his own fucking mission. He was lookin for Queequeg's moby dick!" Candi nudged Mike again and said, "Good thing his name wasn't *Queer*-queg!" She laughed out loud and slapped her knees, and then slapped Mike's knees too.

"Please tell me," Mike said, "You didn't make these jokes in front of Dr. Cagniart."

"Fuck yeah I did! Are you fucking kiddin me? He laughed his French ass off!"

Mike sighed.

"So in the mornin," Candi said, "Cagniart made coffee for us. It was real strong coffee too. He even used an actual French press to make it. You know. Ground those fucking coffee beans right there in his kitchen. It was fucking awesome. And that's when Cagniart said somethin to me that I've never fucking forgotten."

"What?"

"Have you ever had anybody say somethin to you that was so profound that it kinda stuck with you all your life?"

"I can't think of anything right now."

"I reckon," Candi said, "That's what JC's disciples must have felt like all the fucking time."

"I take it you mean, Jesus Christ?"

"Who the fuck else?"

"So what did Cagniart say?"

"Yep. It was a perfect fucking moment. French coffee. Sittin in that unfinished library. Me bummin nasty-ass coffin nails off Cagniart."

"So what did he say to you?"

"He said to me- My dear, you must never pwee-pare your pweasures.

"What?"

"He said to me," Candi said, feigning the lisp, "You must never pwee-pare your pweasures."

"Ok, I get it," Mike said, "You must never prepare your pleasures."

"Yep. Pretty fucking profound, huh? Cagniart told me some French writer said it a long fucking time ago. But I've never been able to remember who the fuck it was."

The quote sounded familiar to Mike. But he couldn't name the writer. Was it Malraux or Montaigne? Or Gide perhaps?

"It's just such good fucking advice," Candi said. "It's kinda my motto for life."

"I'm not surprised," Mike said, "You're a real live-in-the-moment kind of girl."

Candi smiled and said, "Yeah. But it's not just about livin in the fucking moment. It's about not always expectin moments in life to be picture perfect. You know? It's about just acceptin the moment. Takin the good with the bad. And not always havin unrealistic fucking expectations about life."

"Is that what Cagniart told you it meant?"

"Nope. That's all me, pardner." Candi said. "I've thought a lot about those words."

"I agree," Mike said, "It's good advice."

"I wonder," Candi said, "If Cagniart ever made it out west to Wyoming. I wonder if he ever got him a cowboy hat."

Candi turned to Mike and said, "So, pardner. What's *your* motto for life?"

It took Mike a long time to think of a life motto, which turned out to be quote by one of his favorite philosophers, Jean-Paul Sartre. However, it took Mike even longer to explain to Candi the significance of the quote. Which means that what should've been interesting dialogue turned out to be a boring and worthless conversation altogether. Fortunately, for all involved, neither the quote nor Mike's efforts to explain it are recorded in the present volume.

✳ ✳ ✳

Mike and Candi sat at the bar in the Magnolia Hotel. Mike was thinking about how the bellman downstairs had the same name as the bellman in *Catcher in the Rye*. A very cool coincidence, he mused.

"Let's play a game," Candi said. "It's called, The Who Would You Fuck Game." The bartender looked at Candi funny, and then went on making a couple of martinis for a group of men in tuxedos.

"Ok" Mike said, grinning, "This sounds like a game *you'd* be really good at."

"Hey, pardner. At what point in this fucking story are you gonna stop lookin down your fucking nose at me just because I'm a fucking whore?"

The well-dressed clientele around them stopped and stared for a moment.

"Hey, for Chrissakes," Mike said, whispering, "Chill out. I was only teasing you."

"Yeah right. You're one of those assholes who says shit he really means but then claims he was only jokin."

"I *was* only joking, Candi."

"You know what? It must be nice to be a complete fucking washout waste-of-space like you. And yet still live your fucking life on the moral high ground like you're fucking better than everybody else."

"For Chrissakes, Candi. Will you chill out? I don't think I'm better than anybody."

"Except," Candi said way too loudly, "for a whore from Houston, Texas."

The bartender glanced over in their direction and frowned.

"Ok, ok," Mike said in a hushed voice, "for Chrissakes, I'm sorry. I fucking apologize for that comment." Mike watched the bartender carefully out of the corner of his eye.

"Now. That's better," Candi said. "I reckon I forgive you, for now. You sorry sack of shit, motherfucking, cocksucking, bastard." She smiled. "Now. We can play the game."

"Here's how you play," Candi said, then took a drink of her gin and tonic. "There are four questions. First question is- Who would you fuck? And I'm just talkin about a good ol fashioned animal fucking. Strictly physical."

"Second question- Who would you make love to? Now I'm talkin about foreplay. You know. Face-to-face, sweet love-makin that lasts a couple of hours."

"Third question- Who would you take a romantic walk on Galveston beach with? Here I'm talkin about no sex at all. No sex allowed. Just a long intimate conversation. Talkin until dawn."

"Fourth and final question- Who would you marry and settle down with? I'm talkin about somebody you'd want to grow old with. Somebody who makes you laugh. And makes you feel safe. You know? Warm fuzzy romantic bullshit like that."

"So," Mike said, "What's the point of this little game?" He gulped his gin and tonic and signaled the bartender for another.

"Well, pardner. I've got a theory about that," Candi said, sipping her gin and tonic. "I reckon how a person answers these questions. And what a person's three favorite flicks are. Will tell you more about that person than any other fucking questions you could ever ask them. I'm fucking serious."

"Are we going to talk about our favorite films too?"

"Nope. Not right now we're not. Right now we're just gonna play The Who Would You Fuck Game. We'll get to our favorite flicks later on."

Mike gulped his new drink and said, "Ok, but you go first."

"Alrighty. Fine. Go ahead and ask me the first question."

Mike thought for just a second and then said, "Candi, who would you fuck?"

"I love this fucking game," Candi said, rubbing her hands together and smiling. "Well. I'd definitely have a threesome. And it would be fucking awesome."

"A threesome, really? Is that allowed in the game?"

"Yep. Of course its fucking allowed!"

"Ok"

"Anyways. I'd have a threesome with John Wayne and Humphrey Bogart," Candi said, smiling. "Yep. The Duke would wear his cowboy hat, boots, gun belt and spurs. And he would have his dick in my asshole. And then Bogart would be wearin nothin but his fedora. And his dick would be fucking my pussy."

Mike wasn't a prude, but the scenario Candi described seemed cinematically sacrilegious somehow.

"Oh yeah," Candi said, "I almost forgot! William Holden would be fucking me too."

"You've got a *really* active, and perverse imagination. You know that?"

"The other day I was playin this game with my friend," Candi said. "Everybody calls him Black-Jack-in-the-Cardboard-Box. He lives downtown. Anyways. He made me realize that I had an empty fuckhole that needed fillin. William Holden would have his dick in my mouth, down my throat, pumping my tonsils full of his hot cum."

"What's the name of that friend of yours, again?"

"I don't know his real name. Everybody just calls him, Black-Jack-in-the-Cardboard-Box. He's a big black homeless guy. He sits in the parking lot across from the downtown Sears. At the intersection of San Jacinto and Wheeler streets. There's a Jack-in-the-Box nearby. And a lot of people stop and buy him food, drinks, and even fucking milkshakes!"

"And here's the fucking kicker! He doesn't even ask or even beg for any of it. He just sits his big fat black ass right down there, like a wise man on a fucking mountain. Anyways. Me and him were playin this game a few days ago. And he's the one who made me realize that in my ultimate fuck fantasy, nobody even had their dick in my mouth. So I decided it would be William fucking Holden."

"Why does that name sound so familiar?" Mike said. "Who is William Holden?"

"Oh my fucking God! You've gotta be fucking kiddin! You mean you don't know who William fucking Holden is?"

"No"

"He's only the fucking star of the some of the best fucking flicks ever made! *Stalag 17. Sunset Boulevard. The Wild Bunch?*"

"Oh yeah," Mike said, "that guy"

"Yeah, you fucking retard dumbass! *That* guy!"

"Ok, ok. I should've known that." Mike decided to play the devil's advocate and prove he wasn't a dumbass, to make up for not knowing who William Holden was. "Well, let me ask you then," Mike said to her, "Exactly which William Holden are you talking about? The young and brooding William Holden of *Sunset Boulevard*? Or the aging and jaded William Holden from *The Wild Bunch*?"

"Huh, that's a good question."

"I think it's a fair question, don't you?"

"Oh fuck yeah. It's more than fucking fair," Candi said. "Fuck yeah. Now this fucking game just got a lot more fucking interesting." Candi scratched her chin in a melodramatic display of contemplation and then said, "Definitely the aging and jaded William Holden. Because he wore a cowboy hat in *The Wild Bunch*. I'm a sucker for a cowboy hat. And William Holden could wear a fucking cowboy hat too!"

"Ok," Mike said, "Second question- Who would you make sweet love to?"

"The Houston Kid," Candi said, "That's an easy one."

"No threesome this time?"

"Nope. Threesomes ain't allowed on this question. Those are the rules."

"The Houston Kid? Who's that?"

"Rodney Crowell? You know, The Houston Kid? Come on, pardner. He's only the hottest and most famous thing to come out of Houston, Texas. Since Beyonce, that is."

"Never heard of him"

"He's a famous fucking country singer and songwriter. Let me tell you. Rodney Crowell is sooo fucking sexy. And I'll bet he's made love sooo many times to sooo many beautiful women. That he'd really know what he was doin down there." Candi pointed to her pussy. "Know what I mean, pardner?"

"You know he was married to Rosanna Cash," Candi said, "You know, Johnny Cash's daughter. I mean he got to like have Christmas and fucking thanksgiving with Johnny Cash! Wow! And Rosanna Cash supposedly wrote that famous song about him. It's called, *The Seven Year Ache*. And in that song. Rodney sounds like he was a real asshole to be married to. But! He also sounds like he knows how to fucking handle a clit."

Mike was unfamiliar with either country music or Rodney Crowell, and was therefore unimpressed with Candi's answer. "Ok," Mike said, "Third question- Who would you go on a romantic walk on the beach with?"

"Galveston beach," Candi said. "It has to be Galveston beach."

"Ok. Who would you go on a romantic walk on Galveston beach with?"

"Same answer motherfucker," Candi said, "Rodney Crowell."

"You've really got a thing for this Rodney Crowell guy, huh?"

"Yeah, I know. And it's kinda funny actually. Because he's not necessarily that sexy. But like I said before. You know there's a reason so many of the ladies wanna sleep with him. And that's why I wanna make love to him."

"But you said you don't get to have sex on your romantic walk on the beach?"

"I know, I know. Just hold your fucking horses there, pardner. I reckon that not only would Rodney know how to tug on my clit for a few hours. But he also seems really smart too. I mean he's like a country music philosopher."

"I didn't know there was such a thing," Mike said, "or for that matter, ever could be such a thing."

"I'd just love to talk to Rodney about love, life and every other fucking topic that has any meaning at all. He just seems so wise, you know? Like he really takes a lot of time to fucking reflect about his life and shit like that. And think about the choices he's made. Not many people do that, you know."

"I guess I need to hear some of his music," Mike said, feigning interest.

"Oh fuck yeah. You'd fucking love it! You don't listen to much country music, huh?"

"Uh, no. I don't. None actually..."

"Wow. Well you're fucking missin out, pardner."

"Sure," Mike said. "Ok, last question- Who would you marry and settle down with?"

"This is definitely the toughest question of em all," Candi said. "But! I think it would have to be Steve Wilkos. Even though, goddammit, he's already married to his lovely wife Rachelle."

"Who is Steve Wilkos?"

"Really? Not again! Are you fucking kiddin me? You really, and I mean you really need to watch more daytime TV."

"Well, I know that's always been one of my goals in life."

"Oh fuck you, smart ass. Let me tell you. Steve Wilkos is a real American hero. I mean he's the American fucking dream. He served in the Marines. And then he became a Chicago cop. And then he moonlighted as a security guard on the *Jerry Springer Show*. And then! He was sooo popular he got his own fucking show. And now! Steve helps all kinds of people. Especially women."

"Let me guess," Mike said, "He's handsome and sexy too? And he knows his way around, down there?"

"No actually," Candi said. "He's bald and a little overweight. And he's probably not too bright either. Not dumb or anythin. Just not smart, you know? And I'll bet he's a decent, but not a spectacular fuck." Candi paused and then finished her drink. "But! You know what I love about him? I'd fucking marry Steve Wilkos and settle down with him in a New York minute. Why? Because he fucking stands up for people who can't stand up for themselves. And do you know how fucking rare that is?"

Mike watched Candi stare at the liquor bottles behind the bar. She whispered to herself, "And Steve Wilkos doesn't even wear a cowboy hat."

Mike watched Candi watch the liquor bottles.

Candi broke their silence when she leaned forward and asked the bartender, "Is that the new Jack Daniels made with honey?" A couple of minutes later there were two complimentary shots of Jack Daniels Honey in front of them. They downed them. Mike grimaced. Candi licked her lips. "Ok," Candi said, "Your turn, pardner."

They ordered two more gin and tonics. "Ok, pardner," Candi said, "Who would you fuck?"

"I guess I'd have to say Bette Davis."

"You mean the old actress?"

"Yeah. But not the *Whatever Happened to Baby Jane* Bette Davis. The younger hotter Bette Davis. The one from *Jezebel*."

"Why her?"

"It's her attitude," Mike said. "Her attitude was just so damn sexy. Bette Davis was feisty and could be a real, a real-"

"Bitch" Candi said.

"What I mean is," Mike said, "Bette Davis never took shit from anybody. Can you imagine what foreplay with Bette Davis would be like? I'll bet... What I mean is... I'll bet Betty Davis never gave it up without a fight, huh?" As these words escaped his lips, Mike realized that Candi had a way of making him say things out loud he had only ever thought. He looked for Candi's reaction but she didn't even bat an eye.

✳ ✳ ✳

-RAPE – noun

1. the unlawful compelling of a person through physical force or duress to have sexual intercourse.

2. any act of sexual intercourse that is forced upon a person.

3. an act of plunder, violent seizure, or abuse; despoliation; violation: the rape of the countryside.

RAPE - verb

1. to force to have sexual intercourse.

2. to plunder (a place); despoil.

3. to seize, take, or carry off by force.

Origin: 1250–1300; (v.) Middle English rapen < Anglo-French raper < Latin rapere to seize, carry off by force, plunder; (noun) Middle English < Anglo-French ra(a)p(e), derivative of raper

* * *

"Sounds to me, pardner," Candi said, "Like you like your fucking with a side order of rough and tumble. Am I right?"

Mike took a gulp.

"Sounds to me like," Candi said, "You kinda like it when a woman says no a few times before you shove your dick inside her. Maybe even pushes you away a few times before you fuck her? Am I right?"

"Hey," Mike said, "I didn't mean it like that."

"Oh sure you didn't, pardner. Sure you didn't. Don't worry. It's ok. Don't get all fucking defensive on me. It's not a fucking problem. I mean there's nothin wrong with a little rape fantasy once in a while. You know me. I don't fucking judge nobody."

"I just meant-"

"So you ever ask a woman to slap you while you got your dick inside her?"

"What?"

"You fucking heard me. You want me to say it again? Really fucking loud this time so everybody in this classy joint can join in on our little game? And find out what a sick perverted motherfucker you are?" Candi laughed.

"No, please," Mike said, "I heard you, for Chrissakes. I heard you." He took another gulp of his gin and tonic. "And no, I've never asked a woman to slap me during sex."

"Well then. You oughta fucking try that shit sometime." Candi sipped her drink, "I'll bet you'd really like it. In fact. I'll bet it would make your cock harder than it's ever been. And I'll bet you'd cum more than you ever came before."

"Can we please get on with the game?"

"Sure. Ok. You said you'd fuck Bette Davis. Good choice by the way. I always say. You can't go wrong with a black and white flick fuck. Am I right?"

Mike noticed Candi pause when she noticed a man listening in on their conversation and ogling her breasts. Candi winked at the man, smiled and then turned back to face Mike. "Ok. So second question- Who would you make sweet sweet love to?"

"I'd make love to Mia Farrow."

"Ok, it's my turn now. Who the fuck is that? And why the fuck does that name sound so fucking familiar?"

"She was married to Woody Allen. She starred in some of his most famous films."

"Oh yeah! She's the chick who had that Oriental daughter that Woody Allen fucked when she was like ten or somethin, right? What a fucking creeper! Wasn't she his adopted daughter or somethin like that?"

"It wasn't really his daughter," Mike said. "She was adopted by Mia before she even met Woody. And she was almost eighteen when Woody and she got together."

"Yeah. But that shit about adoptions doesn't fucking matter. I mean. He raised her like a daughter. He played the father role in her life. Like on Christmas and birthdays and shit. Let me tell you. There's no point in life when it's ok to say to your daughter- I'm not takin you out for ice cream on your birthday anymore sweetheart, I'm gonna fuck your tight little pussy instead."

"It's way more complicated than that, Candi. Actually, I've read a few biographies on Woody Allen and all of them say-"

"Holy shit," Candi said, "You've really done your fucking homework, haven't you pardner? And either you're the biggest fucking Woody Allen fan in the world. Or you just wanna figure out how you can adopt a little Oriental girl and then canoodle her pussy when she grows up. And then get away with that sick shit because you're a famous fucking writer just like Woody Allen. Or I reckon. Maybe you're both!"

"Do you think," Mike said, "you could cut me a break just once in a while? You're always giving me shit."

"It's because you're so full of shit, pardner. I mean. You make it so fucking easy."

"Thanks"

"So," Candi said, "Why the fuck would you make sweet love to Mia Farrow? She's not even that hot. And worse! She settled for fucking Woody Allen. Gross! I mean she can't be too good in the sack."

"I met Mia Farrow at Yale a few years ago," Mike said. "She hosted a fundraiser for Darfur."

"What the fuck is Darfur?"

"It's a war-torn country in Africa."

"Isn't every fucking country in fucking Africa war-torn?" Candi said, laughing.

Mike shook his head and said, "I'm really glad you weren't at that fundraiser."

"So how much money did ya'll raise for those poor little starvin African fuckers in Darfur?"

"I don't remember"

"Well then how much did *you* give?"

"Uh, I don't remember." Mike recalled that he had not given any money at the fundraiser. In fact, Mike never knew how much money was raised.

"Sounds to me," Candi said, "Like you just went to that fucking fundraiser just to meet Mia Farrow. Am I right?"

"I think Mia would be awesome in the sack," Mike said. "She's so classic." Mike could tell Candi remained unimpressed with his choice. "Plus. She was also married to Andre Previn *and* Frank Sinatra. Can you imagine following in those footsteps?"

"I don't think it's their footsteps you're interested in followin in," Candi said. "So you're tellin me that you wanna make sweet love to Mia Farrow. And it's all because you wanna stick your dick in the same pussy-hole as Woody Allen, Frank Sinatra and some other fucking famous guy?"

"No, for Chrissakes. It's not like that at all."

"Oh it's exactly fucking like that, pardner."

"You do this with every answer I give," Mike said. "I didn't give you shit about your choices."

Candi laughed and said, "That's because my choices were cool and original. Your choices are just fucked up and pathetic."

Mike sighed.

"Hey! I've got another bright idea!" Candi said. "How about you just strap on a dildo. And then you can just fuck Woody Allen right in the asshole. I mean just go right to the fucking source. Just skip fucking Mia altogether. And while you're at it. You can dig up Ol Blue Eyes and butt-fuck his rotten corpse too." A group of people in suits and fancy dresses stared disapprovingly. The women glared at Candi but the men seemed to smile.

"Dammit!" Mike said. "You're ruining this game for me, Candi. Seriously. I'm not going to play anymore if you keep this up. I'm trying to be honest and have a little fun here." He ordered them two more drinks.

"Ok, pardner. I'm sorry for givin you shit about you're stupid fucking choices. I promise I'll behave. And I promise I'll keep my fucking mouth shut. Which is," she leaned back towards the man sitting next to her and whispered, "not how I usually do business if you know what I mean?" Candi nudged the man with her elbow, winked at him, and then popped a lime wedge into her mouth.

Mike felt jealous every time Candi flirted with the room. And yet, hanging out with Candi made him feel good too, in a way no woman had ever made him feel before. Every time Candi flirted with a man and then the man ogled her, Mike felt a surge of both intense jealousy and a kind of masculine pride because she was with *him*, and because *he* was buying her drinks.

Mike hated it when another guy ogled her breasts. And yet, he felt strong because her breasts were with him, facing him, heaving up and down in laughter with him. Mike hated it when Candi flirted, winked, or bent over a little too long so someone could stare at her ass. But the very lust she inspired in other men made Mike feel virile. No other woman had ever made him feel this way.

"Ok, pardner," Candi said. "Third question- Who would you take a romantic walk on Galveston beach with? Now this is a real important question. Remember. It says a fucking lot about a person. Well. They all do. But this one especially."

"Well, now you've made me nervous about my answer."

"No, no, no," Candi said, "Don't you fucking change your answer. Just say what you were gonna say. Just say it. I promise this time I won't make fun of you or give you any shit."

"Ok," Mike said, "It would have to be Simone de Beauvoir." Mike knew Candi would not know who this was, so he explained before she could even ask. "Simone de Beauvoir was a French philosopher. She wrote plays, novels, philosophy and essays. She also wrote a definitive Feminist text called *The Second Sex*. She was brilliant and beautiful," Mike added, "the perfect combination."

"Sounds to me like ya'll would've been two peas in a fucking pod," Candi said. "Well not two peas in a *fucking* pod. Because the whole point of this question is that you only get to walk on the beach with them until dawn. No fucking involved." She laughed at her own joke. "See! I didn't make fun of you that time."

✳ ✳ ✳

Mike considered Candi's comment for a moment- no fucking involved. This made him think of his friend Sonny Quillan.

Sonny had been a Southern Baptist preacher when he was younger. He was charismatic, good-looking and extremely well-spoken. And yet, Sonny never graduated from high school. He earned a GED at the local post office in his home town. And then he went to community college, worked a series of shit-jobs for a few years, and then went back to college. He'd worked his ass off and ended up getting accepted into Harvard, Yale and a bunch of other snooty colleges. Sometimes Sonny wore western vests and rattlesnake-skin boots around the Yale campus. Mike didn't remember Sonny ever wearing a cowboy hat…

When Sonny was drunk or just trying to impress people, he would spin yarns about staging old fashioned church revivals back in his hometown, taking up an offering for some country in Africa nobody had ever heard of, and then keeping all the money for himself. Sonny had this old brown Samsonite briefcase that belonged to his traveling salesman father. He bragged about how he would fill that old briefcase with cash after a series of revivals. When Mike asked him why he gave up the ministry, Sonny would always say- The money was good but the morals in the Bible left a bad taste in my mouth.

Nearly everything Sonny said offended somebody's sensibilities. Even Mike found most of Sonny's comments crass or offensive. And yet, Mike relished every opportunity to hang out with him. Whenever Mike was in close proximity to Sonny, he felt a rare surge of masculinity.

Sonny's every word inevitably offended some environmentalist, or pretentious philosophy major, or feminist, or Buddhist. Take your fucking pick... And every time, as the offended party fumed or sulked away, Mike experienced a two-fisted flush of machismo. Mike knew Sonny was wrong for insulting people. He knew Sonny wasn't interested in being too open-minded and that Sonny was decidedly old-fashioned. And yet, Mike couldn't resist the fantasy to be Sonny Quillan.

Mike remembered being in a class at Yale Divinity School with his girlfriend Lisa and Sonny. It was a philosophical theology class, so naturally there were conversations about God. It was all the academic rage at Yale Divinity School to use gender neutral language for God. This meant that one must never refer to God as *he* or *she*. The way Mike remembered it, and what pissed-off Sonny, was that it was most important that the men never refer to God as he.

Not surprisingly, Sonny refused to play by the academic rules. After repeated warnings from the professor, the female teaching assistant, and even a few of the female students in the class, Lisa could no longer contain her feminist indignation. Lisa called Sonny out in front of the whole class. Lisa called Sonny a narrow-minded and stubborn misogynist.

After class in the hallway, Sonny approached Mike and Lisa and their group of friends. In front of everybody, Sonny asked Lisa, "You know what the smartest thing to ever come out of a woman's mouth was?"

Lisa stared Sonny down and replied, "No, what?"

Sonny smiled and said to her, "Einstein's cock..."

✳✳✳

Once, in a drunken rant, Sonny had bragged to Mike about wanting to fuck Simone de Beauvior. Before that, Sonny and Mike had both agreed that the philosopher Jean-Paul Sartre, who was de Beauvoir's lifelong companion, was an intellectual badass.

"But," Sonny told Mike that night, "Sartre was not a badass because he wrote *Being & Nothingness* or *No Exit*. He wasn't a

badass because he won the Nobel Prize and then rejected it. Nope.
Sartre was a badass for one reason and one reason only, Sonny said.
Because Sartre had fucked Simone de Beauvior.

"It must've been an awesome feeling, huh?" Sonny said, "To
fuck one of the founders of modern feminism! Goddamn, can you
imagine that? If you fucked Simone de Beauvior. And you made her
cum with the sheer power of your dick?" Sonny said. "There would
be nothing in life you wouldn't feel like you could accomplish after
that!"

"And what's more," Sonny added, "After that. You'd never
be able to take a feminist seriously ever again. So whenever
she's rambling on about phallic symbols or quoting *The Second
Sex* all you'd be able to think about was that look on Simone
de Beauvoir's face when you made her cum. Why do you think
Sartre nicknamed her, The Beaver, huh?" Sonny had laughed.

Mike reassured himself. He was certain he had not chosen
Simone de Beauvior for Sonny's reasons. Mike was envious of
the unique relationship Sartre and de Beauvoir had shared. A
few years ago Mike had read two books: *Hearts and Minds: The
Common Journey of Simone de Beauvior and Jean-Paul Sartre* and *A
Dangerous Liaison: A Revelatory New Biography of Simone de Beauvoir
and Jean-Paul Sartre*. After reading these books, Mike fell in love
with the way Sartre and Simone shared such mutual respect, even
as academics and intellectuals. In fact, their mutual respect and
devotion seemed almost too good to be true.

Mike fell in love with Simone de Beauvior when he learned
that in addition to being a strong, brilliant and independent
woman, she had pledged her lifelong allegiance to Sartre. For
Mike, the most amazing thing about Simone de Beauvoir's pledge
was that she felt she could do it and still remain true to herself,
still become one of the great novelists and essayists of the twentieth century, and one of the founders of modern feminism.

It was through her efforts of editing his manuscripts,
encouraging Sartre to finish projects, helping him control his
excessive use of amphetamines, and letting him know through
constant reassurance throughout their lifetimes that he was the
most brilliant person she'd ever known, that Sartre became a
philosophical legend.

It was for this reason and this reason alone, that Mike
wanted to walk down the beach with Simone de Beauvior, and

not fuck her. Mike wanted, perhaps more than anything, for even just a night, to feel that unique level of support, that level of belief and encouragement from another human being, especially a woman. Even a single night of experiencing that kind of intimate reciprocity, Mike thought, would indelibly change him, and perhaps, inspire him towards legendary endeavors.

"Ok, pardner," Candi interrupted him, "It's time for your final question. Who would you want to marry and settle down with? Now. It's gotta be somebody who can make you laugh. And remember, it's gotta be somebody who'll protect you and never leave you alone. It's gotta be somebody who'll come to your rescue. And it's gotta be somebody that challenges you. You know, really makes you think."

Mike sighed, still thinking of that walk along the beach with Simone de Beauvior. "Honestly, Candi," Mike said, "I can't think of anybody…"

* * *

Mike and Candi staggered into room 1905 of the magnificent Magnolia Hotel. Earlier, when the woman at the front desk asked Mike whether he wanted a king bed or two queen beds, Candi chimed in and requested two queens. Ever since, Mike had wondered why.

In fact, ever since the parking lot at Ninfa's when they agreed to go on their odyssey, Mike wondered whether they would sleep together that night. He didn't know whether it was part of the deal they made, meaning a trip together included a fuck. Or, whether he would have to pay her an additional fee for a fuck. Paying her an additional fee for a fuck was fine, Mike reasoned, Candi *was* a whore after all. It was broaching the topic with her that troubled him.

Should he ask Candi for a price? Or should he simply assume that because she had already given him a blowjob, and they had agreed to go on a journey together, and he'd paid for dinner and their drinks at the bar, that a fuck was simply complimentary? Candi seems to like me, Mike thought, so maybe she likes me so much she plans to fuck me for free. Maybe asking for queen beds is Candi's way of teasing me, her way of fucking *with me* until she actually fucks me.

Mike sat down on one of the queen beds and took off his shoes. It was just past midnight. Candi went into the bathroom and yelled, "Oh my fucking God! They've got a Jacuzzi-bathtub in here."

It wasn't long before Mike heard the bath water running. He spotted Candi's naked ass peak out from behind the door as she bent over and pulled off her blue-jean shorts and thong underwear, all in one fatal swoop. Mike saw steam form on the mirror and heard Candi splash as she got into the tub. "Fucking bath crystals too? Holy motherfucking shit! This is a nice goddamn place, pardner. See I told you! *The Houston Press* never fucking steers you wrong."

Right about now, Mike didn't give two shits about bath crystals. He was too busy trying to discern the appropriate whore etiquette for this particular moment. Maybe that's my problem, Mike thought, there is no etiquette when it comes to sex with whores. Maybe I should just go right in there, take off my clothes, get in that tub with her, and fuck her fucking brains out. Candi would probably get a kick out of that, Mike mused. It might even turn her on.

Mike wondered- Does a whore ever get genuinely turned on when she turns tricks? I wouldn't think so, he guessed. But then again, getting turned on is just biology after all. Well maybe some psychology too. No way in hell, Mike thought. Candi must totally disconnect from the sex act. She must disconnect in order to cope. Mike was reminded of how Candi claimed she did her best never to cope.

Mike wondered- What if a whore did get turned on during a trick? Would that change the nature of the transaction? Would Candi then offer herself up to him for free? Just because his dick was payment enough? Mike felt bad for being so crass. He concluded that it must be the gin and tonics doing his thinking.

All things now considered Mike didn't want to jeopardize his chances of having sex with Candi. He didn't want to do anything rash or stupid. He felt like at this point he had a really good chance of fucking with her, of fucking her. Ever since he came in her mouth on the Baytown Bridge, Mike's dick had literally been aching to feel Candi's pussy around it, fucking his dick.

This dickache was a strange new sensation for Mike. For the longest time, whenever Mike desired sex, it always felt more like he simply needed sex as a kind of physical release. Basically he just needed to cum to relieve the pressure, so that he could write a paper or focus on giving a lecture.

For men and women alike, Mike mused, boners are distracting. And for this reason, Mike never understood how people like monks, nuns and Mahatma Gandhi swore off sex so they could concentrate on other more important things. That was supposed to be the whole point of a vow of celibacy. To channel the energy you would be expending on having sex, to other more noble causes like helping to establish the kingdom of God on earth. Not that Mike would ever have disagreed with Gandhi. But how can anybody concentrate on anything, even the kingdom of God on earth, when they haven't cum in a few days?

Mike's desire for physical release wasn't about masturbation either. Actually Mike preferred not to masturbate. Of course, Mike knew certain people, as does everybody, who actually prefer masturbation over sex. It isn't always necessarily the case that these people suffer from a sexual fetish. Some of them simply prefer to be alone. However, in Mike's case, he actually preferred the sensation of pussy around his dick. He preferred the feel of a pussy squeezing, constricting and choking cum out of his dick, over the desperate-forceps feeling of his own gravedigger fingers. Pussy made his orgasm more intense. There was absolutely no fucking substitute. Mike even preferred pussy over a blowjob.

Above all else, Mike desired the oppressive feel of pussy around his dick. And what made this new, dickaching sensation Mike felt for Candi so strange, was that Mike not only desired pussy around his dick, but he desired Candi's pussy around his dick. Her particular pussy around his dick. It had been a long time, maybe never, since Mike had desired a particular pussy. In the past, any pussy would do.

This didn't mean that Mike would fuck just any pussy. It did mean that when Mike desired pussy, the pussy didn't necessarily need to have a face attached to it. And yet, much to Mike's surprise, Candi's face was now attached to the pussy needed to satisfy him tonight. No other pussy would do. There was just something inscrutable about Candi. Something sublime and indelible, annoying and repulsive that made the combination of her face and pussy Mike's perfect fantasy.

Candi called to Mike from the bathroom. "Hey there pardner! Why don't you make us a couple of drinks? Come on in here and sit down. And talk to me while I soak in the fucking tub."

Mike had stopped at the liquor store earlier and bought limes, club soda and Tanqueray. He got up from the bed, grabbed the ice bucket and eagerly went in search of the ice machine down the hallway. This is my chance, he thought. The quicker I make us drinks the quicker I'll be sitting in the bathroom with Candi. And the closer I'll be to fucking her in one of those queen sized beds.

"Dammit," Mike said, standing at the bathroom counter about ten minutes later, "I don't have any way to slice these damn limes. I don't have a knife." All Mike could think was- no drinks, *ergo* no getting drunker, *ergo* no fucking tonight.

"No problemmo, pardner," Candi said, still soaking in the tub. "Hand me a fucking lime and your fucking car keys." Mike reached into his pocket, pulled out his car keys, and handed them to Candi along with a lime.

"Watch and learn, boy." Candi held the lime and with the jagged edge of a key, carefully cut the rind all the way around. Next, she cut through the middle of the lime and then cut the wedges in half again. "Looks just like those limes in the fucking bar downstairs," Candi said. She handed them to Mike. "You better keep those keys out, pardner. I gotta feelin we're gonna need that whole fucking bag of limes tonight."

✻✻✻

Mike sat next to the tub, using the toilet for a chair. He watched Candi's breasts between the soap suds of her bubble bath. He tried several times but never caught a glance of her pussy. Mike gulped his gin and tonic. Candi sipped hers as usual. They'd been talking for about an hour.

"I had a pet tarantula when I was a kid," Mike said, slurring his words. "It was the coolest pet ever."

"Oh yeah?"

"Yeah. I put gravel from a nearby creek into this aquarium. Then I put this piece of tree bark in there for her to crawl on or hide under."

"It was a fucking *she?*"

"That's what my father told me when he brought it home."

"What did your daddy do for a livin?"

"Let's just say he was Willie Loman and leave it at that."

"I don't know what the fuck that meant," Candi said, "but whatever you say, pardner."

"He brought it home to me in a brown paper bag. Actually it was a Whataburger bag. Dammit. I hadn't thought of that in years!"

"It's a gooood fucking thing the gin is all gone."

"So," Mike said, "My father told me to make sure and put the bark in the middle of the aquarium. That way the tarantula wouldn't be able to climb the walls of the aquarium and escape."

"Sounds kinda creepy if you ask me"

"No way," Mike said. "She was the coolest pet ever. I took the metal lid of a Vlasic pickle jar and put it in there as a water bowl. I even pushed the gravel up to the edges of the lid. Creating this nice natural contour. You know. Like it was an actual pond in the wilderness." He chuckled in drunken amusement. "I always wondered whether the water in that lid tasted sour. You know. Like it had a hint of the taste of pickle in it. For Chrissakes! What that tarantula must've thought!"

"Every Saturday I'd catch a cricket. The little guy would wriggle around inside my cupped hands." Mike set his drink on the bathroom floor. He cupped his hands, imagining he held the cricket again. "And then I'd drop that little guy into the aquarium. And then I'd sit on the floor and watch the show."

"Dammit," Mike said. "It was like the moment that cricket hit the gravel. The moment the little guy regained his footing and figured out where the hell he was. It was like in that moment, both the cricket and the tarantula just knew."

"Just knew what?"

"That a deadly dance had started. You know. A deadly dance for survival."

"Holy shit"

"I always wondered," Mike said. "Did that cricket realize his fate had already been decided? Not literally, of course. But what I mean is. Did that little guy realize that it was only a matter of time before the tarantula pounced on him and ended it all?"

"You mean," Candi said, "Did the cricket know it was fucked from the get-go?"

"Yes. Exactly," Mike said, "that's exactly what I mean, goddammit."

"Let's fucking hope not, pardner."

"Have you ever watched a tarantula eat a cricket, Candi?"

"Nope"

"The tarantula," Mike said, "lowers its body over the cricket. Its eight long legs trapping the little guy like hairy prison bars. Then two sharp fangs emerge from its torso. Descending like a claw. The fangs lower and then close. And then pierce the cricket's body."

"That's fucking gross!"

"What I wonder is," Mike said, slurring his words. "In that moment. In that very moment. Did the cricket know he was going to die? Was the little guy aware that over the next hour or so, those fangs piercing its side would slowly drain all of the moisture from its body?"

"Again," Candi said, "Ewwh! Gross!"

"And when all the life is all sucked out of the little guy. The tarantula retracts her fangs. And stands up from her crouched position. And stretches her long legs. And then drops the dried-out, lifeless body of the cricket into the gravel. Until next time, that is." Mike smiled.

"Soooo," Candi said, "You're tellin me you never ever felt bad for any of the crickets?"

"No. I guess not."

"Well I would've been fucking rootin for the cricket. I mean. If I'd been there. I would've ripped the goddamned lid off that aquarium and rescued that fucking cricket."

"But the tarantula would have starved?"

"Well, I reckon that's true too," Candi said. "But I just can't fucking imagine just sittin there. While that poor fucking cricket hopped around in that goddamned aquarium. Without even a fucking chance, you know? I just don't think I could've just sat there and watched. Just let it happen."

Mike didn't reply. He was lost in the past, contemplating a painful childhood memory. He drained his gin and tonic.

"So you gotta tell me, pardner. Of all the goddamned crickets you threw in there. How long did the one live, who lasted the longest?"

"What do you mean?"

"I mean. How long did the toughest cricket last? Before that tarantula got him? A few fucking hours? A few fucking days? I mean. There must've been at least one cricket who just wouldn't fucking get tired and just wouldn't fucking give up. I mean. If just one cricket kept hoppin around that goddamned aquarium. Then maybe that tarantula would've just fucking given up and left the little guy the fuck alone. And then maybe you could've rewarded that cricket for refusin to give up? You know, by rescuin the little guy and settin him free?"

Mike didn't respond to her proposal. He nodded off in a drunken stupor.

Candi stood up and stepped out of the tub. She stood there facing Mike. Soapy water dripped down her naked body, down from her tits along her belly, down from her belly along her pussy and then down her long legs. Candi bent down, picked up Mike's empty glass, and then put it safely on the bathroom counter next to the sink. Candi looked down at Mike. The child-Mike woke up and looked at Candi. However, without a single word, he fell into an inebriated slumber.

Day 2

Chapter 5

The JP Morgan Chase Building in downtown Houston;
The Myth of Theseus & Ariadne; And how Candi cured Mike's
hangover in the underground tunnels while debating the ethics of stealing

Mike and Candi made their way down Texas Avenue towards the JP Morgan Chase Tower. Mike walked with a hangover gait. Even at eleven in the morning, the Texas sun hurt his puffy eyes. He felt nauseous and said, "Candi, I really need to sit down."

"Well you should've eaten some fucking breakfast, dumbass," Candi said, still carrying Mike's copy of *Moby Dick*. "You know what I always say? The best cure for a fucking hangover is a big delicious Texas breakfast at the Magnolia Hotel. They had this breakfast buffet. You should've seen it. It was fucking awesome."

Mike groaned and said, "Can we sit down, please?"

"I ate a fuck-ton of bacon, pardner. Yep. I must've eaten two whole fucking plates of that shit. And it was that good bacon too! You know. That thick-sliced, peppery shit. Not that fucking cheap bacon you can see right through. Yep! Nothin but fucking bacon and black coffee for breakfast." She patted her belly. "Just like the cowboys did back in the Old West."

"Well if that's the case then maybe you should've woken me up so I could've eaten something."

"Trust me. There wasn't any wakin you up, pardner. You were dead to the fucking world."

"I don't even remember going to bed."

Despite his hangover daze, the first thing Mike wondered when he awoke was whether he and Candi had fucked. As he lay there he kicked himself for getting too drunk to remember their fuck. And then, to his great disappointment, he realized they hadn't. Candi had even slept in the other queen bed.

"You don't remember goin to bed," Candi said, "Because you fucking passed out in the bathroom. Yep. Right there sittin on the fucking toilet. Elvis-style!" She laughed. "You're such a fucking pussy. Let me tell you somethin. People like you gulp their drinks for a reason. It's true. Next time you go to one of your fancy-pants Yale parties. Pay attention to who's gulpin and who's sippin their drinks. It says a fuck-ton about a person."

"Oh yeah," Mike said, "What does it say?"

"Well. I reckon it could say a lot of things. It could say they ain't gettin fucked on a regular basis. Or if they are gettin fucked regular, then it could say the fucking ain't any good. Or it could say they got a guilty conscience. Or it could say-"

"I think I've heard enough," Mike said. "Thanks *so much* for that enlightening psychological profile."

"You're a mighty welcome there, pardner," Candi said, feigning a hick-hillbilly accent. "Why thank ya kindly sir. I'm just good country folk, ya know? Yessir! Good country folk!"

Mike hated it when Candi feigned being a country-bumpkin. In his mind, he always equated being trashy with the ignorance that one was trashy. Basically, Mike thought, if you're a country-bumpkin then you'd be too dumb to know that you were in fact a country-bumpkin. In Candi's case however, she seemed not only to know she was trashy, but also revel in it and be critical of it all at the same time.

"If I passed out in the bathroom," Mike said, "then how did I end up in one of the beds?"

"I fucking drug your ass outta the bathroom and hoisted you onto the bed."

"Wow"

"No fucking shit wow. I'm stronger than I look," Candi said, flexing her bicep. "And don't you ever worry, pardner. I won't ever just leave you hangin."

"Honestly," Mike said, "I don't remember much of our conversation last night. What did we talk about? I hope I didn't say anything incriminating."

"Nah," Candi said, "We just fucking shot the shit for a couple hours. That's all." She laughed. "But I gotta tell you this, pardner. The last hour or so we were talkin. You had the biggest hard-on. Well not the biggest. I mean. I've seen bigger. But pretty fucking big anyways. And it was still goin strong even after you fucking passed out."

"Well, I didn't mean-"

"You know what I shoulda done? I shoulda just grabbed your hard-on and pulled you into the bedroom. Kinda like a little red wagon. It sure woulda been easier that way!"

Comments like this made Mike realize that Candi had the uncanny ability to make him feel like such a prude.

"Oh don't fucking worry about it, pardner. It's nothin to fucking be embarrassed about. After all. I'm a cockteaser, plain and fucking simple. What can I say? Cockteasin just comes naturally to me. Always fucking has. I mean. I was fucking naked in the tub right there in front of you. So there'd be somethin fucking *wrong* with your dick if you *didn't* get a hard-on."

"Can we please change the subject?"

"Hold on there, pardner. I'm not done just yet. What I'm tryin to tell you is. I felt really sorry for you. All hot and bothered and passed out like that. So I seriously considered givin you a hand-job right then and there. Just to release the pressure. You know. Just to help you sleep better."

Mike perked up.

"But," Candi said, "then I realized. First off. You wouldn't even fucking remember the hand-job. So you wouldn't really be able to appreciate my gesture." She pumped her fist up and down in the air as they walked, "Get it? My gesture? Get it?" She laughed out loud.

"I get it."

"And second. I figured that me and you. Well we're even-fucking-Steven on the whole sexual favors thing. I mean. I got over the bridge and you got a blowjob. That was our deal, right? Sure afterwards you felt guilty for takin me up on my offer. And so you decided to buy me some lottery tickets and blowpops. But that was all fucking you, pardner! That was all you!"

"But"

"What I'm tryin to tell you is this. Abe Lincoln freed the fucking slaves, pardner. I'm a free fucking agent. You said it yourself before. God gave me a fuck-ton of free will."

"Candi," Mike said, "I just want you to know that I don't expect-"

"Maybe you don't expect and maybe you do expect. But here's what I reckon. You're hopin I'll fuck your brains out before our little odyssey is all said and done, right? Am I right? You're wonderin if because I agreed to take this drive with you. That I was also agreein to be your personal whore along the way. And if it ain't that, pardner. Then you must at least be hopin there's another bridge that needs crossin between here and there."

"It's not like that, Candi."

"Oh for fuck's sake, pardner. Don't be such a fucking phony. A phony is the fucking worst thing anybody can be. Even last night. You were probably wonderin if you were gonna get lucky, right? Am I right? Am I right? Huh? I'll bet you wondered if when I invited you into that bathroom to talk to me. If I was really just sayin come on in here and fuck me in this tub. That's what you were thinkin, right?"

"No," Mike said, "That's not what I was thinking."

"Then you're a fucking faggot," Candi said.

"I'm not gay," Mike said. "I don't have anything against homosexuality. But I'm not gay."

"Well which is it then, pardner?" Candi said. "Are you an impotent little faggot who spends more time thinkin about writin philosophy papers than fucking pussy? Or are you a big strong man? A *real man* who wanted to fuck me? I mean. A real man woulda been thinkin about fucking my pussy ever since he stuck his cock in my goddamned mouth."

"Oh for Chrissakes, Candi! Drop it, will you? And why are you using *that word* for gay people? I never figured you for a homophobe. I thought you weren't judgmental?"

"Hey! Hold up there, pardner. I'm no fucking homophobe. Got it? I got no problem with gay people. In fact! I'll bet I've fucked and fisted more cunts than you have."

"Well then. If you're not a homophobe then don't use homophobic language. It's just that simple, Candi. You can't have it both ways."

"Oh yeah I fucking can, pardner. Me and everybody else in this goddamned world."

"What's that supposed to mean?"

"Listen up, dumbass. I only say faggot when I'm makin a comparison. I'd never call a gay guy a faggot. Or ever even refer to him as a faggot. I only use the word faggot when I'm makin a fucking comparison between a real manly man, and a pussy little faggoty man."

"Oh, well… That explains everything. You're just making a comparison! Of course! It all makes sense now. Oh well. If all you're doing is making a comparison then that makes it all ok, doesn't it? For Chrissakes, Candi. You are so full of-"

"I talk that way because when I was growin up. With my daddy. When it came to men. You were either a real man or a faggot."

"That's no excuse, Candi. Just because you're daddy talked that way doesn't mean you should."

"Hey! Whoa there, pardner. I'm not castin any fucking stones here. In fact. I'm that adulterous cuntbag whore everybody wanted to throw stones at. You remember? The one JC stood up for that time?"

"Yes, I know what you're talking about."

"All I'm sayin is. Sometimes. In moments of weakness. Or just as a fucking kneejerk reaction. We all say things our parents said when we were growin up."

"I disagree," Mike said. "It's always a choice. It has to be a choice. Otherwise-"

"And all I'm sayin is. A real man woulda marched into that bathroom last night. Dropped his pants. Let his hard cock dangle in front of my pretty little face. And then a real man woulda climbed right in that tub and fucked me. Whether I liked it or not. Let me tell you this, pardner. That's what every woman wants from time to time."

"That's not true, Candi."

Candi laughed and said, "I'm just fucking with you, pardner. You're sooo fucking uptight. You know that? I mean can't you tell when a girl is just cock-teasin?"

✳ ✳ ✳

"Can we please just sit down at one of these cafes?" Mike said. "I'm dying for Chrissakes." They had only walked a few blocks but Mike was falling behind.

Candi took his arm in hers. "Just stick it out a couple more minutes there pardner. We're almost to the Chase Tower. You know what my grandma used to say? She'd say- the best thing a body can do for a hangover is just walk it off. Yep. Just walk it off. In fact. She said that advice applied to most situations in life. Just walk it off..."

They turned left on Milam Street and walked a little ways. "Here it fucking is," Candi said, "The Chase Tower in downtown Houston. The tallest building in the world. And the coolest fucking view in the whole goddamned fucking universe."

They stood in the outdoor plaza at the JPMorgan Chase Tower. Mike stared up at a gargantuan post-modern style sculpture in front of the building. "Oh wow," he said, perking up. "That's right. Somebody told me this Miro sculpture was here in Houston. I've always wanted to see it in person. I love the work of Joan Miro. I went to his museum when I was in Barcelona. Isn't it amazing?"

"Your hard-on is showin again," Candi said.

"What?" Mike said, looking down.

"Just kiddin"

Mike and Candi stood at the base of a fifty-five foot tall, steel sculpture cast in bronze then painted in bright primary colors. It is the largest freestanding work of Joan Miro, the Spanish-Catalan artist, in the United States.

"Miro's work is a brilliant example of surrealism," Mike said. "And it's so... anti-bourgeoisie."

"Well I don't know what the fuck that means. But I gotta tell you. It kinda just looks like a really tall colorful dude with an enormous colorful cock," Candi said. "Doesn't it?"

Mike winced and said, "It does now."

***

As they neared the revolving glass doors at the entrance of the JP Morgan Chase Tower, Candi said, "And speakin of enormous cock. Here's a funny fucking joke for you that never gets old." She raised her blowpop near her lips and said, "What's white and ten inches long?"

"I don't know," Mike said.

She sucked her blowpop, popped her lips and said, "Not a goddamn thing!" She nudged his arm hard with her elbow and laughed aloud. "Get it? Not a goddamn thing! Get it?"

"Oh, for Chrissakes"

They entered the lobby of the Chase Tower. Candi ran towards the elevators and pushed the up button. "Oh my fucking God," she said, "I've always wanted to do this."

"Do what?" Mike said.

"Go up to the Sky Lobby of the Chase Tower and fucking see *this* view."

"Hey wait a minute. I thought you said before it was the most amazing view in the world?"

"Well," Candi said, shrugging as she backed into the elevator. She summoned with her finger for him to follow her, "I *imagine* it is."

They got off the elevator on the sixtieth floor and took in the breathtaking views of Houston, Texas. Candi ran over to the tall glass windows. "Looky," she said, "There's the Galleria. And right over there's the Medical Center. And those planes are on their way to Hobby Airport."

Mike was amazed and a little puzzled by Candi's excitement. This was obviously *her* city, he thought, and she loved it more than anything. He couldn't help but wonder why Candi, or anyone else for that matter, could feel this way about a particular city.

It seems an inherent part of the human condition to seek a sense of place. James Joyce was obsessed with Dublin. Woody Allen with New York. Hell, if you think about it, William fucking Faulkner was so desperate for a sense of place he made up an entire county. Not to mention Ernest Hemingway, who was so schizophrenic about seeking a sense of place that he couldn't decide between Florida, Paris, Africa, or Spain; talk about your moveable feast.

Mike thought of something he wanted to put in his novel- In seeking a sense of place, are we as humans merely seeking a place that makes sense?

And what about Candi? Mike wondered if it was really Houston, Texas that she was so enamored with, or was Houston simply a part of some neurosis. Not that Houston was a dismal place, he admitted to himself. Actually, because of Candi's infectious enthusiasm, Mike felt himself falling for the Bayou City.

Still, was Candi's insistence that Houston was the greatest city in the world only because she had so little else in her life to call her own? What more could a whore possess than her city, her street corners and her back-alleys? If she possessed anything at all? Or, Mike thought, perhaps her affection for this city was some kind of pathetic means for Candi to aggrandize a place, and in doing so, vicariously aggrandize her own life. But then again, Mike realized in a moment of self-clarity, whose life doesn't need aggrandizement?

"Isn't this the most beautiful fucking view you've ever seen?" Candi said. "And I'll bet you've seen a lot of beautiful scenery in all your world travels."

Mike hesitated to respond. Normally he would've casually denied that this was the most beautiful view he had ever seen; and then qualified that statement by mentioning he'd traveled to Paris on a Fulbright Scholarship. That he'd rented an apartment overlooking the Eiffel Tower where he watched fireworks on New Year's Eve. Mike knew from personal experience that this was the story of a beautiful view not many people could top. But somehow he knew that Candi just wouldn't be impressed.

Moreover, Mike was really impressed that Candi just expected him to agree with her about the view. That she didn't seem a bit apprehensive at all that he might disagree with her. He'd never met anyone whose enthusiasm overpowered her desire for other's approval. It seemed a kind of insanity to him. And yet, nonetheless, her insanity was somehow inspiring and definitely contagious.

"Well..." Candi said, arms crossed and tapping her foot on the floor, "Isn't this the most beautiful view you've ever seen in your whole fucking life?"

Mike looked out over the beautiful city below. And then he turned and looked directly at Candi, "Yes, yes it is..."

* * *

On the other side of the observation deck, Candi leaned against the glass and fogged it up with her breath. Mike stared at her ass.

"How are you feelin, pardner?" Candi said, and then turned around to face him.

"A little better," Mike said, "but still not great."

"Tell you what, pardner. Let's soak up this here view for a couple more minutes. And then we'll go into the underground tunnels and get you," she raised her hands and made quotation marks with her fingers, "Candi's-Special-Hangover-Cure. How's that sound?"

"Is this some kind of down-home remedy?"

"Oh, yessirree," Candi said in her feigned Southern-bumpkin voice, "It'll damn sure cure what ails ya. Good country folk!"

Mike shook his head and said, "Did you say underground tunnels?"

"Fuck yeah," Candi said, like a kid on her way to the carnival. "There are miles and miles and miles and miles of underground tunnels under downtown Houston. It's fucking awesome. They got every kind of shop and restaurant you'd ever want. It's so people don't have to walk around in the fucking heat and humidity."

"Like an underground mall?'

"Yep. Only these tunnels wind and wind and fucking wind around and around and around for miles and miles and fucking miles. Let me tell you. A person could get lost down there. But at least while you were lost, you could get your shoes shined and eat some sushi!"

"Lost in underground tunnels, huh," Mike said, "like Theseus in the labyrinth."

"Like *who* in the *what*?"

"It's a story from Greek mythology."

Mike was accustomed to making casual literary references and having them immediately acknowledged by his educated, intellectual peers. He was also accustomed to his peers acting as if they understood his references, even when they didn't. It was a definite sign of weakness to reveal to a fellow academic that you didn't understand her obscure literary or philosophical reference.

Thus, when Candi said- like *who* in the *what*? a modest admission of her ignorance, it simultaneously pleased and unsettled Mike. It pleased Mike because he genuinely enjoyed teaching. There was nothing Mike enjoyed more in life than reading a book which interested him, and then imparting that knowledge to others.

Of course, Mike lamented, unfortunately for him, being a graduate student meant reading a syllabus-long-list of books which only interested his professors, and then regurgitating their knowledge back to them in a term paper. Sonny Quillan once told Mike- a term paper written by a graduate student for a professor, is like having to puke after fucking somebody you regret fucking.

Still, despite Sonny's personal cynicism towards all things academic, Mike enjoyed teaching. And Mike even enjoyed teaching people like Candi the more obvious things, like the story of Theseus in the labyrinth.

Mike had never met anyone who was so impetuous when admitting that she had no clue what you were talking about. It was like every single declaration of her ignorance was her own Thermopylae. When Candi asked a question, Mike mused, it always seemed courageously germane to that particular moment and to her personal circumstances within that moment. For this rare Spartan authenticity, Mike both adored and envied Candi. And yet, it was this authenticity which also made him uncomfortable too.

Clearly, Mike thought, Candi was intelligent. She possessed a natural-born curiosity and genuinely desired to know more; uncommon traits for a common whore. And yet, despite all his adoration and envy, it was Candi's devil may care attitude towards her own ignorance which unsettled Mike so much.

Each time Candi confessed that she didn't understand his casual intellectual references Mike felt the sting of what he could only describe in his journal as- *elitist angst*. Like an insect sting, this elitist angst stung most in the moment when a gadfly like Candi took a tiny bite. Of course, once the gadfly had flown, the stinging pain eventually subsided, leaving a numb whelp in its wake. Mike had been trying to make sense of this stinging sensation for a while now. Perhaps, he thought, for almost three years now. Perhaps, he thought, ever since his arrival at graduate school in New Haven.

For Mike, the sting of elitist angst made him feel intellectual guilt. It made him feel guilty for possessing so much specialized knowledge, when so many others didn't possess even the most basic knowledge. Mike viewed this gaping chasm between the very-educated and the very-uneducated or semi-educated as a kind of intellectual affluence. For him, this affluence was akin to the sting that the very-wealthy must occasionally feel, living in a ten million dollar home while the children of their neighbors die in summertime because they can't afford air conditioning.

Sure, Mike always reminded himself, he worked hard for many years in college to acquire this wealth of specialized knowledge. And it was this surplus of ideas which made him an academic, and afforded him the opportunity to teach. And despite his elitist angst, Mike still felt comforted whenever his friends and colleagues in academia nodded in silent acknowledgment at his references to Greek mythology, Latin or Greek words, and the epistemological jargon of Immanuel Kant or phrases like the banality of evil. And yet, Mike couldn't help but feel that all forms of affluence, even his intellectual affluence, was made possible only by the intellectual poverty of others.

Like an insect sting, this elitist angst stung most intensely in the moment when a gadfly like Candi landed on Mike's skin and took a tiny little bite. These days, Mike lamented, the gadflies seemed smaller, but their stings seemed more intense. Of course, once the gadfly had flown, the stinging pain eventually subsided. However, a lingering numbness was inevitably left in its wake. Good thing for Mike, there were time-honored means for numbing the numbness of elitist angst.

At some point in his collegiate crusade Mike had realized that the only reason he was able to make obscure intellectual references in casual conversation, and not be reminded of his elitist angst by an ignorant gadfly, was that he never spent time around any gadflies. Of course there had been Sonny Quillan. But for the most part Mike's friends and colleagues were all cultured, cult-like members of academia.

Mike had also realized that his near-exclusive association with the intellectually affluent was not a random happenstance. It had been a deliberate dividing of the herd on a long cattle drive north, ending in the territory of Yale University. Thus, with every college class attended, every paper written, every footnote cited, every dead language learned, and every obscure tome highlighted Mike had little by little, sequentially defined himself by and for the educated company he kept.

"And considering *your* roots," Lisa once told him, "That's quite an accomplishment!"

"Yep, she's right Mike," Sonny had added, "But remember. Now that you're one of the educated wheat, you're gonna have to divide yourself from the uneducated chaff. That's the goddamned hardest part of it."

Until recently, Mike's hermitic academic lifestyle enabled him to successfully cope with the occasional sting of elitist guilt. Of course, the cloistered walls of the university helped keep the gadflies away. Mike just kept telling himself- for someone like me, elitist angst is simply the price you must pay for success.

Until a week ago, Mike had continued coping; until receiving the horrible news from out West. Mike remembered that precise moment. Mike recalled hearing the horrible news and then feeling the bitter sting of elitist angst. He had never felt the sting so distinctly before. Mike realized two things in that defining moment: that he would never be able to cope with elitist angst ever again, and that he no longer wanted to. It was in that stinging moment Mike decided to abandon his sequestered quest for specialized knowledge, and drive back down south...

"Well, pardner," Candi said, "You just gotta tell me this fucking Greek story."

"You sure you want to know?"

"Fuck yeah. You should know by now. I fucking love stories."

"Alright," Mike said, relishing an opportunity to teach. "A long time ago-"

"How long ago?"

"Well, Candi. This story is from Greek *mythology*. It didn't really happen. It's just a myth."

"It's just a what?"

"A myth," Mike said.

"A what?"

"A myth, myth-"

Candi chuckled, batted her eyes and in an exaggerated, high-pitched female voice said, "Yes???"

Mike was puzzled.

"Oh for fuck's sake, pardner! Come on! You gotta have seen that flick? *The Muppet Movie* is a fucking classic! You know? The original flick where Kermit and all the other Muppets get chased by Doc Hopper. And at the end they finally get to Hollywood

and meet Orson Welles. And then they sign," Candi made quotations marks with her fingers, "The Standard Rich and Famous
Contract."

"Wow," Mike said, "I do remember that. Jesus Christ. I
hadn't thought of that film in years. I mean when I was a kid I
loved that film."

"What in the fuck do you mean when you were *a kid* you
loved that flick? I still love that fucking flick! In my book it's
definitely a once-a-yearer."

"You mean you watch it once a year?"

"Fuck yeah I do! At least once a fucking year. I watch all
my favorite flicks at least once a year. How long's it been since
you saw it?"

"Not since I was young."

"How young?"

"I don't know. Maybe twelve or thirteen years old."

"Holy fucking shit. That's really, really, really, really fucking pathetic."

"Thanks a lot"

"So then you remember that runnin gag about the word
myth in *The Muppet Movie?*"

"Yeah, I do"

"It's just gotta be one of the best runnin gags ever. I mean
it's fucking right up there with the walk-this-way gag in all the
Mel Brooks flicks."

"I remember it," Mike said. "But how exactly did it go
again?"

"Every fucking time Kermit says the word *myth* everybody
thinks he has a lisp. And that he's really sayin the word, *miss.* So
every fucking time Kermit would say the word myth, he had to
end up repeatin himself and say myth, myth, myth-"

"That's right," Mike said. "And every time Kermit repeated
the word myth, myth. That's when... Oh dammit. What was her
name? That's right. That's when Carol Kane always stepped out
and said- yes?"

"Carol Kane, huh?" Candi said. "All I know is she was that
chick who played Latka's girlfriend on *Taxi.*"

"You mean *Taxi Driver*," Mike said, "that Scorsese film?"

"No, dumbass," Candi said. "I'm not fucking talkin about
fucking *Taxi Driver*. Which by the way is one of the worst

fucking flicks ever fucking made. I'm talkin about *Taxi*. That old TV show starrin Andy Kaufman and Danny DeVito. And that guy who played Doc Brown in all the *Back to the Future* flicks. It's a fucking awesome old show. Kinda depressing. But still fucking awesome. You really should watch it."

"It's crazy, you know," Mike said, "I can't believe I forgot about that running gag in *The Muppet Movie*."

"You didn't forget, pardner," Candi said, "You just didn't remember, that's all."

✳ ✳ ✳

A half an hour later, Mike and Candi were still on the observation deck. Mike was bored. He noticed that Candi never seemed to get tired of staring down at the cityscape of Houston. In fact, her eyes seemed to scour the bustling streets below, as if searching for something or someone.

"Candi," Mike said, "You look like you're looking for something."

"Nah," Candi said, still staring down. "I'm just people watchin."

"You're just people watching?" Mike said, "From sixty floors up?"

"Yep"

"You know. If you really want to watch people, we could go back down to street level. Get something to drink and then watch people from there."

"No thanks. This view is just fine."

"All I'm saying is. What's the point of people watching all the way up here? It must be like watching ants."

Candi turned around and leaned against the glass. She stared Mike down, winked, smiled and said, "Actually, more like watchin cockroaches."

A security guard joined them and said, "Excuse me, ma'am. If I have to ask you one more time not to lean against the glass, you will be escorted out of the building."

Candi rolled her eyes and slowly stood up straight.

"I'm really sorry," Mike said to the security guard. "We're about to leave. Thank you for your patience."

"What a fucking prick," Candi said, just loud enough for the security guard to hear her. "Get a fucking *real* job, asshole."

"For Chrissakes, Candi. Can we just go now?"

"Well, motherfucker," Candi said. "We can leave. But first you gotta tell me that Greek myth."

"How about I tell you the story in a patio café across the street? I'll even buy you a drink?"

"Hold up there, pardner. Now don't go tryin to bribe my hot ass with liquor. You're the one who needs a fucking drink here, not me. I mean. If this were a fucking western flick, you'd be Dean Martin in *Rio Bravo*. You'd be diggin coins out of a spittoon just to buy a fucking gin and tonic."

"Thanks a lot, Candi. Nothing like a little emasculation before lunch."

"Emascu-what? Sounds to me like a fancy-schmancy word for turnin a man into a steer."

"A steer? You mean like a cow?"

"Yeah, of course a fucking cow. When you cut off a cow's nuts it becomes a steer. And when you cut off a cowboy's nuts he becomes *you*, pardner."

"Goddammit. You know what, Candi?"

"Awww. Are you gonna compliment me on how fucking clever I can be? Even though you really think I'm dumb as a fucking fence post?"

Mike simmered down.

"Come on! Just fucking say it already. You're such a pussy. Go ahead. Call me whatever it is you really really wanna call me right now!"

"You may be a lot of things, Candi," Mike said, "but dumb is definitely *not* one of them."

"Well, you dumbass fucking steer," Candi said, winking at him, "that makes one of us anyway."

Mike cringed, trying to keep his composure. "So," he said, attempting to change the subject, "If this were the film *Rio Bravo*. And I'm Dean Martin the drunken burnout. Then who does that make you?"

"Are you fucking kiddin me? Who the fuck do you think I am? By this point in our little odyssey I'd think it'd be pretty fucking obvious. I'm fucking John Wayne."

"Why do *you* get to be John Wayne?"

"Because I'm the fucking hero"

"And what makes you the hero?"

"Duh! You're such a fucking dumbass! I'm the hero because I kick over that spittoon before you can stick your shaky hand in it. And then I step up and beat the ever-livin shit outta that guy who made fun of you. And then I give you a tin star and try to fucking save your life. Before it's too fucking late to save."

Mike followed Candi as she walked back over to where they'd first looked out the massive windows. "I wanna take just one more gander at the most beautiful city in the world," Candi said. "I'm sure as shit never gonna get a view like this ever again." She stood in front of the window with her back to Mike. She leaned into the window as closely as possible, her face almost touching the glass. The security guard watched her closely.

Mike maneuvered alongside her. He noticed Candi's eyes were closed. Her lips moved, silently mouthing words that fogged up the glass and her view of downtown. She seemed to be praying or reciting words.

"What is it?" Mike said.

Candi's continued to face the window, ignoring him. After a few more moments her lips fell silent. She smiled to herself and then turned to face Mike. "Well motherfucker," she said, "Are you gonna tell me the story of that Greek myth? Or are we gonna hang out in this fucking place all day?"

"Are you sure you don't want to sit down and-"

"I already told you, pardner," Candi said, "I'm not fucking leavin until you tell me the fucking story of that fucking Greek myth."

Mike glanced at the security guard, then back at Candi. "I'll tell you the story," he said, "If you promise not to lean on the glass anymore."

Candi glared at the security guard, and then frowned at Mike. "Ok. You got yourself a fucking deal," she said, spitting into her palm and then extending her hand to him. "Shake on it?"

Mike took her hand and said, "Deal"

"But," Candi gripped his hand tightly and pulled it towards her chest, "This better be a good fucking story."

"Hey," Mike said, "I didn't make up this story. You can't blame me if you don't like it."

"Oh yes I fucking can blame you. And I'll fucking do it too. Just fucking watch me."

"Hey. You know you're not supposed to shoot the messenger, right?"

"Let me tell you somethin, pardner. If the messenger needs shootin. Then somebody's gotta step up and fucking shoot the messenger. That's just the way life is…"

"Well," Mike said, "I've never heard it put that way before, but-"

"Just shut up and get on with the fucking story already!"

"Ok. There were these two cities in ancient Greece named Crete and Athens. And they went to war against each other."

"Who won the war?"

"I'm getting there," Mike said. "So, Crete won the war. And as a kind of tribute. Every nine years Athens had to send seven young boys and girls to Crete. Where they were fed to a monster called the Minotaur, who lived in a labyrinth."

"The Minotaur? He was that guy with a bull's head right?"

"How did you know that?"

"I've seen *Time Bandits* like a million fucking times. Great flick!"

"Well," Mike said, "There was a man from Athens named Theseus. And he volunteered to go and be thrown into the labyrinth. In hopes of slaying the Minotaur."

"Hey! You never told me what a labyrinth is."

"It's like an underground maze."

"Oh, Ok. That's what I thought."

"Well," Mike said, "When Theseus arrived in Crete, the daughter of the king fell in love with him. Her name was Ariadne."

"Theseus musta been smokin hot. So what did he look like?"

"For Chrissakes, Candi. This was ancient Greece. Nobody knows what he looked like."

"I know nobody knows for sure what he looked like. I'm not a fucking dumbass like you! I just mean. For the sake of *this* story. What does Theseus fucking look like?"

"I don't know," Mike said, "It's not important."

"Listen up, goddammit. If you're gonna tell me a fucking story about some chick who falls in love with some dude at first sight. Then you better tell me what he fucking looks like! And I'm not gonna let you finish the fucking story until you do."

"You've got to be kidding me?"

"Come on. Aren't you supposed to be a fucking writer? You should be good at this shit!"

"Ok, ok! Let's say Theseus looks like-"

"And you better not say *you*!"

"Give me a second. Well. Since Theseus needs to be smoking hot. At least *you* need to think so. Let's say Theseus looks like that country singer slash philosopher you were swooning over last night."

"You mean Rodney Crowell?"

"Yeah, him. The Houston Kid, right?" Mike was proud of his deft and accurate use of colloquialism.

Candi nodded and said, "Fair enough. I'll buy it. I mean. If I lived on some little fucking island in ancient Greece and Rodney Crowell showed up one day. I'd fucking fall in love with him at first sight too."

"May I finish the story now?"

"Wait a second, pardner! I think I fucking changed my mind. This dude's gotta slay some monster right?"

"The Minotaur. Yes, right"

"So he's gotta be smart *and* strong? Right? I mean he doesn't have to be Arnold fucking Schwarzenegger. But he's definitely gotta be in good shape. Right?"

"You've got to be kidding me"

"No, no. This is really fucking important. I need to be able to actually picture what this dude-"

"Theseus," Mike interjected.

"What this dude Theseus actually looks like. And as much as I love old Rodney. He just doesn't strike me as the slay-the-monster-type."

"So what then? He strikes you more as the write-a-song-about-the-other-guy-who-slayed-the-monster-type?"

Candi laughed out loud and said, "You know what pardner? That's the funniest fucking thing you've said since I met you! I guess we're both allowed to be clever along the way, huh?"

Mike really liked *the way* Candi laughed at his joke. He had written and published humorous short stories in several literary journals; and yet, whenever women had laughed at his witticisms in the past, he always sensed it was an inauthentic gesture.

Mike confessed this suspicion to Lisa once and she immediately accused him of not being able to take women seriously, either intellectually or emotionally. He genuinely didn't think this was true about him. But he had had no rejoinder for Lisa back then and no current theories now. "Ok," Mike said finally, "Then you pick. I'm really no good at this. I don't know what to say at this point."

"And that's the first fucking time since I met you that I heard you admit you didn't know somethin." Candi started to lean back against the glass windows and close her eyes but Mike took her arm and stopped her. She smiled and said, "Thanks, pardner."

She closed her eyes and thought for a minute. "Ok," she announced loudly, opening her eyes, "I've got the fucking perfect Theseus!"

"Ok, let's hear it."

"Mike Brady!"

"You mean the dad from *The Brady Bunch?*"

"Hell to the fucking yeah that's who I mean! Mike Brady makes a perfect Theseus!"

"You're kidding, right?"

"Fuck no, I'm not kiddin. Mike Brady is perfect for the part. Ok, hear me out. Theseus has to be really smart, right?"

"Right"

"Well. Mike Brady was an architect. Which makes him really fucking smart. Right?"

Mike could not believe his ears.

"Plus! Mike Brady always had all the answers to everybody's problems. He wasn't just smart. He was fucking wise too."

"You do realize of course, that was *just* a TV show. Right?"

"Hey," Candi said, "At the end of the day. Whether it's the story of Theseus and Ariadne. Or the story of *The Brady Bunch*. Or some fucking piece-of-shit novel you wrote. It's all just a bunch of fucking myths."

"Pun intended?" Mike said.

Candi thought for just a minute. She smiled and said, "Oh fuck! Wow! Now I get it. *Fucking* myths, like myths about fucking. Nope. Sorry. Pun *not* intended actually! But I sure wish I could take credit for it though! See! I'm clever without even tryin to be clever."

"So, it's Mike Brady as Theseus, then?"

"Hold up there, pardner. Not so fucking fast. We've agreed that Mike Brady is smart enough to get in and then get out of the labyrinth. And I think even though it's a close one. He's got the muscle to slay the Minotaur too."

"You're saying that Mike Brady has the muscle to slay the Minotaur? No way"

"Hear me out. First off. Did you see his body when the Brady's went on that vacation to Hawaii? He was fucking ripped and toned. And he probably didn't even go to the gym."

"Then how did he get so ripped?" Mike said, playing along now.

"Duh," Candi said, "Mike Brady got ripped from fucking Carol Brady missionary-style every single fucking night. Let me tell you. That'll keep a man in shape."

"Gross. Honestly. I could've lived my entire life and never heard those words and died perfectly happy."

"Not that that cunt Carol Brady deserved a *real* man like Mike Brady. I mean Carol didn't do shit all day long. Alice did all the housework. So Carol Brady doesn't do shit all day long. But every single night Mike Brady comes home after a long day at the architect's office. And fucks her brains out. Let me tell you somethin. Life just ain't fair, pardner."

"What do you think Carol Brady did all day?" Mike said. This was not the deep abiding philosophical questions to which he was accustomed, he thought, but in this moment of conversation with Candi, it seemed somehow pertinent.

"Who the fuck knows what that worthless cunt did all day," Candi said. "Let's just hope it wasn't Alice! Am I right?" Candi laughed.

Mike just shook his head.

"Let's face it, pardner. Alice always was kinda dyky looking. Wasn't she? I mean. I think she was a total rug-rover. And what about Alice's supposed boyfriend? Yeah right! Sam the fucking Butcher? Always making his alleged late-night meat deliveries? What the fuck ever! I don't fucking buy it for a minute!"

"You know what, Candi," Mike said, "I'm actually really sorry I asked."

"Of course. It kinda ruins it that the guy who played Mike Brady turned out to be gay."

"Really? He was? I never heard that."

"Oh fuck yeah. And by the way, pardner. Did you notice I'm not questioning Mike Brady's manliness? So... *ergo* I didn't use the word faggot. Give a girl some fucking credit where cred-it's fucking due!"

"Well now. That's *really* something to be proud of," Mike said. "What an amazing accomplishment for you."

Candi smirked and said, "What a fucking raw deal that would be, huh? I mean. Just imagine. You're that princess chick on the island-"

"Ariadne," Mike interjected.

"Yeah, her. Just imagine you're some princess stuck on that fucking island. And your prince charmin finally shows up. And he looks like Mike Brady! And with all the answers to all the world's problems too! So of course you fall in love with him at first sight. And then he turns out to be gay? What a fucking raw-deal!"

"So," Mike said, "Does that mean it's got to be somebody else in the role of Theseus, then?"

"Nah, fuck it. It doesn't fucking change anythin for me. I mean even though he turned out to be gay. I can still watch after-noon re-runs of *The Brady Bunch* and finger myself and get a hard clit for Mike Brady. So let's just go with him."

"I guess *I* always thought of Mike Brady as a father figure. Not a sex symbol."

"Well let's fucking hope not. I sure as fuck hope you weren't sittin in your bean-bag chair after school. With your hand in your pants. Whackin it to Mike Brady!"

"Chrissakes, Candi. You know that's not what I meant!"

"I know. I fucking know," she said, laughing. "I just wanted to see the fucking look on your face when I said it, that's all."

"May I finish the story now?"

"What was her name again?"

"Her name was Ariadne."

"Ariadne," Candi said slowly to herself with a smile, "Ariadne. Ok, got it."

"May I please continue the story now? Please?"

"Abso-fucking-lutely," Candi said, and then whispered, "Ariadne," to herself again.

"Ariadne fell immediately in love with Theseus. So that night she snuck into his room. And she gave him a sword and a ball of red yarn."

"Sounds kinky," Candi said. "This is gonna be a great story."

Mike frowned and said, "The sword was so Theseus could slay the Minotaur. And the red yarn was so he could tie it near the entrance of the labyrinth, and then find his way back without getting lost."

"Did they fuck that night before he went into the labyrinth?"

"I don't know, Candi."

"Well does it say in the book or the scroll or whatever that they fucked?"

"No, Candi. I know *you* may find this hard to believe. But Plutarch, the man who recorded this story, doesn't write about fucking on every other page."

"Alright, alright. I was just wonderin, that's all."

Mike thought for a moment and then said, "Actually, Candi, that's not true at all."

"Oh yeah?"

"Well, what I mean is. Plutarch doesn't say whether or not Theseus and Ariadne had sex that night. But Greek mythology is definitely full of stories about fucking."

"Sounds like I need to get my hands on some fucking Greek mythology," Candi said, "pun intended this time."

Mike smiled and said, "In fact. Most of the famous stories from Greek mythology are about sex."

"You mean fucking?"

"Yes, actually. Fucking. Incest. Rape. And even the mythic combination of all three at the same time."

"Trust me, pardner. That's no fucking myth."

Mike started to make the running gag from *The Muppet Movie* but then realized what Candi had just said.

"Are you familiar with Zeus?" Mike said.

"Guys don't usually tell me their names," Candi said, "At least not their real ones anyway."

"I mean Zeus, the Greek god."

"Nope. Never fucking heard of him."

"Zeus was a Greek god who was basically a serial rapist. He would lust after mortal women and then rape them."

"Are you fucking kiddin me? No fucking way! You're makin that shit up."

"I'm serious. And what's worse-"

"You mean it gets worse?"

"And what's worse is Zeus had a bizarre fetish. He would turn himself into animals when he raped women. Once he turned himself into a swan and raped a woman. Another time he was a bull."

"Are you sure this Zeus guy didn't have a floor-show in Tijuana?"

Mike laughed. "No, I'm serious," he said. "These are actual stories from Greek mythology."

"Oh my fucking God. What kind of fucked up religion was that? I mean. Who in the fuck would worship a god who was a rapist? That's just fucking stupid."

"Well, in their defense, the Greeks did live over two thousand years ago and so,"

"Did you just say- in their *defense?*"

Mike thought for a moment.

"Tell me you didn't just say- in their defense. Because that would just be all kinds of fucked up, pardner."

"What I meant was. Historically and anthropologically speaking they,"

"Let me tell you somethin, parnder. I don't give a good goddamn when you lived. It's just plain fucked up to believe in, much less worship a god who rapes anybody. Period!"

"I agree," Mike said, "You're right. There's really no excuse..."

"Kinda makes you wonder," Candi said, "Which is worse? A god who actually rapes women? Or a God who stands by and does nothin while a woman gets raped?"

"I think it's safe to say," Mike said, "that Zeus was a veritable zoological menagerie, when it *came* to rape. Pun intended." He chuckled. "Get it?"

Candi didn't smile. "I reckon," she said, "If some dumb cunt gets raped by an actual god, or just a god who stands by and just watches, it's just her dumb luck, huh?"

"Listen, Candi. I didn't mean to be glib about-"

"Oh my fucking God, pardner! Don't get your little bitch-dick all bent outta shape there. I'm just fucking with you. That's all."

"But let me just say that-"

"You know what? I think I've heard just about enough about the rapist-worshippin, fucked in the head, ancient Greeks. Sounds to me like readin that Plutarch guy is like watchin *Days of Our Lives*. He must've been from the same goddamned trailer park as me!"

"What I'm trying to say, Candi. Is that you asked a good question a minute ago. About whether or not Theseus and Ariadne fucked that night."

"I just think," Candi said, "If Ariadne fell in love with this guy at first sight. And then took the trouble of riskin her life and sneakin into his room in the middle of the night. Then they probably got busy. That's all I'm fucking sayin."

"And all I'm saying is- I think it's a fair question. You're right. They probably did."

"I mean. If I was gonna fall in love with some foreign guy at first sight. And then fucking help him dick over my own country. I'd wanna fucking see the size of his dick first. You know? I wouldn't wanna sail away with this guy and then find out his dick wasn't big enough to even get in the same neighborhood as my clit."

"You know, Candi. You are such a *romantic*. You really are. And what's more. You're ruining this myth for me."

"ruining this what?"

"myth"

"this what?"

"Oh, shit!"

"Gotcha!"

"You know," Mike said, "I'm never going to think of Theseus and Ariadne the same way ever again. You really ruined the romantic aspect of this story."

"Oh, come on. I'm just pullin your leg there, pardner. And by the way," she said as she punched him in the shoulder, "Fuck you, pardner. Fuck you right in the fucking ear with Ron Jeremy's sweaty dick. You know why?"

"Why?"

"Because actually. I'm very *romantic*."

"Oh really? You're very romantic, huh?"

"Yessirree! In fact! I'm a hopeless fucking romantic."

"Pun intended?" Mike said.

"Oh wow!" Candi said. "That's really becomin the runnin gag in our little story. And you know what else it's becomin? Really, really, really fucking annoying."

"Ok, sorry," Mike said, "I'll stop now."

"I really am romantic, you know?"

"What exactly do you mean by that?"

"What everybody means by that, dumbass. I mean I wanna fall in love someday."

Mike was puzzled. One moment Candi could utter the crassest commentary on sex. And in the very next moment express an apparently genuine longing for true love and romance. Mike wondered if someone like Candi, a whore, could really and truly believe in love and romance.

"I am romantic," Candi said, "And I do believe that true romance exists. Out there..."

"Out where?"

"Out there... You know. Somewhere out there on the open prairie."

"Ok"

"I've just never seen it, that's all."

"I believe you"

"Bullshit, pardner! You don't fucking believe me."

"Yes, I do"

"Well. I wouldn't even believe me. So why should you believe me?"

"Why not?"

"Because. If some whore who gave blowjobs for a ride across a bridge told me she believed in true love. I'd laugh in her fucking face. I mean it just doesn't make any goddamned sense. No matter how you tell the story."

"I do believe you"

"Then you're a bigger fucking dumbass than I thought you were."

"How about I finish the story now?"

"Well. What the fuck are you waitin for, pardner? Since I'm not gonna get to hear how Ariadne *got off* on that little island. At least I can hear how she *gets off* that fucking island."

"Ok," Mike said. "Well. Before Theseus enters the labyrinth he professes his love for Ariadne. And he promises her that if he survives he'll take her way with him."

"And they'll live happily ever after?"

"Something like that. Theseus entered the labyrinth with the red yarn and the sword that Ariadne gave him. Now the labyrinth was an underground maze of tunnels running for miles under Crete. So even if you made your way down to the Minotaur. And you were lucky enough to slay it. You might never find your way back. Remember, that's what the red yarn was for."

"I fucking remember"

"Sorry"

"Hey," Candi said, "Do you remember when Tom Sawyer goes in that cave lookin for gold? And then Injun Joe is fucking in there too? And Tom uses his fishin string to find his way back?"

"Yes"

"That story always scared the ever-livin shit outta me when I was a kiddo."

"I thought the only book you ever read was *Moby Dick*?"

"It is," Candi said. "When I was a girl I used to listen to bedtime stories on my Fisher Price record player. Right when I went to bed. I had Tom Sawyer. I had Cinderella and Snow White. I had Pinocchio. I must've listened to the fucking story of Tom Sawyer and all those other records a million fucking times. I reckon. Come to think of it. Looks like Mark Twain was just rippin off that Plutarch guy. I never knew that. What a fucking hack job!"

"I don't think Twain was ripping anybody off, Candi. It's just that-"

"Did you know that Mark Twain's real name was Samuel Clemens? I'll bet you already knew that, huh?"

"Yes, Candi, I knew that. Actually. His real name was Samuel *Langhorne* Clemens."

"Really? I'm gonna fucking remember that one, pardner. That's a pretty good piece of fucking trivia right there. *Langhorne,* huh?"

"Here's another interesting piece of trivia for you," Mike said, gushing over the fact that Candi gushed over his trivia. "In philosophy we use logic. Logic is correct reasoning. A lot of people don't know that in logic, if you follow a certain thread of reasoning to its logical conclusion and arrive at the truth, it's called Ariadne's Thread. Pretty cool, huh?"

"No, not really," Candi said. "But here's a good question for you. Why was the yarn she gave him red?"

"Uh, I don't know."

"Really?"

"I don't think there is a reason, actually."

"Ok. I reckon I just thought it might be symbolic or somethin. Oh well. Now finish the fucking story, will you."

"Just before Theseus enters the labyrinth," Mike said, "Ariadne tells him the secret to getting in and out of the maze of tunnels." Candi moved in closer, rubbing her shoulder up against Mike's, so as not to miss a single word. "Ariadne told Theseus-always go forwards, always go downwards, and never go to the left or right. That was the secret to not getting trapped in the labyrinth."

"That's really fucking cool, pardner. Let me see if I got it right. Always go forwards, always go downwards, and never go to the left or right."

"That's it"

Candi recited it again, "Always go forwards, always go downwards, and never go to the left or right."

"Now you know the secret of the labyrinth."

"Awesome," Candi said.

"So Theseus made his way to the center of the labyrinth. And after slaying the Minotaur, he decapitated it. And then he carried the head back to the surface and became a hero."

"That's a cool fucking story, pardner. You did real, real good." Candi slapped him on the back. "I'm not gonna be fucking shootin the messenger today. I'll tell you that."

"Glad to hear I dodged that bullet."

"Now," Candi said, "finish the story for me Bertie Higgins. Tell me how Theseus and Ariadne starred in an old late-late show, and then sailed away to Key Largo."

"Huh?"

"Never mind. It's just another myth. Now tell me about how Theseus and Ariadne lived happily ever after."

"Well, actually they didn't live happily ever after."

"Cut it out, pardner. You're ruinin the romantic ending here."

"They did sail away. Unfortunately. It didn't take long for Theseus to drop Ariadne off on another island and then head back to Athens. He never saw her again."

"What in the holy motherfucking cocksucking dicklicking hell are you talkin about? You mean to tell me. Theseus fucking abandoned Ariadne? After she fell in love with him at first fucking sight? After she risked her fucking life to save his ass? And after she betrayed her own fucking family and her own country for him? What the fuck? I thought you said Theseus was a hero?"

"I never said that."

"Yeah you did. You fucking said that alright. A minute ago you said. Theseus made it back out of the labyrinth and was a hero."

"I said he made it back. But I never said he was a hero."

"Yeah you did! You fucking did say that you goddamned sonuvvabitch!"

"Oh for Chrissakes, Candi. Why does it matter so much to you? After all. It's just a story. It's just a myth."

"I reckon," Candi said, "I just really get into stories sometimes. It's probably that whole Fisher Price record player thing." She shook her head in disbelief. "He just fucking dropped her off on some island and left her there, huh? Wow! What a fucking asshole! Poor fucking Ariadne"

"You know, Candi. I never promised you a happy ending to this story."

"I know you didn't, pardner. Sometimes it's just kinda hard not to expect a happy ending. Know what I mean jelly bean?"

"I hope this doesn't mean you're going to shoot the messenger?"

"No," Candi said, smiling, "Not yet, anyways…"

✳ ✳ ✳

Mike and Candi left the observation deck and returned to the lobby of the JP Morgan Chase Building. From there they took the escalators down into the underground tunnel system beneath Houston. Candi sat Mike down at a small table in one of the food courts. She patted him gently on the shoulder and said, "I'll be right back, pardner. I gotta appointment with Dr. John."

"What?"

"I gotta appointment with Dr. John. You know. I gotta abort a baby."

"I don't get it."

"I gotta abort this baby," Candi said, patting her belly. "And boy oh boy. He's gonna be a biggun too. I ate way too much fucking bacon for breakfast this mornin."

"I still don't think I get it."

"I've gotta take a big fucking shit, you dumbass!"

"Oh"

"You're such a fucking dumbass. You mean you never heard it called that before?"

"No"

"Wow. What fucking rock have you been livin under?"

"And why exactly are you telling me this?"

"Because. I might be gone awhile, pardner. In fact," Candi said, thumbing through *Moby Dick*, "I think I'll take this time to catch up with my ol buddy Herman Melville."

"Well," Mike said, "You and Melville enjoy your visit to Dr. John's office."

"Oh, we will. Don't you worry about that. This girl can flush a fetus like nobody's business. And when I get back. I'm gonna round up the ingredients for my special hangover cure. We're both gonna be feelin better in no fucking time. Don't you worry."

After what seemed like a half an hour of waiting, Mike began to worry about Candi. He wanted to get up and search for her, but decided against it. He began to think about her abortion jokes, and whether or not they were jokes. He imagined Candi on the floor of the bathroom, crying, curled up in a puddle of blood and torn flesh, alone and dying. He remembered the last thing he said to her- another joke about Dr. John.

After what seemed like half an hour more, Candi came strolling around the corner.

"Where the hell have you been?" Mike said, "I was worried about you, dammit."

"Worried?" Candi said, "About little ol me? Why?"

"Because you were gone for almost an hour"

"Well. You know how doctor's offices are. Especially when you're gettin an abortion. They always make you wait a long fucking time. Because the longer you have to wait, the longer you have to reconsider abortin your little baby. It's those goddamned Southern Baptists here in Texas. They've got their fucking hands in everythin, includin your pussy. To tell you the truth. After all that waitin. I almost decided to keep Mikey Jr."

"What the hell are you talking about?"

"I was gonna tell you before," Candi said. "I decided to name the little guy after you. I reckon I just thought maybe our little odyssey would end up in the suburbs of Houston. You know. In a nice little cookie-cutter house in someplace like Cypress or Pearland or even Clear Lake. You could teach your fucking philosophy classes at the community college. And I could get Mikey Jr. ready for school every day. Let me tell you. With my brains and my good looks, that little guy woulda really gone far in life." Candi frowned. She wiped a make-believe tear from her eye and said, "A lot fucking farther than a dirty toilet in a public bathroom in underground Houston, Texas. That's for damn sure." She laughed out loud.

"I can't believe you're joking about that," Mike said.

"Who says I'm jokin?"

"I'm serious, Candi."

"Yep. Poor little Mikey Jr. I fucking flushed him down the toilet in the prime of his little fucking life. I reckon we can both feel better knowin Mikey Jr. had quite an adventure. While it lasted."

"That's really tacky, Candi."

"I mean think about his little adventure. First off. Little Mikey Jr. cums shootin outta your dick right into my mouth. Right there on the Baytown Bridge. And then I up and swallow little Mikey Jr. And then he wriggles all the way down my throat. Right down into my pussy. And then. Right when Mikey Jr. starts to grow up, his own mama makes him into a fucking hanger steak. Yep, flushes his unborn ass right down the goddamned toilet!"

"I give up," Mike said, "I give up."

"Oh don't be too upset there, pardner. Right before I flushed him. I gave little Mikey Jr. some red yarn. That way maybe. Just maybe he could find his way back." Candi laughed.

"I don't even know what to say."

"Well you can start by tellin me how you like my new purse." Candi set a brand new purse on the tabletop in front of him.

"Where did you get that?"

Candi grinned and pulled two bottles of Coca-Cola and two energy drinks from the purse. "Where do you fucking think I got it, dumbass? I fucking smouched it."

"You what?"

"I *smouched* it. You know. I stole it. And then I fucking smouched this other shit too. Put it right into my new purse here. Just so I could make you my special hangover cure."

"Let me get this straight. You stole a purse. And then you used it to steal more stuff?"

"My poverty entitles me to a few privileges, you know." Candi got up from the table and just as casually as she'd approached, walked over to the corner of the food court and then stuffed the purse down into the trash can.

Candi walked back over to the table, smiling a big gloating smile at Mike the entire time. She sat down and said, "How do you like my new sunglasses?" She tilted them up revealing her baby blue eyes for just a moment. They were cheap-plastic, black sunglasses with hot pink glittery stems. "Kinda makes me look like a fucking movie star, right?"

"I can't believe that you-" Mike hesitated, glanced around nervously, and then continued in a whisper, "I can't believe that you stole this stuff. I would've given you some cash. Even for the sunglasses"

"Whoa there, pardner! I don't fucking need to reach in your pants every time I need somethin. Plus. You bought dinner at Ninfa's. So this is my fucking treat. Besides. My daddy always used to tell me- Go right ahead and smouch a chicken whenever you get the chance. Because even if you don't end up needin it. You can always give it away to somebody who does. And it never hurts to do a good deed whenever you can."

"Sounds to me like just a soft name for stealing."

"Well yeah! Why do you think I fucking call it smouchin?"

"Listen, Candi. I'm not the kind of person who lives on the moral high ground, but-"

"You sure about that, pardner?"

Mike frowned and said, "Like I was saying. I'm not the kind of person who lives on the moral high ground, way above everybody else. But stealing is just wrong."

"Oh yeah? Really? Why is stealin wrong?"

"I can't believe we're even having this conversation."

"Well," Candi said, "You're the fucking one who brought it up. So either you explain to me why stealin is sooo wrong. Or just shut the fuck up about it."

"Stealing *is* wrong. Because if we're going to live in a society, in a civilization where everybody can feel safe and be-"

"Not everybody feels like we live in a fucking civilization," Candi said. "And let me tell you, pardner. Not everybody fucking feels safe either. In fact. Feelin safe is a fucking luxury not everybody can afford. Not all of us can be like you, you know."

"Being poor doesn't justify stealing."

"Spoken like somebody who's never been poor. Pardner, do you know what's on the back of a poor whore when she dies?"

"No"

"Just the clothes of pride. And they're not a bit fucking warmer to her when she's dead than they were when she was alive." Candi leaned forward and said, "You know what flick that's from?"

"Uh, no"

"You really, really need to see *that one*, pardner."

"Don't change the subject," Mike said. "We're not done talking about stealing."

"Well then," Candi said, in her best country-bumpkin voice, "You a better git to learnin me a real quick bout how stealin's wrong. So's I don't end up goin to the bad place when I up and die!"

"You are really annoying, you know that?"

"I do my fucking best."

"Ok," Mike said, gathering his thoughts. "Let's forget for just a minute about the socio-economic angle of this debate."

As an undergraduate in college, Mike captained his debate team in the Southwest Regional Ethics Bowl, winning second place. "Rich or poor," Mike said, "If you choose to steal then you're basically saying to the whole world that you condone stealing. And that everyone should steal, just like you."

"Listen up, pardner. Let's get this straight. I'm not fucking sayin stealin is right. I mean. Everybody who's anybody knows that God said right fucking there in the goddamned Ten Commandments- Thou shall not steal."

"Well," Mike said, "I never said anything about God or divine command theory. But I think you just proved my case. If God said don't do it and you take the Ten Commandments seriously, then how can you sit here and defend stealing?"

"Hey, fuck you. I do fucking take the Ten Commandments seriously. You got me all wrong, pardner. I'm not defendin stealin. Stealin is just wrong. Plain and simple. All I'm sayin is this. Sometimes I steal when I need somethin. Let me tell you. A cowboy can't *always* ride the high country."

"That's just it! Only steal when you *need* something? It's just that! We're not exactly starving here, Candi. It's not like you stole a loaf of bread to save the life of your starving niece. You stole a purse, some Coke, energy drinks and cheap sunglasses for Chrissakes."

"Not for Chrissakes," Candi said, "for my-sakes."

"Ha-ha-ha. Very funny"

Candi seemed puzzled by his comment and said, "Well I don't fucking have a starvin niece. But I'd for fucking sure steal a loaf of fucking bread to save her fucking life."

"And what about all this other stuff?"

"Hey! Me and you are both a little hung over. Especially you. And we really *need* my special hangover cure. And! And! It's really fucking sunny outside. And we're about to go on a road trip. So I really *need* some fucking sunglasses."

"Give me a break, Candi," Mike said, shaking his head in disbelief. "Ok. Let me ask you this question then." Mike paused to think, preparing his Socratic *coup de grace*. "Answer this question for me."

"Shoot"

"When you get to Heaven and you stand before God at the final judgment and-"

"You mean at the Pearly Gates?"

"Sure. So when you get to Heaven and you stand before God at the final judgment. And when God asks you why you stole this stuff, when the Ten Commandments clearly told you not to, what are you going to say?"

"Shit. I've given this one a lot of fucking thought, pardner. If I ever do end up standin at the Pearly Gates someday. I'm gonna fucking hope God will understand all the times I thought it was necessary to bend or even fucking break his commandments. I reckon I'd say to God- a whore's gotta do what a whore's gotta do. Hell! We all gotta do what we gotta do to survive."

"I'm just curious," Mike said, "Why did you use the word *if* I ever stand at the Pearly Gates? Instead of *when* I stand at the Pearly Gates? You do believe in God, don't you?"

"A few years ago," Candi said, "I signed up for a semester of classes at Houston Community College. And by the way. Awesome fucking school. HCC is the fucking best college ever! Now. I only signed up for classes to get a couple of financial aid checks in the mail. Horny Henry who works over at the Happy Lucky Mart told me if you sign up for college classes you could get free money to go to college."

"Horny Henry?"

"Don't even fucking ask"

"Will you tell me about him later?"

"Sure"

"Promise?"

"So here's how it works," Candi said. "When you register for classes the government will pay for them. And then they send you a few checks over the course of the semester. Basically whatever money is leftover after payin for your classes. They just fucking mail it to you. When I heard about that shit I was like- sign my fucking ass up. God bless fucking America, right?"

"But here's the fucking catch. You actually have to go to class. At least for the first few weeks. In order to get that second check in the fucking mail. If you don't then they drop your ass from the class roster and you don't fucking get paid."

"So the way I figured it was. Showin up for class every once in a while would keep me on the class roster. And keep those fucking checks comin in the mail. Free fucking money bitches! God fucking bless America! Let me tell you, pardner. I was livin high on the fucking hog that semester!"

"Anyways," Candi said, "When they asked me what classes I wanted to take. I didn't have any fucking clue. So this girl I knew who worked in the financial aid office. She told me there was this young, smokin-hot philosophy professor at the central campus. And what was even better. His classes were interesting. In fact. This girl told me that he'd made her think about a lot of things. Besides fucking him, of course. So I fucking signed up for his class."

"You never mentioned any college classes before," Mike said.

"You know what?" Candi said. "Goddammit. I can't remember his name now. Dammit. I can't believe I can't remember that professor's fucking name. Dammit. That's really gonna fucking bug me."

"So what did you think of the class?"

"What I do remember," Candi said, "is he wore these sexy aviator sunglasses. And he liked to wear a bandana. Can you believe that shit? A fucking bandana tied right around his head! Just like Willie fucking Nelson or Bruce Springsteen. I mean. Who the fuck does that, right? I mean it's no cowboy hat. But it's awful fucking close in my book. Come to think of it. He kinda looked liked Warren Oates in *Bring Me the Head of Alfredo Garcia*. Smokin fucking hot, pardner. Smokin fucking hot"

"I think we've established," Mike said, "that he was hot."

"You ever seen that flick?"

"No"

"Wow. You really need to see that one."

"Why didn't you tell me you'd taken a philosophy class? I had no idea. After everything we've talked about?"

"It's really not that big of a fucking deal. In fact. I didn't even finish the class. The whole fucking point of this little story is that this professor. And by the way. He *was* smoking hot. I mean. I sat on the very front fucking row of that classroom. And I just stared at his package through his blue jeans. But you know. As sexy as he was. I never saw him get fresh with any of his students."

Mike noticed a security guard walk by their table slowly. She seemed to meander deliberately towards the trash can. Mike's body stiffened and he felt his stomach wretch.

"Stay cool, pardner," Candi whispered to him. The security guard glanced over her shoulder and looked at them. Candi smiled and gently placed her hand on Mike's arm. "Stay cool," she whispered again. "You look like you just fucking robbed a bank or somethin."

The security guard inconspicuously glanced into the trash can and then turned around and walked towards them. Candi laughed out loud and nodded, as if responding to a joke. Mike wanted to look at the security guard but knew his eyes would give them away. The security guard strolled past their table slowly, and then picked up her speed as she walked away, rounding the corner down the tunnel.

Mike exhaled deeply and said, "That was a close one."

Candi leaned back in her chair and smiled, "Oh she'll be back. She fucking knows..."

"Then let's get the hell out of here."

"Aww, don't sweat it. We got a little more time before she gets back. Besides. I wanna finish tellin you about what this professor said about God's final judgment." Mike grimaced and stared at the corner in the tunnel where the security guard had disappeared.

"Anyways," Candi said. "on one of the days I happened to be there. That professor was talkin about the existence of God. And he said somethin I've never fucking forgotten. He said- the most important part of God bein like perfectly good, would be if God was perfectly empathetic."

"Empathetic?"

"Yep, empathetic. And then he said. There's a difference between empathy and sympathy. Sympathy is when you feel sorry for someone. And let's face it, nobody wants anybody to feel sorry for them. Even if it's God. Because when somebody just feels sorry for you it's like they pity you. And that makes you feel shitty. Basically, pity equals shitty."

"But this professor said- if it turns out that God does exist. And you do have to stand at the Pearly Gates and get your ass fucking judged someday. God would be perfectly empathetic. Basically, God would be able to stand in your shoes and understand why you made the choices you made. Because everybody always has a good reason for what they do, right? Even if that reason doesn't make any fucking sense to anybody else"

"Perfect empathy, huh?"

"Yep. Basically he was sayin- God's the only other person in the fucking universe who could really empathize with you. And all the choices you made, good or bad. And if God can see it *your way* like that. Then God would fucking understand. And then fucking forgive you for that shit."

"Well," Mike said, "That doesn't sound to me like the traditional picture of final judgment you hear about in church. And I certainly never heard anything like that at Yale Divinity School."

"No shit," Candi said. "I was like, wow! My preacher never said anything like that. I don't even think the Bible says anything like that. But you know what, pardner? I really fucking like it."

"I suppose," Mike said, "If God does in fact exist, then that scenario *is* logically possible."

"If God exists," Candi said, "Then a lot of fucking things are possible. Hell. I reckon anything's possible, right? Let's just all fucking hope. For all our sakes. That professor's right about the Pearly Gates."

Mike could still not discern how exactly Candi felt about God, religion or the afterlife; especially after this little conversation. His years of studying both philosophy and theology had equipped him with an uncanny knack for quickly identifying other people's personal religious beliefs, and then deftly critiquing them. And yet, Mike could not pin Candi down. She seemed to him a jumble of contradictions, heroically defying the stale philosophical and theological stereotypes to which he was accustomed. Candi was, Mike concluded, an endangered species.

"I still think," Mike said, "That rationally speaking, one must always maintain that stealing is wrong."

Candi huffed and puffed and said, "Oh, please. Don't fucking act like you've never stolen anything."

"Maybe back when I was in high school. Just for a cheap adolescent thrill"

"Well that's the fucking difference between me and you, isn't it? You've never really *had* to do anything. Have you? Everything with you is either a cheap thrill to temporarily make you forget how boring your life is. Or it's somethin that should be an actual accomplishment that just becomes a fucking chore for you. Kinda like your really long research paper you never finished."

Candi opened the two Cokes, drank a little from both bottles, and then poured the energy drinks into each. "Me," she said, "I don't do things like smouch or fuck or anything else because I'm bored. I do it because either I want to. Or because I have to."

She handed him one of the Cokes and said, "Here. Drink this Mr. Ride-the-High-Country. It'll make you feel a shit-ton better. It's the absolute fucking best hangover cure, ever."

Even though she never said it, Mike thought, Candi acted like rich people didn't have any real problems. Mike took a gulp of the stolen Coke. He reached into his pocket and pulled out his orange prescription bottle. He popped a tiny green and white pill, gulping it down with more Coke.

Candi's comments made Mike remember a graduate seminar on Kantian ethics he took at Yale. The professor teaching the class was The Noah Porter Professor of Philosophical Theology, some semi big-name ethicist whose father had been an actual big-name ethicist around the turn of the century. Mike recalled that over the course of the entire semester, the professor had made only two memorable comments.

One day in class the professor said, "There is certain nobility in pushing a broom."

Sonny Quillan, always sitting next to Mike in class, leaned over and whispered, "I pushed a broom most of my goddamned life. And let me just say. If this privileged prick had ever actually pushed a broom he wouldn't be saying that." Sonny had absolutely no ability to whisper. So whenever he did, everyone nearby overheard whatever witty, biting or satirical commentary he happened to be offering.

"My mom couldn't whisper either," Sonny once told Mike. "So whenever my dad used to fall asleep in church. And that was pretty much every Sunday morning and evening service. And during Bible study on Wednesday nights. My mom made sure everybody knew. It was fucking hilarious."

In Mike's opinion, the fact that Sonny knew he lacked the ability to whisper and yet still made comments in class like, "If this privileged prick had ever actually pushed a broom he wouldn't be saying that," made Sonny Quillan one of those characters who was almost too good to be true. It also made him one of those characters you either loved or hated. For this reason and in moments like that one, Mike had considered it both a blessing and a curse to sit next to Sonny in the classroom.

"If you think sitting next to this outlaw in the classroom is a misadventure," Esther Quillan once confessed to Mike, "then you should try sharing a saddle with him."

During his first year at Yale Divinity School, Mike lived in the graduate-student housing on Canner Street in New Haven. And during the first week of classes, Mike met his new neighbors down the hall, Sonny Quillan and his wife Esther. Over the next year, Mike and Sonny attended classes together, and the three of them spent nearly every Friday night together.

Mike recalled the words of Esther's confession, and suddenly realized it had been almost three years since that night. After dinner and a show at the Yale Cabaret, the three of them had cocktails back at their apartment. After polishing off almost an entire bottle of Johnny Walker Black, Sonny had passed out on the couch. He slept with his head resting in Esther's lap. Mike and Esther sat on the couch together.

Esther said to Mike, "I've been married to this cowboy for ten years now. And I've been with him even longer than that. Ever since I was fifteen years old. Can you believe that? And every single day of his life. Of our life together. Sonny gets up in the morning. Saddles up his horse. And somehow figures out a way to pull off a General Custer at Little Bighorn. You're his friend Mike so you know what I mean."

Mike nodded and said, "Yeah, I know what you mean. I see it every time he raises his hand in class."

Esther laughed softly, smiling down at Sonny. She said to Mike, "Have you ever read the poem, *The Charge of the Light Brigade*?"

"Tennyson?"

"The one and only"

"Yes, I've read it. It's been a while, though."

"Well there's this line in that poem that goes- *Ours is not to question why- Ours is but to do or die*. Remember that line?"

"Yes"

"That's the story of Sonny's life," Esther told Mike. "He just charges ahead. He gallops at full speed. Both pistols blazing. Riding into battle ready to vanquish the enemy."

"You're right," Mike said to her, smiling, "That's Sonny alright."

"The trouble is," Esther said, frowning, "Most times when Sonny rides into battle. There's no real enemies to vanquish." She pressed her fingers to her lips and kissed them, and then rested them gently on Sonny's forehead. "That's right. No *real* enemies. It's just Sonny. He's a cowboy riding into battle all by his lonesome. A cowboy with a horse and a pistol and no Indians to shoot at."

Mike watched for tears to well in Esther's eyes, but they never did.

"Every once in a while," Esther said, "when Sonny looks around. And realizes for just a brief moment that there's no enemy. You know what he always does?"

Mike shook his head, and then placed his hand gently on Esther's knee.

"He makes them up. That's right, he just makes them up. I'm pretty sure he's been making up enemies and fighting them all his life. He needs them, you know, enemies. He needs some-body to shoot at."

Mike remembered that day in their Kantian ethics class. After Sonny whispered to Mike, "If this privileged prick had ever actually pushed a broom he wouldn't be saying that," Sonny immediately raised his hand. And when the professor called on him, Sonny repeated his comment, *sans* the prick part, for the edification of the entire classroom.

Later in the semester, that professor made his second mem-orable comment.

It was a personal anecdote. It was an event the professor described as the singular greatest ethical dilemma of his entire life. He told the class that when he was offered the named pro-fessorship he currently held at Yale, he was faced with an ethical crisis, a moral choice. The professor then posed the question he had wrestled with- Should I stay in my tenured professorship at a lesser-known university, or make the move to Yale University? The professor then compared his ethical dilemma to a footnote in *The Groundwork for the Metaphysics of Morals*; or Mike wondered, was it from *The Prolegomena*, Mike couldn't remember exactly...

Mike and Candi took the escalators back up to street level and then walked back towards The Magnolia Hotel.

"Houston fucking sunshine!" Candi said. "I sure am glad I smouched these fucking sunglasses. I'm really gonna need them. And who knows! If my niece is ever starvin to death. And she needs a loaf of fucking bread. Then I can sell these bad boys and save her fucking life." She laughed and nudged Mike's shoulder with her elbow.

Mike didn't respond.

"Oh come on, pardner. That was a pretty good one. You gotta admit."

"Can I ask you a question?" Mike said.

"Shoot"

"What would you say is the greatest ethical dilemma you've ever faced?"

"Ever?"

"Yeah. What's the most difficult moral choice you've ever had to make?"

"Kinda hard to narrow it down, I reckon. Why?"

"I was just wondering."

"Wait a second," Candi said, "I think I know. Yep, I got it. My greatest ethical dilemma. It's gotta be tryin to decide whether or not to suck your dick for a ride across the Baytown Bridge. Yep, that's fucking it!"

"What?"

"You fucking heard me."

Mike glanced down at the pavement.

"Why are you sooo fucking surprised?" Candi said. "I mean. What the fuck? You think I like suckin strange dick? You think I just," Candi made quotation marks with her fingers, "love the taste of a stranger's cum? Oh yeah! I love that salty shit sooo fucking much. I was really, really, really excited about tradin a blow-job for a ride across that bridge? Yep! That's me alright. I get up every single mornin. Lick my pretty lips. And fucking daydream about all the sweaty strange dick I'm gonna get to put in my fucking mouth that day. Wow! You know what? My mouth is literally waterin right now."

"Listen, Candi," Mike said, "I never meant to-"

"Let me tell you somethin, pardner. I fucking hope I have a starvin niece someday. Just so I can go suck a few dicks for a loaf of bread to save her life. Maybe I'll even make it a baker's dozen. Get it?"

"I'm sorry I asked."

"*That's* what you're sorry for? You're sorry you *asked me* about the dilemma? Fuck you motherfucker!"

"For Chrissakes, Candi. What the hell do you want me to say?"

Candi laughed out loud and said, "Lighten up, pardner. I'm just fucking with you again. You didn't think I was serious about the whole givin you a blowjob for a ride was my greatest moral dilemma, did you? Wow! You know what you are?"

"What?"

"A fucking dumbass faggot. All day long!"

"You know I hate it when you call me that."

"Come on. I just love it sooo much when you get all bent outta shape and pissed off at me. I think you're my favorite person in the whole fucking world to tease. You know that?"

"I don't mind a little teasing, Candi. But you're too much."

"I fucking know I am. And I fucking love that shit about me."

Mike sighed, partly from exasperation but partly from relief too.

"So, pardner," Candi said, "What's the greatest moral dilemma you ever faced?"

"I guess I can't say right off the top of my head."

"You know what you shoulda answered, don't you?"

"What?"

"You shoulda answered. Whether or not to just..." Candi paused, gave it some thought, and then said, "You shoulda said. Whether or not to just go ahead and..." Candi hesitated again.

"What is it, Candi? I should've done what?"

"Brain fart!" Candi said. "Wow! I just completely lost my train of fucking thought there. Don't you just fucking hate brain farts? They're even worse than pussy farts, if you ask me. I mean a pussy fart might smell like shit, but at least with a pussy fart you don't forget shit. Am I right?"

✳ ✳ ✳

Later, as they climbed back into the car, Mike said to Candi, "You know. I've faced some real ethical dilemmas in my life. I have."

"I'll bet you been rackin your brain for the past twenty minutes tryin to think of one, huh? You know, pardner. If it takes you that fucking long to think of one. Then there's a good fucking chance it's not gonna be very impressive when you do."

"Who says it needs to be impressive?"

"Come on now! That's the whole fucking point of that stupid fucking question. Isn't it? You ask a person about the biggest moral choice they ever made. And then you're either impressed because their life seems so tough or interesting or what-the-fuck-ever. Or you're not impressed and then you think they don't have any real problems. Am I right?"

"Well, uh, I think there's actually more to the question than that."

"I mean. When you ask a stupid fucking question like that. Are you really interested in what moral choice they made in that situation? Or are you just tryin to use the situation to rubberneck your way into feelin better about yourself?"

"You've got a point, I suppose," Mike said. "But you're doing the exact same thing yourself, right here. When I asked you the question you didn't take it seriously. You made a joke, like usual. And then when you asked me the question, because I couldn't think of anything off the top of my head, you concluded that I must not have any real problems."

"I didn't say I wasn't fucking doin it. I mean we all do it, right?"

"Ok. Maybe we all do it. But that doesn't mean it's an accurate portrayal of a person's life. Or that it represents the sum total of a person's moral choices."

"A person like *you*," Candi said, smiling, "for instance?"

"Yes. A person like me. Or even a person like *you*, for instance."

"So me and you are the fucking exceptions to the rule, huh?"

Mike frowned and said, "Trust me, Candi. Before this little trip is over-"

"You mean odyssey, right?"

"Yes. Before this odyssey is over I'll share with you my greatest ethical dilemma."

"Do you think I'll be impressed?"

"I'll let you be the judge," Mike said.

"But I told you, pardner. I fucking never judge."

"Never say never," Mike said, starting the car. "Where to now?"

"We're ridin northwest."

"By the way," Mike said. "Since you didn't tell me the truth when I first asked you. Are you ever going to tell me about your greatest ethical dilemma?"

"Trust me, pardner," Candi said, tossing her empty Coke bottle out the window. "No matter how bad *your* life gets. You're never gonna know what it's like to have to smouch a skirt, just to have it lifted by some strange man."

Chapter 6

Union Grove Baptist Church; A sign from God;
Candi's sermon on the mound;
A true fucking story; Whitehall, Texas;
And how Mike and Candi struggled and who won

Mike and Candi drove northwest on Highway 290 out of Houston. After passing under Beltway 8 they continued on that same highway for awhile, eventually surmounting the urban and suburban sprawl on the outskirts of Houston.

Mike said to Candi, "You're still not telling me where we're going?"

"Nope"

After awhile Candi said, "Take this exit, right up here." Mike looked up and saw a green sign which read, EXIT 362. Once they exited the highway Candi said, "Turn right up here. And then just keep followin 362. We're about to drive right into the fucking boonies, pardner. You sure you're ready for this?"

"I guess so" Mike noticed they were heading into a rural area. It made him a little nervous to be leaving the city with a stranger. But he kept telling himself it was an adventure. And excellent fodder for his novel. Even if he didn't believe they were actually looking for buried treasure.

After a few more miles Candi said, "Right up here at FM 1488. Take a right turn and then keep goin on 362 towards Magnolia."

"Oh yeah. In a few more miles there's gonna be a fucking Buddhist or Chinese or some kinda Asian lookin temple building. On the right hand side of the road. We're gonna turn left right as we pass it."

"Are you serious about the temple?"

"Yep. It's some kinda spiritual retreat or some fucking bullshit like that. You know. A nice quiet place in the country where weirdos from Houston come and meditate and do yoga and whatever the fuck else people like that do to relax."

Minutes later they drove by a gated enclave of cottages arranged near a chapel. Trees and bushes were overgrown along the fence and around the property. "Huh," Candi said, "kinda looks like it's fucking closed down."

The sign by the roadside read: TINH LUAT.

Mike said, "It's a Buddhist retreat, alright."

"It's actually kinda funny," Candi said. "When they first opened up this place a few years ago. And put up that sign. All the yocals around here were pretty fucking excited. They all thought somebody was openin up an all-you-can-eat Chinese buffet!"

Mike shook his head.

"And then when all these yocals found out there wasn't gonna be any orange chicken and egg rolls for lunch after church. And instead. People were gonna be worshippin Buddha in there. They all started prayin for God to close the fucking place down."

"And let me tell you. If that fucking place ever catches fire those Buddhists are sooo fucked in the ass. I mean. Out here in the fucking boonies. Every man in the volunteer fire department is a fucking Southern Baptist. God's gonna work in mysterious ways, pardner. That's all I'm sayin."

"Buddhists are peaceful, you know," Mike said, "and actually, they don't worship Bud-"

"Right fucking here. Here's our fucking turn motherfucker. Turn left right here. And keep goin on 362. This is Field Store Community."

"You were right," Mike said. "This *is* way out in the country. Are we almost there?"

"Nope. We gotta ways to go yet."

As Mike made the left turn, he said to himself, "And miles to go before I sleep..."

* * *

A little bit later, still driving on 362, Candi said, "Hey! Pull over right up here. Just up ahead on the right side of the road"

Mike slowed down the car.

"Just pull off the road into that gravel driveway where that church sign is. Careful though. There's a fucking gate with a lock on it."

Mike pulled the car over into the gravel driveway.

The gate was a single rusted pole blocking any cars from continuing down the long driveway towards an old country church you could see on the hill.

They got out of the car. Mike watched Candi stare down the long gravel driveway, the Texas wind blowing her dark hair in the afternoon sunshine.

"Be careful, Candi. It looks like you're standing on a fire ant mound."

Candi looked down at the ground. She dug her heel into the soft brown dirt and said, "Nope. Looks like they moved on to greener pastures"

Mike turned his attention to the church sign. It was an old white wooden sign with a little shingled rooftop over it. There was a big red cross on the right hand side. The sign read:

Discover God's Word
UNION
GROVE
BAPTIST
CHURCH

"Where two or more are gathered in My name, there I am also."

SUNDAY SCHOOL 9:45am
SUNDAY WORSHIP 6pm
WEDNESDAY BIBLE STUDY 6:30pm

Below this was one of those signs with removable plastic letters, like you see in front of the car wash or the convenient store advertising a sale on cigarettes. In black plastic removable letters it read:

CELEBRATE THE
FREEDOM TO WORSHIP
JESUS WHILE YOU CAN

Even though Mike had studied philosophical theology at Yale Divinity School he was a little puzzled by the bottom part of the sign. "What's that supposed to mean?" he said. "Is that supposed to suggest that the world is ending soon? So you better accept Jesus and get saved before it's too late?"

"Once upon a time..." Candi said, "Somethin really fucking horrible happened here."

Mike forgot about salvation for a minute. "Really? Did it happen to you?"

"Nope"

"Did you used to go to this church?"

"Nope," Candi said, pulling out a blowpop.

"Well, for Chrissakes. Tell me the story already."

"You know what, pardner. I don't think I should tell you this particular story. It just wouldn't be right, you know?"

"What? Why? What are you even talking about?"

"I mean. You want shit for your novel? You know. People and places and stories, right?"

"Yeah. Isn't that the whole point of us coming out here? People, places and stories. Isn't that what you said you'd give me if I went on this road trip with you?"

"Odyssey, remember?"

"Listen, Candi. You can't just have me pull over in this driveway and then say something like- Something really fucking horrible happened here one time. And then refuse to tell me what happened."

"I'm afraid I'm gonna have to insist on fucking silence this time, pardner. Sorry. You're right though. I shouldn't have teased you with it. It's downright mean. I know. But I guess I just spoke too quickly. Before I really thought about it, you know? It just kinda came outta me when I saw this fucking place again."

"I don't understand," Mike said, "Why won't you tell me what happened here?"

"Because. Some stories about people's lives are fucking sacred. Or at least they fucking should be anyways."

"Listen, Candi. If it didn't happen to you then why do you give a shit about sharing the story with me? Why does it matter?"

"It does fucking matter that it's not about me. It's just that some stories about people and places should be fucking sacred, you know? I mean not every story should be fucking told."

"You, of all people! Are lecturing me about what's sacred?"

"Ouch, pardner!" Candi said. "That hurt like a cheap gag-store dildo."

"I'm sorry"

"No you're fucking *not* sorry. You made a good point. I mean what's a whore know about what's sacred anyways?"

"That's not what I meant. That's not true."

"It is fucking true. I didn't say it wasn't true. I said it hurt like a cheap gag-store dildo."

"I'm sorry, Candi. Listen. I haven't eaten all day and I'm feeling jittery." Mike held his hands up in the air. His fingers trembled. "Look at me. I'm shaky, for Chrissakes. Sometimes I don't even know what I'm saying. You know I didn't mean it that way."

"Well. I don't know for sure that you didn't mean it. But! Seein as I'm standin on private property right now. And this private property happens to belong to JC. And JC's always forgiven me every time I needed it. Whether I fucking deserved it or not. I reckon I'll fucking forgive you. This time"

"Thanks, Candi. I'm sure Jesus is very proud of you."

"You know, pardner. When I said that shit about JC bein forgivin, just now. I wasn't bein *facetious*. I betcha didn't think I'd remember that two-dollar word. Did you?"

"No I didn't"

"And speakin of JC," Candi said. "You know what I've always loved sooo much about him?"

"What's that?"

"Well. It wasn't so much that JC was willin to die on the cross for the sins of the whole world. Now don't get me wrong here. I know that *I'd* never give a shit enough about a bunch of complete strangers to hang on a cross so they could get forgiven for their fucking sins. Let me tell you. I don't care who you are. You gotta fucking admit. That's *real* love right there."

Mike nodded and said, "Well, Jesus did say- Greater love hath no man than he give his life for another."

"Wow. That's pretty fucking cool, pardner. You must've learned a fuck-ton about the Bible at that fancy-schmancy divinity school you went to, huh?"

"I didn't learn it at divinity school," Mike said, "it was in Sunday school. When I was a kid"

"You mean somebody took you to Sunday school when you were a kiddo?"

"Yeah, unfortunately"

"Well, you're one fucky bastard. You know that?"

"I beg to differ"

"I'll bet somebody even took you to Vacation Bible School in the summertime?"

"Again, yeah. Unfortunately"

"Why do you keep sayin, unfortunately?"

"That's a really long story."

"When I was a kiddo," Candi said, "I always wished somebody would take me to Sunday school. And to Vacation Bible School. All the other kiddos got to go. Except me. It always sounded really fun. You know. I mean. You get to make cool crafts outta pipe cleaners and paper plates and glue and glitter and shit. And you get to eat snacks like animal crackers, ice cream and chocolate chip cookies. And you get to fucking sing songs like- 'He's Got the Whole World in His Hands' and 'Jesus Loves Me' and 'The B-I-B-L-E'. And best of fucking all! You get to sit there and listen to somebody read you Bible stories."

"Oh yeah. Tell me about it," Mike said. "I sat there and listened to my fair share of Bible stories alright."

"And you got to do all those other fun things too, right?"

"Unfortunately"

"So why the fuck do you keep sayin, unfortunately?"

"Trust me, Candi. It's not all it's cracked up to be. I told you. It's a long story."

"But you got to do all those fun things, right?"

"Yes, but I-"

"Then I don't give a good goddamn how long of a fucking story it is. You're one fucky bastard! End of story."

"Fine," Mike said, "Whatever you say. I'm fucky."

"Anyways," Candi said, "Like I was sayin before. You gotta give JC props for bein willin to die so a bunch of fucking strangers, perverts and all-around pieces of shit could get forgiven for their sins and go to Heaven."

"Agreed," Mike said. "I think that's the reason most people like Jesus. Or trust him as their savior. Or even just respect him as a virtuous person. But not you, though?"

"Nope. Not me. My favorite JC is the *alive* JC."

"What do you mean?"

"Again, don't get me wrong. I like the bloody-faced, crown-of-thorns, hangin-on-the-cross JC who saves you from your fucking sins."

"Pun intended?" Mike said.

"That street runs both ways, pardner."

Mike chuckled.

"Anyways," Candi said. "I also like the walkin-through-fucking-walls, scarin-the-shit-outta-his disciples, raised-from-the-dead JC who kicked Satan's fucking ass back to the bad place."

"You mean *zombie* Jesus?"

"Hey dumbass! That's not fucking cool. JC was *not* a fucking zombie. You got that? I mean we're at a fucking church here. So try and show some goddamn fucking respect."

"Sorry"

"So. I like all those things about JC. Just like everybody else. But! I've always been the biggest fan of the *alive* JC. You know. The actual flesh and blood real man. The walkin-talkin, wine-drinkin, even had to take a shit once in a while like everybody else, *alive* JC. I mean *before* he fucking died on the cross for all our sins!"

"What I love most about JC," Candi said, "is that when he was alive he was always willin to stand up for people who couldn't stand up for themselves. You know. Like that adulterous cuntbag that everybody wanted to throw rocks at. Remember her? Can you fucking believe those assholes were gonna throw fucking rocks at that adulterous cuntbag and kill her? And then! Just in the nick of fucking time! *Alive* JC just rides right into town on a white fucking horse and rescues her."

"Actually, I think it was a donkey," Mike said, chuckling.

"You know what I always thought?" Candi said. "I always thought. I'll bet that adulterous cuntbag was like- who the fuck is this stranger savin my ass? And what does he fucking want from me in return? She was probably like- this stranger wants to save my fucking ass so he can take me back to his place and fuck me in the ass!"

"Why am I not surprised?" Mike said. "Only you, Candi, would think something like that when you heard that story."

"Let me tell you, pardner. I'll bet that after everybody threw down their fucking rocks and went home to jerk-off. I'll bet that adulterous cuntbag took JC out back of the old barn and offered to suck his dick. Just to thank him, you know."

"Umm, I think it's safe to say," Mike said, smiling, "that's an apocryphal story."

"A what kinda story?"

"Apocryphal. It means it never really happened."

"Well, if it did happen. What I mean is. If that adulterous cuntbag did take JC behind the barn and offer to suck his dick. JC never would've let her do it. Never in a million zillion trillion fucking years."

"Well," Mike said, "According to the Bible, Jesus *was* the son of God. He was supposed to be perfect."

"No, no, no! You're missin my fucking point, dumbass. You're right. JC *was* the son of God. He was fucking perfect. He never fucking sinned. Ever! But! JC was also just a really, really, really, really decent man. A *real man*. I mean. JC fucking stood up for other people. Especially women, you know."

"Honestly, Candi. This is the strangest sermon I've ever heard."

"I mean just think about how JC stood up for that fucking slutbitch that he met by the well that day. Remember that?"

"You mean the Samaritan woman at the well, right?"

"Yeah, that's the one. That's the slutbitch I'm talkin about. She was like the village fucking bicycle. I mean a total fucking tramp. I'll bet she gave everybody and their camel a ride! And what did *alive* JC do when he fucking met her? That's right! Alive JC still stood up for her."

"I always liked that story of the Samaritan woman at the well," Mike said. "And you're right. It does seem like, according to the Gospels, that Jesus was willing to-"

"You mean, *alive* JC, right?"

"Right, sorry. I meant *alive* Jesus. As I was saying. It does seem like alive Jesus was willing to stand up for the subjugated or oppressed members of society, especially women. If you read the gospels, whether you're a Christian or not, you'll realize that alive Jesus didn't mind breaking the religious and social taboos of his day. He was a rebel."

"Fuck yeah he was! Alive JC was the original James Dean."

Mike laughed and said, "Jesus even ate dinner with tax collectors and whores."

"Whoa there, pardner. Hold up there for just a fucking second. What did you just say?"

"I was just pointing out that Jesus was willing to associate with people who were considered social outcasts. Like when he ate dinner with tax collectors and whores."

"That's bullshit. Alive JC never ate fucking supper with a whore."

"What?"

"Nope! Never fucking happened. Never"

"You mean you've never heard that story?"

"Nope, I never heard that story. And you know why I never heard that story? Because. That story ain't fucking true, that's why."

"You're teasing me again, right?"

"Nope"

"Candi, that's a true story. The Bible says Jesus ate dinner with tax collectors and whores. I can't believe you never heard that."

"I told you, pardner. Nobody ever took me to fucking Sunday school."

"It's true. You see. Jesus broke many religious and social taboos. In ancient Judea-"

"That's when alive JC was alive, right?"

"Right. In ancient Judea, being a tax collector or a whore meant you were a social pariah."

"A social *piranha*? You mean like the meat-eating fishes?"

Mike chuckled and said, "Sorry about that. No. Not the meat-eating fish. The word is *pariah*, and it means a social outcast. A person who's despised by society"

"Basically," Candi said, "Somebody who nobody wants to be seen in public with, right?"

"Exactly"

"So are you absolutely fucking sure? And I mean absolutely fucking sure about this story where alive JC eats dinner with a whore?"

"Yes, I'm sure."

"So you're not just makin that shit up, right? Because if you're makin a story like that up. It just might be the one and only sin that raised-from-the-dead JC ain't gonna forgive your ass for. And you know what, pardner? I wouldn't fucking blame him either."

"No, Candi. It's a true story."

Candi sucked on her blowpop, smacked it in between her lips and said, "Wow. I'll bet alive JC would've looked great in a big ol white Stetson cowboy hat. Whatta ya think?"

✳✳✳

"So," Mike said, "Why don't you just go ahead and tell me about that horrible thing that happened here."

"Wow," Candi said, "You really gotta hard-on for that story, don't ya?"

"Just tell me."

"I said, fucking *no*."

"Come on, Candi. It's not that big of a deal. For Chrissakes, it's just a story."

"Stories are important."

"Come on, just tell me. You know you want to. And please don't give me any of that bullshit about it being sacred either."

"Well it is sacred. So fucking drop it, motherfucker."

"You know what *I* think?'

"Stop"

"*I* think," Mike said, "Nothing is sacred. And I think that *you* think it too."

"Speak for your fucking self."

"Come on, Candi. Just give it up."

"No means fucking *no*, pardner."

"I'm not giving up this time," Mike said. "I'm going to make you tell me that story."

"Listen up pardner. If I tell you this story then you'll put it in your fucking novel for the whole fucking world to read."

"Ok. How about this then? If you tell me. I promise I won't put the story in my novel."

"Bullshit"

"No, I'm serious. I promise, Candi. This is the one story on our whole trip that I promise not to put in my novel."

"Bullshit," Candi said. "You won't be able to fucking resist. This is just toooooo good of a fucking story. I mean it's just toooo fucked up. And toooo fucking horrible. And just toooooo un-fucking-believable that you won't be able to fucking resist!"

"I promise. Please, Candi."

Candi gazed back down that long driveway towards the country church on the hill amongst the oak trees. The Texas wind seemed to whisper the story to her.

"Sorry, pardner," Candi said finally, tossing down her spent blowpop stick. "Some stories should just never be told, no matter what. And I ain't takin a chance of this one goin in your fucking novel."

✳✳✳

Mike and Candi had climbed over the gate, walked down the gravel road, around the church, read the Texas Historical Marker out front, and were walking back towards the car along the barbed wire fence.

"You know what, pardner," Candi said, "All this talk about alive JC has got me thinkin."

"About what?"

"Remember when we played the 'Who Would You Fuck Game' back at the Magnolia?"

"Yeah, sure"

"And you remember how I said before that I'd marry and settle down with Steve Wilkos?"

"Yeah," Mike said, chuckling, "Yeah, I do."

"Well. No offense to Steve Wilkos or his lovely fucky wife Rochelle. But! I think I fucking changed my fucking mind about who I wanna marry and settle down with."

"Please don't say what I think you're going to say."

"Yep. I wanna marry and settle down with JC."

"You mean *alive* Jesus, right?"

"You betcha, pardner. I mean I'm not gonna marry and fucking settle down with nails-through-his-fucking-hands JC. Or raised-from-the-fucking-dead-all-glowy-and-shiny JC!"

They laughed together as they approached the rusted gate.

"Not that alive JC ever would've popped the fucking question," Candi said. "I mean. He didn't really seem like the marryin kind. Am I right? And plus. He had a lot of fucking work to do. His father's work, I mean."

"I think you're right about Jesus not being the marrying kind. But I must admit, Candi. If there was any woman in the whole world. Who might have been able to make Jesus forget all about his father's work, get married and settle down. It would definitely be you."

Candi stopped and turned to Mike. She took his hand and said, "Well thank you, pardner. That was really fucking sweet. I didn't know you had it in you."

"Well, I do. And I mean it…"

Candi continued holding his hand. She squeezed it and said, "Well. You know what I think?"

"What?"

"I think it'd be really, really, really weird to fuck JC." She dropped Mike's hand. "Even if he was my fucking husband!" She turned and kept walking towards the gate.

"Candi, you always know exactly what to say."

"I mean fucking think about it for a second. Don't you think it'd be really really weird to have JC's hard cock inside you?"

"I really can't believe I'm having this conversation."

"I mean don't fucking get me wrong. I'm sure JC had a big huge Moby-sized dick. And I'm sure if JC shoved his hard throbbin cock in my pussy. I'd cum like there was no tomorrow. And I bet he'd cum over and over and over and over again."

"You know Candi. This gives a whole new meaning to the second *coming* of Christ." Mike chuckled.

"Not cool, pardner," Candi said, frowning. "I already fucking told you to watch your fucking mouth here. We're on private goddamned property."

"Sorry"

"All I'm sayin is. That it would kinda be weird to fuck JC. That's all. I mean it would kinda be like gettin fucked by God."

Mike really wanted to make a joke, but hesitated.

"Course," Candi said, "I reckon a lot of people in this world feel like they've gotten fucked by God. And they *didn't* fucking mean having sex with JC."

"Well," Mike said, "So much for me trying to be reverent."

"Whatta ya think, pardner? You think alive JC would've ever wanted to fuck his wife up the ass? You think JC was that kinda guy? Not that I'd mind of course. Hell. If JC was my hubby he could fuck me in the ass and not even use any fucking lube. I mean I'd just let him dry fuck that shit if he wanted to. Course. I'm pretty fucking sure JC would've been a gentleman, and at least spit on his dick first."

"Do you ever," Mike said, "listen to yourself when you talk?"

"Hey," Candi said, "I'm just askin the big questions. You're a philosopher. Isn't that what ya'll do? Ask the big questions? I mean didn't you go to fucking Yale Divinity School?"

"Yeah, I did. But believe me. We never asked any of the big questions while I was there. Everybody just pretended to already know all the answers to all the big questions."

"Well the only fucking thing I do know," Candi said, "is that I don't know shit."

Mike thought about his hero Socrates.

"You never answered me before," Candi said. "You think JC would've wanted to fuck his wife up the ass?"

"I think if *you* were his wife," Mike said, "then Jesus would've been a *fucky* guy."

"You're just full of sweet little nothins today, aren't ya?"

"I guess you just bring it out of me."

"Kinda like I brought all that cum outta your dick with my goddamned mouth on The Baytown Bridge?" Candi winked and smiled.

Mike grimaced and frowned.

They climbed back over the gate and stood next to the hood of the car.

"My daddy always told me," Candi said. "Girl, you got the worst taste in men that I ever seen. And I fucking reckon he was right too. I mean looky at the two men I said I'd settle down and get married to. A cop and carpenter. Oh well! I reckon I've always had a stiff-clit for the workin man."

***

"Candi," Mike said to her, "I've got to ask you a question."
"Shoot"
"Would you say that you're a Christian?"
Candi thought for a moment, smiled and then said, "You ever heard that song, *Walking in Memphis* by Marc Cohn? Not the fucking version by Cher. I'm talkin about the only real version of that song worth listenin to. *Walking in Memphis*. You ever heard that song?"
"No, I've never even heard of it."
"You really need to listen to that song," Candi said, and then started singing, "They got catfish on the table..." She closed her eyes, raised her arms up over her head and then snapped her fingers and sang, "They got gospel in the air..."
Mike watched her wriggle and writhe her body as she sang. He noticed the way Candi arched her back and swayed her arms above her head, and noticed how her tits gently jiggled.
"Anyways," Candi said. "In that song. He fucking goes down to this night club in Memphis. It was called The Hollywood. Where this chick named Muriel plays piano every Friday. And they ask him to do a little number. You know, sing a fucking song. And then Muriel sings to him- tell me are you a Christian child? And then he sings back to her," Candi paused and sang, "Ma'am I am tonight!"
"So," Mike said, "What is that supposed to mean?"
"Dumbass," Candi said. "It means that sometimes you just get all caught up in the moment, you know? Like when you go to a fucking funeral or a church service. And you hear one of those old hymns like *Amazing Grace* or *Washed in the Blood* that you used to sing when you were a kiddo. And all of a sudden you get all caught up in the music. And you just *feel* like a Christian. Yep. Right in that goddamned fucking moment. You just *feel* like a Christian. I mean it just fucking happens."
Mike marveled at Candi's sweet, simple, gentle, *dumb* imagination.

"It's like he sang in that song- Ma'am I am, *tonight*! Sometimes you're just a Christian because you feel like one. Because you just can't fucking help yourself but feel like one. That's the way I feel about it anyways."

"Candi," Mike said, "compared to Valechka you're a Schlegel, and compared to Charlotte you're a Hegel."

"What the fuck does that mean?"

"It's Nabokov"

"If you say so, pardner"

✳ ✳ ✳

"Ok. Since I didn't tell you that story about the horrible fucked up thing that happened here," Candi said a few minutes later, "I'm gonna make a little true story happen right now. Right here. Just for you. Just so you can fucking put that shit in your novel."

Candi walked over to the church sign and stared at the removable plastic letters. They read:

CELEBRATE THE
FREEDOM TO WORSHIP
JESUS WHILE YOU CAN

Mike noticed that Candi seemed to be reading and rereading the words on the sign. He wondered if she was conjuring another dark memory of this place.

Suddenly Candi said, "Hurry up and get your ass in the fucking car!"

"Huh?"

Candi rushed towards the sign and yelled, "Hurry up and get in the fucking car! Crank up that fucking engine. And get ready to fucking peel outta here!"

Mike obeyed her, climbed into the car and started the engine. He watched Candi slide the removable black letters on the sign in and out of the grooves, quickly arranging and rearranging them. Candi yelled, "I'll give you a true fucking story to put in your fucking novel."

Candi tossed the excess letters over the barbed-wire fence into the grass. She laughed out loud and bolted away from the sign towards the car. Candi jumped in and yelled, "Let's get the fuck outta here, pardner!" The tires spun gravel as they peeled away onto the road.

The sign now read:

CELEBRAE THE
FREEDOM TO WORSHIP
CUNT WHILE YOU A

As they rode away from Union Grove Baptist Church, Mike and Candi laughed out loud together.

True fucking story...

* * *

Not far down the road Mike and Candi stopped in Whitehall, Texas.

"It basically amounts to a big old beautiful abandoned cotton gin and the Whitehall Grocery Store," Candi said, "which doubles as a gas station."

They pulled up and parked in front of the grey building with cedar posts propping up the front porch. Mike saw white chickens foraging in front of the store next to a TEXAS LOTTO sign.

"You hungry there, pardner? How about some free-range fucking chicken?"

They went inside Whitehall Grocery Store. An old woman sat behind the register, smoking like a chimney. Candi inhaled deeply, leaned over to Mike and whispered, "You don't find too many stores these days that still smell like coffin nails. It's kinda like payphones and cowboys. They're a dyin fucking breed."

Mike got a Diet Peach Snapple. Candi got a Coors Light and a sour-apple blowpop.

They drove on down 362 for a few more miles, passed a cemetery on the right, crossed some railroad tracks, and then turned left on Highway 105 towards Navasota.

"Once we get to Navasota," Candi said. "We'll drive north on Highway 6. Then we'll cross the Navasota River into Brazos County. And then we'll get to the twin cities of College Station and Bryan. And then, pardner, we'll be half-way fucking there."

* * *

A little later, as they crossed the Brazos River, Mike reached into his pants pocket and pulled out his orange prescription bottle. Before he could open the bottle Candi snatched it from his hand. They struggled. Mike tried to hold on to both the steering wheel and the prescription bottle. The car swerved. Mike shouted at Candi and then pleaded with her. Candi wrested the bottle from him. She rolled down her window and tossed the orange bottle off the bridge.

It all happened so fast neither of them could remember exactly what was said and done. Except for when Candi rolled up her window and said, "Maybe now you'll be a little nicer to me, pardner. Not so fucking jittery." She patted Mike on the back and said, "And get your fucking appetite back too. You need to eat, pardner. And I'm gonna make sure you do."

Chapter 7

College Station, Texas;
How Mike and Candi ended up drinking at Dudley's Draw;
Mike's satirical tribute to Hemingway

On their way to College Station and Bryan, along Highway 6, Mike and Candi drove by the sleepy little communities of Millican and Peach Creek.

Candi said to Mike, "Before we get done with our little odyssey. Be sure to remind me to tell you the story of old Clifton Clowers."

"Who's that?"

"Oh just some old man who lives around these parts. His farm is over near Wolverton Mountain." She snickered to herself.

"What's so funny?"

"Nothin"

"I had no idea there were any mountains around here."

"Oh fuck yeah. Lots and lots and lots of fucking mountains. Lots of fucking farms. And lots of fucking woodpiles on those farms."

"Woodpiles?"

"Yessirree, pardner," Candi said solemnly, staring out the window. "Here in Texas. Woodpiles are where families keep their secrets. And let me tell you this. There's a fuck-ton of secrets buried in some of these old woodpiles round here."

✳ ✳ ✳

College Station, Texas is affectionately known as Aggieland. It is home to Texas A&M University, Kyle Field and the fightin Texas Aggies. In this great city everybody bleeds maroon and nobody locks their doors at night. College Station is also home to the George H. W. Bush Presidential Library.

"And let me tell you," Candi said, "If you go to that fucking library on the 4th of July. When the Brazos Valley Symphony fucking Orchestra is playin. You'll see the *second* best fireworks and patriotic music show in the whole fucking world."

"Only the second best?"

"Duh, you fucking dumbass. Everybody and their fucking mother-in-law knows that the best fireworks show in the whole wide fucking universe is in Mountain Home, Arkansas. On the grounds of the ASU Campus there. Fucking amazing!"

"You mean you're not going to tell me that the best fireworks are in Houston, Texas? Wow. Saints and angels preserve us."

"Hey! Houston can't be the fucking best at everything, you know."

Mike smiled at her.

"Right up here," Candi said as they rode into town. "You're gonna wanna take Business 6 through town. Or as it's called in these parts, Texas Avenue. And then you're gonna wanna turn left when you get to University Drive. Pardner, I'm takin you to Northgate for a drink."

Across the street from Texas A&M University, on the way out of town towards both Easterwood Airport and the buzzing metropolis of Snook, Texas, the thirsty-weary traveler will find what the locals refer to as Northgate.

"It's nothin fancy," Candi said. "Just a couple of city blocks lined with bars, beer joints, restaurants and cafes. Oh yeah. And did I mention the bars and beer joints?"

"I could really use a gin and tonic," Mike said.

"There's no fucking way you can visit College Station and not have a beer at the Dixie Chicken. It's world fucking famous!"

When Mike thought of famous places to have a drink, places like the Café de Flore in Paris, even though it wasn't a bar, or The Hotel Carlyle in New York City came to mind. It was puzzling, and yet, somehow appealing to Mike, that Candi thought of places like the Dixie Chicken at Northgate in College Station, Texas instead.

Mike and Candi walked out of the Dixie Chicken into the afternoon sunshine. "Well shit!" Candi said, "I didn't remember them only sellin beer. I reckon it figures. Like the guy inside fucking said- this is a *beer* joint."

Mike felt queasy and said to her, "Candi, I really need a cocktail."

"I can't fucking believe you don't fucking drink beer. You're such a fucking pussy." Mike noticed a young couple with two kids. All four of them were wearing maroon, and glaring at Candi. "I could really fucking use a goddamned Shiner Bock right about now!"

"Hey, Candi. For Chrissakes. Keep your voice down. There are kids right over there."

"Fuck you and fuck those kiddos too. I'm not the one who didn't use a condom. So I shouldn't have to be the one who watches her fucking language. Am I right?"

"You're a real class act, Candi. You know that?"

"Hey don't blame me! If you drank beer like every other red-blooded American. Like a real man. Then we wouldn't be standin on this fucking sidewalk. In this fucking hot sunshine. And I wouldn't be fucking cussin in front of these motherfucking cocksucking little kiddos right here."

The couple and their kids quickly walked away.

"Pardner," Candi said, "You gotta have the only cootch West of the Pecos that's bigger than mine. And I'm a busy girl too. If you know what I mean."

"I will drink beer," Mike said. "I just prefer a cocktail or a glass of wine. That's all."

"Well then, pardner. It's our fucky day!" She pointed to a sign on the building next door and read it aloud, "Dudley's Draw. Right next door. And I'll betcha they make one hell of a-" she raised her hands and made quotation marks with her fingers, "*cock*tail."

"Let's check it out then," Mike said.

"Sure thing. If you can drag your big fucking *mangina* that far!"

Mike and Candi went into Dudley's Draw and sat down at the bar. There were only a few other people there, regulars mostly, middle-aged men and women who probably got off work early.

The bartender was a college girl wearing a maroon Aggie t-shirt, tight Wrangler blue jeans and red cowboy boots. She said, "Welcome to Dudley's, ya'll."

"You know what sweetheart," Candi said to her, "That's exactly the kinda sexy Southern accent that drives Hank Williams Jr. wild."

"Why thank ya," she said to Candi. "I wish more men would use a pick-up line like that."

Mike frowned, feeling sick to his stomach.

"Call me Candi- with an i," she said to the bartender. "And this here's my pardner, Mike. We're on a drive together. Headed up north"

"Nice to meet ya'll," the bartender said.

Mike still frowned.

"Well. I'll take a Long Island Iced Tea, please," Candi said to her, and then turned to Mike. "You're shootin awful straight today, pardner. See. I'm gonna have to go with you on this one. Fuck beer. A fucking cocktail does sound pretty fucking good."

"And for you, sir?" the bartender said.

"Make mine a gin and tonic," Mike said, "with Tanqueray."

"Real sorry, sir," the bartender said, "I'm all out of gin." She poured the several liquors that make up a Long Island Iced Tea into a metal shaker. "Can I getcha somethin else?" she said.

She started chatting with Candi. She told Candi that she was a Geology major at A&M. And that she only had a few more days left at this job because she was going on a geological dig in Yellowstone National Park.

Mike leaned over to Candi and whispered, not so quietly, "What kind of bar doesn't have gin? This has got to be the only fucking bar in the world that doesn't have gin."

"Hey there, pardner. Watch your fucking mouth, goddammit. You're in the presence of ladies. Why don't you just order a margarita? Or a Long Island Iced Tea like me? They're fucking deliiiiiicious."

The bartender slid Candi her drink and said to Mike, "I make the world's best margaritas. I guarantee you'll like it."

"Can you make it with Patron tequila?"

"No way," the bartender said. "Patron's overrated. I've got somethin way better than Patron." She turned around and grabbed a bottle of Hussong's tequila off the shelf. Mike noticed that the back of her t-shirt read: GIG EM AGGIES. "Trust me," she said to him, "You're gonna think this is the best margarita ever."

Mike shrugged, resigned to his fate. "Sure. Whatever. Just give me a drink for Chrissakes."

Dudley's Draw has the feel of an Old West saloon. That is to say, it's authentic Texas *kitsch*. It's dimly lighted and adorned with Lone Star Beer and Shiner Bock signs. And the walls are decorated with dusty taxidermies- stuffed and mounted dead animals. The wildlife menagerie includes, but is not limited to whitetail deer, javelina, antelope, wild goats and even a jackelope.

Mike asked Candi, "What's a jackelope?"

"You see that over there?" Candi said to him, pointing to the corner of the place. There was a stuffed and mounted jack-rabbit on the wall, with horns protruding from its head just behind its ears. "It's like a fucking cross between an antelope deer and a jack-rabbit. It's a fucking rabbit with horns! Can you fucking believe it? You only see them in Texas. Mostly in west Texas. Mostly west of the Pecos. I think they're actually an endangered species these days."

"Oh yeah," the bartender chimed in, "She's right. Jackelopes *are* an endangered species."

Mike stared at the bizarre looking animal. "You've got to be kidding me. That just can't be for real."

"Well, dumbass. You're fucking lookin right at one. You know. I've never actually seen one in the wild. Not too many people have. That's how rare they are."

Mike studied the jackelope. "I guess it's an evolutionary anomaly. Kind of like a platypus," he said. "It's just so strange looking. I've never seen or heard of-"

Candi and the bartender laughed out loud at the same time. "Oh my fucking God!" Candi said. "That was sooo fucking perfect!" Candi gave the bartender a high-five. "Wow! I'm just shittin you. Dumbass. There's no such thing as a fucking jackelope! It's an old Texas joke. Taxidermists make a fucking fortune off of em. You can fucking buy those things at any roadside flea market!"

Mike didn't laugh along with them. And to make matters worse, his margarita was the worst margarita ever. Mike never knew whether it was the tequila, or that the bartender didn't like him, or that he had to drink a margarita made by a bartender who didn't like him while being mocked and called a dumbass.

Candi didn't mean any harm by the joke, Mike thought, she was just being Candi. However, he wouldn't say the same for the bartender. And to make matters even worse, his amphetamines were beginning to wear off. Mike was exhausted, starting to get hungry, and now, glaring over the bar at this woman.

"You ever do any huntin, pardner?" Candi said.

The bartender returned to the other side of the bar to chew the fat with the locals, which made Mike feel a little more congenial.

"No," Mike said, "I've never killed anything in my life."

"My daddy used to take me huntin when I was a little girl. I killed my first deer when I was like thirteen years old. We were at this huntin lease near Taft, Texas. It belonged to a friend of our pastor. Anyways. Me and my daddy sat up in the fork of an oak tree together for about five hours that mornin."

"My daddy had this old single-barrel 4-10 shotgun. It belonged to my granddaddy. Not many people in Texas hunt deer with a shotgun, you know. But we were usin 4-10 slugs. And let me tell you. Those motherfuckers pack a fucking punch. Anyways. To make it easier for me to aim the goddamned thing, my dad put a piece of masking tape on the barrel. And then he took a pencil and marked the dead center of it with a straight line. My daddy was real good at shit like that. It was fucking awesome."

Mike gulped down his margarita.

"So. After about a thousand hours of waitin and waitin and waitin and waitin. And let me tell you this. You have to be absolutely fucking quiet when you're deer huntin. Or else you'll scare them away. So after about five hours of waitin this deer finally comes walkin by us. Right under our tree."

"It was a doe. And she stopped to fucking nibble on a bush right below us. So me and my daddy are literally ten feet above her. Anyways. I take aim along that pencil line my daddy drew. And then I fucking shoot her right smack in the fucking shoulder. Right where my daddy showed me. And she fucking dropped like a sack of fucking potatoes. Never knew what fucking hit her!"

"Next few seasons I got a buck every single year we went huntin. You know what," Candi said, slurping down the remainder of her drink, "My daddy always took me huntin every season. But I never saw *him* hunt. I mean *his* daddy took him huntin and taught him how to do it. But I never saw my daddy *actually* hunt or kill anythin. I mean my daddy would pull out his Old Timer pocket-knife and clean and gut a deer. So we could take it home for supper. But I never saw him kill a deer. He always told me- It's important you learn how to hunt, everybody should learn how to hunt."

"My favorite writer is Ernest Hemingway," Mike said.

"Never heard of him. Is he famous?"

"Yes"

"Why's he your favorite?"

"Well," Mike said, "I mentioned him because he wrote a lot of stories about hunting. He was a big hunter. He traveled all over the world hunting and fishing and writing stories about his adventures."

"He sounds pretty fucking cool to me. So why the fuck do *you* like him so much?"

"What's that supposed to mean?"

"Oh don't get your panties all in a bunch," Candi said. "All I mean is. This Hemingway dude seems kinda opposite of you. I mean *you've* never been huntin, right?"

"No"

"Ever been fishin?"

"No"

"And you never killed anythin? Anythin at all?"

Hemingway killed, Mike thought. Hemingway spilled fresh warm blood in the dirt and on his boots. Just like Candi and her daddy and her daddy's daddy. And just like Candi had never read Hemingway, neither her daddy nor her daddy's daddy probably ever read him either. It was funny, Mike thought- they didn't need Hemingway, like Mike needed Hemingway.

In a moment like this, Sonny Quillan would've said to Mike, "I guess you like Hemingway's *pose*, better than Hemingway's *prose*."

Candi said to Mike, "Ok, Mr. I-never-killed-anythin-but-I-like-to-read-stories-about-killin. How about this?"

"Candi, please. If you're going to tease me or provoke me, please don't. I'm not feeling that great right now."

Candi smiled and said, "You ever had somebody shove a fucking pistol in your face?" She made a gun with her hand and pushed her fingers into Mike's forehead. "And I mean right in your fucking face. Cock it," she moved her thumb back slowly, "and then tell you that you're about to fucking die?"

Mike pulled away from her and said, "For Chrissakes, Candi. Of course not! When would that have ever happened to somebody like me?"

"Somebody like *you*, pardner? You're right. Probably never" Candi stirred the ice in the bottom of her glass with her straw and then slurped it dry again. "But! I guaran-goddamn-tee you, pardner. That if anybody ever fucking does that shit to you. You'll never fucking be the same. I mean trust me. You won't have to write any fucking stories to prove you're alive. Or read them either. Trust me, pardner. If that shit ever happens you'll fucking *know* you're alive."

There were fleeting moments when Candi made Mike a little nervous, even a little frightened. In these brief moments Mike glimpsed in Candi's baby blue eyes just a flash of what he could only describe as a kind of desperate abandon; the self-same expression he imagined a hunted, wounded animal would have just before it turned around and charged its hunter. This was one of those moments...

As an undergraduate Mike worked as the editor of *Persona*, the literary-arts journal at his college. During that time he wrote a short story which he submitted to *Esquire*. It was rejected for publication, but included the most encouraging rejection letter he'd ever received; it was even hand-signed by an editor. The story was a humorous satire of his favorite Ernest Hemingway story. Here is that story, attenuated and edited for inclusion in the present volume:

The Short Happy Wife of Francis McCucumber

a short story by
Michael Curd

It was dinnertime now and they were all sitting under the dark green flap of the dining tent, pretending nothing had happened. "What'll ya'll have to drink?" Sonny Quillan asked, his lean chiseled face was lambent with masculinity beneath the wide brim of his cowboy hat. "I'm havin another Old-Fashioned."

Being a professional game hunter and rugged outdoorsman had toughened the middle-aged Texan. Especially considering the dozen or so African tribesmen, who cooked his meals, pitched and unpitched his camp, chauffeured him around in a fashionable safari jeep, walked ahead of him into the bush when there was a possibility of danger and cleaned and gutted the animals he and his wealthy clientele killed. Pulling the trigger on some shiny rifle and berating helpless black natives was a man's job, and by God, Sonny Quillan was a *man's* man.

"I'll have a gin and tonic," Francis McCucumber said, "with Tanqueray." He was still embarrassed by the events of earlier that day. Francis McCucumber was an American and a pickle of a man, dill with a slightly vinegar flavor. He was the kind of man any domineering woman would relish. In high school Francis was perpetually picked last for kickball, lettered in entomology and was forced by his unpopularity to take his cousin's yearbook photo to his senior prom.

Still, despite the scars of his formative years, Francis had worked long hours to earn three college degrees, publish a handful of scholarly papers, and write a book nobody's ever heard of. He was now a named professor at an Ivy League university where he was paid six-figures to teach just two classes a week; thus affording him the luxury to jet-set around the world and eventually pay for an African safari; where Francis would finally prove to everyone, including his therapist, that he was a *real* man.

"Better make mine a Johnnie Walker Black, double, neat," Lisa McCucumber said. She adjusted the leather string that held her straw hat about her tobacco brown hair. "God knows I need something after that..." Lisa McCucumber was a handsome, strong woman, with silky blue eyes, oval face and ample bosom. She was a short beauty, standing only five feet tall; and when sitting, even shorter than that. Before marrying money, Money was Francis' nickname; Lisa had been a lingerie model in New York, a folk singer in San Francisco, a feminist scholar at Sara Lawrence and a longshoreman in Oregon.

Lisa McCucumber glared at Francis with gunner's eyes, disgusted by him. She had always known that Francis was not John Wayne; however, today he had proven he was a eunuch, in the truest sense of the word. At dinner parties Lisa was fond of saying that when she had married Francis and settled down, she never realized that she'd really just settled. She wasn't Donna Reed and did not pretend to be. "Francis," she said, "I still can't believe you shot that lion as many times as you did. A blind man with a sling shot would have been more effective."

Francis McCucumber blushed, bit his bottom lip, and then stared down at the dry African dirt beneath his boots. "Hunting is *not* a spectator sport," Francis mumbled to his wife, "I forgot the gun was on safety. And then the lion bolted and ran before I could get off a shot."

"In the time it took you to get off that shot," Lisa said, snickering, "I balanced my checkbook, did my hair and makeup and read *Anna Karenina*, twice!" One of the natives brought their drinks over on a tray, set them on the table and then walked away without a word.

Sonny Quillan lifted his glass, hoping to lighten the mood with a toast. "Here's to the lion," he said, "and a damn good lion." As Sonny Quillan watched the couple, he realized both McCucumbers approached life in very much the same way they approached their drinks. Francis cradled his glass, sipping timidly at the marriage of club soda and gin, while his wife threw back her scotch, slammed the glass on the small table and promptly demanded another. *You'd think she'd be embarrassed for him*, Sonny thought, *you'd think she'd at least try to make him feel better about it.*

"It's a good thing Mr. Quillan was there," Lisa said, "Or we'd all have been mauled by a lion that looked more like Swiss cheese than the king of the jungle." She drew her shoulders up, shuddered and said, "That poor creature. I'll bet when his alarm clock went off this morning he was not thinking to him-self- Today is the day some bored American invertebrate having a mid-life crisis is going to blow my head off." One of the natives set another scotch in front of her. She chuckled. "For God's sake, Francis. I thought you were going to wet yourself like that one time when..."

"Can we *please* stop talking about the lion, Lisa?" Francis McCucumber said, "I wish you could forget about it."

"Forget about it?" she said, "I only wish I had pictures to show my mother." She threw back another scotch and laughed.

"It really ain't all that unusual," Sonny Quillan said, though in his mind he could not agree with her more, "Most folks get frightened the first time they see a lion."

"Do most people get frightened when they see lions at the zoo?" Lisa said, shooting her husband an accusing glance, then smiling back at Sonny Quillan. She shook her head and said, "Francis sleeps with a night light on. Does that tell you anything?"

"You try shooting a lion sometime and see how you hold up," Francis said.

"If I were a man," Lisa said, "and I may be closer to it than some people at this table. But. If I were a man, I wouldn't need to kill defenseless animals to prove it."

"Oh they're hardly defenseless," Sonny Quillan said. "Lions are fierce creatures. Especially when provoked and cornered." Now she was insulting him too, Sonny Quillan thought. "Huntin is a primal urge, ma'am," he said, "It's just part of bein a *real* man."

Lisa McCucumber laughed out loud, a mocking, condescending laugh that made Francis shiver and Sonny Quillan fume. "You call *this* hunting?" she said. "Chasing down animals in a jeep? And then shooting them from two hundred yards away? And then letting them nearly bleed to death while you smoke and reload your guns in the shade of a tree?" She smirked. "Sorry *boys*! And I say that with all sincerity. But I just don't buy it. I may have been born yesterday, but it wasn't last night."

Francis McCucumber contemplated considering the possibility of perhaps telling his wife to shut her mouth. *She enjoys mocking me. If only*, Francis thought, *I could find a hobby I enjoyed that much.*

Sonny Quillan was disgusted with both of them. *Francis ain't a real man*, he thought, *he's a spoiled little American boy who never grew up. Never really became a man. And no amount of dead lions*, Sonny concluded, *or copies of the Sports Illustrated Swimsuit Issue for that matter, would ever change that. And his wife! So cruel and selfish. So conniving and vicious.* Such a one dimensional character. *But then again*, Sonny Quillan thought, looking her up and down, *she was a woman after all. And a damn beautiful woman at that...*

In Sonny Quillan's experience, when it came to women, wealth and beauty were a deadly combination. Especially when it came to American women. And still. Despite the fact he loathed her very presence. Sonny Quillan could not help but undress Lisa McCucumber in his mind. She was a *real bitch*, he reassured himself, but he desperately wanted to fuck her.

Later that night Francis McCucumber lay on his cot inside his tent, mulling over the events of the morning. His wife lay sleeping quietly in the adjoining cot, an opened copy of *Madame Bovary* in her hand. Francis remembered the lion. How beautiful the creature had seemed, prowling through the bush in the early morning sunshine. If only he had remembered the safety switch on the gun, he lamented, then he would have had a clean shot and maybe the animal would not have suffered so much. *I never intended the poor lion to suffer. I'm not a cruel man. I shouldn't have stepped forward to aim, and then the lion wouldn't have seen me and ran.*

Francis could not erase the gruesome scene from his mind. It played over and over again. How the lion's flank ripped away from the bone and how it bled from his careless gunshot. And yet, the lion kept running. And to make it worse. The lion had mustered the strength to sprint from the grass where it lay bleeding, charging him with a queer courage and fortitude that Francis McCucumber still could not understand.

Could it be, Francis puzzled, that the lion possessed a courage and fortitude he himself had never felt before? The kind of courage and fortitude even a Platinum American Express card could not buy? A sleeping bag of guilt enveloped Francis as he drifted into a restless slumber.

Francis McCucumber awoke in the middle of the night and found his wife's cot empty. He lay still for nearly two hours, not moving, listening to the sounds of darkest Africa.

Lisa McCucumber finally returned. She lifted the tent fold, removed a cigarette from her lips and then tossed it to the ground. She blew a final stream of cigarette smoke into the air and then slipped quietly into the tent. She raised the mosquito net draping her cot, and then lay down. "Where have you been?" Francis snarled.

"Oh just having a midnight snack."

"Is that what they call it in Texas? I have trouble killing *one* lousy lion and you go sleep with the first man you find?"

"I wasn't sleeping," she said. "Besides. Mr. Quillan wasn't the *first* man I found. None of the tribesman wanted to risk losing their jobs." She smiled at him and said, "Don't worry sweetheart. Trust me. Despite what Mr. Quillan may think. It wasn't anything to write home about."

"Oh I'm sooo sorry," Francis said. "Next time I'll hire a Frenchman to take us on safari."

"How sweet of you, my darling. You may be a putz, Francis. But at least you're a considerate putz." She rolled over and pulled her blanket up near her chin. "Now. Let's go to sleep. I'm exhausted."

"I'll just bet you are." For the first time in a long time Francis McCucumber was almost but not quite on the verge of thinking about being somewhat upset enough to confront his wife. He fell asleep instead, and dreamed of tall timid women.

Just before dawn the McCucumbers walked silently together towards the breakfast table which was illumined by two lanterns hanging from a tree.

Sonny Quillan was all smiles, a smoldering Montecristo cigar between his lips. "Mornin, you two," he said to them as they sat down. "As soon as you take care of your breakfast we can be off and shoot some buffalo. It's a great day for shootin buffalo." He smiled over at Lisa. "And how did you sleep, Mrs. McCucumber?"

"Well. I would have slept a lot better," Lisa said, scooping apricots onto her plate, "If *someone* had let *me* finish too." She smiled at Sonny Quillan. "You know what they say about men who carry *really* big rifles, don't you?"

Of all the men in the world that Francis McCucumber hated, besides his mother-in-law of course, Francis McCucumber hated Sonny Quillan the most. He hated Sonny Quillan's tanned, chiseled face. He hated his cowboy hat, his tight Wrangler jeans and his bloodstained boots. Not to mention the fact that Sonny Quillan had almost-but-not-quite given his wife an orgasm.

As Sonny Quillan glanced at Francis McCucumber, he felt as if he had just dropped a lobster into a boiling pot of water. *There's nothin that makes a man feel more like a real man*, Sonny mused, *than fuckin another man's wife. But why is Francis mad at me? I mean who does he think I am, Mahatma Gandhi? I mean it's not my fault his wife won't stay where she belongs. Fuckin is a primal urge*; Sonny reminded himself, *part of bein a real man.*

"So have you got your ammunition ready?" Sonny Quillan said to Francis. "Along with some buffalo, we might also get a shot at a wild boar."

"A wild boar?" Lisa said. "I'm already sitting next to one."

Francis frowned.

"Now come on, partner," Sonny Quillan said, trying to share some male solidarity with Francis, "Let's not spoil the safari with hard feelins. I mean. If you've got somethin to say to me then just go right ahead and say it out loud."

"Trust me," Lisa McCucumber said, "You don't have to worry about that Mr. Quillan. Francis only knows how to say two things: *please* and *thank you*." She buttered her toast and called over one of the tribesmen. She said to him, "I'll take another vanilla soymilk latte. But this time. Not so much froth. And a little more cinnamon sprinkled on top."

Damn! She's one nasty bitch, Sonny Quillan observed. *I should ask Francis if he wants me to slap her around for him. After all. Slappin women around to show them whose boss is a primal urge. Part of bein a real man.*

"Come on now, partner," Sonny Quillan said to Francis, "What's say we let bygones be bygones?" He patted Francis on the shoulder, "Let me tell you. You'll feel a hell of lot better after you kill somethin."

"I suppose it's the thing to do," Francis said.

When Sonny Quillan insisted on riding in the back seat of the jeep with Lisa, Francis McCucumber never protested. And when Sonny Quillan unrolled one of the blankets and laid it over their laps, despite the sweltering African heat, Francis McCucumber let it slide. And when Sonny Quillan pulled the blanket up over their heads and Lisa started kicking the back of his seat and moaning, Francis McCucumber rolled with the punches.

A little later Sonny Quillan and Lisa were finishing their cigarettes when Francis McCucumber spotted a herd of buffalo running ahead of the jeep. "Let's shoot them from right here in the jeep," Francis yelled.

"We can't shoot em from the jeep," Sonny Quillan said.

"Why not?"

"It just ain't done that way, partner," Sonny Quillan said. "Don't worry, though. We'll speed up the jeep and head em off at the pass."

"Oh, of course not!" Lisa said. "Shooting them from a jeep would be cheating. Because stepping out of the jeep first, and then shooting them from two hundred yards away with their backs turned is *sooo much* manlier!" She laughed her laugh again and both men cringed.

Nearing the herd of buffalo in their jeep, they watched two old bulls straggling behind the rest of the herd. "There's our buffs, partner," Sonny Quillan yelled. "Better get your rifle ready!"

"What Mr. Quillan means, Francis," Lisa said, "Is to make sure the safety on your rifle is off this time. So that it will actually fire when you pull the trigger. I'd hate to see you screw up like the last time. It really embarrasses me, you know."

Francis McCucumber was too busy thinking about the buffalo to pay attention to his wife. *I'm ready this time*, he told himself, *I know I can do this*. Francis watched as the old bulls slowed a little more, outrun by the jeep and exhausted from their attempted escape. As the jeep screeched to a halt, the men clambered out and Francis raised his gun.

A shot rang out across the African plains and the larger of the two buffalo fell to its knees. "Damn good shot, McCucumber," Sonny Quillan yelled, "Right in the shoulder! That's how it's done! Let me tell you, partner. That kinda shootin will win you a cupie doll at the carnival every single time!"

Another shot rang out and the other buffalo tumbled in a bloody spray into the grass. "Damn good shootin, partner! You bagged both of em! We'll break out the champagne and party poppers when we get back to camp!" They loaded back up in the jeep and drove over to where the buffalo had roamed.

"Damn good shootin," Sonny Quillan said again. He patted Francis on the back. "Damn good! Damn good!"

"Is there a broken record in this jeep?" Lisa said.

Francis McCucumber was a statue now; a stoic satisfied stone figure savoring his triumph all alone. He was proud of himself, maybe for the first time in his entire life. And in this statuesque moment, he didn't care what either of them thought.

Lisa waited for the men in the jeep, because in these types of stories that is what women do best. In the meantime, the two men took their guns and walked over to where the buffalo had been shot. One of the bulls lay dead in a large puddle of blood near the edge of the high grass. "Damn good shootin," Sonny Quillan said. "You dropped that buff like a real huntin buff."

"Where's the other buffalo?" Francis said, looking around.

"Looks like the other buff made it into the high grass over there," Sonny Quillan said. He pointed to a trail of blood. "Here, hold this for me." He handed his rifle to Francis and walked over to the edge of the grass. "Well. Unless you gotta lawn mower under your pith helmet there. We should probably wait a while and let that buff stiffen up and die before we go in there after him."

"But I want to go in there now," Francis said.

"Better not," Sonny Quillan said. "That buff is wounded and right about now is feelin cornered and desperate. It'll damn sure turn and attack us."

"But I don't want to wait. What I mean is. I've been waiting my whole life for this."

Sonny Quillan sensed something different about Francis McCucumber. Since the safari began Sonny had never heard Francis insist on anything. There seemed to be a new fire in Francis' boyish eyes, as if he was seeing the world differently now, with more optimism. *Maybe the boy's family jewels are finally droppin*, Sonny Quillan thought to himself, *maybe I was wrong about how many dead animals it would take to make him a real man.*

"I reckon," Sonny Quillan said, "We could go in after him. It'll have to be just us two, though. Me and you." Sonny Quillan glanced back at the jeep. "Our driver's a young man and he's never been in the bush before. He'll have to stay with your wife."

"Me and him both," Francis said, smiling.

Sonny Quillan chuckled and smiled back at him.

"Let's go into the bush," Francis said to him, "and finish this, *partner*." Francis handed Sonny Quillan's rifle back to him and they stalked slowly forward into the bush. Everything was quiet except for the sound of the bloody, dry grass which cracked and crumpled beneath their boots.

After a couple of minutes they heard a heavy guttural breathing. And then they spotted the massive body of the wounded buffalo. It jumped to its feet and charged the men with desperate abandon. Blood dripped from its lips as it snorted and reared its giant head, two sharp horns swinging wildly like wielded swords. Sonny Quillan was closer to the buffalo and raised his rifle, taking perfect aim. Being a trained hunter, he waited for the buffalo to get closer before taking his shot.

As the feral buffalo charged nearer, Sonny Quillan gently squeezed the trigger of his rifle with a calm forged from a thousand previous kills. No shot rang out. His rifle did not fire. Sonny jerked the trigger this time, but still no shot rang out. And then just as Sonny deftly lowered his rifle to check the firing mechanism, the buffalo bore down upon him, plunging its deadly horns deep into his gut.

Sonny Quillan screamed like a madman as the buffalo trampled him into the dry African dirt, its horns wildly ripping and tearing his flesh from his bones. Suddenly a shot rang out. The buffalo dropped dead in its tracks. Francis McCucumber stood nearby, gripping his still-smoking rifle. He smiled at Sonny Quillan again, just like he'd smiled at him right before they went into the bush.

Francis walked casually over to where Sonny Quillan lay dying. The buffalo's horns had torn Sonny Quillan's stomach open. And both his hands and one leg were crushed, broken and mangled. Sonny Quillan's breathing was desperate and guttural, just like the buffalo's had been. "I'll never make it, partner," Sonny said to Francis as he coughed up blood. "The nearest hospital is miles away. I think I'm a goner for sure."

Francis McCucumber was a statue again. His face betrayed neither sympathy nor satisfaction. He bent down and picked up Sonny Quillan's rifle. "It hurts real bad, partner," Sonny Quillan said. "Tell you what. How about you go ahead and put me down, partner. I mean help me out me here. Put me outta my misery. A real man shouldn't have to die like this."

"Sorry, partner," Francis said. "I should probably wait a while. And let you stiffen up first. Don't you think?"

Sonny Quillan glanced up at his rifle, the one he'd handed to Francis right before they went into the bush. He saw that the safety latch was on. Sonny Quillan stared up at Francis. And then back at his rifle. And then back at Francis, who just stood there smiling again. "But I never put my rifle on safety, ever," Sonny Quillan said, choking on his words.

"Well, partner," Francis said to him. "You know what they always say. There's a first time for everything." Francis turned and walked away. Sonny Quillan tried to yell for help, tried to scream in pain, but his mouth went dry and his strength was failing him. Sonny Quillan knew it would take him quite a while to stiffen up. And he knew it would take him even longer to die.

Francis McCucumber left the bush and met his frantic wife. "What happened in there?" Lisa said to him, "I heard screaming. Where's Mr. Quillan?"

Francis didn't answer her. He only stood there staring down his short beautiful wife. "Answer me dammit!" Lisa yelled at him. "Where's Mr. Quillan?"

"Well," Francis said, still smiling, "It looks like I got to bag a wild boar after all."

A look of fear swept over Lisa's face. She had never seen Francis smile like that before. "What have you done, you dumbass? What the hell happened in there?"

"Calm down, calm down," Francis said to her. "It's only a joke. Mr. Quillan is hiding in the bush right now. We thought it would be funny to scare you. It's all just a joke."

"Dammit! That's not funny Francis," Lisa said. "I mean when are you going to grow the hell up?"

"Sooner than you think, my dear," Francis said to her. "Oh. Here. Will you hold Mr. Quillan's rifle while I go back in the bush and get him?" Francis handed her the rifle with the barrel facing her. As Lisa reached for the rifle, the trigger caught on Francis McCucumber's finger and a shot rang out across the African plains.

A little later that afternoon, in the shade of a nearby acacia tree, Francis McCucumber sat smoking a Montecristo cigar, savoring the exotic colors of the African sunset. After the second shot had rung out, the young native driver sped off in the jeep. Francis had finally killed. And Sonny Quillan was right. It did make him feel better. *Revenge*, Francis mused, *is a primal urge. Part of being a real man.*

✳✳✳

"You know," Mike said to Candi as he gulped down the remainder of his margarita, "I once wrote a short story about hunting."

"Oh yeah," Candi said, "Did it have a happy endin?"

Mike never answered her and Candi never asked the same question twice.

So a little bit later, Mike paid their bar tab in silence. And as revenge for the lousy margarita, and a whole host of other injustices recently suffered, Mike didn't tip the bartender.

Chapter 8

Hearne, Texas;
Supper and a showdown at Johnny Reb's Dixie Café;
An etymology of a the word nigger; Candi's family tree;
And what Mike and Candi discovered in Calvert, Texas

Mike and Candi drove away from College Station and headed north on Highway 6.

"Be careful, pardner," Candi said as they approached the city limits of Hearne, Texas, "There's a hill right up here. Right as you head into town. And it's a famous fucking speed trap. I mean the speed limit fucking drops from 70 mph to like 55 mph just like that," she snapped her fingers. "And trust me. You don't wanna spend this night or any other fucking night in jail in this fucking one-horse town."

Mike realized that Candi was always on the lookout for police, even when she wasn't doing anything wrong. He assumed it was because of her line of work. And yet her fear seemed somehow more irrational than that, as if she always felt like she was being hunted. Mike had never been arrested, never been in jail, and couldn't remember the last time he broke the law. But riding with Candi made him feel like an outlaw, which unnerved and excited him all at once.

The town of Hearne has been referred to as the Crossroads of Texas, owing this moniker to its central geographic location within the Lone Star State and the fact that there are more railroad tracks that meet and cross there than any other town in Texas. For this reason, years ago it was a bustling economic metropolis facilitating the transport of cotton and other Southern trade goods.

Also for this reason, during World War II, Hearne was the home of Camp Hearne, a prisoner of war camp. During those war years thousands of captured German soldiers were shipped by train to Hearne where they lived out the remainder of the war. These days, Hearne is no longer a bustling economic metropolis, and Camp Hearne was closed years ago.

"But! I'll tell you this, pardner," Candi said. "You can still fucking hike in the ruins of Camp Hearne. And it's pretty fucking creepy too."

"Wow," Mike said, "I had no idea that was here."

"And now its suppertime," Candi announced. "And that means me and you are gonna eat at Johnny Reb's Dixie Café. And you're gonna try the fucking best chicken fried steak in the whole goddamned world."

***

Mike noticed that the sign for Johnny Reb's Dixie Café had a Confederate flag in its background. And once inside, he noticed that the walls of the restaurant were lovingly ornamented with pictures of Confederate soldiers and oversized portraits of Confederate generals.

Mike and Candi sat at a table adjacent to a large portrait of General Robert E. Lee. Their waitress was a young Mexican woman with tattoos. Her nametag read: Irais V.

"Oh for Chrissakes," Mike said, looking at a menu, "Not again. They only have beer."

Candi ordered two bottles of Coors Light.

"You know," Mike said, "They put condom lubricant in light beer."

"No fucking way"

"It's true"

"Huh, is that right? Well I thought it tasted familiar!"

They laughed.

Along with the beer their waitress brought a red plastic basket of hot rolls, butter and corn bread muffins.

"How about we order up some cheese fries?" Candi said.

"Sure, whatever," Mike said, shrugging his shoulders. "All I know is that I'm a long way from Le Procope in Paris. But what the hell, right?"

"Hey, pardner. Trust me on this one. Nobody wants to read a fucking novel about people eatin supper at some snooty-ass restaurant in Paris. I'm telling you. That shit has sooo fucking been done."

"You keep saying that, Candi. But if you've only read one book in your entire life, then how do you know it's already been done?"

"I just fucking know." Candi globbed butter on a roll and stuffed the entire thing in her mouth. "These rolls and cornbread muffins are fucking fantastic. Holy shit! This shit is goooood!"

"You know, Candi. You're a real demur Southern belle," Mike said, smiling, "You know that don't you?"

"Why thank ya kindly good sir," Candi said in her best feigned Southern accent. Her mouth was still full of half-chewed roll. "You wanna sit a spell on the front porch of my daddy's cotton plantation with me? I could sip on lemonade and you could drink a mint julep. And later on after everybody's gone off to bed. You could eat out my pussy like a good Southern gentleman."

"I should've seen that coming," Mike said.

"Pun intended?" Candi said. She laughed out loud, swallowed the rest of her roll and then took a swig of her Coors Light.

Mike shook his head and took a cautious bite of a cornbread muffin. "Wow," he said, "These are *actually* really good."

"You always fucking say that, you know?"

"Say what?"

"You always fucking say- this or that is *actually* good. Like you're always fucking surprised that shit is good"

"Huh. I guess I do say that."

"You fucking do. And it's fucking annoyin. And fucking rude too"

"Rude?"

"Fuck yeah it's rude. You say it in front of waiters and bartenders and pretty much fucking everybody. You just better be glad that you didn't say it after that blowjob I gave you."

The waitress walked by, frowned at them, and then kept on walking.

"Cause if you had. I'd of bitten your fucking dick off right then and there."

"Well," Mike said, taking a more generous bite of his cornbread muffin this time, "They are *actually* good."

"Damn straight they're good. Do you know what makes for really good cornbread?"

"What?"

"Well. Really fucking good cornbread is just a little bit sweet. Almost like cake. But not too sweet where you can't taste the cornmeal. But just a little sweet where it tastes like fucking cake. And you just can't stop eatin it."

"You might have to write that recipe down for me."

"I swear to fucking God. My daddy used to make the best fucking cornbread ever. And I mean ever. He musta put like ten pounds of white sugar in every fucking muffin."

The waitress brought their cheese fries and set them down on the table. Candi asked the waitress, "Would you mind bringin us a little bit of Ranch dressin? Thanks so much, sweetheart."

"I can't believe I'm about to say this," Mike said. "But you know what else is *actually* really good?"

"What's that?"

"This beer. I haven't had beer, much less a domestic light beer, in years. But it actually tastes really good."

"Fuck yeah, it's good. And! It's good for you, too. Let me tell you, pardner. You drink waaaay too much straight liquor. Not that there's anythin wrong with that. You know me. I don't judge. But some days you really oughtta lay off the sauce a little bit. And just have a few fucking beers with your supper." Candi raised her beer bottle above the table and said, "A toast, pardner."

"What are we toasting?" Mike said, raising his bottle.

"To just how fucking good a light beer can taste sometimes. It's the simple things in life, you know." Candi clanked her bottle loudly against his and drained it. Mike chuckled and did the same.

The waitress brought the Ranch dressing and asked them if they were ready to order. Candi snatched Mike's menu away from him. "No fucking way, pardner. Tonight. I'm orderin for you. I mean if I don't look out for you. You'll probably end up orderin some faggoty ass salad with a side of prescription pill dressin."

Mike noticed the waitress choking back her laughter. Candi set the menus down in the booth next to her and announced, as if making a royal decree, "My friend and benefactor here. Or in other words, my sugar daddy. He'll have your famous chicken fried steak. With fried okra and mashed potatoes. And be sure to dump a shitload of cream gravy on that steak and potatoes."

Mike wanted to protest but he decided he wasn't going to further entertain their waitress.

"And!" Candi said, "Do ya'll still have your all-you-can-eat fried catfish on Fridays?"

The waitress nodded.

"Then that's what I'll have. And keep the beers comin, please. Thank you."

Mike waited for the waitress to walk away and said, "Candi, I try to avoid fried foods. It's my stomach."

"Oh my fucking God. Just when I thought you're cooch couldn't get any bigger. You go and say wimpy shit like that."

"I'm serious, Candi. If I eat fried food right now, I'll be sick."

"Ok, no problem," Candi said, grabbing the menus. She handed one to Mike. "Let's me and you take a gander at these fucking menus together. And see if we can't find you somethin that's not fried. I mean I've gotta look out for you, pardner."

"Thanks," Mike said. He opened his menu and stared down into its plastic laminate pages.

"How's about a fish taco?" Candi said, and then quietly put her menu back down on the table. "Do you like fish tacos?"

"It depends"

"Yeah," Candi said, "I reckon it all depends on just how fishy the taco is, huh?"

"Exactly"

"Hey, pardner. Here's somethin you don't see every day," Candi said, still smiling, and still not looking at her menu. "They got somethin here called a *pink taco*. Does a pink taco sound good?"

"Uh, I don't know. What does a pink taco come with? Actually, I don't see the tacos anywhere on the menu."

Candi chuckled and said, "It looks like the pink taco comes with sour cream."

"I don't see it"

"Well," Candi said, "If you're not a fan of eatin fish tacos, then maybe you'd like to eat a *ham flap*. You ever eaten a ham flap, pardner?"

"No," Mike said, still flipping through his menu. "It sounds like something you eat for breakfast."

"Yessirree. A man sure could definitely eat him a ham-flap in the mornin. I mean if he wanted to"

"For Chrissakes. I don't see breakfast on the menu either."

"You don't see it? It's right there next to the *blue waffle*."

"I still don't see any of that." Mike finally looked up at Candi and noticed that she wasn't even looking at her menu.

Candi smiled and said, "How about you eat a *fur burger*? And then for dessert. You can eat you a slice of *poon-tang pie*?" She laughed out loud.

Mike slammed his menu shut and said, "For Chrissakes, Candi. I should've known you were being way too nice to me."

"Oh my fucking God! That was sooo fucking hilarious! You had no fucking clue. The whole fucking time! You're such a dumbass!"

"I already asked you," Mike said, "Please don't call me that."

"I can't help it," Candi said. "And you even asked me- What does a pink taco *come* with! What does a pink taco *cum* with?" She laughed even harder and louder than before. "You mean to tell me that with all your college education. That you never learned *pussy-speak*?"

"No, Candi. I never learned *that* language. Sadly. I only studied Latin, Greek, French and German in college. Unfortunately for me, Yale University doesn't offer a course in *whitetrash-speak*."

"Ooooh! Ouch!" Candi said. "Good one there, pardner. You're gettin better at that shit all the time. I reckon I'm rubbin off on you." She smiled, leaned forward and said to him, "Of course. That would only be fair since you already rubbed one off on me. Remember? Right in my fucking mouth. Pun fucking intended"

"For Chrissakes, Candi. Can we just try to have a good time tonight?"

"What the fuck are you talkin about, pardner? I'm havin a great fucking time tonight!"

"You always do"

"So. Tell me some more about all those languages you learned in college. I mean that shit is sooo fucking sexy, you know. I'll bet all those college girls cream their panties every time you name off all those languages you learned."

"Can we *please* just drop it?"

"You know. I kinda find it hard to believe that old Yale doesn't offer a single class in pussy-speak. I reckon that means they don't offer a class on how to talk like a white-trash whore, either?"

"Knock it off, Candi."

"I'm just fucking with you, pardner. But you gotta admit. That was pretty fucking funny. Wasn't it? You were all lookin through your menu. And I was just sittin here rattlin off every word for pussy that I could think of that sounded like it could be food."

"You're quite the wordsmith."

"It's weird, huh? I mean how many words for pussy sound like somethin you can order at a fucking diner?"

"Well," Mike said, chuckling, "Everybody's gotta eat, right?"

Candi laughed and said, "How about you, pardner?"

"What about me?"

"Do you eat fish tacos?"

"Yes, I do"

"But do you *like* to eat fish tacos?"

"Like I said before. It depends."

"On what?"

"Like *you* said before. It all depends on how fishy the taco happens to be."

"I am very wise," Candi said, smiling.

"What about you?" Mike said.

"Sure. I've eaten my fair share of fish tacos."

"And do you like eating them?"

"Sure I do"

"Which do you like better? Fish tacos, or uh, or do you like-"

"The word you're lookin for is *dick*."

"I know. I was just trying to maintain our clever food metaphor."

"Trust me. It ain't really all that clever."

"So," Mike said, "Which do you like better?"

"Oh for fuck's sake," Candi said. "That's a fucking easy one! I always prefer dick, pardner. I've always been a sucker for a big hard dick."

"Pun intended?"

"Abso-fucking-lutely"

"Candi. There's actually something I've been wanting to ask you. Something I've been wondering about since we met, but I don't know just how to phrase it."

"Well then don't phrase it," Candi said, "Just fucking say that shit right out loud. Just like little ol me."

"Listen. I'll understand if you don't want to answer my question."

"Shoot, pardner"

"Do you ever get turned on," Mike said, "when you give a customer a blowjob?"

"Do I ever get turned on," Candi said, "or, do I ever cum?"

"Either, I guess"

"Is that all you were gonna ask me? Wow. And I was worried it was gonna be somethin really, really personal."

"Are you being *facetious*, again?" Mike said.

"Nope. I pretty much get turned on every single time I have a dick in my mouth. Let me tell you. My clit is like clockwork when it comes to suckin dick. Always has been."

Mike felt his hard-on return. He placed his menu down in his lap.

"But," Candi said, "When it comes to cummin. If I'm givin a man a blowjob. That only happens every once in a while. I mean it really depends."

"It depends on what?"

"It all depends on the Mobyness *and* the fishiness of the dick."

***

Mike caught a whiff of the plate of cheese-fries and winced.

"What's wrong with you?" Candi said.

"It's just that fried food really irritates my stomach."

"You know what fucking irritates your stomach, don't you? And it's not fucking fried food." She dipped a cheese-fry into the cup of Ranch dressing, ate it and then said, "You ever figure that maybe? Just maybe? Missin three square meals a day and drinkin too much gin and poppin those fucking prescription pills just *might be* what's irritatin your stomach? Dumbass" Candi licked the Ranch dressing from her fingertips. "I mean maybe you should try poppin deep fried, hand-breaded okra for a change."

The waitress brought them two more beers.

"I'm already not feeling good," Mike said. "Fried food will just make it worse."

"Seems to me like you're feelin a fuck-ton better. You've even got a little color back in your face, pardner." She reached over and pinched his cheek. "Yep! Pretty soon. I'll have you workin with your fucking hands. Doin an honest day's work out in the sunshine. Instead of just sittin at a fucking desk tryin to be creative. And tryin to write papers and shit."

Mike desperately wanted to change his order. But he knew the waitress had overheard Candi's derogatory comments about him wanting to order a salad. So he drank his beer instead.

Candi tore a cheese-fry away from the heaping pile on the plate. She drenched it in Ranch dressing and then raised it up to Mike's lips. "Here motherfucker," she said, "Eat this cheese-fry. It's fucking deliiiiiiiiiiiiicious."

"No thanks," Mike said, pursing his lips.

"I swear to fucking God. If you don't fucking eat this cheese-fry. I'm gonna smother it all over your goddamn face. Right here in the fucking restaurant. All down the front of your faggoty little fucking shirt too." Candi smiled her devilish smile. "And you fucking know I'll do it, too."

Mike opened his mouth and received the cheese-fry.

"Well," Candi said, "It ain't exactly the fucking body of Christ. But I reckon it'll do for now."

✳✳✳

"Well look at you, pardner. I'm proud of you," Candi said. "You ate your whole chicken fried steak. And all your mashed potatoes. And all your fried okra. And you even sopped up all your fucking gravy with two pieces of Texas toast! And I reckon you even ended up fucking eatin almost all my cheese-fries too."

"I never thought I'd say this," Mike said, "But I think that was the best meal I've ever eaten. I actually feel really good now."

"See! I told you I'd take care of you," Candi slid her finger across the empty plate, sopping up leftover cheese, grease and Ranch dressing. "Yummy"

As Candi licked her fingers clean, a group of rednecks started laughing at a nearby table. They were all sunburned, disheveled, dirty, and smelled like asphalt. When they first came into the restaurant they slowly walked by the booth, ogling Candi. And ever since they sat down they'd been winking and cat-calling the waitress, and adjusting their hard-ons in their blue jeans.

And then, in a voice just loud enough for Mike and Candi to overhear, one of the rednecks said to his buddies, "Hey fellas. How do ya know that Noah was a white man?" He paused, chuckled, and then answered, "Because there ain't no *nigger* who could stay on a boat for forty days and not eat the chickens!" All the rednecks laughed loudly.

"And speakin of The Good Book," the redneck said, "Ya'll ever heard this one? It's a good'un. When God created Eve, how do ya know Adam wasn't a nigger?"

His buddies shrugged.

"You ever try to take a rib away from a nigger?" They all laughed together.

Another redneck said to him, "Hey man! Them kinda jokes ain't cool. I mean I happen to really like niggers. In fact! I used to have me some friends who were niggers."

"Oh yeah? What happened to em?"

"Well my daddy up and went and sold em all one day!" They all laughed.

"Oh yeah," another redneck said, still laughing. "How long does it take for a nigger-bitch to take a shit?"

"How long?"

"About nine months!"

"I got another good'un," the original redneck said, looking over at Candi. "How does a nigger-cunt fight crime?"

They all shrugged again, still laughing.

"She gits an abortion!"

All of them laughed.

✱✱✱

NIGGER, noun

1. Slang: Extremely Disparaging and Offensive
a. black person.
b. a member of any dark-skinned people.

2. Slang: Extremely Disparaging and Offensive: a person of any race or origin regarded as contemptible, inferior, ignorant, etc.

3. a victim of prejudice similar to that suffered by blacks; a person who is economically, politically, or socially disenfranchised.

Origin:
1640–50; < French nègre < Spanish negro black

   Langston Hughes once wrote: "Used rightly or wrongly, ironically or seriously, of necessity for the sake of realism, or impishly for the sake of comedy, it doesn't matter. Negroes do not like it in any book or play whatsoever, be the book or play ever so sympathetic in its treatment of the basic problems of the race. Even though the book or play is written by a Negro, they still do not like it. The word nigger, you see, sums up for us who are colored all the bitter years of insult and struggle in America."
   One of Hemingway's fictional characters refers to Othello as a nigger.
   Huckleberry Finn refers to his friend Jim, the escaped black slave, as a nigger.
   Other notable, non-fictional transgressors include: James Joyce, Henry Miller, Harper Lee, Tony Morrison, Rudyard Kipling, William S. Burroughs, and Joseph Conrad, with several Nobel and Pulitzer Prize winners among them.
   Many of these books have been bowdlerized in recent years; and the word nigger excoriated from their canonical pages, often replaced with words like: slave, black, and more recently, hipster.
   When Mark Twain, the granddaddy of American literature, wrote his classic novel, *The Adventures of Huckleberry Finn*, he managed to pen the word nigger a whopping two hundred and nineteen times, setting the record for its use in a single work of fiction.

✳✳✳

One of the rednecks said to the others, "How bout this one, fellas? How come nigger-bitches always wear panties to picnics?" He coughed up a little fried chicken trying to keep from laughing. "To keep the flies away from their fried chicken!"

"Oh shit, man. That ain't nothin. Ya'll hear bout the new Nigger Barbie doll? Yep. She comes with twelve kids, AIDS, and a fucking welfare check!"

"I got one even better than that. Why do niggers have flat noses? Because that's where God put the heel of his cowboy boot when he was pullin off their fucking tails."

"Holy fucking shit! That was a real good'un! Kinda reminds me. Why are chimps always frownin when you see em at the zoo? Because in a million years they know they're gonna turn into niggers."

Mike hadn't heard the word nigger spoken out loud in years. He cringed every time one of the rednecks said the word nigger. And he couldn't bring himself to turn around and face them, much less turn around and glare in disapproval. Mike wanted to speak up. He wanted to at least frown in their direction. Instead, Mike leaned forward over the table and whispered to Candi, "Come on. I think we should leave now."

Candi didn't budge. She finished off her beer and set the bottle in front of her on the table. "Hey pardner," Candi said loudly, loud enough for the rednecks to hear her. "I gotta great fucking joke for you. What do you call a bunch of white guys sittin on a bench?" She paused and then shot the rednecks her trademark devilish smile. "The NBA" She laughed out loud.

Mike noticed that the rowdy rednecks suddenly got quiet. And he could almost feel their angry eyes boring through the back of his head. Mike leaned forward and whispered, "What the hell are you doing, Candi?"

"Well, pardner. I reckon somebody's gotta do somethin."

"Let's get out of here, right now."

"Or how bout this one?" Candi said to Mike, even louder than before. "Oh fuck yeah! This here's a real, *good'un*! What does a white man do at the night club?"

The rednecks stared her down in silence.

"He just fucking sits there and watches while all the niggers in the place bump and grind their ten-inch nigger cocks against his white-bitch girlfriend." Candi slammed the table with both hands and laughed aloud.

"How bout you, pardner?" Candi said to Mike, still as loud as ever. "You know any good jokes about nigger cock?" She smiled and winked at him, nudging him under the table.

Mike frowned at her. He shook his head in silent response to her question. And then he searched frantically for the restrooms sign, hoping to excuse himself from the table.

"Now, now, now. Come on, pardner," Candi said. "I know for a fucking fact that you know at least one good joke about nigger cock. I mean don't you remember that big-ass sculpture we saw in downtown Houston? Remember that?"

Mike thought back to the sculpture outside the Chase Building downtown. He recalled the joke Candi told him in the plaza. "Please, Candi," Mike whispered again, "Let's just get the hell out of here. *Please.*"

The rednecks remained quiet, listening to their every word.

Candi lowered her voice and whispered back at Mike, "Come on, pardner. This is your fucking chance. I mean this is your chance to be the fucking hero in this little story. This is your fucking chance to be a real man. This is your chance to be the man who steps up and *does somethin* about fucked-up evil shit. Instead of just *writin papers* about fucked-up evil shit."

"Please, Candi. Let's just go."

"Come on, pardner. It's now or fucking never. Let's me and you give these rednecks a taste of their own fucking medicine."

"I mean it, Candi," Mike whispered. "Just ignore these assholes like everybody else. "

"Come on, pardner. It's just like one of those western flicks. I mean this here's a classic fucking showdown between the good guys and the bad guys."

"Candi, *please*"

"Look right over there," Candi said, pointing to the opposite wall. "There's a picture of General Robert E. Lee. And over there is General Stonewall Jackson. And over there is a picture of a bunch of Texas Rangers. And all of them are watchin me and you right now. Lookin down on us, pardner. And all them are wonderin if me and you are gonna man-up and stand up for what's right. Just like all of them did."

Mike pressed his finger against his lips, hushing her. "Shut up, Candi. Please"

"Don't you wanna be a fucking hero?"

"I'd rather be alive."

"Come on, pardner. Let's me and you give these rednecks a good ol fashioned hark from the tomb. Let's wake em the fuck up."

"No"

Candi frowned and said, "Well, pardner. Somebody's gotta do somethin. So I reckon that means me, huh? I reckon I gotta be the one who mans up and puts on the tin star. Oh well. At least you're gonna get another fucking story for your novel. Am I right?"

Candi turned her gaze back to the rednecks, staring them down again. "Come on, pardner," she said, even louder than before, almost yelling now. "I know you've heard *this joke* before. But I'm gonna fucking tell it again anyways. But only because I know you like it sooo fucking much! Remember back in Houston when you asked me," she made her voice really deep, "What's white and ten inches long? Remember what I said?"

Mike finally mustered enough courage to glance back at the rednecks. They looked pissed off.

Candi feigned her best Southern belle accent and said, "And I said to back to you- Well I dooooo declare, Colonel. Whatever in the world could possibly be white and ten inches long? And then you answered me- Not a goddamn thing, sweetheart."

Candi laughed aloud, slamming her hands down on the table, rattling the plates and beer bottles. And then she said in her regular voice, "You sure said a mouthful, didn't you? And I should fucking know about a mouthful of nigger cock! I mean. Nigger cock is my favorite flavor ice-cream!"

The rednecks stared down Candi. Their initial puzzlement over her switching to racist jokes was now replaced with anger. One of the rednecks said to the others with him, "Oh yeah, fellas. And speakin of nigger cock. How can you tell if a nigger is well hung?" He shot back a glance in Candi's direction. "If you can't git your fucking finger between his neck and the rope."

More notable transgressors: Ian Fleming, Ken Kesey, Feodor Dostoevsky, Ralph Ellison, Jack London, Zora Neale Hurston and Thomas Pynchon.

Mike was in shock. The families at nearby tables moved to another part of the dining room. Even their waitress hadn't returned to their table to pick up the check.

Candi leaned back in her seat. She began moaning loudly, fondling her tits and stroking her lips. "Oh my fucking God!" she announced. "Did somebody just say nigger cock? Oh holy fucking shit! That gets my pussy sooo fucking wet." She licked her lips and the rednecks quieted back down.

"You know what I love most in the world, pardner?" Candi said. "I just love it when a nigger shoves his big ol black nigger cock right into my pussy. Hell! I don't even fucking care if I'm wet yet when he does it. I mean there ain't no woman in the world can resist the feel of nigger cock in her pussy."

"You know why rednecks make so many nigger jokes, don't you, pardner? Because every redneck in this fucking goddamned world fucking knows. That while he's at work layin asphalt on the highway for minimum wage. And sittin on the tailgate of his pickup makin nigger jokes with his buddies. He knows that some nigger is back at his trailer fucking his wife's white pussy. And I don't mean fucking like a redneck fucks either. No sir! I mean that nigger is givin his wife's little white pussy a deep nigger dickin like only a nigger can."

The rednecks fumed.

Mike leaned forward and said, "For Chrissakes, Candi. Let's get the hell out of here."

"In fact!" Candi said, still doing her best redneck voice, "I just realized that I got me a bad hankerin for some nigger cock right about now. Yessiree! I gotta find me a big ol nigger who can fill up my pussy with his big ol nigger cock. Goddammit!"

"My pussy is a gonna be soooo stretched out by the time that nigger gits done with me. I mean after that nigger gits done fucking me with his big ol nigger cock. My redneck hubby ain't even gonna be able to feel my pussy round his little white peckerwood dick. Yessirree! Boy howdy! My redneck hubby is a gonna have to fuck my asshole iffin he wants to feel anythin a rubbin up against his little white peckerwood dick."

niggers, but niggers are *real* men. Yep. Real fucking men. Not just a bunch of Kansas City faggots drivin pickup trucks and wearin John Deere caps."

The rednecks got up from their table and walked over in Mike and Candi's direction.

Still more notable transgressors: Dashiell Hammett, William Golding, James Baldwin, Dorothy Allison, Charles Dickens, Harriet Beecher Stowe, William Faulkner and Kaye Gibbons.

"How about this, pardner?" Candi said aloud as the rednecks approached their booth. "When I'm all done gettin nigger-fucked by a nigger with his big ol nigger cock-"

The rednecks got closer.

"How's about me and you send that same nigger out to the parkin lot right here at Johnny Reb's Dixie Café-"

The rednecks gathered round their booth, staring them down.

Mike could only sit there and watch Candi, a look of horror on his face.

"And then," Candi said, still looking at Mike, pretending the rednecks didn't exist. "And then! That same nigger can whip out his nigger cock. And then he can corn-hole him a bunch of rednecks. Just the way they fucking like it!"

The original redneck who told the very first joke leaned forward over their table. He had a packet of Levi Garret chewing tobacco in the breast pocket of his flannel shirt. His dirty beat up old cap read: PRODUCER'S CO-OP. He pursed his lips and let tobacco juice drain slowly down into Candi's ranch dressing dish. He chuckled and the others joined him.

Mike noticed Candi's hands. She dandled her empty beer bottle with her right hand, and her steak knife with the left.

Candi still ignored the rednecks, pretending they weren't even there. She smiled and said to Mike, "You know somethin, pardner. All this talk about niggers. And nigger fucking. And nigger cock. And nigger cock fucking in the pussy and the ass-hole." Candi paused. She acted like she was looking around the restaurant, still pretending the rednecks were invisible. "If there did happen to be any neighborhood rednecks around. And they heard me talkin like this. You know. All about niggers. And nigger fucking. And nigger cock. And nigger cock fucking in the pussy and the asshole. I bet every single one of them rednecks would get a tiny little white peckerwood hard-on in their Wrangler blue jeans. Don't you think so?"

Mike shrunk down in the booth.

The rednecks turned and walked away slowly towards the front of the restaurant.

"Yep! I can picture it now, pardner," Candi yelled. "A bunch of white-trash redneck pieces of shit! Gettin their little white assholes nigger-fucked by a fucking nigger!"

The rednecks paid their bill at the front counter and turned towards the front door.

"Yep! They'd all be a bunch of nigger bitches! And they'd fucking love every nigger fucking minute of it too!" Candi laughed out loud, slamming her fists on the table, rattling the plates and beer bottles again.

✳ ✳ ✳

"You are totally insane!" Mike said to Candi.

They drove north on Highway 6 leaving Hearne. Mike's heart still raced and his hands were shaking. "Those men might've killed us back there."

When leaving Johnny Reb's Dixie Café, Mike had been afraid the rednecks would be waiting for them in the parking lot. However, by the time Candi and Mike got to their ride, the rednecks were already gone. But for the last fifteen minutes Mike had watched his rear-view mirror, thinking the rednecks might catch up to them for some revenge. For now, though, the coast seemed to be clear.

"Oh, hell,' Candi said. "They wouldn't of done shit about shit. Rednecks are all talk. Most of the time"

"Most of the time? Most of the time? Are you crazy? What if we'd been the exception to the rule?"

"Like I said before. They're just a bunch of fucking redneck white-trash losers. Who blame niggers and everybody else for how fucking miserable and poor they are. I mean. They fucking act like if there wasn't any black people or Mexicans. Then they might've actually graduated from high school. And might actually be makin more than minimum wage. Let me tell you. These days. Most poor white guys are really fucked in the head when it comes to that shit. You know? I'm actually really fucking surprised that the Klan hasn't made more a comeback."

"You are crazy," Mike said. "And I still can't believe the way you kept saying," he hesitated for a moment, *"that word."*

"What word?"

"You know what word I mean."

"Nope. Sure don't, pardner. What word do you mean?"

"Come on, Candi," Mike said. "You were brilliant back there! You were like Jonathan Swift when he wrote *A Modest Proposal.*"

"Was this Jonathan Swift guy a whore?"

"Uh, no"

"Then I have no fucking clue what you fucking meant by that."

"I mean," Mike said, "The way you used *satire* back there. The way you started using *that word* the same way those men were using it in all their racist jokes. The way you ended up using *that word* so much it finally made *them* uncomfortable. So they stopped and then they just left."

"You mean the word, fuck?"

"I'm not going to say *that word*, Candi. I know that's what you're trying to get me to do. And don't get any big ideas about punching me in the nuts either!"

"Good one there, pardner," Candi said, laughing. "Oh! I think I know what word you're talkin about. You mean *that word?* You mean, nigger?"

Mike nodded, acknowledging her sarcasm. "That's not a word you hear spoken very often anymore."

"That all depends, pardner," Candi said, "on what kind of company you're keepin."

"Yeah. The wrong kind of company"

"Depends, I guess"

"Depends on what?"

"Depends on whether or not you hang out with white racist assholes. If you do. Then you're gonna hear the word nigger all the time. But if you hang out with most black people. Then you're gonna hear the word nigger all the time too. It's kinda funny if you think about it. You can hang out with completely different people. And you can still end up hearin the exact same fucking word."

"Actually," Mike said, "I think there is a difference."

"I don't think so, pardner. The only difference is what part of town you're in and how you pronounce it."

"What do you mean?"

"I'd be willin to bet good money," Candi said, "That you've never ever said the word nigger in your whole fucking life. Am I right?"

"Well then you'd win that bet. Because I haven't"

"And how about all your smarty-pants friends in college? You ever hear any of them ever say the word nigger?"

"Of course not," Mike said.

"Even you're black friends?"

"Of course not"

✳ ✳ ✳

Mike recalled that even Sonny Quillan never used *that word*. In fact, during the American Pragmatism class they took together at Yale Divinity School, Sonny became fast friends with their African-American professor. Sonny had once said to Mike, "Me and him both hate what we like to call- the heroic irrelevance of academia."

Sonny lived his life standing on a soapbox. And Sonny's soapbox rants soon became the stuff of legend at Yale University. And when the topic of racism came up in conversation, whether in the classroom or at a cocktail party following a lecture, Mike remembered Sonny's favorite soapbox rant. "Poor whites and poor blacks have more in common than rich whites and rich blacks," Sonny always said. "In my opinion, socio-economic profiling is just as big a goddamned problem as racial profiling."

To prove his point, Sonny liked to tell this story: "I was driving through Houston, Texas once. It was real late at night. Like around two or three in the morning. I was on my way to my aunt's house to stay with her for a few days. She lived on Darcus Street. Just off Bellaire in the Southside Place neighborhood. Her husband's a big-name neurosurgeon. And you know what that means." Sonny always rubbed his fingers together to suggest the big bucks.

"The Southside Place neighborhood is right next door to the West University neighborhood. Both of them full of swanky, million dollar homes. They even got their own police force. And goddamn me if they sure as hell know how to use it too."

"Well. Back in the day. I was still living in Austin and delivering pizzas. And my ride was this rusty old piece-of-shit. Don't get me wrong. I loved that goddamned car. Believe me. But that old car was a certified, pre-owned piece of goddamned shit. I think the only thing holding it together was bailing wire and JB Weld."

"So I'm driving through West U. And I hadn't been in that neighborhood for five minutes. And all of sudden I see cop lights flashing in my rear-view mirror. Now keep in mind. My car might've been a piece of shit. But she was street legal. All my lights worked. I was going the speed limit. And I hadn't run any stop signs. So I pull over my piece-of-shit car and the cop car pulls right up behind me. And guess what? Not a minute later *another* cop car shows up too."

"When cops pull you over they're supposed to tell you why they stopped you. You know, give you a reason. Well guess what? They didn't. They just drug my ass out of my piece-of-shit car and then cuffed my hands behind my back." Sonny always swung his hands around behind his back for dramatic effect.

"And then those cops made me sit down on the curb, with my goddamned hands cuffed, while they searched my piece-of-shit car. The only thing I can figure is- some rich prick's house must've been burglarized that same night. And those cops must've figured that a piece-of-shit car like mine meant that the person driving it didn't live in that rich neighborhood. And! Was probably being driven by the kind of piece-of-shit person who burglarizes swanky million dollar homes."

"Well. The cops searched my piece-of-shit car. And guess what? They didn't find any Picassos or Rolex watches. They even ran my driver's license too. But I was clean. So finally they uncuffed me and put my ass back in my piece-of-shit car. And then! One of the cops leaned down into my window. He points down the street. Stares me down and says- that's the way outta this neighborhood."

"And you know what? Both of those cops followed behind me until I'd left the neighborhood. I'm telling you," Sonny always said as he brought his story to an end. "Those cops didn't stop me because of the color of my skin. Hell! I was as white as them. Nope. Those cops stopped me because I was poor. And they knew it just by looking at my piece-of-shit car."

"I'm telling you. Poor is poor whether you're white or black. And rich people don't want either one of them in their rich neighborhoods. And *that's why* I've got more in common with that young black guy Robby who mops the floors here at the divinity school, than Cornell West ever will. But don't get me wrong," Sonny always added, "Nothing personal against Cornell West."

Mike also knew a lot African Americans at Yale. Even though, admittedly, there were more of them mopping the classrooms than attending classes in the classrooms. One semester, as an elective, Mike had even taken an African American Literature class.

Every time Cornell West came up in conversation, Sonny would say to Mike, "You remember when you got that first edition of *Black Theology and Marxist Thought* signed by him after that lecture we went to?"

Mike was extremely proud of his signed books collection. And Yale had provided a steady stream of academics, celebrities, and academic celebrities to autograph them. The shelf over Mike's desk was an academic shrine, ornamented with books signed by intellects such as Richard Swinburne, Alvin Plantinga, John J. Collins, Miroslav Volf, Stephen Greenblatt, Seyla Benhabib, Jurgen Habermas, Harold Bloom and Judith Butler.

"The only drawback to your little collection of books," Sonny once pointed out to Mike, "or should I say, collection of relics. The only drawback is that not too many normal people know who any of these academics are. What I mean is- only academics can appreciate just how impressive your little collection of academic books really is."

Mike said, "And that's a problem, how?"

"Well, huh," Sonny said, "I guess you're right. That's the whole goddamned point."

It wouldn't be until shortly before Mike fled from Yale to Houston, that he truly appreciated Sonny's comment that day...

A month ago Mike had lunched with one of his favorite philosophy professors at Yale. As always, they met at Bangkok Gardens just down the street from Connecticut Hall. Their conversation meandered from one philosophical topic to another, until finally they discussed Martin Heidegger's essay, *Der Ursprung des Kunstwerkes*. Mike had recently become fascinated by Heidegger's use of the German word, *holzwege*.

"Since you've been at Yale for over forty years," Mike said, "Did you ever get to meet Heidegger before he died in 1976?"

"No," Mike's professor said, "But I did have *the chance* to meet him once. My friend Hans Gadamer knew Heidegger very well. And Hans offered to introduce me to Heidegger on one of our many trips back to Germany."

"What?" Mike said. "How could you turn down the opportunity to meet one of the most famous, not to mention, one of the most infamous philosophers of the twentieth century?"

"I guess I'm just not into academic tourism," his professor had said.

Mike had remained uncharacteristically quiet in his African American Literature class. Normally, he was assertive and well-spoken in the classroom; and these qualities always served him well as intellectual weapons against other aspiring academics. Mike lived and died by the unwritten law of the academy- the student still standing at the end of the semester skirmish, is awarded letters of recommendation by doting professors.

Mike was a sharpshooter amongst the intelligentsia; and had acquired the necessary recommendation letters from eminent professors to prove it. And yet, during the entire semester in his African American Literature class, Mike never even fired a single shot.

The course description for the class in African American Literature at Yale looks something like this:

> The literary reaction to slavery; the evolution in form from slave narratives to autobiographies and fictions; the incorporation of folk and popular materials into formal literature. Authors include Phyllis Wheatley, Jupiter Hammon, Frederick Douglass, Harriet Jacobs, France Ellen

Watkins Harper, Charles Chestnutt, Paul Laurence Dunbar, and James Weldon Johnson.

"I'm not afraid of saying the wrong thing," Mike once told Sonny, "I just,"

"You just don't know the right thing *to say*."

"How is that different?"

"Who the hell knows?"

Near the end of that class, Mike realized that he felt more comfortable commenting on the society and culture of Ancient Greece, a people who lived two thousand five hundred years ago, than on the social and cultural experiences of African Americans who lived right alongside him in the present day.

✳ ✳ ✳

"Well how bout your parents?" Candi said, "They ever use the word nigger?"

"Not that I can remember."

"How bout your grandparents then? They ever use the word nigger?"

"No"

"Well. Let's see here then," Candi said, scratching her chin, "You ever had any horny Thomas Jefferson-types in your family? You know. Maybe one of your ancestors who had him some jungle fever? Lurkin around in your family woodpile somewhere? I'll just bet there's an old woodpile on your family plantation that's got a few juicy nigger-stories in it."

"The rednecks are gone, Candi," Mike said, "So I think you can stop saying *that word* now."

"What word? The word, Thomas? Or the word, Jefferson?"

"Oh for Chrissakes, Candi. You know exactly which word I'm talking about."

"You mean the word, nigger?"

"Cut it out, Candi."

"So, you want me to stop sayin the word nigger, then? So what you're tryin to tell me is that you wish I would stop sayin the word, nigger? Nigger is the word you mean, right? Nigger? Right? So we're agreed then that it's the word nigger, right?"

"I don't understand you, Candi. I mean after you did such a brave thing back there by standing up to those racist assholes? Why are *you* acting like such a racist?"

"Hold up there, pardner. How the fuck can I be fucking actin like a racist?"

"It's racist to use *that word*. And it doesn't matter who you are."

"I can't fucking believe. That you can't even *say* the word nigger out loud. Even when you're just talkin about *using* the word nigger, you can't even say the word nigger. What are you sooo fucking afraid of?"

"I'm not afraid. I'm just not a racist."

"Come on, pardner. Me and you both fucking know what white people always call a black person after they leave the room. Am I right?"

"No. I'm afraid I don't know."

"A nigger," she said, and then chuckled. "That's another, *good'un.*"

"Oh for Chrissakes, Candi. Not everybody is a racist."

"Please! You know and I know. Hell! Everybody and their fucking mother-in-law knows. There's just two kinds of white people. Those who say the word nigger when they *think* it. And those who think the word nigger but never *say* nigger out loud."

"I happen know a lot of white people who haven't done either one. Including me. I told you. I'm not a racist."

"You are too a fucking racist. I mean look right fucking here in your fucking book box of books." Candi reached into the cardboard box in the back seat. She pulled out a red soft cover book. "What about fucking Mark Twain? I mean he used the word nigger all the fucking time. Right?"

"Wait a second. Don't tell me. Let me guess," Mike said, exasperated with her argument. "I'll bet you're going tell me that while you were in that Greyhound Bus Station, you just happened to read *The Adventures of Huckleberry Finn* too! Wow! What a surprise!"

"You know somethin, pardner? You might never *think* the word nigger. And you might never *say* the word nigger. But dammit if you don't know how to make a person fucking *feel* like a nigger."

"It was fifteen minutes before I could work myself up to go and humble myself to a nigger; but I done it, and I warn't ever sorry for it afterwards, neither. I didn't do him no more mean tricks, and I wouldn't done that one if I'd a knowed it would make him feel that way."

"Ok, Candi," Mike said finally, "I'm sorry for what I said back there."

"A few years ago," Candi said, thumbing through the book, "I heard em talkin about *The Adventures of Huckleberry Finn* on the news. A bunch of uptight parents in New York or somewhere like that were tryin to get this book removed from school libraries. They said it was a racist book. And all because it had the word nigger in it like a thousand fucking times."

"Actually," Mike said, "Mark Twain used *that word* two hundred and nineteen times."

"So what do *you* think?" Candi said, still thumbing through the pages. "You think this book is racist or what?"

"Of course not," Mike said. "This book isn't racist. Even though *that word* gets used over and over. It's used in a proper context to *expose* racism, not promote it."

"Now wait just a fucking second there, pardner. How the fuck do you know what was goin through Mark Twain's head when he fucking wrote this book? I mean maybe he *was* a racist. Maybe he just filled up his book with the word nigger because he really and truly was a fucking racist? And puttin the word nigger in this fucking novel was the only way for him to use the word nigger and fucking get away with that shit?"

"Oh, for Chrissakes"

"I'll bet he even got a fucking kick outta writin the word nigger over and over and over and over. Because nobody could say shit to him about it! Because it's just a fucking novel!"

"Jesus Christ," Mike said, "It's like taking a road trip with Alan Gribben."

"You ever think that maybe Mark Twain put all that racist shit into a kiddo's mouth so nobody could tell whether to take it seriously or not?"

"What the hell are you talking about?"

"I mean. Kiddos say the darndest things, right? It's like when a kiddo says somebody is fat. Or a kiddo makes a racist comment. Or says some other rude shit no respectin grown-up could ever say in polite company. When that shit happens, usually the kid's parents just gently correct the little bastard. And then everybody just laughs it off. Kiddos say the darndest things, right?"

"Ok"

"So maybe Mark Twain made the character of Huck a kiddo *on purpose*. So he could say nigger all he wanted and nobody could say shit about it? I'll just bet if Huck's character had been a grown-up, ol Mark Twain couldn't of gotten away with that shit! Am I right?"

"Candi. That's got to be the biggest load of bullshit I've ever heard in my life. You really, really don't know what you're talking about. You are so way out of your league on this one. You don't know anything about the art of the novel or about classic American literature."

"Hey! Just because I've only read one book in my whole entire fucking life. Doesn't mean I don't know how people are."

"I didn't say you don't know how people are. I said you don't know a damn thing about the art of the novel. Or about great literature. Or about what it means to craft characters for a story."

"You're right, pardner. I don't know the first goddamn thing about writin a fucking novel. And guess what? I don't wanna fucking know either! But I *do* know that books are written by people. And I *do* know people."

"Well before you lecture me on the art of the novel. How about first you try reading more than one novel! I don't know. How about maybe reading *The Adventures of Huckleberry Finn!*"

"Wow," Candi said. "You just fucking did that shit *again*!"

> "It most froze me to hear such talk. He wouldn't ever dared to talk such talk in his life before. Just see what a difference it made in him the minute he judged he was about free. It was according to the old saying, "Give a nigger an inch and he'll take an ell." Thinks I, this is what

comes of my not thinking. Here was this nigger, which I had as good as helped to run away, coming right out flat-footed and saying he would steal his children – children that belonged to a man I didn't even know; a man that hadn't ever done me no harm."

"You know what, pardner? You are one stuck-up sonuvabitch. I mean. You really know how to ride your high horse."

"I think the word you're looking for is narcissist," Mike said, and then chuckled at her.

"You're such a fucking phony," Candi said. "You and your smarty-pants college crowd are all such fucking phonies. You call rednecks racists because they say the word nigger. But you make an exception and you let whiteys like Mark Twain say it. And whoever the fuck else you read and study in college get away with saying nigger as many times as they fucking want. And why? All because you call it a classic of American fucking literature. You and your college crowd are such a bunch of fucking phony bullshitters."

"I give up, Candi. I give up, for Chrissakes. I'm not going to argue with you anymore about this. Clearly, you're dead wrong. And you don't know what you're talking about here. You can't always win every argument, you know?"

"Well, den, dey ain't no sense in a cat talkin like a man. Is a cow a man? –er is a cow a cat?"
"No, she ain't either of them."
"Well, den, she ain't got no business to talk like either one er the yuther of em. Is a Frenchman a man?"
"Yes."
"WELL, den! Dad blame it, why doan he TALK like a man? You answer me DAT!"
"I see it warn't no use wasting words- you can't learn a nigger to argue. So I quit."

✳✳✳

A few miles down the road, Candi said, "You know. I got more than a few juicy nigger-stories in my family woodpile, "You wanna hear some of em?"

Mike was still fuming over their argument. However, at the prospect of mining Candi's colored life experiences for more belletristic gold, he resolved to perk up and listen. "Well," Mike said, "For the sake of my novel and the future of American literature, I'm willing to let bygones be bygones."

"Fuck you with a corncob pipe full of cowshit, pardner," Candi said. "And fuck your fucking bygones too."

"This novel," Mike said, "Just keeps getting more and more Southern Gothic."

"Well? You wanna fucking hear some of my family woodpile nigger-stories or not?"

"Sure. Let's hear some."

"Well, first off. You should know. My family tree has more than a few knots in it. And a few rotten branches too. And mum's the fucking word on this one, pardner. But let me tell you. There's cattle egrets *and* grackles roostin up in these branches, if you know what I mean?"

Mike didn't know what Candi meant. Somewhere along their little odyssey it had become apparent to Mike that no amount of Faulkner novels or Flannery O'Conner stories could've prepared him to accurately translate Candi's commanding and copious use of Southern colloquialisms.

Mike wondered if Candi was suggesting there were criminals or outlaws in her family. No shock there, he surmised. Or was Candi suggesting that some of her family stories weren't the whole truth? Again, if so, he wouldn't be surprised. And what did Candi mean by cattle egrets and grackles? What was she hinting at? And what the hell was a cattle-egret or a grackle anyway? And why did Candi keep mentioning wood piles in association with family secrets?

Mike recalled Candi singing along to a song on the radio earlier that day, *"I'm part hippie, a little redneck- I'm always a suspect- my bloodline made me who I am."*

Mike cautioned himself with a proverb he'd just made up-
*When you're in a rental car with a whore; too many questions make a
man look like a dumbass.* Mike decided against volunteering his
ignorance about cattle egrets, grackles or even woodpiles. Mike
penned another proverb off the top of his head- *Even a fool appears
wise if he keeps his fucking mouth shut.*

"My granddaddy was pretty racist," Candi said. "Granddaddy
used the word nigger sometimes. In fact, Granddaddy's favorite joke of all was- Why do niggers keep chickens in their back
yards?"

Mike sighed with dissatisfaction at Candi's insistence on
using *that word* again. He shrugged.

"To teach their kiddos how to walk," Candi chuckled a
little.

"I don't get it," Mike confessed, forsaking both his proverbs.

Mike decided to break down and ask Candi to explain the
joke, for several reasons:

First- After both the showdown at Johnny Reb's Dixie Café
between Candi and the rednecks, and the showdown between
Candi and him concerning Mark Twain, Mike decided he was
going to include at least one racist character in his novel. This
racist character would facilitate a contemporary literary dialogue
on racism.

Second- Mike realized that in order to write a racist character for his novel, he needed the racist jokes he was hearing.

Third- Mike realized that not only did he need these racist
jokes; but also, he needed to understand them if he was going to
put them into his novel.

Fourth- Mike realized that he needed to understand these
racist jokes in anticipation of the questions asked him during an
interview with *The New York Times.*

Fifth- Mike also realized that he needed to understand these
racist jokes because all classic works of American Literature are
eventually annotated with commentary and footnotes.

"I don't get it," Mike said.

"Well I can't stand up right now," Candi said, "So I can't
show you exactly. But every time my granddaddy told that joke
he would bob his head forwards and backwards." She mimicked

the gesture. "You know. Kinda like you're doin the Egyptian dance. And then Granddaddy would swagger his arms and legs at the same time. You know. Like some jive nigger!"

"I still don't get it."

"Never fucking mind you fucking dumbass," Candi said, unwrapping a blowpop.

Mike cringed and said, "Do you mind not calling me, dumbass?"

"Sure, dumbass. Whatever you fucking want!"

Mike decided to go back to his policy of not asking questions. He consoled his ignorance with the assurance that he'd already gleaned more than enough racist jokes from the rednecks back in Hearne.

"So you grew up in a racist family?" Mike said.

"I guess that all depends on what you mean by racist," Candi said. "Not everybody in the South is a fucking racist, you know. Not everybody throws the word nigger around willy-nilly. Just sayin- nigger, nigger, nigger, nigger, nigger, nigger, nigger, nigger, nigger every other fucking word. Like every fucking chance they get." She chuckled.

"I just meant your *granddaddy* was a racist," Mike said, savoring his opportunity to recite such a quaint epithet as granddaddy. Mike reminded himself that the use of colloquial dialect is one of the hallmarks of great American literature, especially Southern literature. Lucky for me, Mike observed, Candi is a walking, talking dictionary of Southern slang.

"Yep. Granddaddy liked to tell an occasional racist joke. And sometimes Granddaddy would even say things like- Never trust a nigger as far you can throw a chicken wing! And this too- Be careful when you're drivin at nighttime else you run over a nigger, because you can only see a nigger at nighttime if he's smilin."

"But most times," Candi said, "Granddaddy didn't even use the word nigger. Nope. Most times Granddaddy used the word *colored*, not nigger. You know. Like, colored folks. Or like, look over there at that colored fella."

Candi pursed her lips and appeared to be contemplating. "I don't know why," she said, "and don't get me wrong here. But it always seemed a little less racist to me to say colored fella instead of nigger."

Candi's musings on the nature of racism made absolutely no sense to Mike. He decided that rather than disagree, he'd just change the subject. "So, did you ever know anybody in the Ku Klux Klan?"

"Of course not!" Candi said, "I mean look at me. Who do you think I fucking am here? The Klan is just a bunch of ignorant white-trash assholes!"

What never ceased to amaze Mike is how one minute Candi would be tossing around racial epithets like nigger or white-trash, and the very next minute distance herself from the very characteristics commonly attributed to both groups. A whole host of these plebian characteristics came to Mike's mind: lack of education, poverty, use of bad grammar, refusal to use birth control, promiscuity, illegitimate babies, broken homes and an overall lack of culture, etc.

"My granddaddy," Candi said, "never would've hurt anybody. Or lynched anybody either. Or burned crosses in anybody's front yard. Granddaddy wasn't *that kind* of racist."

Mike was troubled by what Candi had just said. And yet, he was done arguing with her and decided to play Socrates instead. "What exactly do you mean- *that kind* of racist?"

"Like I said before. Granddaddy liked to tell an occasional nigger-joke. And he honest to God didn't like bein around em. And he didn't trust em either. Remember the chicken wing joke? But let me tell you. Granddaddy never would've hurt one."

"So what you're saying is- there are *different degrees* of being a racist? That two people could *both* be racists, but one of them is *more* racist, and therefore a *worst* racist?"

"Yep," Candi said. "I mean take my Uncle Tom for instance. He was an even *worst* racist than my granddaddy."

"Uncle Tom?" Mike said. "Was that really his name?"

"Yeah it was. Why?"

"Nevermind"

"Well. Like I was sayin. Uncle Tom was an even *worst* racist than Granddaddy. Don't get me wrong. I love my Uncle Tom to death. He was the best fucking uncle ever! He used to take me and my cousins to get ice cream and candy in the summertime. But I'd have to say. In all honesty, Uncle Tom was definitely a worst racist than my granddaddy."

"What made him worse?"

"Well, for one thing. Uncle Tom pretty much *only* used the word nigger. I mean I never heard him say Negro, or colored guy, or spook, or jiggaboo, or coon, or anythin like that. Nope. Uncle Tom pretty much decided to just say nigger."

"Oh yeah," Candi said, "and you're gonna fucking love this shit. Uncle Tom always carried a nigger huntin license in his wallet. He always used to show it to me and my cousins when we were kiddos."

"A what?"

"Oh, you know. A nigger huntin license. It's a novelty item. It's a little laminate license. Like a deer huntin license you get during deer season. And they put your name and address on it and everything. Uncle Tom bought it at a flea market in Cut n Shoot, Texas. There's a bunch of racist assholes around there. They all live back there in the piney woods and get their jollies by dressin up like Klansman or Nazis."

"Is there really a town named Cut n Shoot, Texas?"

"Yep"

"You're kidding, right?"

"I'm not fucking kiddin, pardner. I went to a flea market there one time. And almost every fucking booth had Nazi or Klan shit for sale."

"Well, goll-darnet. Look at my ass. I fucking live in Cut n Shoot, Texas" Candi said, feigning her famous country bumpkin dialect. "Instead of a GED I got me a criminal record. Yessir! And now I can't work nowhere but MacDonald's. So I reckon I'm a gonna blame the fact that I'm such a fuckin loser on niggers, kikes and spics. Yessirree! I'm a gonna git me a bunch of Nazi tattoos. And I'm a gonna salute ol Adolf Hitler while I'm at it." Candi laughed and said, "What a bunch of white-trash losers!"

"You *really* think that's why most of those people do that?" Mike said, "Because they feel like losers?"

"I don't fucking think, pardner. I fucking know. I've met a fuck-ton of these assholes. And they're all the same. They're fucking pissed off at the world because they started with nothin. And now they got nothin. And they're goin nowhere with nothin fast. And they ain't never gonna have a pot to piss in."

"I mean don't get me wrong. It's no excuse for bein a racist asshole. I'm not sayin that. But even you, pardner. You'd be pissed off and angry at the whole fucking world. If you'd been born some white-trash piece of shit. And then raised in some nowhere hick-town. We got ghettos in the country too."

Mike couldn't help but wonder yet again, how Candi seemed to offer such critical insight into her own species, while at the same time, ostracizing herself from them.

"You know, pardner. If you weren't so busy listenin to Beethoven. And whoever the fuck else wrote that elevator music you love sooo much. And goin to jazz clubs. And snooty fucking wine bars. Then you just might notice that country music and rap music have a whole hell of a lot in fucking common. There's a fucking reason for that shit, you know."

Mike was resolved to remain Socrates for the moment, which meant ignoring Candi's predictable personal attacks on his lifestyle. "So what else made your Uncle Tom a *worst racist* than your granddaddy?"

"I don't know," Candi said. "I mean. Uncle Tom wouldn't even be in the same room with one of em. One time my cousin showed up at my grandparent's house. With a friend who was one of em. And Uncle Tom got right up and went to his room. And didn't fucking come out until they were gone."

Candi tossed her blowpop stick out the window and said, "Don't get me wrong here. My Uncle Tom never woulda actually hurt one of em either. My grandma always told us kids that Uncle Tom was a really sensitive guy. And smart too. I don't believe Uncle Tom would've ever really hunted a nigger with his nigger huntin license. Even if he had the chance"

"Why do you think he had it then?"

"Who the fuck knows! I mean why the fuck does anybody have any fucking thing? I'm a fucking whore not a fucking psychiatrist... Get it? Fucking whore? Fucking...whore? Get it?"

"I get it."

"Now my great-granddaddy. He was an *even worst* racist than Uncle Tom."

"Really? This I gotta hear"

"Oh, fuck yeah. You're definitely gonna wanna hear this story. My great granddaddy told me and all my cousins this story at a family reunion one year. Course. All growin up my daddy only took me to that one family reunion. So you're fucky I even heard this story at all."

"I'd love to hear that story," Mike said, wondering what could possibly be worse than carrying a nigger hunting license around in your wallet, and throwing the word nigger around all the time.

"Ok," Candi said, "This is a damn good fucking story. And you know what makes this story even more fucked up and creepy? My great granddaddy had that surgery where they remove part of your throat. And your fucking voice-box too."

"A tracheotomy," Mike said.

"Yep, that's it. Anyways. My great granddaddy had a huge gapin hole in his throat. And he had to hold a damp handkerchief over the hole. And then he'd fucking swallow a bunch of air. And then burp up the air and that's how he fucking talked." She grimaced. "It was the grossest goddamn thing. And what made it even worse. It was a hot Texas summer day when we had our family reunion. And they were guttin and cleanin catfish up to fry. And the fucking flies were buzzin all around great grand-daddy's neck and face. I mean the fucking flies were crawlin all over that hole in his throat. Great granddaddy was old as dirt by then. I think he must've died pretty soon after."

"But! Even though he had a big fucking hole in his throat. My great granddaddy was tall, lean and one tough motherfucker. Nobody in the family gave him any lip. Ever. Even when he was old as dirt. Even my Uncle Tom. Who was one bad-ass mother-fucker himself. Was afraid of Great Granddaddy."

"I guess I don't need to tell you. Great Granddaddy didn't even know any other word to use besides nigger. I mean it never would've even fucking crossed his mind to use any other word. Anyways. Here's how my great granddaddy told us kiddos the tale:"

"Years back," Great Granddaddy said, "I was workin on a construction site in Wellborn, Texas. We was buildin a building for old man Junek. It was summertime then. And hot as the bad place."

"Hold on for a coon's moon, Daddy," Great Grandma interrupted him, "Git all the kiddos gathered round over here. They need to hear this story." There must've been at least twenty kiddos at our family reunion that day. "Go on now, Daddy," Great Grandma encouraged him, "Tell em your story now."

"Well," Great Granddaddy said, "Back in them days they had one bucket of drinkin water for the white folks. And another one for the niggers. Ya see," Great Granddaddy said, "in the olden days niggers knew their place. A nigger didn't drink from the same bucket as white folks. And a nigger didn't use the same water fountain neither."

"A nigger didn't eat supper in *the front* of the restaurant with white folks neither. In fact. Them niggers had a separate door they used *in the back* of the place. Where they could eat their supper. Or just pick up their supper and go back home. You wanna see how it was back in them days? Martin's BBQ is still open today. Course. Things have changed regardin niggers and white folks. But that building is still the same as it was when I was young."

"Yep. Go on over to Martin's BBQ sometime. Near the corner of Villa Maria and College Avenue in Bryan. That ol building's still got the same door in the back them niggers used. Our family's been eatin supper and drinkin beer there for years. Ain't that right Tom?"

Uncle Tom saluted Great Granddaddy with his beer can.

Great Grandma swatted flies away from Great Granddaddy's throat and said, "Git on with the story, Jack. Tell em what you done to that uppity nigger."

"Well. I was workin in Wellborn, Texas on this construction site. I forget what we was buildin. Anyways. Back in them days they had metal buckets full of water. With big ol wooden ladles in em for us to drink from. It was as hot as the bad place that day."

The young dark-haired girl sitting at Great Granddaddy's feet interrupted and asked, "What's the bad place, Great Granddaddy?"

"Hush up, girl," Great Grandma said, "Let your great granddaddy tell his story."

"Where was I, ma?" Great Granddaddy asked her.

"Go on and tell em bout what that uppity nigger done, Daddy," Great Grandma said.

"Oh yeah," he said. He bent over and dipped his handkerchief in a glass of ice water. Great Granddaddy sat back up straight. Shewed the flies away. And then pressed the cool damp handkerchief over the hole in his throat. "We was all sittin there havin lunch under a live oak tree. Us white folks, I mean. And them niggers was all gathered under another tree nearby. Them niggers knew their place back in them days."

"The drinkin buckets were under the back of the wagon to keep em cool. In the shade, I mean. It was hotter than the bad place that day. So we was all sittin there eatin lunch. Us white folks, I mean. And then! This uppity nigger just gits up from under that shade tree. Walks hisself right over to the wagon," Great Granddaddy paused and made a motion with his free hand of somebody lifting a ladle to their lips and taking a drink. "And then by God. That nigger took him a drink from the white folk's bucket!"

"Well. All them other niggers was shakin in their boots. And all us white folks were shocked all to the bad place. I don't think none of us, white folk or nigger, ever seen nothin like that before. What I mean is. Nobody did nothin about it. I mean everbody just sat there not knowin what to do. And that uppity nigger just stood there with the white folks ladle in his hand. And the white folks water just a drippin down from his fat ol nigger lips."

"Well. That's when I figured somebody better do somethin bout that nigger. I reckoned a nigger's gotta know his place. Am I right?" Great Granddaddy paused. He was distracted by the sight of Uncle Tom, who was battering up some mountain oysters in cornmeal and poppin open another can of Pearl Beer.

"Don't ya cook them cow nuts too long, boy," Great Granddaddy said to Uncle Tom, licking his lips. "And slow down on them beers. This here's a day for family! And I ain't gonna tolerate no drunks at a family picnic, ya hear!" Uncle Tom nodded, chagrined, and set his beer aside for now.

Great Grandma chimed in and said, "I sure was blessed by the good Lord to git me a man like Daddy here. I mean he ain't never took a drink in his life. And he always hung up his hat at home. Yep. My mama always said that's the best a woman can do in this here life. Find a real man like this. A real man like Daddy right here." She patted Great Granddaddy on the shoulder. She took his free hand in hers, kissed it and then squeezed it affectionately. "Go on and finish your story, Daddy," she said. "Tom's bout to drop them nuts in the fryer."

"So I reckoned," Great Granddaddy said, "Somebody had to do somethin. I mean back in them days it was us white folks job to keep them niggers in line. Now don't git me wrong. Most niggers was real decent folk. And they knew their places. And there weren't never any problems. Back in them days niggers wasn't like they are today. Back in them days I never knew a nigger who wasn't a hard worker. And didn't fear God and know his place."

"But *this* nigger was uppity, by God." Great Granddaddy paused, contemplating. "Course. I reckon it's possible that nigger coulda been a Mongolian idiot. I mean I never did find out for sure. I mean nobody ever told me so."

The dark-haired girl interrupted again and asked, "What's *that* Great Granddaddy?"

Great Grandma said, "Ya know, girl. A Mongolian idiot. Like a moron or a retard. Somebody who ain't right in the head since they was born. Now hush up!"

"I never did find out *why* that nigger did what he done," Great Granddaddy said. "All I know was that nobody was doin nothin about it. So I reckoned I'd better do somethin. So I git up from the shade of that ol oak tree. Ya know somethin? That ol oak tree is still right there in Wellborn. Near the old post office building. I could show ya right where it happened."

"Anyways. I git up and put on my tool belt. I always took it off durin lunch. Anyways. I put on my tool belt. I walked right over to where that nigger was standin. Him still holdin the white folk's ladle in his hands. And then. I pulled out my ball-peen hammer. Yep. And nobody did nothin neither. I mean everbody, white folks and niggers alike, just sat there and watched me do it."

"Well I pulled out my ball-peen hammer. And then I up and hit that nigger smack in the left temple of his nappy head. And I mean I hit him hard too. Real hard. And back in the day. I was a danged good shot with that hammer too. Well. I hit that nigger square in the temple of his nappy head. And he hit the ground like a sack of taters."

"Well I watched that nigger tremblin there in the dirt for a few minutes. And then. That nigger just stopped movin altogether. And lay there dead still. There was blood on my hammer. And it was then I reckoned that I'd just killed that nigger, dead as a door-nail."

"Anyways. I took the white folks ladle outta that dead nigger's hand. But I didn't put it back in us white folk's bucket. On account of him drinkin from it and all. I mean I knew nobody was about to drink after no nigger."

"You mean you killed him, Great Granddaddy?"

Great Grandma nodded her head and said, "He sure did, girl. Your great granddaddy stood up for what was right. Yep. Ain't nobody else was gonna do it." Let me tell you, pardner. Us kiddos were all gathered around Great Granddaddy as he told his story. I mean our eyes were watchin him like our eyes were watchin God or somethin.

"Well. The sheriff showed up not too long after that," Great Granddaddy said. "And I told him everthin what happened. Yep, the Gospel truth. And all the white folks and all the niggers backed up my story too."

"I told the sheriff I never intended to kill that nigger. Just scare him a little bit. Ya know. Give him a little hark from the tomb. Make a lesson of him for them other niggers. Well. Me and the sheriff growed up together. I mean as boys we gone to the same school in Millican. So he knowed me as a straight-shooter. So nobody did nothin bout me killin that nigger in Wellborn. Cause back in them days, things was just understood."

Near the end of Great Granddaddy's story, Uncle Tom let his younger brother Don take over the fryer while he went over into the garage. Uncle Tom came out of the garage holdin a ball-peen hammer in the air. "Here it is right here," Uncle Tom announced to everybody, "We still got it Great Granddaddy. Keep it right here in the toolbox in the garage."

"You ever still use it?" Great Granddaddy said.

"I still pull it outta the toolbox from time to time," Uncle Tom bragged, "Whenever something needs fixin."

Great Grandma chimed in, "That ball-peen hammer's a family heirloom kiddos. Yep, a family heirloom."

✳ ✳ ✳

"Are you telling me that's a *true* story?" Mike said.

"Yep! True fucking story, pardner. I was fucking there at that reunion," Candi said. "Can you fucking believe my great granddaddy got away with that shit? Those were different days back then, huh?"

"Oh my God," Mike said. "I think I'm going to be sick."

"What?"

Mike pulled over the car on the side of the road. "I've never heard anything so fucked up in all my life."

"What?"

"Candi, you just told me that your great grandfather killed a black man. And that he was bragging about it at your family reunion."

"Oh yeah, that," Candi said. "I reckon I'm just so used to the story by now. You know? I mean even though it's a horrible fucking thing. I reckon it's just kinda hard for me to have a normal reaction to it. You know?"

"That's totally fucked up too, Candi." Mike rolled down his window for some fresh air.

"You gonna be okay there, pardner?"

"I just need a minute. I'm so sorry for you, Candi. I just can't fucking believe you had to hear that story when you were a kid."

For Mike, Candi's gratuitous use of the word nigger was now beginning to make some sense. In Mike's mind, because of her family tree, Candi could somehow be exonerated for her gratuitous use of the word nigger.

Sitting at the feet of her Great Granddaddy at that picnic. Summertime visits to Uncle Tom's house. Racist witticisms and nigger-jokes told by her granddaddy. They all seemed reason enough to forgive Candi, in much the same way it seemed reasonable to forgive Huckleberry Finn, who sat at the feet of his Paps...

"I can't believe you grew up in a family like that," Mike said.

"Now hold on a coon's moon, pardner," Candi said. "Just because my great granddaddy did somethin like that. Doesn't mean I'm ashamed of my family. We're not," Candi raised her hands and made quotation marks in the air, "*bad people.*"

Even though he disagreed with Candi, Mike resisted the urge to argue with her. Instead, he asked, "How about your dad? Was your dad a racist too?"

"My daddy was a good man. He worked real fucking hard with his hands. Out in the fucking sunshine everyday of his life." Mike noticed what seemed like a kind of peacefulness wash over

Candi's face, a tranquility he'd never sensed from her before. "And after a long fucking day my daddy," Candi said, "he always hung his cowboy hat up at home."

"But was he a racist too?"

"I never heard my daddy use the word nigger," Candi said, "Not even once."

"Was your daddy at the reunion that day?"

"Yep. My daddy was there that day. But it was like I told you. It was the only family reunion we ever went to. When I was a kiddo I always wanted to go. I mean I loved playin with my cousins. And havin a catfish fry. And makin homemade ice-cream. Anyways. My daddy drank a few beers with Uncle Tom and helped him clean some catfish for the fryer. They weren't speakin much by that time."

"Why not?"

"Lots of reasons, pardner. But that's a whole other fucking novel"

Mike smiled.

"My daddy always told me- Girl, it's best to call a person whatever they wanna be called, no matter who they are. So I remember my daddy never usin the word nigger. He mostly used the word Negro. And Black too. And even African-American. Even though he never seemed to like that last one very much. Somethin about the liberal media and political correctness. I don't fucking remember."

Candi shrugged, chuckled and then said, "Ain't it funny how my daddy and his brother Tom could be raised in the same exact house by my Granddaddy? And then both spend summertimes with my Great Granddaddy? And still turn out so different from each other? I don't fucking understand how that works. Do you?"

Mike resisted the urge to weigh in on the issue. Now, more than ever, he was resolved to play Socrates. This role included the Herculean task of refusing to argue with Candi, despite her indefatigable provocations. And yet, this resolve was yielding a bountiful literary harvest.

"I don't know," Mike said, "I don't think anyone knows."

Mike realized that after their little odyssey was over, he would have a long literary row to hoe. For when he finally sat down at his Olivetti Lettera 32 typewriter, yet another Herculean task awaited him- sifting the wheat from the chaff on the threshing floor of his novel. Mike knew that when it came to Candi's stories, even the stories she insisted were true, there would inevitably remain the chaff of half-truths, or *chaff-truths.*

"Wait a second," Candi said, "I almost fucking forgot. Now this should be good shit for your novel. And this is true too. Remember how I told you that my daddy never once used the word nigger? But my daddy *did* have this old record that belonged to my granddaddy. It was one of those old racist Johnny Rebel records. You know what I'm talking about?"

"No, I don't."

"It was a song called *The Flight of the NAACP.* I think my granddaddy bought it in Lose-iana from a bunch of racist Cajun assholes."

Johnny Rebel is one of the pseudonyms for Johnny Pee Wee Trahan, a Cajun musician who made famous songs like:
Nigger, Nigger
Nigger Hatin Me
Some Niggers Never Die (They Just Smell that Way)
Move Them Niggers North
Kajun Ku Klux Klan
Coon Town
His most popular song *Lookin for a Handout* was so successful, he penned a popular sequel, *Still Looking for a Handout.*

"Anyways," Candi said, "Granddaddy used to play that record for my daddy and Uncle Tom when they were boys. And then Uncle Tom got the record when Granddaddy died. And he would play it for me and my cousins when we visited him in the summertime. Well. When Uncle Tom finally died, my daddy got the record."

"The thing about it is," Candi said, "My daddy kept Granddaddy's record til the day he fucking died. But he never played it. Not even once. And he wouldn't fucking let anybody else play it either."

"Of course. I'd already heard it at Uncle Tom's house about a thousand fucking times. All growin up. But still. I guess it's gotta mean somethin that my daddy never played the fucking thing. Like I said before. My daddy was a good man. A *real* man. A real good man."

"What happened to your granddaddy's record?" Mike said. "It's got to be some kind of collector's item by now."

"I was afraid you were gonna fucking ask me that. Fuck me. I mean fuck me right in the ear with a stolen dick. And then! And then goddamn me to the bad place for fucking ever and ever!"

"Why?"

"My daddy left me that record when he died. He never had much. In fact. He only ever had two things that were worth anything at all. So my daddy didn't have much to leave me. But he sure as shit left me that fucking record."

"What happened to it?"

"Remember that 4.10 shotgun I told you about before? You know. The one my daddy put the tape on and marked with a pencil? So I could kill my first deer?"

"Yeah"

"Well. My daddy left me that shotgun too. But it was stolen when somebody broke into a storage unit where I'd put all my shit when I was movin. Just like that!" Candi snapped her fingers, "a piece of my fucking childhood, gone! And I mean fucking gone forever! I swear to fucking God. If I could ever get my hands on those cock-sucking, mother-fucking, thieving sons of bitches I'd fucking kill every single one of them. Slooowly and paaainfully."

Mike observed that Candi seemed to always say aloud everything she was thinking. This rare quality made her both attractive and intriguing to him. And yet, what she said aloud, particularly her penchant for violence, sometimes made him uneasy too.

"Anyways. Just like my daddy. I never played my granddaddy's record. And I never let anybody else fucking play it either."

"So what happened to it?"

"Well. One day me and this piece-of-shit I was fucking at the time. We got really, really fucking drunk. And then we got into this knock-down, drag-out fist-fight."

"You mean he hit you?"

"Oh, fuck yeah he hit me. I was bein a total fucking cunt that night. Of course. He was bein a total fucking dick too. So I fucking hit him back! I mean it's not like I'd never been hit before." Candi leaned over and punched Mike in the shoulder.

"Ouch, Candi. For Chrissakes!"

"You ever been in a fistfight, pardner?"

"No," Mike said, rubbing his shoulder.

"Didn't think so"

"So what happened with your boyfriend?"

"Whoa there, pardner! You got cotton in your fucking ears, or what? He wasn't my fucking boyfriend. Like I said before. He was just some dick I was fucking at the time."

"Ok, sorry," Mike said. "So what happened with that dick you were fucking?"

"That's better. Well. I fucking met him at a David Allan Coe concert. Which should've been a big fucking red flag right there. I mean. It's one thing to *listen* to David Allen Coe. But only fucking lowlife, white-trash assholes actually *go* to his fucking concerts."

"So what were *you* doing there?"

"Hey! Don't bother me with details. You wanna hear this story or not?"

"Sorry"

"So I met him at this David Allen Coe concert. We danced. He had a few beers. And fifteen minutes later I sucked his dick in one of those porta-potties. And you know what I regret the most?"

"What?"

"My favorite David Allen Coe song is *You Never Even Called Me By My Name*. You know it?"

"No"

"Didn't think so. Well the whole reason I was fucking there at that concert was to hear that fucking song. And wouldn't you know it? That's the fucking song! Of all his songs! He had to go and fucking sing while I was suckin that guy's dick."

"*That's* what you regret the most?"

"Yep. But in my defense. That asshole had a really pretty face *and* a whale of a dick. Let me tell you. If that guy woulda gone to a nude beach. Fucking Japanese whalers woulda seen his dick and tried to harpoon it. It was sooo huge. I mean usually it's one or the other. Pretty face or humongous Moby dick. Am I right? But this guy fucking had both."

"Anyways. It's all my own goddamn fault about my grand-daddy's record. I mean there's nobody else to blame but little ol me. So anyways. Me and this piece-of-fucking shit were tearin up his fucking apartment one night. Breakin furniture and dishes. We smashed the TV. We smashed the kitchen table. I mean he was beatin the ever livin shit outta me. And I was fucking givin it right back to him. Let me tell you, pardner. I might *have* a fucking pussy, but I've never *been* a fucking pussy!"

"Anyways. In a fit of fucking rage I grabbed my granddaddy's record. And then I fucking broke it right across that motherfucker's pretty face. I mean I cut his pretty face up good too. Sliced his fucking pretty face right up." Candi ran her finger like it was the blade of a knife down along Mike's cheek slowly. "All the way from his fucking eyeball, right on down to his upper fucking lip. And let me tell you. He wasn't pretty no more after that, pardner, I guaran-goddamn-tee ya that!"

"Course. Like the pussy with a dick he turned out to be. *He* fucking called the cops. And guess what? *Only* yours truly," she pointed to herself, "went to the Harris County Hotel that night."

"You mean they only arrested you? Not him?"

"Yessirree. And all because of this goddamned fucking pussy of mine right here between my legs! Let me tell you somethin, pardner. My fucking pussy is a blessing and a curse. It's got me in and outta trouble my whole fucking life."

✱✱✱

Mike and Candi drove on northwards on Highway 6. Eventually they pulled into Calvert, Texas. Much to their surprise, at the heart of this sleepy little Texas town furrowed along both sides of the main street with antique and junktique stores, Mike and Candi discovered a gourmet chocolatier.

"COCOAMODA," Candi said slowly, reading the sign aloud, "Wow. Sounds fancy, huh? This place is new! Well I'll be damned. Of all the places in the fucking world to find a fucking gourmet chocolate shop. I never expected it to be right here in Calvert!" At Candi's insistence they stopped at Cocoamoda.

Inside Cocoamoda you will discover a beautiful wooden bar where they serve coffee and scones. A full dinner menu is offered and the ambiance is stylish and tasteful. They don't serve alcohol; however, it is BYOB, so you may bring a bottle of wine to enjoy with dinner. Cocoamoda serves as a chic oasis where the weary traveler or literary tourist may enjoy a brief respite from the sundry joys and travails of a Texas road trip.

"Wow! Look at all this fucking chocolate," Candi said. She leaned against the glass of a massive case displaying dozens of flavors of gourmet chocolate, "It's kinda like we died, pardner. And it turned out we actually got to go to the good place, huh?"

"Get whatever you want," Mike said. His deft and profitable use of the Socratic Method in their last conversation had put him in a good mood.

"I always do," Candi said, swaying her hips sideways and bumping against him. "So these are truffles, huh? I've always wanted to fucking try one."

A man walked up behind the case, smiled and said, "How may I help you?"

"They all have such cool fucking names," Candi said, pressing her finger against the glass. "What's that one? And how do you say it?"

"Cassis," Mike said.

"What's in it?"

The man behind the case said, "It is dark chocolate flavored with currant."

"Ok," Candi said, "So what's that?"

Mike chimed in, "Currant is a berry, kind of like a grape. It's a-"

"So then it's like chocolate with grape flavorin? I reckon that could be good. As long as the grape flavorin doesn't taste like that grape flavorin they put in cough syrup. I fucking hate that shit."

Candi didn't seem to notice that the man behind the case simply smiled, listening carefully to each of her comments, all the while her breath fogging up the glass as she studied the truffles. Mike did notice his smile, and couldn't decide whether to be chagrined or gratified by Candi's companionship.

"What's that one?" Candi said. "Look there, pardner. They call that one, Inspiration. Cool name for a truffle, huh?"

The man behind the case said, "It is white chocolate, madam, infused with rose petal."

"You're shittin me, right?"

"No, madam"

Candi turned to Mike and said, "Is this guy tryin to fucking pull a fast one on me? I mean did you put him up to this while I was in the fucking bathroom?" She playfully punched

Mike in the chest and laughed. "I swear to fucking God. If this is your idea of gettin back at me for the jackelope thing then-"

Mike raised his hands, stilled Candi's fists and said, "It's not a joke, Candi. It's not uncommon to infuse candies, foods or even wine with roses."

"It's uncommon in Calvert fucking Texas, pardner!"

The man behind the case laughed along with her. "Would madam care to sample the Inspiration truffle?"

"You mean to tell me that that truffle is white chocolate? *And* it fucking tastes like roses?"

The man behind the case nodded.

"Well then. No samplin necessary," Candi said, providing a drum roll on top of the display case, leaving smudge marks on the glass. "I'll take *two* of the," she raised her hands and made quotations marks with her fingers, "*Inspiration* truffles." She turned to Mike and smiled. She leaned over and whispered in his ear, "Thanks, pardner."

Mike felt her breath on his ear as she whispered to him. It was hot and sexy.

The man behind the glass case said, "Anything else?"

"Anything else?" Mike asked her, "Anything?"

"Nope," Candi said, slapping Mike's ass playfully, "I got everythin I need already."

After they left Cocoamoda they walked down the main street of Calvert. "Can you believe they fucking wrapped up this chocolate in tissue paper? And then they fucking put it in a fancy little box. And then they put it in this beautiful fucking gift bag!" Candi held up a black gift bag with string handles bearing the name Cocoamoda. "All that fuss over fucking chocolate! I feel like I just went shoppin at Neiman Marcus in the Galleria."

Mike watched her strut towards the car, swinging the bag playfully.

"Maybe on our way back to Houston," Candi said, "We'll stop back by here in Calvert during business hours. And go to a few antique stores. I wish they didn't close so fucking early in small towns. That's the only drawback to livin in a small town. Well," Candi said, "maybe not the only drawback..."

"So you like antiques?" Mike said.

"Well I like antique stores," Candi said. "Don't worry though, pardner. I don't wanna buy anythin. I never buy anythin in antique stores. I just like to look at all the cool shit from the good old days. These days, you know. They just don't make shit like they did back in the olden days."

"Sounds good to me," Mike said. "I actually like antiques stores too."

"Yep," she said, "Goin to an antique store is like goin to a fucking museum. Except it doesn't cost an arm and a fucking leg to get into an antique store."

They got to the car. Mike unlocked it and they opened the doors. The inside of the car was like an oven and the Texas heat hit them both in the face.

"This chocolate is gonna melt if I don't eat it real quick," Candi said. They got into the car. Mike started the engine and turned up the air conditioning. "Just so you know," Candi said, "I'm not fucking sharin my chocolate with you." She reached into the bag. Mike smiled and watched her dig through the white, brown and black tissue paper.

Candi finally pulled out the little box and opened it quickly. She pulled out a truffle and took a bite. "This is the best fucking chocolate I've ever had! Ever!"

"Can I have a taste?" Mike said.

"Sorry pardner," Candi said. "You just don't deserve white chocolate flavored with roses…"

✳ ✳ ✳

Later on down the road, Mike saw something along the highway. It reminded him of their conversation earlier that day, when they were just leaving Hearne.

It also made him recall the paper he wrote for his African American Literature class at Yale. Even though the *The Adventures of Huckleberry Finn* was not on the class syllabus and therefore not required reading, at Mike's request the professor allowed him to write his semester paper on it. For the topic of the paper Mike decided to address Twain's literary reaction to racism, with a careful analysis of the narration, use of primary and secondary character voice within the narrative, and uses of the word nigger.

Mike recalled a crucial passage from the final chapter of *The Adventures of Huckleberry Finn*, at the very end of the novel, when Huck says:

> "The first time I catched Tom private I asked him what was his idea, time of the evasion? —what it was he'd planned to do if the evasion worked all right and he managed to set a nigger free that was already free before? And he said, what he planned in his head from the start, if we got Jim out all safe, was for us to run him down the river on the raft, and have adventures plumb to the mouth of the river, and then tell him about his being free, and take him back up home on a steamboat, in style, and pay him for his lost time, and write word ahead and get out all the niggers around, and have them waltz him into town with a torchlight procession and a brassband, and then he would be a hero, and so would we."

"Can you fucking believe I broke my granddaddy's record?" Candi said to Mike, interrupting his recollection. "Goddamn me for it too. Just like that. I broke my granddaddy's record." She snapped her fingers like a noose around her own neck, "Goddamn me. Yep. I went and broke my granddaddy's record…"

Chapter 9

Bremond, Texas; Beers at the Dry Bean Saloon;
How Mike and Candi related to Lonesome Dove;
And the Ballads of Leonard Wallace and Christopher Paulsen

After driving northwards on Highway 6 for a little while longer, Candi said, "Here. Take Highway 14 right up here."

"How much farther until we get to where we're going?" Mike said.

"You're almost there," Candi said.

✳ ✳ ✳

Candi flipped through Mike's copy of *Moby Dick*, reading passages aloud. She flipped a few more pages and then said, "Oh my fucking God! This part makes me think of you, pardner!"

Mike tried to note the page number but couldn't see it.

"This is the part where Ishmael talks about how whalin ships gave him his education. You know. And how whalin taught him everythin about life. Anyways. Ishmael says right here- For a whale-ship was my Yale College and my Harvard. Pretty cool, huh? Melville talks about your fucking school right here in this famous book."

"I guess," Mike said, "you've never heard of *The Great Gatsby*."

"*The Great*, whatsy?"

"*The Great Gatsby*. It's just one of the many classic American novels that mention Yale."

"Oh really?" Candi said. "Who's it by?"

"Why do you want to know?"

"I don't know. I just thought I'd ask."

"It's by F. Scott Fitzgerald"

"Hey, pardner. Wait a sec. Why the fuck did you just ask me why I wanted to know who the author of that fucking book was?"

"I guess I just thought you wouldn't know anyway. So why bother asking."

"You know what I think? I think that you think, just because you know certain things like who F. Scott Fitzgerald is. That that makes you smarter than people who don't?"

"Not smarter, I guess. But definitely more educated."

"More educated about what though?"

"More educated meaning you have an education. A college education doesn't necessarily make you smarter than others. But it definitely broadens your horizons. It exposes you to new ideas, information and opinions that you might never have considered before. That's all I meant."

"I don't buy it, pardner. I don't think that's all you meant. In fact. I fucking think you meant a whole lot more than you're sayin out loud."

"Oh really? Like what?"

"*I* think that *you* think. That you're really *better* than other people. All because you know shit like who F. Scott Fitzgerald is. And what the word theodicy means. And what Samuel Clemens middle name was. *I* think that *you* think. That knowin shit like that makes *you* better than other people. *Smarter* than other people"

"I already told you. It's not necessarily about smarter. It's about more educated."

"No fucking way, pardner. If it was all about just bein more educated and havin broad horizons or whatever. Then you wouldn't always be trottin out your trivia. And sittin up on your high horse all the fucking time. I mean fucking listen to yourself for once. Goddammit. Who are you tryin to fucking impress with all that worthless trivia?"

"Just because you don't know it, Candi, doesn't make it worthless. Education, learning and knowledge are never worthless."

"You're dead fucking wrong, pardner. I think education can be a complete waste of your fucking time. Let me tell you. If all your education gets you is a piece of paper to hang on your wall. And a hard-on for how much more you know than other people do. Then it's a complete waste of time in my fucking book. I mean look at you? You're educated. And when I found you at that truck-stop you were fucking lost. Hell! You were ABC remember?"

"That's ABD"

"Whatever! You were depressed. Drugged and fucking miserable. And how much did that fucking Yale education cost you, pardner? Cause I'd demand my fucking money back if I was you!"

"Why do you always do this, Candi? For Chrissakes. You always turn everything we talk about into a personal attack on me."

"Oh take it like a real man for once in your fucking life. You know why I fucking do it? Because I gotta constantly remind you. That I'm not as impressed by you as everybody else is. I know that you knowing all that fucking trivia impresses your usual group of smarty-pants college friends. In fact. I bet that's exactly why they're your friends. But out here in the real world, pardner. That shit just makes you seem like a pretentious asshole. That's all I'm sayin. Don't fucking take it personal."

"What? Don't take it personal? Are you fucking kidding me? Ok. Well how's this for personal? You're just a dumb- you're just a dumb..."

"I'm just a dumb what?"

"You're nothing but a dumb-"

"Come on you pretentious fuckwad. Say it! I'm nothin but a dumb what?"

Mike couldn't bring himself to say aloud the word he was thinking.

"Dammit, pardner. You'd feel a hell of a lot better if you'd just for once. Go right ahead and say what you're thinkin out loud. I mean you're not gonna hurt my fucking feelings. Dammit. And I really thought I had you there for a minute, too. I really thought I was gonna get you to say it out loud."

"Just leave me alone, Candi."

"Hey, pardner. When I said before that you didn't impress me. I meant the things you normally do for all your smarty-pants college friends. You know. I mean quotin philosophy and dishin out worthless trivia just doesn't fucking impress me. But there are a few. Just a few now. Things about you that *do* fucking impress me. I mean do you think I would've invited you on this," she raised her hands and made quotation marks with her fingers, "*odyssey*, if you hadn't impressed me?"

"Really? Like what things?"

"Well I'm not gonna fucking tell you! Don't ya know? A genteel Southern lady never *sucks* and tells."

Mike chuckled.

"Hey," Candi said, "Just one more thing. I was gonna say it a minute ago." She opened back up the copy of *Moby Dick*. "You know what's kinda hilarious?"

"What?"

"Actually, it's *really* fucking hilarious. And kinda pathetic too"

"What?"

"Ok. We both know Ishmael is a man of the world, right? I mean he's really had some real adventures. And he fucking knows how people really are. Am I right?"

"Right"

"And that's the whole fucking point of him sayin that a whalin ship was his Yale College and his Harvard. Am I right?"

"Right"

"But *you*, pardner," Candi said. "If *you* had to say somethin like that. You know. Somethin that summed up all your adventures. And explained how you learned all about the real world. And how people really are. Well you'd be forced to say- *Yale College* was my Yale College and my Harvard!" She laughed at him. "I mean seriously. That's all you *could* say! Am I right? *Yale College* was my Yale College and my Harvard. You get it?"

"Oh for Chrissakes, Candi. And just when I thought we were-"

"Oh for Chrissakes your fucking self! Don't get your panties all fucking bunched up in your pussy again. I was just teasin you."

Candi continued to flip through the pages of *Moby Dick*. "If it makes you feel any better, pardner," she said, "*I'd* probably have to say- A stranger's dick in my mouth was *my* Yale College and my Harvard. Am I right? I mean that's all I *could* say, right?"

✳✳✳

"It's a hot one... And I fucking need a cold one," Candi said as they rode into Bremond, Texas. "Take a right up here on Jack

Street. See that little street right up there. I'm in the mood for a few beers at the Dry Bean Saloon."

They parked on the corner of Jack and Main Street. Mike quickly realized that this bar was not a tourist destination. And there was certainly nothing *kitsch*, Texas or otherwise, about the Dry Bean Saloon in Bremond, Texas.

"I wonder," Candi said, "if ol Leonard Wallace is still warmin a bar stool inside? He was like an uncle to me."

"Uh, I don't know about this place, Candi. Maybe we should just find another place to get a drink. I imagine they don't get many people from out-of-town. I mean look at us, for Chrissakes."

"Look at *us?*" Candi looked Mike up and down, and then looked herself up and down too. She pulled her blue jean shorts down about a half an inch lower on her ass. "Ok, pardner. I reckon you're right! We don't exactly look like yocals."

"You mean, locals?"

"Nope. Not round these parts I don't. I fucking mean, *yocals.*"

"See. That's exactly what I mean. Let's just go somewhere else and-"

"Hell no, pardner. This is gonna be fucking fun. I mean these yocals don't get out much. So they need all the entertainment they can fucking get. And we're gonna give it to em too. I mean fucking look at us! You! You look like a fucking carpet baggin faggot. And me! Me! I look like your fucking Texas roadtrip whore."

"Carpet bagging faggot?"

"What? You fucking do! I mean let's face it. You are a carpet bagger. Am I right? I mean the only fucking reason you're down in these parts is so you can smouch my stories. And then write that shit in your novel so you can make a million fucking bucks, right?"

"I guess I didn't think you knew what carpet bagger really meant."

"Oh I know what it fucking means, pardner. I just never saw one in real life, that's all. You wanna hear somethin funny?" Candi chuckled. "My daddy used to call everybody who lived north of Dallas a carpet bagger. Whether they smouched from us or not."

"But what about the faggot part?"

"I told you already, dumbass. You never fucking listen, do you? Ok. Try to fucking pay attention this time. When I call you a faggot. I don't fucking mean you like dick in your mouth or up your asshole. I know you like pussy. What I mean is that you're a fucking faggot- a steer. You know. Not a real man."

"Oh thanks a lot. I'm really, really glad I asked."

"I reckon I just thought you'd be used to it by now."

"Trust me, Candi. That's something a man never gets used to."

"Hey, pardner. You oughta know me well enough by now. To know that I don't fucking judge anybody. I mean. Take a gander up and down at me. These yocals are gonna think I'm nothin but your fucking Texas roadtrip whore. And I guess they'd be almost right, huh? After all. We are on a roadtrip."

"You mean, odyssey?" Mike said.

"Yep. Oops. I forgot. Odyssey, that's right. And *I am* a fucking whore. We both know that's the God forsaken truth. And sure. I did suck your dick when we first met. But that was only for a ride over the Baytown Bridge. So technically. I'm a whore, but not a *fucking* whore." Candi leaned over towards Mike, their faces close. She scratched the bottom of his chin softly and said, "Not yet, at least."

Every time Candi touched Mike or brushed up against him he got turned on. And he knew it was only getting worse for him. He hoped that a hotel room tonight would mean they would finally fuck. And the way Candi was acting, his hopes were getting higher.

Candi slid her hand down Mike's chest and then pushed him away. "Don't get any big ideas, pardner. I'm just a good ol fashioned cock-teaser. And don't you ever forget it."

Mike had never used *that word* to describe a woman before. However, he was beginning to agree with Candi about it, and about her. "So," Mike said, "Are we going somewhere else to get a drink?"

"Don't sweat it, pardner," Candi said. "It's not just me. We're all cock-teasers, man or woman, every single last fucking one of us."

A few minutes later, as the Texas sun began its long descent over the idyll town of Bremond, Texas, Mike asked Candi again, "So are we going somewhere else to get a drink?"

"Fuck no, pardner," Candi said. "Forget every other place we ever had a beer together. This is the real fucking deal right here. I'm tellin you. The Dry Bean Saloon is about as Texas beer-joint as a beer-joint gets!"

"That's what I'm afraid of, Candi."

"And if ol Leonard Wallace is still hangin round these parts," Candi said, "He'll make the best goddamn character for a novel anybody ever wrote."

"No, Candi," Mike said without thinking, "I think that's *you*."

Candi perked up and looked straight at Mike, as if genuinely surprised by his comment. "Well, thanks pardner," she said, patting him on the back. "Honest to fucking God. That's really and truly gotta be the nicest thing anybody's ever said to me."

✳✳✳

It was dark and cool inside the Dry Bean Saloon. As the front door opened, the locals leaned back on their barstools in what appeared to be perfect, choreographed synchronicity to catch a glimpse of the strangers entering. Mike and Candi sat down at the bar. Candi still carried the copy of *Moby Dick* with her.

"Well I'll be damned to the bad place," Candi said, patting the old-timer sitting next to her on his back, "If it ain't the world famous rodeo clown, Leonard Wallace! After all these years! Do you remember me?"

The old-timer studied her face for a minute, took a swig from his bottle of Natural Light beer, and then grinned. "Well I'll be damned to the bad place too. You're Don's little girl ain't ya? And all growed up too"

"Yes, sir," Candi said, "That's me. In the fucking flesh"

"Don's little girl!" he said. "Well I'll be damned all the way to the bad place!"

Candi smiled and said, "Yep that's me!"

"Now don't tell me your name. I know I can recall it."

"Candi," she said, quickly, "Candi with an *i*."

"Candi," Leonard said to himself, "Well now. That name don't sound right to me at all."

"Yes, sir," she said, the same respectful tone in her voice, "Don's little girl. Candi, with an i. You remember me, don't you? My daddy used to bring me up here with him after work. And you used to buy me RC Cola and a moon pie."

"Candi just don't sound right to me at all," Leonard said, and then took another long swig from his bottle of beer. "You sure your name ain't Joanna?"

Candi frowned and said, "No, sir. My name's Candi, with an *i*. You remember? Don's little girl, Candi, with an *i*."

"Candi," Leonard recited it to himself again. He finished his beer and then ordered another. "Don's little girl, Candi. Well I'll be damned to the bad place. It is you. Candi! Don's little girl!"

Candi smiled.

"Well I ain't seen you since you was knee-high to a grass-hopper!" Leonard gave her a hug.

"Leonard Wallace, I'd like you to meet Mike," Candi said, "Mike Hemingway." She shot Mike a furtive smile and winked. "Yep. Mike Hemingway here is a big-game hunter. Mike's been huntin and fishin all over the whole wide world. He's hunted and fished in Africa. And in Paris, France. And in China. And even in the forests of fucking Timbuktu. Yep. Mike's pretty much hunted and fished everythin there is to hunt and fish."

Leonard looked Mike up and down. He offered him a hand-shake and said, "Wow! Pleased to meet ya, Mr. Hemingway. You must be one tough hombre!"

Without thinking too much about the charade, Mike accepted Leonard's handshake. *Tough hombre*, Mike thought, *me*, a *tough hombre*? Mike held on to Leonard's handshake as long as possible. Mike savored the firmness of this man's leathery handshake, the macho esteem patent upon his sunburnt face, the approbation apparent in his weathered smile. Mike Hemingway was beside himself elated by this handshake.

"Yep," Candi said, "Mike came to these parts all the way from Houston. Just to kill somethin. He doesn't know what yet. But he's gonna kill somethin before it's all said and done."

* * *

"Coors Light for both of us, please, ma'am," Candi said to the woman behind the bar. Candi turned to Mike and said, "Looky at that black and white picture above the bar right over there. You fucking better know who those guys are, Mr. Worthless-Trivia."

"Sure I do," Mike said. "That's Tommy Lee Jones and Robert Duvall, starring in the film *Lonesome Dove*."

"Nope. You're dead wrong, pardner," Candi said. "I think you mean. That's Captain Woodrow F. Call and Captain Augustus McCrae, Texas Rangers."

"Yeah," Mike said, "Those are the *characters* that Jones and Duvall play in the film."

"They're not *just* characters in a flick, pardner. Those men are larger-than-fucking-life! I mean they're fucking legends."

"Which men are we talking about? The actors or the characters?"

"*I'm* talkin about Captain Woodrow F. Call and Captain Augustus McCrae, Texas Rangers."

"Ok. So we're talking about the characters then," Mike said. "Well, Candi. I hate to break it to you like this. But those men were characters in a novel *before* they were characters in a film. In fact, Larry McMurtry wrote *Lonesome Dove* in 1985. And it won the 1986 Pulitzer Prize. The television mini-series, starring Tommy Lee Jones and Robert Duvall, didn't come out until 1989. Can I hear a round of applause for Mr. Worthless-Trivia man?"

Candi didn't clap. "Well how'd you like that flick?"

"Actually, I never saw it. But I did read the novel."

"What the fuck? What do you mean you never fucking saw that flick? But it's fucking awesome!"

"You think it's better than the book?"

"I never read the book, dumbass," Candi said. "I just figured the book couldn't ever be better than the flick was. So I never fucking bothered to read it. I mean Gus and Call will always be my fucking heroes. They just don't make real men like them anymore."

"That's just it," Mike said, "They're not *real* men. They're just fictional characters."

"Fuck you," Candi said.

"In fact, I'd say that's *why* they're heroes. Because those kinds of heroes. I mean those kinds of real men only exist in fiction. Not in real life." Mike realized his comment upset Candi, so he decided to seize this rare opportunity and get the best of her. "Captain Woodrow F. Call and Captain Augustus McCrae, Texas Rangers," Mike made sure to elaborate their names and titles just like she did, "Are only *real* men and *real* heroes because they don't *really* exist. And they never did."

"That's not true, fuckwad," Candi fired back at him. "I happen to know that Captain Woodrow F. Call and Captain Augustus McCrae, Texas Rangers," she made sure to elaborate their names again, "*were* based on *real* men who really lived back in the Old West."

"Actually, Candi. You're partly right. McMurtry based the character of Woodrow F. Call on a *real* Texas Ranger named Charles Goodnight. And the character of Gus McCrae was based on a *real* cattle-rancher named Oliver Loving."

"Yeah? Well fuck you for bein able to remember their real names," Candi said. "But I was right! You just proved my fucking point. Those characters were based on *real* men. They even went on a real cattle drive. And that Loving dude really died from an Indian attack with the other dude by his bedside. Just like in the fucking movie"

"You mean, just like in *the novel?*"

"I mean. Just like...fuck you fuckwad." Candi ordered them two more beers. "And by the way, pardner. How in the bad place does a carpet-baggin, faggoty-ass Yankee like you know so fucking much about *Lonesome Dove?*"

✳✳✳

Mike recalled taking the class, *Life and Literature of the American Southwest* as an undergraduate in college. The professor for that class was a man named Christopher Paulsen. Mike remembered his curly graying hair, and a kind of Mark Twain mustache. Paulsen would occasionally wear a gray felt cowboy hat. And sometimes he would tuck the pant legs of his dressy slacks into dress cowboy boots. Paulsen was originally from the East Coast, so he never wore them exactly right.

Christopher Paulsen was a Charles Olsen scholar, a literary critic and a published poet. Mike remembered Paulsen telling a story about meeting Alan Ginsberg at some academic conference. Ginsberg, he'd told the class, shocked everybody by showing up at the conference with a naked young man. Mike remembered thinking that someday he would like to have stories like that to tell his students. Thus, over the next few semesters, which included a poetry class and a creative writing class, Christopher Paulsen became Mike's hero.

Mike learned to love reading, and then learned to love the art of the novel under the lectures of Christopher Paulsen. For the class Mike read and studied the works of McMurtry, Cisneros, Anaya, Momaday, Castaneda and Cormac McCarthy, whose novel *Blood Meridian* had changed his life.

Christopher Paulsen was the first true sophisticate Mike ever met. Paulsen spent his summers in the French countryside, and was a connoisseur of fine wine and food. One day in class Paulsen described how he often made a European stir-fry using fresh vegetables, olive oil and cilantro. "And you must use a wooden spoon!" Paulsen had insisted, "Never stir it with anything else."

Enchanted by this novel recipe, Mike took copious notes that day. And on his way home from class he stopped at the local Kroger. It must have taken me hours, Mike reminisced, to wander through the produce section and find all those fresh vegetables and exotic spices. And it must have taken me even longer to cut them up and fill the skillet.

Like a faithful disciple Mike dug a wooden spoon out of the kitchen drawer. "Never stir it with anything else," the master had enjoined him. Back then Mike still lived at home with his parents, who gathered at the small kitchen table that night to gawk at their son and this bizarre ritual. Mike had grilled outside many times with his father. However, he'd never cooked anything on the stove before.

Mike propped his college notebook up next to the stovetop. The ingredients for the European stir-fry were scrawled in the margins of the notebook alongside class notes on *The House on Mango Street*. Mike had regaled his parents about Christopher Paulsen many times. And in response his mother had said things like, "What good is a poetry class, anyway?" and his father had simply made a taciturn face.

So when Mike came home with grocery bags that evening, his parents relished their opportunity to persecute Paulsen's young disciple. To this end, Mike's parents jeered and japed as he awkwardly stirred the fresh vegetables, overheated the olive oil and used way too much spice. His mother said something like, "Who cooks with olive oil, anyway?" and his father simply shook his head in disapproval.

When Mike finally finished, his concoction looked more like paste than a fresh vegetable stir-fry. Undaunted by the quaint rabble sitting in judgment at the kitchen table, the young zealot dipped the sacred wooden spoon into the skillet.

It tasted terrible. And even worse, Mike recalled how the surprised look of disappointment on his face betrayed to his parents just how truly terrible is was. They laughed.

And the European stir-fry would continue to taste terrible until, it must have been months later, Mike finally learned to cut the fresh vegetables just the right size, not overheat the olive oil, and use just the right amount of spices. In fact, anon, Mike would even nuance Paulsen's European stir-fry with his own culling of exotic vegetables and spices, and even eventually learn to pair it with just the right French Bordeaux.

However, that fateful evening, Mike dumped his first stir-fry down the disposal in the sink. He ended up eating his mother's Hamburger Helper for supper.

Mike wondered whether he still had that notebook in a box somewhere. It would be cool, he mused, to thumb through its olive oil spattered pages once again.

Christopher Paulsen had also been a member of a renegade band of environmentally minded Texas poets known as the Eco-Tropic Gang. Other notorious gang members included Paulsen's literary compatriots John Campion and John Herndon. Mike had never even known anybody who recycled before. But with a gusto that lasted only for that semester, he began writing poems about the environment.

One day Paulsen announced to the class that John Herndon would pay them a visit. When that fateful day finally arrived, Mike sat on the front row of the class, as close as he could get to the two men, pen and paper in hand.

Paulsen and Herndon sat together in front of the class that day and simply had a conversation. Mike had never heard anybody talk the way they talked. It was as if there were suddenly and miraculously *two* Christopher Paulsens in the room at once. It was then that Mike realized there were more people in the world like Christopher Paulsen, and perhaps more importantly, someday he could be one of them.

What Mike had always remembered being so magical about Paulsen and Herndon's conversation was the enthusiastic ease with which the two men simply talked about poetry, literature and life. They were like two aging Texas Rangers in a San Antonio beer-joint, recollecting early adventures and misadventures.

Paulsen and Herndon's parley seemed too perfect to be true; as if every single word and every single insight had somehow been scripted by a venturesome novelist. But the wondrous and preternatural thing about their conversation was, Mike had relished that day, that it was *not* scripted.

Like a devoted disciple, Mike scribed down one of their repartees in his notebook. It went like this:

"Writers are thieves," John Herndon had said, "and poets are even worse."

"Yes," Christopher Paulsen had replied, "But what a beautiful thing to steal."

Of course, that evening after class Mike bought two of Herndon's books of poetry and got them signed.

Mike hadn't seen Christopher Paulsen in nearly fifteen years. Mike wondered. If he saw Christopher Paulsen again today, would he still feel the same way about the great master? After all these years, Mike still felt it was Christopher Paulsen who had inspired him to go into academia. It had been Christopher Paulsen who taught him that there was more to poetry than *Gunga Din*. And it had been Christopher Paulsen who made him see books as more than just something to get signed.

And yet, these days, Mike was given over to moments of quiet rage wherein he alleged that Christopher Paulsen was everything that was right *and* everything that was wrong with academia. These moments always made Mike feel guilty, kind of like Judas Iscariot must have felt.

Of course, Mike reflected, the allegation that Christopher Paulsen was *both* everything right and everything wrong about academia, might not be such a bad thing after all. Perhaps the academic life is just like any other life. Perhaps the academic life is fraught with pitfalls for *both* authenticity and inauthenticity, providing opportunities to *both* affirm and deny the real world.

Christopher Paulsen, Mike concluded, might be everything wrong about academia; *but*, unlike Mike and so many others, at least Paulsen was everything that was right too. Somewhere along the way Mike had lost the part that was right, and now, everything was just wrong.

For Mike, fifteen years later, there was only the logic of an existence which is capable, never comprehensible. He wondered if Christopher Paulsen would agree…

"Let me guess," Candi said, "You took a class and wrote a fucking paper?"

"Pretty much," Mike said to her.

✳ ✳ ✳

"Goddammit," Candi said, gazing at the picture above the bar. "I love me some Captain Augustus McCrae, Texas Ranger." She took a swig off her beer. "Remember that part in *Lonesome Dove*? When Miss Lorena gets kidnapped by that half-breed Indian outlaw Blue Duck? And then she gets raped by all those Indians and Mexicans. And those two white-trash buffalo hunters too? And then Jake Spoon, who promised to get her out of Texas, just fucking forgets all about her. And nobody really gives a shit because she's just a whore? Remember that?"

"Yeah, I remember"

Candi sighed and said, "Wouldn't it be great to know. That if you got kidnapped by a bunch of assholes. You could fucking know that somebody like Gus was gonna to leave the herd. And ride off and single-handedly rescue you?"

"I think I'd prefer not getting kidnapped," Mike said.

"I gotta admit," Candi said. "I never wanted to be Marsha Brady or Rory Gilmore. Or any of those other fucking cunts on TV. Nope. All growin up. I just always wanted to be Miss Lorena from *Lonesome Dove*."

"I don't know," Mike said. "I think you would've made a great Marsha Brady. Of course," he said, elbowing her, "If you'd played Marsha, then *The Brady Bunch* would've become *The Wild Bunch*." Mike laughed.

"You know what, pardner?" Candi said, laughing, "I think that's the second nicest thing anybody ever said to me. You're on a fucking roll today. Keep that shit up."

Mike raised his beer bottle up for a toast. Candi raised hers too and they clinked them together.

"Yep. I always wanted to be Miss Lorena and have Gus come save me." Candi grimaced and said, "Unfortunately. All I've ever fucking met was a bunch of Jake Spoons."

"Even though Jake Spoon was a bad guy," Mike said, "I could never believe it when Gus and Call hung him. I mean how could you hang your own friend? Even if he was a bad guy and a criminal?"

"That's why, pardner. You'll never fucking be Gus. And you'll never even fucking be a Texas Ranger. Like Jake Spoon was when he was younger."

"That's fine with me. Danger's definitely not my middle name." He raised his beer bottle for another clink, but Candi just stared at the picture above the bar.

"Hey," Candi said. "Remember the part in *Lonesome Dove?* When that uppity bartender in San Antonio is rude to Gus and Call? Remember that? He complains about cowboys draggin in so much dust. And then he calls Gus an old-timer. And then Gus puts the coin on the counter to pay for the whiskey. And when that uppity bartender reaches for the coin Gus grabs his fucking hair. And then swings his fucking face down on the bar," Candi slammed her hand down on the bar, "and breaks his motherfucking nose." She smiled. "I fucking love that fucking part."

"You would," Mike said.

"And then Gus pulls out that really really big fucking pistol of his. And then sticks it," she made a gun with her hand and pressed her barreled fingers against Mike's cheek, "sticks it like this and then," she shoved Mike's face sideways towards the picture over the bar. "And then turns that uppity bartender's bloody face towards that picture of him and Call hanging up in the bar. And then Gus says to him- Back in the old days we were heroes. And people respected us."

Mike jerked his face away from her gun hand. "Stop it, Candi."

"I fucking love that part. And then Gus just orders another drink like nothin fucking happened. And then that uppity bartender says- You just broke my nose you damned old sonuvvabitch! And then Gus just fucking smacks him," she slapped Mike across the face.

"For Chrissakes, Candi! Cut it out!"

"I mean Gus just smacks that uppity bartender with his pistol. And knocks him the fuck out. I fucking love that fucking part!"

"Jesus Christ, Candi," Mike said, rubbing his face.

"You're such a pussy." She studied Mike's face. "You know what, pardner? You kinda remind me of that uppity bartender sometimes." She took a swig from her beer.

"Very funny,' Mike said.

"Ok, Mr. Smarty Pants Worthless Trivia guy," Candi said. "If you're sooo fucking smart. Then why don't you tell me what kind of gun Gus had?"

"What do you mean what kind of gun?"

"I mean what kind of gun did Gus carry? You know. That big fucking pistol he hit that uppity bartender with."

"I don't know," Mike said, "Happy now? There's actually something I don't know."

"It was an 1847 Walker Colt," Candi said. "The biggest and most powerful black powder repeating handgun ever made!"

"And how do you know that?"

Candi smiled and said, "I took a class."

✱✱✱

Leonard Wallace leaned back on his barstool. He looked Candi up and down and then said, "You gotta real nice ass there, sweetheart!"

"Knock it off, Leonard," Candi said playfully, yet respectfully, "I think you've had a few too many Natty Lights there, pardner."

"Nah, I'm serious, sweetheart," Leonard said, ogling her breasts. "Why don't ya bring that sweet ass right over here," he patted his knee, "and sit right here on my lap?"

"I said knock it off, Leonard."

"Aww, come on sweetheart," Leonard said, adjusting his hard-on. "I gotta big ol pistol right here in these Wrangler blue jeans. And you can play with it if ya wanna."

Candi frowned at him. "Seriously, Leonard. Cut it out. That's just gross."

Mike finished off his beer, hoping Candi would suggest they go.

"You can sit right here on my lap and make my day, sweetheart."

"Oh, I'll make your fucking day alright, pardner," Candi said to Leonard, "Just like Gus made that uppity bartender's day."

"Simmer down there," Leonard said. "A girl shouldn't wear what you're wearin, and not expect a real man to ask her to sit on his lap for awhile."

"*You* simmer down," Candi said. "Why don't you just go home and sleep it off."

Mike noticed the bartender and few of the locals watching them now.

"Gimme another round," Leonard said to the bartender. "And give these folks here another round too. On me!"

"No thanks," Candi said to the bartender, "I've had just about enough."

Candi started to get up off the barstool, but hesitated. "Hey Leonard," she said, "You ever read *Lonesome Dove?*"

Mike was glad she changed the subject.

"Nope," Leonard said.

"You ever read *Moby Dick?*"

"Nope"

"Anybody in here," Candi said loudly, and then stood up from her barstool and yelled above the din of the bar, "Anybody in here ever read this book, *Moby Dick?*"

Nobody answered. Everybody mostly looked puzzled.

Mike placed his hand gently on her arm and said, "Candi, don't you think we should be getting back on the road?"

She gently removed his hand. "Anybody in here," Candi yelled again. "Anybody in here ever read the book, *Lonesome Dove?* And watchin the movie doesn't fucking count either!"

Nobody answered. Again, everybody mostly just looked puzzled.

"But they're classics!" Candi announced to everyone. "I mean they're fucking classics of American literature!" She shot Mike a smirk and then said, "For Chrissakes!"

"Hey," Mike whispered to her, "Why the hell are you picking on me? I didn't do anything!"

"I got me a classic of American literature right here," Leonard said, fondling his hard-on and chuckling. *"Moby Dick,"* he grunted, "dick."

Candi sat back down on her bar stool. She frowned and then finished her beer.

"So, Mr. Hemingway," Leonard said. "You ride up here all the way from Houston?"

"Yes I did," Mike said.

"Let me tell ya what. Houston is nothin but a cesspool these days," Leonard said. "I hate it. It's worse than goddamn jail if ya ask me."

"Well nobody asked you," Candi said, and then whispered under her breath, "You damned old drunken fool."

"Nope. I'd never go back to Houston," Leonard said. "I been workin in the cemetery here for darn near twenty-five years now. And I don't reckon I need nothin else. And I especially don't need to ever go back to Houston, Texas. It's worse than goddamn jail."

"But you used to love Houston, Leonard," Candi said, resting her hand affectionately on his shoulder, "You remember that, don't you? Back in the old days?"

"That ain't true. I never did like Houston none. It's a cesspool now," Leonard said, sermonizing from his mount atop the barstool. "Houston's nothin but a big ol cesspool full of junkies, queers, spooks and whores. What they need is one of them hurricanes like hit New Orleans. Just wash all that filth right outta the city. Yep. Nothin but junkies, queers, spooks and whores."

"Hey, Leonard. Remember when Daddy and me went with you to the Houston Livestock Show and Rodeo, that year? And you won that award for bein the bravest rodeo clown in all of Texas?"

"Yep. I sure took a lot of tumbles in my time."

"Remember, Leonard. When you used to say to me- Make sure the tumble that finally gets ya is the tumble ya take off an *unbroken* horse? Remember that? I never forgot it."

"Houston ain't got nothin these days," Leonard said, "but a buncha steers and queers."

"My daddy used to say you were the bravest cowboy there ever was," Candi said. "And that you weren't afraid of nothin."

"When I was young," Leonard said, "I used to brag that I wasn't afraid of nothin. Except livin too long." He polished off his beer and then ordered another. He chuckled and said, "Good thing I ain't done that yet!"

The bartender leaned over the bar and asked Candi, "You folks want another round?"

"No thanks, ma'am," Candi said. As the bartender turned around Candi caught her arm and asked, "Ya'll still sell RC Cola and moon pies in here?"

"Nope," the bartender said, "not in years."

Candi stared intensely at Leonard, who was beginning to nod off on his barstool. Mike heard Candi whisper to herself, "Nope. Not in years..."

✱✱✱

Mike and Candi stepped outside the Dry Bean Saloon into the harsh sunlight and dusty streets of Bremond, Texas. "Sorry about Leonard," was all Mike could think to say to Candi.

"Forget about him," Candi said, "I already have."

Mike unlocked the car and they got in. He noticed Candi cradling *Moby Dick*.

"Goddamn Leonard to the fucking bad place!" Candi yelled. "Cock-sucking, mother-fucking, bastard, sonuvvabitch, dick-head, washed-up, dried-out, asshole, asswipe, drunken old fucking pervert!" She stomped her feet and threw *Moby Dick* against the dashboard. It fell on the floorboard of the car. "Fuck! Fuck! Fuck! Fuck! Fuck!!"

"Calm down," Mike said, "What's wrong?"

"You know what's fucking wrong, pardner? When it's all said and done. And you cut through all the fucking bullshit. Life's just... Well life's just all about dick. I mean the human fucking hunt for dick!"

She kicked *Moby Dick*, crumpling and tearing some of the pages. "I mean nobody ever wrote a novel called, *Moby Cunt*! Am I right?"

Mike shrugged.

"Trust me, pardner," Candi said. "Life is like this fucking book right here. Everybody. And I fucking mean men *and* women. Everybody's just lookin for dick. And at the end of this fucked up story. We all just wanna find dick. And get as close to dick as we fucking can. And then fucking hold on to that dick for dear fucking life!"

✱ ✱ ✱

A few minutes later Mike and Candi were still in Bremond, Texas. They sat in the car, stopped at the railroad tracks, waiting for a slow-moving train to go by. Following Candi's tantrum, neither of them had said another word.

"Oh by the way," Candi said, breaking their silence. "Remember when you pointed out to me that *Lonesome Dove* was a novel *before* it was a flick? Remember that?" She leaned forward, bent down and then picked *Moby Dick* back up. She cradled it in her lap again, straightening some of its crinkled pages.

"Yeah," Mike said, "I remember"

"Well, pardner. You were dead fucking wrong about that one."

"I don't think so, Candi."

"Yep. Dead fucking wrong. And here's why. *Actually...* Way the hell back in 1972. Larry McMurtry first wrote *Lonesome Dove* as a flick script. Back then he was gonna call it *The Streets of Laredo*. Thank fucking God *that* didn't turn out to be the title!"

"Anyways," Candi said, "They were gonna make a flick off this script for fucking *Lonesome Dove*. And guess who was gonna fucking star in it?"

Mike shrugged his shoulders.

"John Wayne was gonna play Woodrow Call. And get a load of this shit. Jimmy Stewart was gonna play Gus McCrae! Jimmy fucking Stewart?" Candi laughed. "Can you fucking believe that fucked up shit?"

"I mean don't get me wrong! I fucking love me some Jimmy Stewart. I mean. *The Man Who Shot Liberty Valance* is a fucking classic. Please don't tell me you haven't seen that one?"

"I think I did," Mike said, lying to her, "But it was a long time ago."

"Well thank fucking God for that! Anyways. Jimmy Stewart playin Captain Augustus McCrae, Texas Ranger? What the fuck?"

In her best Jimmy Stewart voice, Candi drawled, "Uh, yeah, uh… It ain't dyin I'm talkin about, Woodrow, it's livin!" She slapped her knees and laughed. "Anyways. John Wayne backed out. And then the whole project went to the bad place. So McMurtry put that script on his shelf. And then in 1985. He went and wrote it all down as *Lonesome Dove*, the novel." She crossed her arms and smiled.

"So see pardner. You were dead wrong all along. Captain Woodrow F. Call and Captain Augustus McCrae, Texas Rangers," she made sure to elaborate their names like they did before. "They were both characters in a flick *before* they were characters in a novel!"

"I had no idea," Mike said.

"Yep"

"Wow"

"Well," Candi said, "Aren't you gonna ask me?"

"Ask you what?"

"Ask me how *I* know so goddamn much about *Lonesome Dove?*"

"Actually," Mike said, "I *was* going to ask you that."

"So ask me then, motherfucker"

"Candi," Mike said, "How do you know so goddamn much about *Lonesome Dove?*"

"Well. Funny you should ask me that, pardner. My daddy taught me everythin there is to know about *Lonesome Dove*. He was kinda like the biggest fucking *Lonesome Dove* fan ever. And well. You see. My daddy read the novel *and* he watched the flick."

Chapter 10

Trapped at a railroad crossing;
How Mike was reminded of an obscure short story;
and Candi related the crimes and misdemeanors
of her Uncle Bill; The Ballad of Twat-Legs Tracy;
And how Candi argued for the nobility of suicide
but Mike remained silent and unconvinced

Thirty minutes later Mike and Candi still sat in the car at the railroad tracks in Bremond. You see, that slow-moving train had eventually crawled to a screeching halt, trapping Mike and Candi there. And nobody in town even seemed to notice.

"O Muse! the causes and the crimes relate;
What goddess was provok'd, and whence her hate;
For what offense the Queen of Heav'n began
To persecute so brave, so just a man"

✳✳✳

"Well, pardner," Candi said, "Looks like we're gonna be trapped here together for a spell. So I got a great fucking idea. Why don't *you* tell *me* a story for a change?"

"I don't think I know any stories off the top of my head."

"This? Comin from the jerk who wants to write a fucking novel? You know. If you really want this novel to be good. Then you're gonna need more than just," she raised her fingers and made quotation marks in the air, "*my* stories."

"Thanks so much for the advice," Mike said. "What are you my editor now?"

"Editor?" Candi said, "Oh fuck no. I'm your white chocolate inspiration, pardner. Kinda like that truffle, remember?"

"How about we consider you my *muse*?" Mike said.

"Sure. As long as that's not some fancy-schmancy word for cunt"

Mike chuckled. "It's not, Candi. You see. The ancient Greeks believed the Muses were goddesses who inspired their poets and musicians."

"Really? Huh. That's kinda fucking cool. A goddess, huh? Me? A goddess?"

"There were different Muses. The Muses inspired men through dance, music, poetry and extemporaneous speeches."

"Extempa-what-kinda speeches?"

"Extemporaneous," Mike repeated the word slowly to her. "You know. Like a story that suddenly and inexplicably just comes to your mind."

"Kinda like when you're a little kiddo. And you ask your daddy to tell you a story right before bed? You know. Not the kinda story you read in a fucking book. But the kinda bedtime story you just make up. Right off the top of your fucking head. Am I right?"

"Sure"

"Well. Sounds good to me, pardner. Ok, then. I'll be your motherfucking Muse. And you're gonna tell me a fucking bedtime story."

"What?"

"Don't get me wrong," she said, and winked at him. "I'm not sayin we're goin to bed together. I just mean we're gonna pretend I'm a little girl. And that you're my daddy. And it's my bedtime. And let's pretend I just asked you to tell me a bedtime story."

"I don't know, Candi."

"Come on, pardner. And it has to be a bedtime story you just make up. Right off the top of your fucking head. You know, ex-temper-your-anus-ly..."

"I told you already," Mike said, "I don't know any stories off the top of-"

"That's just it. This is gonna be the kinda story you don't have to know off the top of your head. Just fucking make that shit up as you go along. It's easy." She turned in her seat to face him, sitting cross-legged. "Don't sweat it, pardner. I'm your mother-fucking Muse, remember?"

Candi raised her hands, made quotation marks in the air, and then lowered her hands slowly towards him, wriggling her fingers as if casting a spell. "I'm your motherfucking Muse," she said, as if uttering a magic incantation, "I'm your motherfucking, cocksucking Muse... I'm your fucking Muse..."

"Ok, for Chrissakes," Mike said. "I'll tell you a story."

"A bedtime story"

"Right, a bedtime story"

"And be sure," Candi said, "It has lots and lots and lots and lots and lots and lots and lots of violence in it. Let me tell you. I just fucking love a story with lots of blood and guts and gore. Come on, pardner. Really gross me out, ok?"

"Somehow, Candi. I think grossing *you* out might just be impossible.'

"Remember. I'm your fucking muse."

"Ok. Just give me a second to think of how the story starts. You know, Candi. The first line of a novel is the most important sentence in the entire book," Mike said, echoing his undergraduate creative writing seminars.

"I'm waitin," Candi said. She yawned an overdramatic yawn, cupping her hand over her mouth for emphasis. "Come on Mr. Hemingway. It's a fucking bedtime story not a," she made quotation marks with her fingers, "*classic*, of American literature."

"Ok," Mike said, "It starts with these two brothers who-"

"No wait! Start the story with- Once upon a time..."

"Are you going to let *me* tell this bedtime story or not?"

"Sure," Candi said. "It's just. It's just that all the best stories I ever heard. In my entire fucking life. Especially bedtime stories. Well they all started with- Once upon a time... That's all I'm sayin."

"Ok, fine. Once upon a time..."

Candi smiled and settled back into her seat.

"Happy now?"

"Yep"

"Now," Mike said, "Once upon a time... There were these two brothers. They were headed home after working at a cotton gin for about a month. This was during the Great Depression. In the nineteen-thirties-"

"I fucking know when the Great Depression was."

"Sorry. So these two brothers are in the middle of nowhere. Way out in the woods. And one night they decide to pitch camp and get some sleep. In the middle of the night the younger brother wakes up and decides to use the railroad tracks for a pillow. He thinks that if a train approaches he'll hear it and have plenty of time to move off the tracks."

"What a fucking dumbass!" Candi said. "Everybody and their mother-in-law knows that trains hardly ever blow their horns way out in the fucking country. I mean they only blow their fucking horns in the city! I'll bet he never even saw it comin!" She raised her arm, dragged her finger across her throat like the blade of a knife and made a gurgling noise.

"Do you mind?" Mike said. "Let me tell the story, for Chrissakes."

"Alright"

"Well later that night the train did *not* blow its horn," Mike said, chagrined, "because *apparently* everybody knows that trains only blow their horns in the city."

Candi smiled, winked at him, and then giggled with satisfaction.

"Later that night the older brother was awakened by a thundering train passing by. Now listen to this." Mike felt a surge of excitement. "The train never saw him sleeping on the tracks. So the train never even slowed down. The younger brother's body was torn all to pieces. Body parts everywhere. Blood all over the trees and the grass. Guts strewn all over the railroad tracks."

Candi purred as she nestled into her seat like a child into her bed. She folded her hands, resting her face on them like a pillow. "Go on," she said, her eyes closed now.

Mike felt pride and said, "The body was torn to shreds. But somehow the head had been severed clean and rolled near the older brother's backpack."

Candi opened one eye and said in a childish voice, "Holy motherfucking shit, Daddy! This is the fucking awesomest bedtime story ever!" She closed her eyes again, still smiling.

"So the older brother awakens and finds the severed head right there next to him. After a few hours of shock the older brother hears coyotes howling in the distance. So he knows he must do something."

"He realizes that he can't take the body back home for burial. It's just too shredded. So he decides to take the severed head home. So at least his parents will have something to bury. He empties his backpack and dumps his supplies into the bloody grass. And then he puts the head inside. He knows it will take him at least three days to reach home."

"I thought you said you never saw that flick?"

"What?"

"I thought you said you never saw *Bring Me the Head of Alfredo Garcia* before?"

"I haven't"

"Are you sure you're makin this story up right off the top of your head?"

"Yeah, I am. You're my muse, remember?"

"Oh yeah"

"So after a day's walk, the brother stops to sleep for the night. He builds a campfire and makes dinner. And then, during the first night, his younger brother's severed head starts talking to him. And when he pulls the head out of the bag it-"

"Daddy," Candi said in the same childish voice as before, "How's the younger brother's severed head able to talk?"

"That's never explained"

Candi opened her eyes and said, "What do you mean it's never explained?"

"It's just never explained"

"Hold up there, pardner," Candi said, and then sat up from her mock slumber. "There's gotta be an explanation for how a severed head talks. I mean maybe a wicked witch cast a fucking spell? Or maybe the older brother is a fucking wizard and knows magic? Or maybe an angel came down from fucking Heaven and worked a miracle? I mean fucking think of somethin!"

"There doesn't always have to be an explanation, Candi. You see. In literature, in some stories, events like talking severed heads don't have to be explained."

"They fucking do if you want your story to be believable."

"It's a literary genre," Mike said. "What I mean is. It's a kind of story. It's called magic realism. In magic realism strange events take place, usually to illustrate a particular point the author is trying to make. And no explanation is ever offered."

"The characters in magic realism stories act as if talking severed heads," Mike paused to conjure up other notable examples, "or old men with enormous wings, or the ghost of a murdered daughter, or an Indian boy with a huge dripping nose and telepathic powers are simply mundane, everyday events. No explanation is ever given."

"Well, why the fuck not?"

"The author of the story is trying to make a point about how humans perceive reality."

"But that's *not* reality. I mean none of that shit you listed is really real reality. So how come the author doesn't make a fucking point about reality using oh, I don't know, reality maybe?"

"Never mind, Candi. Just forget the whole story. For Chrissakes. Sometimes talking to you is like talking to, like talking to-"

"A severed head in a backpack?" Candi laughed and slapped her knees.

"It's absolutely incredible to me," Mike said. "You have absolutely no aesthetic sensibilities, whatsoever."

"And you know what else I don't have, pardner? I don't have a motherfucking clue what you just said to me. Oh I know. It was probably another one of your literary," she raised her hands and made quotation marks, "*john rahz.*"

"Candi. Don't you remember when we talked about our favorite films? And I told you about that branch of philosophy called aesthetics?"

"Yep, I remember"

"Aesthetics asks the question- What is beauty?"

"Fuck yeah, I remember that. That's when I told you my three favorite flicks were *The Wild Bunch* and *Pat Garret and Billy the Kid* and *Blazing Saddles*. And your favorite was, uh... What the fuck was it called again? Some fucking foreign flick, right?"

"Yeah. It's an Italian film by Federico Fellini. It's called-"

"I reckon I just don't fucking understand why people like foreign flicks so much," Candi said. "I mean to me. Flicks should have lots and lots and lots and lots and lots and lots and lots of explosions. And even more fucking. And then more fucking explosions. And then even more fucking. Kinda like that flick *Sky Scraper* with Anna Nicole Smith. Not one of my favorite flicks. But a damn fucking good one."

"And I said you didn't have any aesthetic sensibilities," Mike said, smiling, "What was I thinking?"

"And those annoying fucking subtitles! Let me tell you, pardner. Any fucking flick with subtitles is pure fucking shit in my book."

"Well I can see why you wouldn't be a big fan of subtitles," Mike said. "I mean after all, they do require reading."

"Fuck you, pardner."

Mike smiled at her.

"It's just fucking weird to me, you know," Candi said. "I just don't get people like you. It's like you only watch flicks so you can try to figure out what they mean. You're always lookin for some hidden meaning. Everything is fucking symbolic. Or a fucking metaphor. Or some fucking puzzle!"

"It's like your favorite flick. That stupid fucking *La Dumbass Vita* flick. Or whatever the fuck it was called. I mean you musta yacked on and on about that fucking flick for fucking ever. You were like- What does that statue of Christ flying over Rome *really* mean?"

Candi raised her hands up, as if to the heavens, and said, "Who gives a *flying* fuck! Who gives a shit what the fucking statue represents or stands for? Who fucking cares? I mean whatever happened to just sittin back in front of a flick with some popcorn? Holdin your girl's hand? And just fucking bein entertained?"

"It's like I told you, Candi. Aesthetics is the philosophical inquiry into what is beautiful. It's about expressing the human condition through a chosen medium like film, or the novel."

"You wanna see somethin beautiful? I'll show you somethin beautiful."

Mike shrugged and said, "Sure, I guess."

Candi leaned back against the passenger side door of the car. She spread her legs, pulled one side of her short's leg up and over to the side, revealing her pussy.

Mike stared at her pussy until she finally sat back up straight.

"I may not have any, *aesthetics*," Candi said, struggling with the pronunciation of the word, "But I've got the most beautiful pussy east or west of the Pecos, pardner. Am I right?"

Mike shook off the image of her pussy long enough to say, "How *very* Georgia O'Keefe of you."

"How very what?"

"Georgia O'Keefe"

"Did you just say- Georgia o *queef?*"

"No," Mike said, "Georgia O'Keefe. She was an artist who painted flowers that everybody claims look like vaginas."

"Oh my fucking God," Candi said. "I can't fucking believe this. I just fucking showed you my pussy. My beautiful pussy! And all you can do is make smart-ass comments about flowers and fine art? I mean. That's what you say to a woman after she shows you her pussy? Wow! Let me tell you somethin, pardner. You're the one with no aesthetic sensibilities."

✳ ✳ ✳

Mike and Candi were still trapped at the railroad crossing.

Candi crossed her legs Indian style and said, "I'll tell you a fucked up bedtime story about a train way out in the country. If you wanna hear it? And unlike your story. This fucked up shit really fucking happened."

"Only if you tell me the," Mike lifted his hands into the air, making quotation marks with his hands, "*john rah* of your story?"

"Oh I'll show you some fucking aesthetics," Candi said. She spit her gum out the window and said, "Anyways. The story starts-"

"Hey, wait a second, there," Mike said, "What about- Once upon a time? I thought all the best stories began with- Once upon a time?"

"Like I was sayin. This story starts with this twelve year old girl. Way out in the sticks. One day she was just wanderin from cow pasture to cow pasture. Just lookin for somethin, anythin she could shoot and kill with her trusty old 22 rifle."

"It was almost dark. And she was about to give up and head back home. So she decided to cut across her uncle's property. And follow the railroad tracks home."

"So she wouldn't get lost?" Mike said.

"Now look who's interruptin." Candi mimicked his voice, "Are you gonna to let *me* tell this bedtime story or not?"

"Ok, sorry"

"So this young girl crosses her uncle's pasture and goes into the woods. She finds the railroad tracks and starts followin em home. Then she rounds this sharp bend in the tracks. And right smack dab in the middle of the railroad tracks she spots her uncle. He's just sittin there in a green lawn chair. Right *on* the tracks. He's holdin a half-empty bottle of Kessler's in one hand. And the Holy fucking Bible in the other hand. And he wasn't wearin his cowboy hat that day either."

"What's Kessler's?"

"It's a real cheap whiskey, pardner. You know. Kinda like Texas Spirit. Not really expensive like Jim Beam or Jack Daniels. So anyways. There they were. Just starin each other down. Her uncle had that sickness you get from smoking. Where you cough up blood and then you fucking die."

"Emphysema"

"Yep, that's it. Anyways. A few weeks before. This girl overheard her daddy say that her uncle didn't have too much longer to live. And her uncle was a real man, too. I mean he'd been a real life Texas Ranger. You know. A real fucking hero. He even had his fucking name on a plaque in the Texas Ranger museum in Waco."

"And get this. When he was a kiddo growin up in Peach Creek over near College Station. The famous outlaws Bonnie and Clyde stopped by his parent's farm. They even drank right outta their well. Then Clyde gave the family some of his stolen cash. You know. Bonnie and Clyde were like Robin Hood or Jesse James. Real heroes"

"Oh yeah, I'm sure," Mike said, "real heroes."

"Anyways. This girl's uncle had been a real man back in the day. Sort of an Andy Taylor meets Augustus McCrae, if you know what I mean. But that day. Sittin on those railroad tracks in that green lawn chair. Her uncle was nothin but a shriveled up pathetic piece of shit. Coughin himself into his goddamned fucking grave."

"That seems a little harsh, Candi. I mean he *was* sick, after all. Right?"

"And let me tell you. That girl's uncle knew right where to sit too. Right there on that wooded bend so the train wouldn't be able to stop in time. Everybody always said he was a real sharpshooter. And he still had his mind too," Candi tapped her index finger up against her temple, "That's what was sooo goddamn sad about it. He still had his mind."

"So her uncle asks her- Girl, do ya recollect when you was just a little girl? That summer day when I put down your dog? Ya wasn't but ten years old. Remember? When your dog got runned over by that pickup truck? And ya carried him up to the house. By God! That dog was split right in two. And you was cryin. And that dog was howlin and whimperin and yelpin. And bleedin all over your blue-jean shorts. You remember that, don't ya, Girl?"

"The girl nodded. And then her uncle says to her- Ya think that was easy for me to take my rifle and put down that dog of yours? Shoot your dog right in the head. Right between the eyes? And I had to put down your dog while you was screamin and bawlin and beggin me not to do it. Ya think that was easy for me, Girl?"

"What a cruel thing to ask a child," Mike said.

"He wasn't bein cruel to the girl," Candi said. "Nope. *On that day* there was tenderness and courage in his eyes. I know it might seem cruel. But it was brave of him. And damn merciful too. It took a real man to raise that rifle, stare down the barrel and put down Copper."

"So then her uncle says to her- Ya been lookin for somethin to shoot all day long, haven't ya, Girl? Well I reckon God works in mysterious ways now, don't he?"

"No way, Candi. This is *not* a true story."

"I swear to fucking God it is. And if you fucking interrupt me one more goddamn time. I'm gonna punch you in the nuts so fucking hard you'll be yellin cunt til JC comes back." Mike winced at the thought. "And yeah, pardner. It's a true fucking story. Not everybody has a perfect life like you. And yet still manages to somehow be miserable."

"Ok, sorry"

"Anyways," Candi said, "The girl's uncle says to her- Ya been huntin all damn day for somethin to shoot, haven't ya, Girl? Ya know what? If ya did it, they'd never catch ya for what ya done. Ya know I was a Texas Ranger, don't ya? I was a detective for em for dern near twenty years. So I know me a crime scene, Girl. And nobody'd ever figure out it was you who did the puttin down today."

"Long as ya make sure my body's on the tracks after you do it. That train'll do the rest. Nobody'll notice a tiny ol .22 bullet hole. Oh hell, Girl. They'll be body parts strewn all over these here woods! Ain't nobody gonna find nothin!"

"Then her uncle says to her- Ya know, Girl. It ain't wrong to kill a person if ya gotta good reason. In fact. Sometimes killin another person can be the right thing to do."

"What I mean is. If somebody's done somethin like killed or raped somebody else. Then it ain't wrong to kill that person. Eye for an eye and a tooth for a tooth is what *this* book says. Her uncle held up the Bible."

"And it ain't wrong to kill a person neither, when they gonna die anyways. It weren't wrong for me to put down your dog, was it Girl? Nope. It weren't wrong. In fact. You were damn lucky I was there and willin to do the puttin down. And some day. You're gonna grow up and thank God above I did what I did for ya. And for that dog of yours too. And someday you might even have to do some puttin down of your own."

"Her uncle took a long swig from that plastic bottle. Then her uncle says to her- Killin is easy, Girl. Hell. I've done it more than once. Back in the day I kilt the Hannon brothers. They was two white-trash boys over in Navasota who raped a colored girl. They wasn't much older than twenty, I reckon. And them Hannon boys thought they was gonna git away with it too! All because their uncle was the sheriff over in Grimes County. And he was a damn racist sonuvvabitch too. And a deacon at Harmony Baptist Church too! Goddamn shameful if ya ask me. Enough to make a body ashamed of the human race!"

"Anyways. I got there too late to stop them Hannon boys from rapin that colored girl. They'd just got done with her and she runned off back home through the woods. Them Hannon boys still had a glimmer in their eyes when I got there. So I got outta my patrol car. And then I shot them white-trash pieces of shit right in between their eyes. Killed both of em dead as doornails."

"And when that Grimes County sheriff showed up. I just shook the hand of that old racist sonuvvabitch. Gave him a little wink. Grinned. And then told him it was all in self defense. And that's what Old Judge Thom Abe said it was too. All because he knew me since we was boys."

"But me and that sheriff both knew good and well them Hannon boys were little shit-asses. And never woulda tried nothin on me that day. Hell! Them Hannon boys didn't even have guns with em. That's why I always kept a few spare pistols from the pawn shop in my patrol car. I mean they damn sure had guns on em once the sheriff got there."

"That old Grimes County Sherriff always told his drinkin buddies that he was gonna git revenge on me someday. He liked to brag that when I wasn't lookin, he was gonna put two bullets right between my eyes. One for each of his nephews. The girl's uncle laughed and then coughed up some blood. And to tell the Gospel truth of it. Knowin that made me even happier bout the whole thing. Her uncle smiled at her."

"Then her uncle says to her- Nope. I never felt bad about killin them Hammond boys for a single day in my life. And I still don't! Hell! I figure killin them Hannon boys who probably woulda gone rapin more girls was akin to puttin down a sick dog. Just like yours, Girl."

"In fact. Ya shoulda seen the way that colored girl's mom hugged me when she found out what I done. Ever Sunday afternoon right after church, til the day that colored woman died, she fed me fried chicken right on her front porch."

"Just goes to show ya, Girl. I reckon sometimes it ain't wrong to kill. Her uncle rubbed his withered hand across the leather cover of his King James Bible. Well Girl, what'd ya say? Ya wanna help me out and put down your old uncle?"

"So the girl raises her rifle and takes aim," Candi said. "I mean the girl's only standin about six feet away from her uncle. It's an easy fucking shot. And by this time her uncle is all smiles. I mean he's smilin like he's about to give JC a big fucking hug at the Pearly Gates." Candi paused and then pulled out a blowpop. She unwrapped it and stuck it in her mouth.

"Well," Mike said, "Finish the story. What happened?"

Candi sucked on the blowpop for a minute and then said, "Well. The girl lowered her rifle. And then just went home for supper. And her uncle. Well that cowardly sonuvvabitch just staggered home all alone that night. He died chokin, coughin and pissin himself in the fucking hospital three months later."

"What the hell?" Mike said, *"That's* how the story ends?"

Candi shrugged and said, "I told you it was a true story, pardner. You know. No matter what your fucking literature classes teach you in college. Real life ain't nothin like fiction."

Mike never revealed to Candi that he had *not* made up the story about the two brothers and the severed head. In a creative writing seminar at Yale, Mike had studied the Southern Gothic genre of literature. And one day, amongst the dusty shelves of the library, in a long forgotten, now long out-of-print anthology of Southern stories, Mike discovered the story about the severed head.

And now, thousands of miles from the cloistered, ivy-league halls of academia, Mike passed the story off as if it were his own, ironically becoming a plagiarism of himself.

✳ ✳ ✳

Sometime later, still trapped at the railroad crossing, Mike said, "You know, Candi. I've thought about killing myself before."

"So why didn't you man up and do it then?" Candi said.

Mike shrugged and recalled a passage from Hesse. *Every one of them knows very well in some corner of his soul that suicide, though a way out, is rather a mean and shabby one, and that it is nobler and finer to be conquered by life than to fall by one's own hand.*

"I guess existing is better than not existing," Mike said, "even if you're in pain."

"Now what the fuck is that supposed to mean?"

"I mean that even being alive and in pain, is better than being dead and feeling nothing."

"You really think so?"

Mike thought of Dostoyevsky's character in *Notes from Underground.* Of course, he knew Candi was ignorant of the work, so the reference would be lost on her. However, Mike suddenly felt up to the challenge of teaching her, of making her understand this existential motif. Maybe, Mike hoped, it would turn out to be what he called a teaching moment, a moment where he felt particularly connected with his students, when he felt his lectures really hit home with them.

"There's this famous Russian book," Mike said, "about a man who feels really alone in the world. He's called, The Underground Man. This man feels alienated from everyone around him. Which makes him feel spiteful and angry. And yet, he-"

"Maybe he's just pissed off because he lives underground?"

"Candi, he doesn't *actually* live-"

"I know! I figured as fucking much. I'm just fucking with you, pardner."

Mike shrugged it off and continued. "In the midst of all these feelings of dread, anxiety and rage, The Underground Man reflects on the seemingly insignificant fact that he also has a toothache. It's only a tiny pain. In fact, it's more of an annoyance than agony. But," Mike said, "This physical pain reminds him that he is alive. And that he is human. That's what I mean, Candi. It's better to be alive and in pain, than dead." Mike smiled with satisfaction. This was definitely, he appraised, a memorable teaching moment for him.

"That is by fucking far," Candi said, "without a fucking doubt. The stupidest goddamn fucking thing I've ever heard anyone say in my whole entire fucking life."

"What?"

"Let me tell you somethin, pardner. You are sooo full of horse-shit."

"What the hell are you talking about, Candi?"

"My daddy used to say- Only a jackass, or a dumbass, carries a burden they don't wanna carry. Sounds to me like your underground man was a little bit of fucking both, huh?"

"I don't think you underst-"

"Pardner. You're one of those people who's sooo afraid of life. That you don't really wanna live it. But you're still clingin to it like a toddler suckin on his mama's titty."

"Clearly, Candi, you didn't understand my point."

"And you know what else you are, pardner? You're one of those annoying pricks. Who thinks that just because somebody disagrees with you. That means they must not have understood you. Because if they'd understood you, they never woulda disagreed with you!"

"Making a choice," Mike said, recalling his lecture notes, "Making a choice to exist *despite* my circumstances is a virtue and strength. Refusing to commit suicide, even in the face of insurmountable odds, is the noblest of human endeavors."

"No fucking way, pardner. What you're talkin about is a fucking weakness in my book. And it's downright fucking stupid too."

"Oh really? How so?"

"Because. When you do what you're talkin about. Then you become a fucking prisoner in your own fucking life. I mean. If you're unhappy with your life, then suicide is like a brave escape. In fact. I think suicide is the fucking bravest thing you could ever do. It actually takes a real man with balls to step up and just fucking commit suicide."

"I'm not following you, Candi. How is it brave to-?"

"Let me put it to you this way, pardner. After I left Huntsville. I met this chick who everybody in the neighborhood called Twat-Legs Tracy. Me and her were stayin at this halfway house near Montrose and Westheimer in Houston. Just off Branard Street. Now. Twat-Legs Tracy was only like thirty years old. But she looked way older. Like sixty. You know the kind. Like my granddaddy used to say- She looked like she'd been ridden hard and put up wet, one too many times."

Mike made a mental note to remember that particular colloquialism for his novel.

"Anyways. Twat-Legs Tracy had been a full-time crack addict and part time whore. Ever since her hubby abandoned her ass. And after eight years of fucking marriage too! She told me they tried for five years to have kiddos. Five fucking years! But it turned out she just couldn't have any. Well we both fucking know how that usually turns out. Am I right?"

Mike nodded.

"Well. Not long after I met her, Twat-Legs Tracy finally got clean."

"I'm sorry, Candi," Mike said, "But I must ask. Why did everybody call her *that*?"

"Call her what?"

"You know what I mean."

"I know. I just thought we might play that game again. And I'd get to punch you in the fucking nuts again."

"Let's not, please"

"Don't sweat it there, pardner. No, it's a fair question. Everybody called her Twat-Legs Tracy because she'd been fucked and raped so many times. With so many different things. You know. Like baseball bats, liquor bottles, tire irons, flashlights. You know, the usual shit whores get fucked and raped with. Anyways. Twat-Legs Tracy had been fucked and raped so many times. With so much shit. That her poor worn out twat just dangled right down outta her pussy."

Mike winced and said, "Oh my God."

"Yep! It was the God-damndest thing I ever fucking saw in my life. And I've seen some pretty fucked up shit too. I mean her fucking worn out twat just dangled right outta her pussy. Looked just like a piece of liver you might see at the fucking grocery store. Or you know when you get a slice of ham at the deli counter at Wal Mart? It kinda looked just like she had a piece of that sliced fucking ham hangin right down outta her pussy."

"Well. Everybody in the neighborhood used to tease her. And they'd all say that her poor worn out twat hung down so far, that you could hear it flappin against her legs whenever she walked." Candi laughed. "Course. You couldn't really hear anythin. But still. Everybody always joked that way. They'd all say. You never gotta worry about Twat-Legs Tracy sneakin up on you!" Candi laughed.

"You think that's funny?"

"Hell yeah I think it's fucking funny. Sometimes pardner. You just gotta laugh that shit off. You know what I mean, jelly bean?"

"Not really"

"Anyways. Twat-Legs Tracy finally got herself clean. Which doesn't happen too often. I mean she was a real success story. No more suckin dick for cash or crack. No nothin. She was fucking ready for a," Candi made quotation marks with both hands, "*normal* life."

"The only problem was. Twat-Legs Tracy wouldn't check outta the half-way house. It was weird. It was like she was too scared of the outside world to leave. Even though she was totally clean. And even though that half-way house was a miserable fucking shithole. Yep. Twat-Legs Tracy just refused to fucking check out on her own terms. I mean. It was like she'd gone from one fucking prison to a whole other fucking prison. Except there weren't any bars on the doors this time."

"Well. Because she wouldn't check out on her own terms. Twat-Legs Tracy got fucked in the end. Yep. She got fucked because she was weak. Because she fucking chose to stay there even though she was fucking miserable."

"So what happened to her?"

"Well it's like I said before. When I met Twat-Legs Tracy she'd gotten clean. She was eight months out of prison and clean as a fucking whistle. But! Because she wouldn't check out on her own terms. Those fucking rat bastards at the halfway house ended up kickin her ass to the fucking curb."

"They can do that?"

"Fuck yeah, pardner. They don't give a handful of horse shit! After all, she was a fucking whore. Anyways. They kicked Twat-Legs Tracy to the curb. And I mean literally kicked her! I watched them physically drag her ass outta the front door. Kickin and fucking screamin. And what do you think happened to her after that? Yep! Not six weeks later. I was walkin home from the mini mart and I spotted Twat-Legs Tracy. She was behind a dumpster suckin some stranger's dick." Candi made a fist and pumped it up and down near her mouth, pressing her tongue against one of her cheeks. She smiled. "You know what I mean, jelly bean?"

"Thanks for the dramatization," Mike said.

"So. What's the fucking moral of this little story? I'll tell you. If you're unhappy with your," she raised her hands and made quotation marks, "*existence*, then fucking check outta this roach motel. Fucking check out on your own goddamned terms. Or else… Or else life's gonna kick your ass to the fucking curb. And then you'll end up suckin strange dick behind some fucking dumpster."

If Candi had ever read Hesse, she might have recalled this passage- *Let suicide be as stupid, cowardly, and shabby as you please, call it an infamous and ignominious escape; still, any escape, even the most ignominious, from this treadmill of suffering was the only thing to wish for.*

"I still can't believe you're actually advocating suicide," Mike said. "Ok. If you think suicide is so brave, then why don't *you* do it? Why haven't you committed suicide then?"

"You haven't been listenin to a goddamn word I've said, dumbass." Candi said. "What I said was- if you're *unhappy*. If you're unhappy then you best just check the fuck out, on your own terms. Me? I'm not unhappy. Not yet at least."

"*You're* happy?"

"Fuck yeah, I'm happy! Why is that sooo hard for you to believe? I mean. Even though this world is pretty much just one fucked up roach motel. And we're all a bunch of fucked up cock-roaches. I fucking love livin here. And I *wanna* be here right now. I mean I'm havin a great fucking time!"

"In fact," Candi said, "It makes me think of that song by The Houston Kid. It's called *Earthbound*. Now that's a fucking philosopher for you!" Candi hummed for a minute to get down the tune, and then sang aloud:

> "Someday I'll be leavin'
> but I just can't help believin'
> that it's not today."

> "Every golden moment I have found
> I've done my best to run right in the
> ground
> Earthbound."

"It's like this, pardner. Me and Rodney make the most of every single fucking moment. We don't *expect* every moment to be golden. We fucking *make* it golden!"

"You on the other hand," Candi said, "You're fucking mis-erable. And why? Hell if I know! I just can't seem to fucking figure that shit out. You know what I think your problem is? You just don't wanna be here, that's all. But you stick around *just because* you think that stickin around is all noble and whatever."

Mike frowned.

"Let me tell you, pardner. If *I* was that underground man. I woulda just fucking pulled out that sore tooth. Instead of just sittin around tryin to make it sound all philosophical and noble. I reckon, pardner," Candi said with a laugh, "You're not the only one who writes papers about pointless shit nobody gives a fuck about!"

"On any other day," Mike said, "I'd be flattered to be com-pared to Dostoevsky."

"You know. That's the fucking difference between me and you, pardner. I'd just pull the fucking tooth out instead of bitchin about it. And when I'm done livin it up. In the right here and the right now. I'll be fucking brave enough. And strong enough too. To check the fuck out of this roach motel. On my fucking own terms. Nobody's kickin my ass to the fucking curb!"

"You on the other hand," Candi said. "You're just weak. Just like Twat-Legs Tracy. I mean. You'll just write a fucking philosophy paper about your toothache. While you piss and moan about your," she made her quotations marks, "*existence.*"

"And guess what? You'll never really live it up a single goddamn day in your whole life. And then one day. Somebody's gonna drag your ass outta this half-way house. And you'll be fucking droolin and pissin all over yourself. And mumblin some meaningless shit about the meaning of life. That pardner! Is the difference between me and you."

Mike remained silent and unconvinced.

Mike wanted to teach Candi. As a teaching fellow at Yale for two years, Mike lectured on French existential philosophy. He focused on the writings of the philosopher Albert Camus, with particular attention given to his novel *The Stranger*, and his seminal essay, *The Myth of Sisyphus*. Mike wanted to teach Candi how Albert Camus appropriated the ancient Greek myth in order to illustrate the absurd paradox of human existence.

According the story, Sisyphus angered the gods. And then, as a kind of obscene and poignant punishment, the gods condemned Sisyphus to roll a stone up to the top of a hill, only to have it roll back down, where Sisyphus would have to repeat the absurd task for all eternity.

"Now class," Mike would say in every lecture, right on cue, "Just so we're all clear. His name was Sisyphus, *not* syphilis." This joke, Mike mused, never ceased to solicit laughter from the class. Yet another cherished teaching moment.

Mike wondered if Candi would laugh at the joke.

Camus interpreted this myth, Mike wanted to explain to Candi, in order to illustrate how humans are condemned to exist. And not only to exist. But also to make choices. Thus, every choice you make is a single shove of the stone up the hill. And to wit, just as the stone always rolls back down afterwards, and the task of shoving it back up atop the hill is never accomplished, so human existence is an equally absurd kind of penalizing trap.

You did not choose to be born and exist, Mike would herald in his lectures. And yet, here you are, condemned just like Sisyphus. And as if this were not bad enough. Like adding insult to injury, you must also acknowledge that the only choice you *do not* have, is that you *must* make choices.

If the gods did exist, Mike often burlesqued in his lectures, Sisyphus' punishment proved the gods possessed a pretty fucked up sense of humor. This was a joke at which nobody in the class ever laughed.

And yet, Mike thought Candi probably would've laughed at that joke.

Camus said that the only way to overcome this absurdity of human existence is to claim ownership of your choices. Because in the end, your choices are all you really have in life. At this point Mike wrote these words on the chalkboard- *Your choices define you*. You must make yourself every moment, by the momentary choices you must make.

Camus believed that you could gain significance, *despite* the absurd paradox of life, by actually embracing your condemnation. You could infuse your absurd task of choice-making with a kind of strength and nobility.

Every time Sisyphus shoves the stone, in defiance of the gods, he should declare- This is my stone! Mike always brought his lecture to a crescendo at this point. Just like Sisyphus, Mike would exhort his students, you should *embrace* the anxiety and pain of your own existence. Even if it all seems like an absurd joke somebody played on you.

To refuse to shove the stone is tantamount to suicide. And it is *this refusal*, Mike wanted to tell Candi, which is the real admission of weakness and defeat. For to choose to commit suicide in order to avoid making more choices, Mike would tell Candi, is ultimately to affirm the absurd paradox of human existence, not overcome it.

Mike wanted to explain to Candi how Camus concluded-the only truly important philosophical question is- Why should I *not* kill myself?

Mike realized that Candi would ask a completely different question. She would ask- Why *should I* kill myself?

Mike watched Candi sitting there sucking on her blowpop, savoring the evening breeze blowing softly into the car window. Mike desperately wanted to teach Candi. He wanted to make her understand him...

And yet, as the train finally began to screech slowly forward, eventually freeing them to ride on northwards, Mike remained silent and still unconvinced. All Mike could think about was Twat-Legs Tracy, that crack-head whore, on her knees behind that goddamned dumpster, giving that stranger a blow-job.

Chapter 11

Kosse, Texas; How Candi proved NPR was full of shit;
And what Mike saw and heard in Candi's hometown

After finally escaping from that railroad crossing in Bremond, Mike and Candi drove north on Texas Highway 14 again. "So," Mike said, "which way do we go from here?"

"How do you fucking think we go? Don't you remember?"

"Uh, no"

"Always go forwards, always go downwards, and never go to the left or right." She smiled at him.

"Oh yeah, sorry. I guess I forgot."

"You didn't forget, pardner. You just didn't remember."

Mike chuckled. "So, Candi. What are you really trying to tell me, here? Are you really trying to tell me that if I can kill the Minotaur, and make it out of this labyrinth alive, then you'll give me your word that you'll sail away with me? And maybe, just maybe we'll live happily ever after this time?"

"Not gonna fucking happen. I'm not givin you shit."

"How about just giving me a sword, then?"

"Nope," she said. "You already got a sword, pardner. I know because I sucked it back there on the Baytown Bridge, remember?"

Mike winced, but still wanted to have the last word. "How about just giving me some red yarn, then? To help me find my way back?"

"Trust me, pardner. You're gonna need way more than fucking red yarn to fucking find your way back…"

A little ways up the road Mike and Candi drove through Kosse, Texas. At the intersection of town, right across the street from The Kosse Café, they spotted an old carwash. On the wall of the carwash was a banner which read:

AMERICAN SOLDIER
HIGHLY DECORATED 20 YEAR VETERAN
SENTENCED TO PRISON FOR <u>SAVING</u>
AMERCIAN LIVES
FLAWED DETAINEE AND RELEASE POLICY ALLOWS
TERRORISTS TO KILL REPEATEDLY
JOHN HATLEY FOUGHT FOR US... LETS FIGHT
FOR HIM
*PAID FOR BY PATRIOTS OF THE UNITED STATES

As they drove by Mike asked, "What the hell is that about?"
"No fucking clue," Candi replied.

* * *

A little later, right around Groesbeck, Texas, Candi shouted, "Oh my fucking God! I love this song! Turn it up!" She cranked up the volume on the radio. It was Lynyrd Skynyrd's anthem, *Sweet Home Alabama.*

"Please," Mike said, grimacing, "Turn off that racist shit."
"No fucking way, pardner! I love this song!" She sang along-

Big wheels keep on turning
Carrying me home to see my kin
Singing songs about the Southland

"You know this song is racist, right?" Mike said above the music.

Candi yelled back over the music. "Shut the fuck up so I can listen to this song!" She tapped her bare feet on the dashboard.

Mike turned down the volume. "Not while you're riding with me."

Candi kicked the windshield with both feet. Mike couldn't believe she didn't break the glass. Candi reached for the volume knob on the radio. She turned it up even louder than before. And then she jerked the knob off and threw it out her window. "Turn it down, *now*, motherfucker!"

Candi leaned forward, drumming on the dash. "Sing it with me, pardner! Sweet... Home... Alabama!"

A few minutes later when the song ended, Candi used her long fingernails like pliers to turn the radio volume back down. She smiled and said, "Sorry about the volume knob, pardner."

Mike sulked.

"Oh come on!" Candi said, "Don't pout. I mean it's not completely your fault."

"Not completely *my* fault?"

"Sure. After all. You're just a goddamned, carpet-baggin, faggoty Yankee. How were you supposed know? You never. And I mean fucking never ever come between a Southern girl and *Sweet Home Alabama* playin on the radio."

Mike stared forward and said, "For Chrissakes, Candi. That was overkill. Even for you."

"Oh trust me, pardner. You haven't fucking seen overkill, yet."

"Did you really have to throw the fucking knob out the window to prove your point?"

Candi laughed and said, "Well, you'll never make that mistake again. Now will you?"

Mike stepped on the brake slowly. He pulled the car onto the shoulder of the highway. "I need some fresh air," he said. "I'm going to walk around for a couple of minutes. *Alone!*"

"I wouldn't pull over right here on the shoulder if I were you," Candi said. "You're gonna pick up a nail or some broken glass in the tire. Nope. I'd wait just a couple more minutes. I know this part of the country really well. There's a roadside park just ahead."

"Will you please," Mike said, "*Please,* shut the fuck up?"

"I'm warnin you. Just wait just a couple more minutes." The car was already on the shoulder of the highway slowing to a stop. Suddenly there was a loud pop. The rear left tire made a flopping noise. "I fucking told you, dumbass."

The car came to a limping halt on the shoulder of the highway. Mike gripped the steering wheel with both hands, more tightly than before. He leaned his head forward and sighed in exasperation.

"Real nice work, dumbass"

"I've asked you this before, Candi. And I really mean it this time. Will you please not call me dumbass anymore?"

"You know what's really fucked up?" Candi said. "Even when you're angry, you're polite." She mocked-up his voice, making it even whinier than usual. "Candi," she said, imitating him, "Will you *please- please, pretty please* shut the fuck up? Candi will you *please, with cherries on top*, not call me a dumbass anymore?"

Candi laughed as she settled back into her seat. She unwrapped a blowpop and said, "By the way, pardner. Why does it bother you so fucking much when I call you a dumbass? I mean. I call you lots of names. But nothin seems to get your goose quite like dumbass."

"Just don't call me that word anymore, okay?"

"Sorry, dumbass. But that was *way too* polite. You're gonna have to man up and do better than that if you want me to stop callin you dumbass."

"I'm not playing one of your games, Candi. And I'm not going to let you provoke me either."

"You know what, pardner? You must have some negative associations with the word dumbass. You think that might be true, dumbass?" She chuckled and poked him on the shoulder with her trigger finger.

"Alrighty, pardner. Here's a fucking game for you. Let's role-play. You're gonna play a pathetic washout. Which should be a real easy one for you. And me? Well I'm gonna play your fancy-schmancy therapist."

Mike groaned.

"And I'll ask you a bunch of stupid fucking questions. You know. About whether you want to fuck your mother. Or some other psycho-babble bullshit like that. And then-"

"You are *so* full of shit, Candi. You know that don't you?"

"Not a bad start there, pardner! But if you want me to stop callin you a dumbass once and for all. Then you're gonna have to be a lot meaner than that. And a whole lot fucking louder too."

"I told you. I'm not playing this game with you, Candi."

"Oh it's not a game pardner. At this point in the story. It's a fucking matter of life or death for you."

"What the hell is that supposed to mean?"

"So," Candi said, "When you were a boy. Did your Uncle Chester the Child-Molester call you a dumbass while he dry raped your tight little asshole without any lube?"

"You're really sick sometimes"

"Is that it? Nope? Ok. Well maybe some chafed twat you were fucking called you a dumbass? Right before she fucking left you for a *real man*? Maybe that's it! Am I right?"

From the corner of his eyes Mike watched Candi study him. Her eyes staring him down like a predator does its wounded prey. He saw her glance back at the box in the backseat.

"Or maybe," Candi said, "just maybe you don't like to be called a dumbass by somebody like me? Because I'm just some dumb whore? Is that it? Because when somebody like me calls you a dumbass. It kinda takes away the only thing in life you really have to be proud of. And that's bein smart, not dumb! Am I right? Am I right?"

"Please leave me alone, Candi," Mike said, wincing as he realized he'd just said *please* again.

"You know somethin, pardner. It must really fucking suck to know that all you are is smart. I mean that's gotta be really fucking depressin. All you are is smart."

Mike sighed.

Candi shrugged him off and said, "Well it's gonna be dark soon." She rolled down her window, pulled herself up and out the window of the car without opening the door, and said, "*Dukes of Hazard* style, motherfucker."

"Where are you going?" Mike said.

"I'm gonna go change that flat tire. I mean somebody's gotta man up around here. And it sure as shit ain't gonna be you…"

✳✳✳

On any other evening Mike would've said something like this- I don't know which is more breathtaking, *Willows at Sunset* or the Texas countryside at dusk. And on any other day Mike's usual friends and colleagues would have nodded in gushing appreciation of his intellectual reference. However, on this evening Mike was foundered alongside a flat tire somewhere on Texas Highway

14, keeping his cultured commentary to himself. Candi wouldn't know Picasso from Pollack, much less Van Gogh. So as he stood leaning against the car, Mike recalled something from his childhood church days about casting pearls before swine; and this recollection made him feel a whole lot better.

Candi was down on all fours on the hot pavement next to the flat tire. She sat up and then bent over again, tightening the lugnuts on the tire. Her hands, arms and knees were dappled with grease.

Each time Candi tightened a lugnut, Mike stared down at her taut ass. He was reminded of how much he regretted getting the blowjob from Candi in exchange for a ride across the bridge, instead of actually getting to fuck her. Again Mike wondered if tonight they would finally fuck. Again he wondered if Candi would be offended if he offered her money for a fuck. Or if she would be offended if he simply made a move and didn't offer to pay for services rendered.

Candi tightened the last lugnut and then sat down on the pavement. She leaned back against the car. "There. All done, pardner. It would figure that *I'd* have to change this fucking flat tire. You know. I never thought I'd meet a man who was too smart to know how to change a tire. Or too much of a dumbass to let a woman do it for him!" She laughed.

Candi wiped sweat from her brow. Her arm left a streak of grease on her forehead. "I know! Why don't you write a philosophy paper about changing tires." She laughed.

"You never give up, do you?" Mike said.

"Give up on what?"

"On being a... On being a bitch to me"

"Ooooh! Bitch, huh? Nice one, pardner!" She pretended to respectfully tip the brim of her invisible cowboy hat to him. "Look at you. Callin me a bitch is a really big step forward for you. Especially since I wasn't punchin you in the nuts to make you do it."

"No, Candi. All you have to do, is just be you."

"Yep! That's me! Remember? The greatest goddamn character for a novel anybody ever wrote! That's me!"

Mike laughed and then said, "Yep. That's you alright, *sweetheart!*"

"Ooooh! Sweetheart, huh? Wow, pardner. You're just full of surprises today. Next thing I know you're gonna swagger over to me John Wayne style. And then order me to," she feigned her best John Wayne style drawl, "Git down off that animal little lady! And then take me back to your huntin cabin in the woods."

"Oh really?" Mike said. "And just what exactly would John Wayne do to you? Once he got you back to his hunting cabin in the woods?"

"Well. First off The Duke would slap me around a little bit. But not too much, you know. Then. The Duke would take off his cowboy boots. Unbuckle his blue-jeans. Drop them down around his ankles. And of course. He'd leave his cowboy hat on. And then. Whether I wanted him to or not. No matter how much I struggled and said no and refused. The Duke would just fuck my fucking brains out. Like a *real man*. There aren't many things you can be certain of in life, pardner. But here's one of them. John Wayne would fuck me and make me cum til I screamed."

"And then," Candi said, "The Duke would say to me," she did her best John Wayne style drawl again, "Git off my dick little lady. And git your ass into that fuckin kitchen. And make me a goddamn sandwich." Candi laughed. "And not too much fucking mayonnaise either, Pilgrim!"

"And what would you say?" Mike said.

"I'd fucking do it, of course. I'd fucking do anythin The Duke fucking told me to do."

"I guess I never saw *that* John Wayne film before."

"Oh shit. Come on, pardner! That's *every* goddamn John Wayne flick! That kinda shit always happened right *after* The Duke saves the bitch from the Indians!"

"You mean the damsel in distress?"

"Whatever! I mean you just don't actually get to see that shit. Because it always happens right after they fucking kiss. You know. Right after the fucking music swells. And they kiss. And then they ride off into the fucking Texas sunset together."

"So you'd do it, huh? You'd make him the sandwich?"

"You mean would I let John Wayne slap me around? And then fuck my brains out? And then order me to make him a fucking sandwich? Abso-fucking-lutely, pardner!"

"Wow"

"And any woman who says she wouldn't, is a fucking liar." Candi tapped her temple with her index finger. "Trust me, pardner. That's what every woman really wants. That's what we all want. We all just want John Wayne's hard dick inside us."

"You really think so?"

"But don't get too excited there, pardner," Candi said. "Remember. First you gotta ride off into the sunset with a woman. And that, pilgrim, is the *hardest* fucking part of all."

***

Candi sat on the trunk of the car sucking on a blowpop. "So, Mr. Smarty-Pants," she said. "What the fuck were you talkin about back there? What did you mean when you said that *Sweet Home Alabama* is a racist song?"

"You know what I've learned on our little drive, Candi? I've learned that it's never a good thing for me, when you begin a sentence by calling me Mr. Smarty-Pants."

"Well. Maybe it wouldn't be so fucking bad for you. If you weren't such a fucking dumbass. You ever think of that, Mr. Smarty-Pants?"

"You're always pushing my fucking buttons. I told you already, for Chrissakes. I'm warning you, Candi. Don't call me that or else-"

"Or else what?"

For a just split second Mike made a fist with his hand; but just as quickly released it.

"Whoa there, pardner! I fucking saw what you did just then." She pointed down to Mike's hand. "I saw you! You fucking made a fucking fist with your hand. Sure! It wasn't much of a fucking fist. But good for you, pardner. Good for you! Now all we gotta do is get you to hit somethin or somebody with it. And then you'll be on your fucking way to bein a *real* man."

"I'm not going to hit *anything*. At this point. I wouldn't give you the satisfaction."

"Well then. If you're gonna be a pussy and not hit anything. Then don't fucking warn me not to call you a dumbass. Because you better listen up, dumbass. When you threaten somebody like me. And then I call your fucking bluff. You fucking better have the *cojones* to back that shit up. Like a real man. And if you don't. Then keep your goddamn mouth shut from now on. Got it?"

"All I want you to do is *plea*," Mike stopped himself, and then started over. "All I want you to do is stop calling me *that word*."

"Well. I gotta say. I'm fucking impressed. You didn't say *please* that time. Good for you, pardner! And to show how impressed I am with your tryin to be a real man. I reckon I'll fucking reward you by not callin you a, *dumb*," Candi stopped herself, and then started over, "by not callin you *that word* again."

Candi tossed her spent blowpop stick onto the pavement. "Trust me, pardner," she said. "You gotta long fucking drive ahead of you, if you wanna get to where *you're* goin. Unfortunately for you, *we're* almost there..."

* * *

A few minutes later they were driving north again.

"So," Candi said, "And don't you worry none. I'm not gonna hurt those delicate feelins that you keep inside your man-gina by callin you Mr. Smarty-Pants, or *that other word*."

Mike sighed with relief. Candi had an uncanny ability, he observed, to pussy-foot insults into her comments right alongside what seemed to be her genuine attempts at being nice, or simply calling a truce. I think I can deal with her comments about my metaphoric vagina, Mike resolved, as long as she doesn't call me *that word* again.

"Thank you," Mike said, "I really do appreciate that."

"At least," Candi said, "I can still talk about your man-gina. I mean that's somethin, right?" She laughed and winked at him.

Mike laughed too. And if he had ever written his novel, he might've described Candi as a playful nymph casting a whimsical spell of high-spirited jest, even when confronted by the most obscene and absurd of circumstances.

"So, pardner," Candi said, "What the fuck did you mean back there when you said that *Sweet Home Alabama* is a racist song?

"It is a racist song. Everybody knows that."

"Umm, nobody fucking knows that because it's fucking not."

"Haven't we *already* covered this territory, Candi?"

"What territory? Lynyrd Skynyrd or racism?"

"I think you know which one I mean"

"Hey. Listen up here, pardner. That song is not racist!"

"I hate to break it to you, sweetheart. But that song is definitely racist. It was written *in defense* of George Wallace, the racist governor of Alabama who supported segregation."

"Where the fuck did you hear that shit?"

"A few years ago NPR did this piece on *Sweet Home Alabama*. It was part of a series where they explored the juxtaposition of pop-culture, racism and Southern Heritage."

"What the fuck is NPR?"

Mike recalled the pearls and swine, and then said, "NPR. National Public Radio. They did a piece where they discussed the controversy surrounding that song. I'll bet you didn't know that Neil Young wrote a song called *Southern Man* where he criticized racism in the South. And then in response to Neil Young's song, that guy in Lynyrd Skynyrd wrote,"

"You mean Ronnie Van Zant?"

"Yeah, that was his name."

"He was sooo fucking hot," Candi said. "He wore those old t-shirts that were way too small for his beer-gut belly. And that long messy hair. Sooo fucking hot! Am I right?"

"Wasn't he way *before* your time?"

"Yeah he was. But I've fucking seen the videos. Anyways. I'd have totally fucked every single member of Lynyrd Skynyrd in one night. If I'd been there back then. I mean I woulda ripped my fucking clothes off and told Ronnie Van Zant- just go ahead and pick any fuck-hole you like!"

"Why am I not surprised that you would've said something like that? Tell me, Candi. Is there *anybody* you wouldn't fuck?"

"Sure there is," she said. "*You...*"

"What?"

"Hell, pardner. I'd dig up Ronnie Van Zant's rottin stinkin corpse. And fuck it way before I'd let you stick your dick inside me."

"Oh yeah," Mike said. "Well you seem to have conveniently forgotten about that *little ride* I gave you across the Baytown Bridge?"

"Oh I haven't forgotten, pardner. And you're right. It was a *little* ride, alright!" Candi licked her lips and said, "Trust me, pardner. *That little* of a ride ain't soon forgotten."

"You're just trying to change the subject."

"Hey! You're the one who fucking brought it up. And unfortunately for me. Stuck it in my mouth too!" She laughed.

"Can I just finish telling you about that song, *please?*"

"You fucking said *that word* again"

"Dammit! Ok. What I meant to say was- I'm going to finish telling you about that song now." He smiled and added, "So shut the fuck up you stupid bitch and let me talk!"

Candi seemed surprised.

"Just kidding," Mike said, "You know that right?"

"I am sooo hot for you right now. Pull over right now and fuck my brains out."

"Really?"

"Just kiddin," Candi said, "You know that right?"

Mike frowned.

Candi laughed and said, "So hurry up and finish tellin me all about that fucking racist song already."

"Van Zant wrote the song *Sweet Home Alabama* in response to Neil Young's criticism of racism in the South. Maybe if you weren't so busy drumming your bare feet on the dashboard. And thinking about fucking long haired rednecks. Then you could actually listen to the lyrics of the song. Van Zant clearly says- *In Birmingham they love the governor*. He's talking about George Wallace, who was a racist!"

"And," Mike continued, "Van Zant actually calls out Young by name in the song and says- *I hope Neil Young will remember. A Southern man don't need him around anyhow*. I'll admit it's a catchy song. But it's racist, plain and simple."

"Huh," Candi said, "I never fucking heard that before."

"And it's sad and pathetic that ignorant people from the South still wave Confederate flags and listen to crap like that."

Candi unwrapped a blowpop. She shook her head in disapproval and said, "Do me a big fucking favor, pardner. Will you? If we ever stop in some honky-tonk bar on this little odyssey of ours. Promise me that you'll repeat that exact same speech really loud. So everyone in the bar can hear you. I mean I'd just love to watch a wild bunch of rednecks kick your lily ass all the way back to fucking Yankeeland."

"With all your talk about prejudiced rednecks and ignorant white-trash," Mike said, "I thought you might want to learn what that song really means?"

"Where on the radio did you say you heard this shit about *Sweet Home Alabama*?"

"NPR. National Public Radio. You know, Candi. Maybe you should try listening to NPR instead of country music once in a while. It's good for the old IQ." Mike winked at her, tapping his temple with his index finger. "And who knows, Candi. If you listen to NPR then you might eventually one day be able to pick up a copy of *The New Yorker*. And maybe, just maybe you'll be able to understand the table of contents." Mike laughed at her.

Every time that Mike fired off a putdown at Candi, he felt an initial recoil of remorse. And yet, as the gunsmoke settled, Mike felt somehow justified in his cruelty towards her. After all, Mike reasoned, *his* putdowns were only a strategic retaliation for all the times Candi fired a flagrant barrage of insults at him, including *that* word. Mike was only defending himself.

But Mike also relished the idea that his putdowns were a kind of revenge for all the times Candi disagreed with him, and then got the best of him. It was not that Mike felt Candi *won* their arguments, only that she got the best of him, which seemed different to him somehow.

Nevertheless, Mike speculated that somebody like Candi had been put down most of her life. And this awareness made Mike inevitably regret every one of his putdowns. Maybe it was the very the fact that Candi had been put down most of her life; Mike presumed, that made it somehow easier for her to endure his putdowns? Of course, and Mike quickly disavowed this other possibility; there was the dangerous contingency that Candi had endured so many putdowns in her life, at some point she might be unwilling or simply unable to endure another.

"I hope you're enjoyin your little intellectual jokes at my fucking expense," Candi said.

"Oh," Mike said in his best John Wayne style drawl, "don't ya worry none about that, little lady. I am!"

"You know somethin? It's too fucking bad that you and your fucking NPR are totally full of fucking shit."

"Oh please, Candi," Mike said, "Don't even try to get the best of me this time." He patted her on the shoulder. "We've both had our fun at the other's expense. And we both fired off a few good putdowns. But how about we call this one a truce? Tell you what? Since I won this round, I'll be gracious and we'll just call it even."

"No fucking way, pardner. This stand-off ain't over yet. Not by a long shot. In fact. I'm about to head ya off at the fucking pass!"

"Did you really just say- *head you off at the pass?*"

"Sure did! And that's what I'm gonna do too!"

"Clearly, you weren't listening when I told you about that lyric supporting Governor George Wallace, who was a notorious racist and pro-segregationist. And as if that weren't enough. What about that lyric denouncing Neil Young's *Southern Man* song? You've got nothing this time, Candi."

"Actually," Candi said, "If you listen to the fucking song. Ronnie says- *In Birmingham they love the governor (boo boo boo)*"

"Oh that's just Van Zant making some sound effects"

"Nope! What Ronnie's sayin is- Lots of men in the South are racists and they love the governor. But! Ronnie is personally *booing* Wallace for bein a racist asshole."

"Are you sure he says *boo boo boo?*"

"And Ronnie was just pissed off. Because Neil Young is a fucking Yankee prick tryin to tell people in the South how to conduct their business. And what's worse. Neil Young named that song *Southern Man*. Basically sayin that *all* Southern men were racists. Sounds like a fucking stereotype to me!"

Mike struggled to recall the episode of NPR.

"Ronnie was just sayin- I'm a Southern Man *and* I ain't no racist. And I don't need Neil fucking Young or anybody else from the North to tell me how it is down here in the South."

Mike reconsidered the lyrics again, frowning this time.

"I'll bet you didn't know that Ronnie was buried in a Neil Young t-shirt, did you? Yep! Ronnie Van Zant was actually a fucking Neil Young fan."

"I didn't know that"

"Yep. Ronnie agreed with Neil Young that racism was bad. Ronnie just didn't like it that a goddamn fucking Yankee was criticizin Southerners. You know. It's like how you can talk shit about your own family and that's ok. But it pisses you off when other people talk the same shit about your family. That's what Ronnie meant."

"How did you figure all this out?"

"I just listened to the fucking song. And then gave it some fucking thought. Unlike a certain *dumbass* I happen to know. Of course. I won't reveal his *true* identity."

This time Mike felt strangely liberated by Candi getting the best of him. "Let me guess," he said, "is this certain dumbass, a *handsome* man?"

Candi seemed genuinely surprised by his reaction and said, "Yep"

"And is this certain dumbass a *brilliant* man?"

"Well he sure as fuck thinks he is"

"And is this certain *dumbass*, in your humble opinion? Anywhere close? And I do mean anywhere close at all? Even in the ballpark close? To being a *real man*?"

"We'll see, pardner," Candi said. "We'll have to just wait and fucking see about that..."

✳✳✳

"So tell me," Mike said, "Where did you really hear all that about Ronnie Van Zant and *Sweet Home Alabama*?"

"What? You think just because I didn't go to college that I couldn't think up all that shit for myself? Some of us don't need professors to tell us everything, you know. "

"Ok. How about Van Zant being buried in a Neil Young t-shirt? You didn't just think that shit up? Unless," Mike said, "You *made* that shit up?"

"Hey, fuck you, you fucking fuckwad. That shit is fucking true!"

"Ok then. Where did you hear it?"

"Ok. Fucking fine. Have it your way! I'll spill the beans. Truth is I was fucking this guy once. And he was fucking obsessed with Lynyrd Skynyrd. It was sooo goddamn pathetic! I mean this guy would rather listen to Lynyrd Skynyrd than cum on my tits!"

They laughed together.

"Of course," Candi said, "He'd never actually cum on my tits before. So he didn't really fucking know what he was missin. I mean look at these tits," she said, placing her hands under her breasts and then pushing them up to accentuate her cleavage. "These are perfect tits for putting your dick in between, don't you think? I mean. Can you fucking imagine your hard, throbbin dick right in between these babies? I mean seriously. My tits are perfect for cummin on, don't you think?"

"Perfect"

"All I'm sayin is. If he'd known what he was missin. He never would've listened to another Lynyrd Skynyrd song ever again. He would've been too busy-"

"No wait, let me guess," Mike said, "cumming all over your tits?"

"You've got a filthy fucking mind there, you know that, pardner? Do you fucking kiss your mama with that fucking mouth?"

"So let me get this straight," Mike said. "for posterity's sake. Everything you know about Lynyrd Skynyrd and *Sweet Home Alabama*. You learned from some guy you were fucking. But who never knew the pleasure of cumming on your tits?"

"Yep, pretty much"

"Ok. I just wanted to be clear on that character exposition. For my novel, of course."

"Well then. Quote me on this, pardner. Unlike a certain *dumbass* that I happen to know. Even though I learned everything about Lynyrd Skynyrd and *Sweet Home Alabama* from some random asshole. I don't need anybody from Yale or NPR or the fucking *New Yorker* to tell me what's what."

"Hey," Mike said, "I thought we were being nice to each other for a little while? You know. Just a little friendly fire, for once."

"Turns out you and your snooty NPR know-it-alls have somethin in common with a bunch of dumb racist rednecks from the South. None of you is smart enough to figure out for yourself what Ronnie was really sayin in that song. Talk about fucking irony, right?"

"For Chrissakes, Candi. What happened to a little friendly fire?"

Candi made a pistol with her hand, pointed her barrel fingers at him, fired at Mike, making a *bang* sound, and then blew the gunsmoke off the tips of her fingers. "In my book, pardner," she said, "There's no such thing as friendly fire..."

✳✳✳

A few miles down the road Mike said to Candi, "You were right, you know."

"Right about what?"

"About why I don't like to be called a dumbass"

"Forget it, pardner. I don't wanna fucking know."

"I was accepted into both Harvard and Yale. On full scholarship"

"I said, fucking forget about it"

"I am smart, Candi. But-"

"Forget about it, pardner. Listen up. I don't give a good goddamn whether you were accepted into Harvard or Yale."

"But all I want to say is-"

"Just keep your shit to yourself. Got it? Listen up. Here's the deal. I'll promise I'm not gonna call you Mr. Smarty-Pants or dumbass anymore. And you promise to keep your shit to yourself. So I guess that solves our little problem, huh?"

"But all-"

"Oh, yeah," Candi said. "And one more part of the deal. You're changin the next fucking flat tire and I'm writin a fucking paper about it."

Mike smiled, thinking again of pearls and swine.

✳✳✳

As dusk settled Mike spotted a green sign along Highway 14 which read:

MEXIA, TEXAS
Population 6,563

A few yards away there was another sign, hand-painted by the local Lyons Club. It read:

MEXIA
A Great Place to Live, No Matter How You Pronounce It!

Mike mouthed the name of the town silently to himself, wrestling with its pronunciation. He said to Candi, "Are you familiar with this town? Do you think we can find a decent hotel here?"

"The only hotels I know of only rent by the half-hour and the hour."

"You're quite the comedian, Candi. But I wouldn't quit your day job."

"Oh, fuck no. Why would I quit my *dayjob* when I've already got a great, *blowjob?*"

Mike laughed.

"Anyways. I'm way too happy in my current *position*. You know the one, pardner. Where I put my head in a stranger's lap and then suck his sweaty dick?"

Mike winced and said, "Yeah, Candi. I know the one."

"Hey, pardner. I've been wonderin somethin for a while now. Why the fuck do you get sooo bugged at me whenever I mention that blowjob I gave you on the Baytown Bridge?"

"I'm not bugged."

"Yeah you are."

"Uh, no. I'm really not."

"Yeah you fucking are. I mean every fucking time I bring up that blowjob. Or any other blowjob, for that matter. You get all bugged."

Mike resisted the urge to say what he really wanted to say.

"Well," Candi said. "I don't fucking know what *you're* sooo bugged about. I mean. After all. I didn't see you suckin a stranger's dick. And *you're* the one who got to cum. Not me!"

"Can we please just drop it, Candi?"

"All I'm sayin, pardner. Is what goes around comes around. Pun fucking intended"

Mike remained silent.

"Oh fucking Hell. I'm just jokin with you, pardner," Candi said, punching Mike on the shoulder. "And speakin of jokes. Slow down here and then turn the car around."

"What? Why?"

"Just turn around right here,' Candi said. "Where that dirt road is." Candi pointed, leaning over towards Mike. Her tits stoked his shoulder. He slowed the car, turned around in the dirt drive, and then headed back south. "Now," Candi said, "just go back down the highway a little ways."

Mike felt Candi's hard nipples press against his arm through her threadbare t-shirt. He stole a quick glance at her tits and noticed that Candi had unusually large areolae.

"Right here," Candi said, "turn around again, right up here." As Mike turned the car around Candi lost her balance, and leaned harder into him. She quickly regained her composure and then leaned back in her seat. "Now right up here. Just pull over off the highway a little bit. Not too much, now. Remember what happened last time? And remember. We both know who's changin the fucking flat tire this time!" She laughed.

Mike depressed the brake pedal, slowing down the car. He pressed his legs together both to conceal his hard-on from Candi, and dandle it against his inner thigh. Mike wondered if Candi had been aroused by their brief friction too.

Candi was all about sex. Evidenced by the way she constantly talked about sex, described sex, and for no apparent reason, brought up sex in casual conversation.

"Right up here, pardner," Candi said. "Pull off and park so we can see that sign for Mexia."

And what kind of message was Candi sending? Pushing her tits up in my face like that? And then asking me about what it would be like to cum on her tits? Or showing me her pussy? Surely she must know by now, Mike mused. I really want to fuck her.

"Hey, pardner. Pay closer attention! I said don't pull too far off the road."

Mike remembered back in Bremond when Candi issued her stern but beguiling warning- I'm a cockteaser. He glanced over at her again. She didn't seem aroused. And what was worse. She didn't even seem aware of his arousal. She could've at least been cognizant that her tits had pushed up against his shoulder. She could've at least realized what that might do to him. She could have at least entertained the possibility that she might give him a hard-on. And even if she wasn't aroused, at least she could've teased him about it like usual.

Mike pulled the car off the highway just a little and then came to a stop not far from the sign for Mexia.

"Now," Candi said, "I just gotta tell you this joke. Right here, right now."

Mike killed the engine.

"It's like the only clean joke I know"

Mike felt his hard-on depreciate.

"It's a joke about these two travelin salesmen"

"You know, Candi," Mike said, doing his best to forget about the brute-force of her tits, the brawn in her nipples, and her oversized areolae. "I don't think I've ever met anyone who tells as many jokes as you do."

"Well, it's funny you say that. Because my Uncle Tom always had a new joke to tell me every time I'd see him. And they weren't always racist jokes either."

"Well I guess that's something," Mike said.

"Yeah. But come to think of it. Most of them were. And most of them were pretty fucking dirty too."

"Why am I not surprised?"

"Anyways. Every time I'd see him. Uncle Tom would announce that he was finally getting married to his longtime girlfriend, Maria Tortilla."

"What?"

"Yep. Uncle Tom didn't much care for Mexicans either. So every single time. And I do mean every single fucking time I'd see Uncle Tom. He'd proudly announce his upcomin marriage to Maria Tortilla. And then Uncle Tom would always go on and on and on and on about the details of the wedding. You know. Really draggin out the suspense of the joke."

"Uncle Tom would go on and on and on and on. About him and Maria Tortilla gettin married. At this outdoor flea market called Jockey Lot on the outskirts of College Station. He picked that place because it wasn't like flea markets in the good ol days. It was mostly just fucking Mexicans sellin cheap Mexican shit from fucking Mexico. To other fucking Mexicans."

"And then Uncle Tom would always brag about how him and Maria Tortilla were gonna raise a *familia*. And have a whole passel of little *Messkin* jumpin beans." Candi laughed. "And how he was gonna give his kiddos names like Pedro, and Nacho, and Taco, and Pico de Gallo, and Double-Decker Burrito from Taco Bell. I mean he'd really go on and on and on. Laughin his fucking ass off the whole fucking time"

"And then Uncle Tom would tell me that someday. Him and Maria Tortilla would decide that a baker's dozen of little *Messkin* jumpin beans just wasn't enough. Nope! Uncle Tom would swear up and down that him and Maria Tortilla would have just *Juan* more little jumpin bean."

Mike sighed.

Candi laughed, nudged Mike and said, "Get it, pardner? *Juan* more Mexican! Get it?"

"Oh I get it"

"And then Uncle Tom would go on and tell me that one of his little jumpin beans might need to get glasses someday. And that's when he'd take the little fella up to see the eye doctor. And the eye doctor would give the little fella a pair of glasses and say," Candi paused, and then sang the punch line of the joke to the tune of the national anthem, *"Jose* can you see?"

Candi sang it again, nudging Mike, *"Jose* can you see? You know? By the dawn's early fucking light!"

"I get it, Candi, for Chrissakes. Are you done yet?"

"Wait for it…" Candi said. "Anyways. After Uncle Tom went on and on and on and on. And you know. It was all part of the whole joke. For me to listen the whole time and play along like he was serious. Anyways. When Uncle Tom was all done. He'd look at me and wait for me to ask him the same question every fucking time. Right on cue… And every single fucking time I'd ask him, right on cue- So when are you and Maria Tortilla gettin married?"

"And right on cue Uncle Tom would always answer- Me and Maria Tortilla are gettin married on the first day of April. It's gonna be a spring wedding. Just like Maria Tortilla always wanted."

"And then I'd ask him, right on cue- But isn't that on April Fool's Day?"

"And then Uncle Tom would say- Damn straight! And then he'd laugh his fucking ass off." Candi smiled and said, "Goddammit! Uncle Tom really loved that fucking joke."

"All of that," Mike said, "For that?"

"Yep"

"You know. For such a long joke, that's not much of a punch line."

"I know," Candi said, laughing, "It's a God-awful fucking punch line!"

"Then why are you laughing?"

"I'm laughin because some jokes ain't about the punch line, pardner. Some jokes are just about gettin *to* the punch line. And about all the little jokes you happen tell along the way."

"Sorry," Mike said. "I still don't think it's a funny joke."

"I reckon it's just one of those jokes where you just had to be there."

"I thought you said your Uncle Tom didn't *just tell* racist jokes?"

"He didn't"

"But,"

"That joke just always reminds me of him. It was sooo him."

"So you think your Uncle Tom is the reason you tell so many jokes?"

"I never really thought about it. But yeah, I reckon so. Uncle Tom always said- Nobody ever tells any good jokes anymore. Back in the good ol days when I was younger, men told jokes all the time."

"Back in the good old days, huh?"

"Yep," Candi said. "So after Uncle Tom told me that. I always tried to show up to his house with a good joke to tell him. Course. I always had to wait until after we did the whole Maria Tortilla joke. But you know what, pardner. Come to think of it. I remember that when I started tryin to get a hold of good jokes to tell Uncle Tom. That's when I realized he was right. About nobody tellin good jokes anymore."

"Of course," Mike said, "You weren't even alive *back in the good old days*. Like your Uncle Tom was. So how do you know? Maybe nobody ever told good jokes?"

Candi shrugged and said, "I reckon I just fucking took his word for it. I mean I never really thought about it until just now."

"I guess," Mike said, "I don't really know any good jokes."

"Trust me, pardner. If you walked a mile in my high-heeled plastic moccasins. Then you'd know a fuck-ton of good fucking jokes." She nudged his arm and said, 'Get it? I said, *fucking* jokes?"

"Yeah, Candi. I get it."

"I mean jokin is just like bleedin out your pussy once a month. Just a part of a life. Kinda like fucking and suckin and eatin. And even fucking breathin."

"Well," Mike smiled and said, "I'm afraid if you do them in that particular order, then you won't be doing any of them for very long." He nudged her arm this time and said, "Get it?"

Candi thought for a moment and said, "Well shit, pardner. I reckon you're fucking right about that shit. But I'm still gonna put fucking before eatin!"

Mike laughed and said, "What about sucking?"

"Well I reckon that's gonna depend on how many bridges I still gotta cross."

Mike frowned.

"Or should I say- How many bridges *we* still gotta cross?"

"I suppose I should've seen that one coming, huh?"

"Pun intended?"

Mike winced and said, "No, actually"

"And you said you didn't know any good jokes!"

"I know. Why don't you tell me that joke about the traveling salesman now?"

"Good job changin the fucking subject," Candi said. "Oh and by the way. Fucking pun intended right there..."

"Just tell me the traveling salesmen joke, already."

"Ok, ok. But first I gotta say. This joke about the travelin salesmen is very," Candi raised her hands and made quotation marks with her fingers in the air, "*app-pro-po.* That's why I had you turn the car around." Candi seemed to be thinking through her pronunciation for a brief moment. She asked him, "Did I say that word right?"

"You said it perfectly, *very* apropos."

"Nice!" Candi was all smiles. "Anyways. Here's the fucking joke. Sooo there were these two travelin salesmen."

"Was one of them named Willie Loman, by any chance?"

"Huh?"

"Nevermind," Mike said, chuckling to himself.

"Sooo these two travelin salesmen are drivin north along Texas Highway 14. That's right, pardner. This very fucking highway right here. And they passed by *that* sign over there." She pointed to the Mexia sign. "And I mean that same exact fucking sign you're lookin at right now."

"So one of the men notices that there sign and says to the other man- strange name for a town, huh?"

"And the other guy says- Yep, it's a strange name for a town. With an even stranger way of pronouncing it."

"Oh yeah?"

"Yep! It's pronounced, *muh hay uh*."

"And then the first man says to him- No fucking way! You're just fucking with me. I bet it's pronounced just like it's spelled, *Mex ee uh*." Candi chuckled, as if already thinking about the punch line.

"Anyways. These two guys go back and forth and back and forth and back and forth arguin about it. And neither of them is givin a fucking inch.

"So once they drive into town. The first man says- Pull into this place and we'll go inside. And we'll ask one of the yocals how to pronounce the name of this town. That'll settle it."

"So they agreed. They pull into a place along Main Street. They park the car and then both go inside the place. They walk up to the counter. And then one of them says to the young woman workin there- Me and my buddy here disagree about how to pronounce the name of this place. Could you tell us how to pronounce the name of this place? And say it *real slow*. So I'll know my friend is full of shit?"

"So the young woman is lookin real puzzled. She leans over the counter. And then she says very slowly- *Dairr eee Queeen*." Candi erupted with laughter, kicking the dashboard.

✳✳✳

"We made it, pardner," Candi announced in a triumphant tone, "We're finally fucking here!"

"We're where? You mean?"

"Mexia, Texas!" Candi said. "Here's where the treasure is buried!"

"You better not be joking!" Mike said.

"I swear to fucking God!" Candi said, and then leaned over and punched Mike on the shoulder. "We're fucking here. This is the goddamned place. This is the end of our little fucking odyssey."

"Wow," Mike said. "I can't believe we actually made it."

They drove into town as darkness fell over the Texas countryside.

"So what do we do now?" Mike said.

"We find a fucking motel," Candi said. "So we can get rested up for tomorrow. I mean. We're gonna need our fucking sleep. If we're gonna dig for buried treasure tomorrow."

Mike didn't believe there was any buried treasure. And right now he didn't care that Candi still insisted there was. All he cared about was his hard-on hugging his thigh once again. All he cared about was the possibility of fucking Candi in a motel that night.

"Well you did it, pardner," Candi said. "You rode on your first cattle drive north. And you fucking survived it...so far." She turned to him, leaned over near his face and said, "So how does it feel to have ridden across so many rivers and still be alive?"

Mike felt his hard-on pressing against his thigh and said, "It feels great."

"But does it feel, *fucking* great?"

"Yeah, it does actually. It feels *fucking* great!"

Candi hugged Mike for what seemed to him like an eternity. She leaned back in her seat and said, "I just hope you're fucking ready for this shit."

Mike's hard-on swelled.

"I mean this is where it all fucking happens. Where the shit finally hits the fan. Where we dig up buried treasure and fucking get rich. And then build us a fucking ranch and settle down. I mean this is where our little fucking odyssey comes to the fucking end."

"I still can't believe we made it," Mike said. "I can't believe that I made it."

"Hold up there, pardner," Candi said. "Don't get down outta your saddle just yet. Our cattle drive ain't over just yet." Mike watched Candi's eyes deliberately turn downwards to his crotch. She stared down his hard-on and said, "You got one more river to cross, pardner..."

Chapter 12

Mike's dream;
which encompasses a prelude;
The execution of a whore and a faggot; Sacred passages read in tandem;
The Ballad of a Bedtime Story; The contest explained;
A panegyric upon Sarai;
The contest and a postlude

There is an ancient legend told by priests and scriveners, of an empty grave in the field of Machpelah in Hebron, in the land of Canaan. They say it was marked with a simple stone. But alas, the words once etched upon it are now long erased...

* * *

"Quiet down ya goddamn sons of bitches! I'm The Judge," he hollered above the clamor of his crowded saloon. He slammed his infamous wooden gavel down on the bar in front of him. Behind him were all kinds of plastic whiskey bottles, black and white photos of cowboys, and a jackelope. He slammed down his gavel again and hollered, "I said quiet the fuck down you surly sons of bitches!"

There was a young woman leaning against the front of the bar, dressed in lingerie. With a demur, Southern belle smile, she faced the throng of unruly cowboys gathered in the saloon. They all hooted, hollered and cat-called right on cue. The Judge even reached over the bar and spanked her ass.

Despite the din and commotion of the saloon, the young woman lifted her arm in a sweeping motion, extended it backwards towards The Judge in a grandiose gesture of presentation, and then announced, "The man, the legend, The Judge!"

The herd of cowboys cheered the legendary Texan everybody called, The Hangin Judge.

The young woman clapped with equal enthusiasm, shaking her ass and flaunting her ample cleavage. She yelled, "The Law West of the Pecos!"

The Judge grimaced with disapproval. He leaned over his bar and hit that young woman square in the back of her head with his gavel. "Stupid fucking whore," he chastened.

The saloon went quiet.

She collapsed to the floor. Blood and pieces of her skull and brain lay spattered on the bar.

The Judge faced the men gathered before him. He held his gavel aloft, like a scepter, for them to see. Blood, hair and pieces of the woman's skull hung off the hammer end of it. "What that stupid fucking cunt-whore should've said was," The Judge decreed, "I'm *The Law*- no matter what side of the river I'm standin on!"

The saloon erupted with rowdy applause.

Two cowboys hurried over to the front of the bar. They reached down and grabbed the young woman's arms, tugging them upwards in order to drag her body away.

The young woman's body convulsed violently and the cowboys dropped her quick. One of them said, "Judge! I don't think this whore's all the way dead!"

"Boys," The Judge decreed, "There's nothin that'll limp a man's dick quicker than a hard-headed whore!" He leaned over the bar and stared down into her face, studying every spasm and death pang.

Her eyes remained open wide, staring upwards as if staring him down. The Judge knew she could no longer see him. He smiled as he watched her bloody, gaping mouth open and close dumbly. "Ya know what boys?" The Judge said, chuckling. "I think that blood oozin from her fucking cunt-whore mouth kinda matches the color of her fucking cunt-whore lipstick! Don't ya think?"

Every man cheered, laughed, and then clinked their beer bottles.

"All for the better, anyways," The Judge decreed, sitting back down behind the bar. "That pet bear of mine just loves a fresh cunt-whore steak for dinner! Of course," he corrected himself, "I reckon there ain't really nothin *fresh* about it. Am I right?"

One of the cowboys said, "Ya mean ya want us to feed this here whore to the bear?"

The Judge jumped up from his seat and hollered, "Ya got cotton in your fucking ears ya ignorant, fucking, redneck piece-of-shit?"

"No sir, your honor!"

"Then drag that fucking cunt-whore outside and feed her to my goddamn bear!"

The herd of cowboys cheered the legendary Texan, who famously kept a black bear chained up as a pet outside his saloon.

"Boy oh boy," The Judge said, "That pet bear of mine is gonna be happier than a kiddo in a fucking candy store! Yep. He's gonna tear into that cunt-whore's bloody pussy like it was a fucking sirloin steak cooked up rare on the goddamn grill."

The cowboys obeyed him. They dragged the woman's bushwhacked body across the saloon floor, leaving a streak of blood in their wake.

"Ok," The Judge decreed, "Now that that cunt-whore is gone. It can be just us real men and we can-" He noticed a strange man in his saloon, sitting at a table in the corner all by himself. He noticed this strange man was dressed up like a cowboy, except, he wasn't wearing a cowboy hat or cowboy boots. He noticed there was no bottle of beer or glass of whiskey in his hand. And that the dingy lamps in the saloon cast this stranger's eyes in a queer light.

"Like I was sayin before," The Judge said, "It can be just us *real* men." The Judge drew his pistol, and raised-up the barrel with finesse, took casual aim, and then decreed, "Except for that faggot over there!" A single shot rang out from The Judge's pistol.

The strange man slumped down in his chair. The bullethole between his eyes hemorrhaged blood onto his face and the table. As the body went limp and fell forward, the stranger's face smacked the tabletop before it buckled onto the floor.

"Honestly boys," The Judge pondered aloud, "I don't know which one I hate worse- a faggot or a cunt-whore!"

The herd of cowboys cheered the legendary Texan.

The Judge fired his pistol into the air a few times. He holstered it and then sat back down behind the bar. He grabbed his gavel, pounded it on the bar and shouted, "Let's fucking get our little contest started!"

* * *

"Preacher!" The Judge hollered, "Get your fucking ass over here and read us a few goddamn passages! Everybody fucking knows ya can't have our little contest without first readin a few passages from a sacred book or two."

An old man shuffled over to the bar. He held two sacred books in his alcoholic hands. He opened the first sacred book and read aloud from it:

> "God said to Abraham, as for Sarai your wife, you shall not call her Sarai, but Sarah shall be her name. I will bless her and moreover I will give you a son by her. I will bless her and she will give rise to nations, kings of peoples shall come from her."

"Amen, amen," The Judge recited impatiently.

"Amen," everybody in the saloon echoed him.

The old preacher closed that sacred book and placed it on the bar next to The Judge's pistol. He then opened the other sacred book, and read aloud from it:

> "It was early in the morning, Abraham arose betimes, he had the asses saddled, left his tent, and Isaac with him, but Sarah looked out of the window after them, until they had passed down the valley and she could see them nomore."

"Amen, amen, amen, goddammit," The Judge decreed.

"Amen," everybody in the saloon echoed him.

The old preacher shut the sacred book and placed it on the bar next to the other one. Then he shuffled back to his seat and back into his beer bottle.

"Well boys. Now that we got that goddamn kingdom-of-Heaven-on-fucking-earth bullshit outta the way," The Judge decreed, "Let's get to our little fucking contest!"

✱✱✱

Mike was in a little girl's bedroom. He sat on the edge of her bed. Candi lay nestled beneath a quilted comforter. Her head rested on her pillow. She opened her sleepy eyes and said, "Mike, will you tell me a bedtime story, please?" She tugged the edge of the comforter up to her chin.

Mike rested his hand tenderly on Candi's shoulder and whispered, "Let me try"

Candi nodded, smiled and then shut her eyes.

"Once upon a time…" Mike made sure to begin this time, "There was a woman. And when she was a little girl she heard the beautiful story of how God tested the man Abraham. And how as an exemplar of faith and obedience, Abraham got back that which he offered to God. Namely, his only son Isaac."

When Candi began to snore softly, Mike slid his hand gently down over the comforter, from her shoulder down to her waist.

"Now," Mike continued his palliative narration, "When the girl grew older she heard the story again. And she wondered for the first time in her life about how Abraham's wife must have felt. After all, it was *her* son, just as much as it was Abraham's, whom God had required as a sacrifice on distant Mount Moriah."

Mike moved his hand softly down over the comforter, this time from her waist down to her hip.

"As the girl grew older still," Mike said, his voice lilting like a child's nursery rhyme, "Her enthusiasm for the story never waned. And yet she felt somehow that she understood it less and less and less. Soon her enthusiasm for the story consumed her. And she imagined a hundred different scenarios starring the wife of Abraham. Each imagined scenario became a story of how Abraham's wife must have felt when she discovered what he had done atop Moriah."

Mike moved his hand gently, sliding it down off her hip and across her thigh. And then, down farther to the side of her bed, where it rested at the edge of the comforter. Candi's eyes remained closed in slumber.

"In time," Mike brought her bedtime story to an end, "The woman's sole desire was to wonder along with Abraham's wife at what the venerable patriarch had done. To share in her sense of betrayal. And to shudder at the loss of a husband who after returning from Moriah was now a ghost. An unreal man she believed at once to be the supreme sinner and the most sacred saint..."

As Mike turned off the light he gently lifted up the comforter, and buried his hand beneath it.

Once upon a time, there was a woman...

* * *

The Judge thundered his gavel and decreed, "I've been waitin my whole goddamn life for our little contest! Feels great, don't it boys?"

The cowboys in the saloon shouted, "Feels great!" echoing him and banging their beer bottles on their tables like gavels.

"Wait a second!" The Judge decreed, "Actually! It feels *fucking* great!"

"Feels *fucking* great!" they echoed him again.

"Well," The Judge proclaimed, "Bring in them famous cunts!"

Every man cheered as the saloon doors opened. A group of cowboys strode in, swinging their ropes like whips, driving a group of naked women into the saloon like cattle into a corral.

"It's been a long drive to have this herd of famous cunts assembled here in my saloon," The Judge bragged. "Guess ya could say it's been a *labia* of love!"

The saloon fell silent.

"It means like a woman's clit, ya know? Get it? It's been a *labia* of love? Get it? Her fucking dirty clit!"

All the cowboys cheered.

"Dumb fucking shitkickers! Ever last one of ya," The Judge said. "But our little contest is gonna be worth every fucking Texas mile."

The cowboys arranged six women in a side-by-side line facing the bar.

"Well boys," The Judge heralded, "Today we're finally gonna have us our little contest!"

Every man cheered.

"Yep," The Judge said, staring down each of the women. "We're finally gonna have us our little fucking contest. One by one, ya see. Each of these cunts is gonna make her case before the judge." He grinned, "That's me!"

Every man cheered.

"Anyways. Each of these cunts is gonna get her chance to tell her sob-story. What I mean is. Each cunt is gonna get her chance to plead her case. And try and convince me just how terrible it is to be a cunt. And at the end of our little contest, *I'm* gonna pick the winner."

Every man cheered.

"But there can only be one winner in a contest like ours," The Judge said. "So ya cunts better argue your cases pretty goddamn well. Because I'm gonna shoot every single one of the losers right in between her fucking cunt eyes!"

Every man cheered.

"But to the winner of our little contest goes a very special prize," The Judge decreed with a macho gleam in his eyes.

One of the cowboys asked, "What prize ya gonna give the winnin cunt, Judge?"

"Well boys," The Judge decreed, rising up from his seat. "The winnin cunt," he adjusted the hard-on in his blue-jeans, "I'm gonna rape the fucking shit outta the winnin cunt. And ya boys get to watch me do it!"

Every man cheered.

"So let's get to it, boys," The Judge urged them. "Let's hear from the first one of these cunts and git our little contest goin! So," The Judge decreed, "let The Contest for Unhappiest Cunt Who Ever Lived," he banged his gavel, "Begin!"

* * *

PANEGYRIC –noun

1. a lofty oration or writing in praise of a person or thing; eulogy

2. formal or elaborate praise

It was near dusk on the day when Abraham and Isaac returned from distant Moriah. The descending sun dipped like an azure lathe into the desert horizon. When the woman discovered from her anguished son Isaac what had happened on the mountaintop, she turned around and faced for the first time in her life, not her trusted husband and lover, but a deceiver.

A hundred misgivings assaulted the walls of the woman's mind. Why did you hide this from me? Did you think that I wouldn't have let Isaac go? I trusted you a thousand times before when you came to me with messages from God! How did you watch me kiss my son goodbye for what you knew would be the final time and say nothing? I trusted you with my life, with my son, with everything. She wept and fled from the deceiver who stood before her....

Every man cheered.

It was near dusk on the day when Abraham and Isaac returned from distant Moriah. The descending sun dipped like an azure lathe into the desert horizon. When the woman discovered from her anguished son Isaac what had happened on the mountaintop, she turned around and faced for the first time in her life, not her trusted husband and lover, but a murderer.

I've loved him all my life! He is my husband! But I hate him too! He is a criminal! She realized, then, that she wanted to embrace him, welcome him home from his ordeal. But in that same moment she realized she could kill him for what he had done. After a few moments she collapsed into the sand, unable to do either...

Every man cheered.

It was near dusk on the day when Abraham and Isaac returned from distant Moriah. The descending sun dipped like an azure lathe into the desert horizon. When the woman discovered from her anguished son Isaac what had happened on the mountaintop, she turned around and faced for the first time in her life, not her trusted husband and lover, but an enigma.

I put my faith in you and all the promises that you told me God made for us! You were the voice of God for me! I knew love and faith in you! But now I can't understand your faith. And if I can't understand your faith then I have none! I was everything in you and now I am nothing...

Every man cheered.

* * *

"It's fucking judgment day, ya cunts!" The Judge blazoned from behind his bar. "I go on a fucking Texas cattle drive. And I manage to cross a thousand fucking rivers," he lamented. "And I manage to assemble a line-up of the most famous cunts that history has to offer. And for what? So I can hear the same old cunt sob-story every man's heard a thousand fucking times before?"

Three women already lay dead on the floor, shot between the eyes.

"If I hear one more cunt whine about her faithless lover. I swear to fucking God," The Judge picked up his pistol and aimed it at the remaining three women. "I better start hearin some sadder fucking sob-stories from you cunts, or else!"

One of the cowboys whipped the next woman and she stumbled forward.

"So why the fuck should I give ya the prize for the unhappiest cunt who ever lived?"

"The sheriff murdered my husband and," she said, and then broke down crying, "and my fourteen children too!"

"Not bad, not bad," The Judge decreed. "But what did *you* *do* to deserve it?"

"What?"

"Well ya must've done somethin to piss off the sheriff?"

"He said I was too proud for my own good."

"You were too proud for your own good, huh?" The Judge said. "Well shit. Listen here, sweetheart. Every man knows there ain't nothin that kills a hard-on faster than an arrogant cunt. Maybe if you'd have just sucked his dick. Or let him fuck ya up the ass. Then your goddamned husband and kids would still be alive, huh?"

"But," the woman protested.

"Shut the fuck up ya dumb cunt! I've fucking heard enough from ya! You can step back in line for now. I'm not gonna shoot ya, just yet."

The woman hobbled back into the line.

"Which one of these fucking cunts is up next?"

A woman limped forward. Her bare feet left bloody footprints on the floor from the long cattle drive.

"Well let's hear it!" The Judge urged.

"The sheriff said my brother's body couldn't be buried in the town cemetery. And that his body should just be left outside of town to be eaten by coyotes. So I judged," she raised her chin slightly, pushing her hair from her face, "I judged for myself that this was unjust. And so I went ahead and gave my brother an honorable Christian burial in the cemetery. But I was caught. And they threw me in jail for my crime."

"Sounds, *almost* noble to me," The Judge said. "So what part of the story are *you* leavin out? I mean why the fuck was your brother refused a decent Christian burial?"

"My brother was betrayed by another man. And then they had a feud. During their feud they killed each other. The sheriff was a close friend to the man who betrayed my brother. It's as simple as that."

"No story is ever as fucking simple as that!" The Judge hollered. "Especially if the story is told to ya by a cunt-whore!"

"I had to bury my brother all alone!" the woman pleaded. "My own sister wouldn't even help me! Somebody had to do somethin!"

"Sounds like your sister knew her fucking place," The Judge said. "So am I a fucking dumbass? Or am I missin somethin here? Remind me again. Why are *you* the unhappiest cunt who ever lived? I mean. Ya don't sound a bit sorry for buryin what ya shouldn't of buried? Am I right?"

"I am unhappy," she said, "Because I did what was just, but all I suffered was injustice for doin it."

The Judge leaned forward over the bar. He grinned and said, "You are one shifty fucking cunt, ya know that? Ya think ya can get the best of me? Well ya better saddle a faster horse in the mornin if ya wanna get the best of me! Listen up cunt. I know more about *you* than ya think I know. In fact! I'm way smarter than you cunts think I am!"

"What do you mean?"

"You recall your daddy?"

"I do"

"And you recall your mama?"

"I do"

"And you recall how your mama was *his* mama? Your daddy's mama, I mean?"

"Yes," she confessed, and then hung her head in shame.

"So let me get this straight. Just for the fucking record. Your daddy fucked his own mama. And then! Outta that unholy fucking inbred union your sorry cunt-ass was born? Did I fucking miss anythin?"

The woman made no response.

"So why should somebody smart like me?" The Judge reasoned out loud, "A man with both book learnin and balls. Trust the judgment. Much less take the word of. Some poor ignorant white-trash cunt like you?"

The woman didn't defend herself, silenced by her shame.

"Step back into line," The Judge ordered her, "Ya trailer-trash piece-of-shit cunt!"

The woman obeyed him, stepping back into the line.

"Only one famous cunt left? Our little contest here is gonna be over sooner than I fucking thought!"

One of the cowboys whipped the final woman forward. Despite her bleeding feet, bruised knees and torn knuckles, the woman stood tall before the bar.

The Judge dandled his pistol on the bar in front of him.

She was armed only with what might be described as a kind of desperate abandon.

"So get to it cunt!" The Judge decreed. "Let's hear your sob-story. Why are *you* the unhappiest cunt who ever lived?"

The woman remained silent.

"For Chrissakes," The Judge said. "Just tell me your goddamn story ya stubborn fucking cunt!"

"My husband murdered our only son. *My* only son..."

"Why'd he do it?"

"Because my daddy told him to..."

"You're a lyin cunt. Because I happen to fucking know that your son *didn't* die that day."

"My son *was* murdered that day. And so was my husband..."

"And you're sayin your daddy didn't do nothin about it?"

"Nope"

"Your lyin again! Because I happen to know that your daddy *did* do somethin about it."

"My daddy was murdered that day too."

"You're a lyin cunt! And ya ain't told a lick of fucking truth since ya first opened your goddamned cocksuckin mouth…"

✳✳✳

There is a story avowed by old-timers and bartenders, of an empty grave near Mexia, Texas. They say it is marked with a simple stone. And the words etched upon it are from a sacred book and read:

"A woman's dialectic is remarkable, and only the person who has had the opportunity to observe it can imitate it, whereas the greatest dialectician who ever lived could speculate himself crazy trying to produce it."

DAY 3
Chapter 13

Mexia, Texas;
Jim's Krispy Fried Chicken;
And what became of Mike and Candi at lunch

Mike woke up in the Best Western Motel in Mexia, Texas. He opened his eyes and felt a chilly sweat up and down his body. He saw daylight streaming in through the curtains and heard the TV. From his bed he saw Candi sitting Indian style on the floor watching TV. She pumped her arm up and down chanting- "Jerry, Jerry, Jerry!"

"Wow," Mike said, "I had the worst fucking nightmare last night."

Candi turned around, smiled and said, "You sure sounded like it, pardner. You even woke me up a few times with all your moanin and groanin. Course. I just thought you were firin off a few rounds from the ol pocket pistol." Candi chuckled.

Mike wiped his sweaty brow with the bed sheets.

"You know. Shootin off the old six-shooter?"

"Yeah, I know what you mean"

"You know. Pumpin the old shotgun?"

"I get it"

"You know. Firin off the old flesh musket?"

"For Chrissakes, Candi. I get it already."

"As for me," Candi said, "I already dotted my i this mornin. If you know what I mean?"

Mike threw off his covers and took a few deep breaths.

"So what was your fucking nightmare about anyway?"

"I, uh, don't remember..."

"Don't you hate it when that fucking happens? Course. If it's a really bad fucking nightmare. Then you probably don't fucking even wanna remember it. Am I right?"

"I'm starving," Mike said. "Let's go downstairs and get some breakfast."

"It's too fucking late for breakfast here, pardner. You nearly slept till noon. Besides. Breakfast in these places will kill you faster than a bullet. Or a stank pussy on a ten dollar whore."

"Ok," Mike said, "then let's go somewhere else and get some breakfast."

"Fuck breakfast, pardner. Let's go rustle us up some grub at Jim's Krispy Fried Chicken. Let me tell you. They make the fucking best fried chicken. The fucking best homemade yeast rolls. And the absolute best fucking hush puppies in the whole fucking world!"

"I can't believe I'm saying this. But that actually sounds really good to me."

"I sure am glad to see you finally grew a pair. And now you're gonna stop orderin fucking salads. I told you I'd have you eatin like a real man before our little odyssey was over."

"Can we just go, please? I'm starving."

✳✳✳

Mike and Candi rode up into the parking lot of Jim's Krispy Fried Chicken, on East Milam Street in Mexia. Mike looked at the brown brick building with a red shingled roof. The sign read:

Jim's Krispy Fried Chicken
Old Fashioned Homemade Yeast Rolls

10 PC MIX
2 MED SIDES $15.99
MC VISA DEBIT

"Everything here is good," Candi said. "So I'll tell you what to get. And then you go on inside and rustle us up some grub. I'll wait right here in the car."

"Why aren't you going inside with me?"

"I know way too many fucking people in this one-horse town, pardner."

"We'll only be in there a couple of minutes. I don't think-"

"And I used to fucking work here too. So trust me. I fucking know everybody."

"Well then let's go somewhere else and eat."

"No fucking way, pardner. We're not gonna ride all the way to Mexia, Texas. And not eat at Jim's Krispy Fried Chicken."

"So we're just going to eat lunch in the car?"

"Sure! Why the fuck not? I mean that's how cowboys on a cattle drive used to do it in the Old West. They'd rustle them up some grub from the chuck wagon. And then eat right there sittin in the saddle. Sittin right up on their fucking horses."

"So what you're saying is. That never once. Never in the history of the American West. Did cowboys ever eat meals just sitting by the campfire, like in the movies?" Mike chuckled.

"Nope, dumbass. That's not what I'm fucking sayin. Cowboys only sat by campfires when they were tellin stories. Everybody and their fucking mother in law fucking knows that!"

"Ok, fine. Just tell me what's good and I'll order-"

"Like I said before- *everything* is good"

"Ok. So what the fuck, then?" Mike said. "You just want me to fucking order everything on the fucking menu, then?"

"I really like it when you talk that way, pardner," Candi said, "You know that, don't you?"

"I guess you're finally rubbing off on me"

"Better than you rubbin one off in my mouth... Am I right?"

"Oh very funny"

"Oh yeah," Candi said. "I may wanna listen to some tunes while you're gone. So just leave the keys in the car with me."

✱✱✱

Staring at the menu above the counter, Mike was glad Candi hadn't recommended he order either the fried chicken livers or chicken gizzards. The place was packed for lunch. The red and white booths inside Jim's Krispy Fried Chicken reminded Mike of the booths in a Dairy Queen, which reminded him of Candi's joke about Mexia. He chuckled to himself.

A young blonde woman behind the counter smiled at Mike. She said to him, "How can help ya, sir?" Her nametag read: Marylin.

Mike couldn't help but smile back at her. He ordered half a chicken, four rolls, a side of mashed potatoes and a side of fried squash. And some fried jalapenos and hush puppies.

And it wasn't long before Mike had two bags of food in his arms. Food had never smelled so good to him. His stomach growled. He walked outside into the parking lot, looked up, and then realized that both Candi and his ride were gone.

✳ ✳ ✳

When Candi asked him to leave the car keys with her, it had never dawned on Mike that she might be planning a getaway. How could she do this to me? Mike thought. And why would she do this to me? She didn't need to ride with me all the way to Mexia fucking Texas in order to steal my car. She could've done that in Houston. Of course. Maybe she knows somebody here in Mexia who buys stolen cars? Maybe that's why she brought me here? But if she was going to pull something like this, wouldn't she at least rob me too? I mean take my wallet? And my money and my fucking Rolex too?

Mike reminded himself that any attempt to understand Candi's behavior by applying rationality was a fool's errand. After all. She was a whore. Ignorant and irrational and sometimes it seemed, even half crazy. And even though Mike felt as if he'd gotten to know Candi over the last few days, he reminded himself that she was still just a stranger. I should've never left those fucking keys with her! Mike thought. She was right. I am such a fucking dumbass!

Mike said to himself, out loud- I can't believe that fucking bitch-whore did this to me! And after everything I've done for her? And after how generous I've been to her too?

Just then, Mike heard a car honking and looked up. Candi drove into the parking lot and pulled up alongside him. She rolled down the window, smiled and said, "Hey there, pardner.

I'm writin a fucking novel about some stupid fucking roadtrip bullshit. That nobody's ever gonna read. Or ever gonna give two shits about. But I tell you what. If you eat out my pussy, then I'll give you a ride across that bridge over yonder."

Mike sighed and said, "I thought you were gone, Candi."

"Well I *was* gone, pardner. I was gone down the street to the corner store. To get us some beers to have with our grub"

"No. I mean I thought you were really *gone*. Like really gone"

"What the fuck?" Candi said. "You mean you actually thought I'd stolen your ride? And just fucking left you stranded out here?"

"Uh, well. I mean. I just panicked and then-"

"Fuck you for that, pardner! I mean after all we've been through together? Fuck you with a stolen dimestore dick!"

"I'm sorry, Candi. I'm really, really sorry"

"You fucking know I really hate it when you talk like that, pardner. You're just makin it worse."

"I'm sorry"

Candi opened the car door and got out. She stood face to face with Mike, leaning into him. She stared him down. "Let me tell you somethin, pardner. When you ride with a man you stick with him. And if you can't fucking do that. Then you're like some goddamned fucking animal. You're fucking finished!"

She mumbled something else under her breath. She grabbed the bags of food away Mike and then went around to the passenger side of the car. She opened the door and said, "Well, pardner... let's ride."

✳✳✳

When you leave Jim's Krispy Fried Chicken in Mexia, take a left on East Milam. Once you get back to Highway 14, take a right and head northwards. A few miles down the highway you'll see North Rosse Avenue, an inconspicuous country road on the right.

Mike and Candi pulled off the highway there. They parked near the intersection of these two roads, and then ate their lunch together.

"There's nothin better in the whole fucking world," Candi said, "than washin down Jim's Krispy Fried Chicken with an ice cold Coors Light."

"This is quite possibly," Mike said, stuffing a homemade yeast roll in his mouth, "the best fucking meal I've ever eaten in my entire fucking life."

"Hey," Candi said, "You didn't say it was *actually* good that time."

"Yeah. I guess I didn't," Mike smiled and took a swig from his beer bottle. He raised up the bottle, offering a toast. "To my pardner, Candi. Thanks for the beers!"

Candi raised her bottle and clinked it against his. "Yep. That's me. The founder of the fucking feast"

"By the way," Mike said, "I would've given you money for the beer."

"I didn't need any money," Candi said, winking at him.

"Let me guess, then. You *smouched* these beers too?" Mike was again proud of his deft use of one of Candi's colloquialisms—more belletristic gold for his novel. "But how did you manage to smouch a whole six pack of beer, for Chrissakes?"

"Nope. No smouchin this time, pardner."

"So if you didn't have any money. And you didn't smouch. Then how the hell did you get a six pack of beer?"

"I traded for it," Candi said. "You know. Like they did back in the Old West"

"Do you mean you traded for, uh...services rendered?"

"Services rendered? Did you really just fucking say that? Come on, pardner. You'd think at this point in our little odyssey. After this long of a ride together. You'd just come right out and say what you really mean. So what do you really wanna know?"

Mike hesitated, took a chug from his beer and said, "So you sucked some guy's dick for this beer?"

"Eeww," Candi said, grimacing, "That's fucking gross! You are one sick fucking pervert, you know that? I mean everythin with you is either about fucking or suckin. Or fucking cummin. Or blowin or goin down. Or fucking gettin it up. Or chokin the chicken. Or just eatin some fried chicken." She took a drumstick from the bag and pumped it back and forth in her mouth. She shoved it hard against the back of her throat and choked a little.

"Hey you're the one," Mike said, "giving a drumstick head. And *I'm* the sick fucking pervert?"

Candi gagged on the drumstick. She tugged it from her mouth and then spit on the floorboard of the car.

"Are you alright?"

"Well. Now that's fucking embarrassin," Candi said. Her eyes were red and watery now. "Be sure not tell anybody what just happened here, pardner. I mean. If that shit gets out. It's bad for my business, you know?" She laughed, still coughing a little.

"Seriously...Are you alright?"

"Course I'm alright! I just need a quick swig of beer." She tipped her bottle and finished what was left, "And then I'll be right as rain. And ready for more hot meat in my mouth. Just like usual." She laughed and grabbed another piece of chicken.

"Ok," Mike said, smiling, "But no more giving head to drumsticks."

"Don't worry, pardner. It's a *breast* this time."

They laughed together.

"So," Candi said, "You really think I gave some guy a blow-job for this beer, huh?"

"Well. I, uh-"

"Yes or fucking no?"

"Yes"

"I fucking knew that's what you were fucking thinking! You know. I just wanted to hear you say it out loud. Right to my fucking face." Candi thought for a moment. She smiled and said, "Hey! Get it? My *fucking* face... Get it? My pretty little face that fucks stranger's dicks for beer? Get it?"

"Pun intended?" Mike said.

"I'm not sure, actually. I'll have to get back to you on that one, pardner."

"You didn't have to do that, Candi. You should've just driven back and picked me up. I would've paid for the beer."

"Well, pardner. It's like I told you before. I don't need to reach into your pants every fucking time I need somethin. I've gotten along just fine my whole goddamned life without your fucking wallet in my hand. Or your fucking dick in my mouth."

"I know you have, for Chrissakes. That's not what I meant. And you fucking know it." Mike ate a hushpuppy and took a swig of beer.

"Hey! I'm the fucking one who should be upset here. I mean I show up with a six pack of beer. And you just fucking assume that I sucked some stranger's dick for it."

"For Chrissakes, Candi. What else am I supposed to think?"

"There's lots of things you could've fucking thought, pardner. I mean maybe I panhandled outside the store. You know. And got some Good Samaritan to give me money? Or maybe I ran into an old friend I knew when I lived here. And she owed me money? Or maybe the store clerk or some redneck just thought I was fucking hot. And bought me some beer? Just because I'm sooo fucking good at cock-teasin? Or maybe I,"

"Ok, for Chrissakes. I get your point!"

"Or maybe God in his heaven knew this little whore needed some beer. And so he dropped it right down into my fucking lap. Just like he did with all that bread in the desert?"

"Candi, will you just..." Mike punched the dashboard. "Will you just fucking shut the fuck up?"

"Like I told you before, pardner." Candi placed her hand on his clenched fist. She gently scratched his knuckles with her pink plastic fingernails. "I fucking love it when you talk like that."

Mike felt the swelling of his sudden hard-on numb the pain in his knuckles and arm.

"Maybe next time," Candi said, moving her hand over to his knee. She scratched her fingernails slowly up his leg onto his thigh. "Maybe next time you'll really man up. And grow a pair and hit somethin *besides* the fucking dashboard?" She smiled at him and then removed her hand from his leg. "You look like you could use another beer, pardner."

"Yeah, I could"

"Anyways," Candi said, popping the bottle cap off his beer. "Just so we get the story straight. For your book, you know. I didn't fucking give anybody a blowjob for this beer."

"Then how did you-"

"I mean don't get me wrong. I did get down on my knees. But there wasn't a blowjob involved. In fact. To tell the gospel truth of it. It *was* God who did it. I mean it was a fucking real-life miracle! You see. When I realized I didn't have any cash for beer. And that we really, really needed beer. If we were really, really gonna enjoy our Jim's Krispy Fried Chicken. I made a vow to God right then and there."

"Yep! Right then and there in the parking lot of that convenient store in Mexia, Texas. Of all places! I got down on my knees. And I made a vow to God. So I got on my knees and prayed to God. And I told him that if he'd drop a six pack of Coors light and a bag of blowpops down from heaven into my lap. I'd never suck a strange dick ever again."

"And you know what fucking happened next? Well. A six pack of Coors Light and a bag of blowpops suddenly appeared. Poof! Right there in my fucking lap. Just like that! Poof! And let me tell you this. I don't care what anybody says. God still fucking answers prayer. And he still works fucking miracles!"

"And you know what's even more amazin? The beer was cold! I mean. I didn't even think to fucking ask for cold beer. But God knew that's what I needed. Because God fucking knows everything. Listen up, pardner. I don't give a shit what anybody fucking says. I mean fuck atheists right in the ear with a shitty bloody dildo. Because God is fucking awesome!"

"Are you sure," Mike said, "that you didn't just suck a dick for this beer?"

"Why?" Candi said, smiling, "Is that a more believable story?"

"Definitely more believable"

"You know what? I should be fucking insulted right now."

"Why?"

"Well. I should be fucking insulted right now. Because what you're really suggestin is this. You're suggestin that my blowjobs are only worth a six pack of beer and a bag of blowpops. I mean don't you think if I had given some guy one of my world-famous blowjobs? That I'd get a little more than a six-pack of beer and a bag of blowpops for it?"

"Candi. I don't think I'm going to answer that question."

"Well why the fuck not, pardner? I mean. You of all people should have an opinion on this one. After all. You sampled the fucking goods. So how much should my world-famous, legendary blowjob be worth?"

"Definitely more than a six pack of beer and a bag of blowpops."

"Well duh! Tell the world somethin they don't fucking know already."

"Hey. I answered your question. And if you ask me, Candi. If you really want to know what I think? Well I think you got fucking cheated and robbed if you gave some fucking asshole a blowjob for this fucking beer!"

Mike rolled down the window of the car. He grabbed the last remaining beer from the six pack and threw it out the window. It shattered and spilled on the pavement. "You really want to know what I fucking think about you, Candi? Well I'm fucking pissed off at you right now. You know why? Not for being a whore. But for being such a *cheap* fucking whore! There! I fucking said it..."

"You know what, pardner?" Candi said. "I fucking take back what I said before. Back in Bremond outside the Dry Bean Saloon. I changed my fucking mind. What you just said to me, just now. *That's* the nicest thing anybody ever told me." She put her hand gently on his cheek and smiled. "But you know what?"

"What?"

Candi drew back her hand and slapped Mike's cheek. "Sometimes. And only sometimes these days. You're still a fucking dumbass."

Mike rubbed his cheek and said, "What the fuck was that for?"

"Well, pardner. You went and threw our last cold beer out the fucking window. And now! No matter how hard I pray on my knees. I don't think God's gonna send us anymore."

✳ ✳ ✳

It was mid afternoon now. Mike and Candi still sat in their parked car along the highway.

"Just so you know," Candi said. She chewed the pink bubble gum off the blowpop stick. "I didn't really give anybody a blowjob for the beer and blowpops."

"You're not going to tell me another story about how God still answers prayer and works miracles, are you?"

Candi laughed and said, "Hell no, pardner. And you know what? I didn't get it any of those other ways I mentioned either. In fact. If you really think about it. Those other ways might just be more unbelievable than God answerin my prayers."

"Why is that?"

"Well to start with. I never fucking panhandle. Never. Never have and never will. Beggin is for bums, losers, crackheads and charity cases. Nope. Not me. My daddy raised me up better than that. Plus! There's really no such thing as a Good Samaritan. Know what I mean, jelly bean?"

"No, I don't"

"It's funny, you know. Of all the stories in the Bible that people find unbelievable. You know. Like when God parted the waters of that ocean?"

"The Red Sea"

"Yep, that's the one. Or when God made the sun stand still. Or when JC turned water into wine. Or when he raised up his buddy from the dead. What was his buddy's name again?"

"Lazarus"

"Or even when JC rose from the dead. I mean. I just think it's weird how it's always *those stories* from the Bible that people find so unfuckingbelievable."

"Why is that weird? After all. They *are* unbelievable stories."

"I guess for me it just doesn't seem all that unbelievable. I mean this is fucking God we're talkin about here. I reckon God oughta be able to do any of those fucking things. Right?"

"I mean if ol Cecille B. Demille can part the waters of that sea in that flick *The Ten Commandments*. And make it look sooo real. And that flick was made a really long fucking time ago too. It seems to me like it would be a fucking sinch for God to do it." Candi tossed her spent blowpop stick out the window and grabbed a fresh one. "You're probably wonderin how an ignorant whore like me knows who fucking Cecille B. Demille is? Am I right?"

"Well, yes," Mike said. "But not in those exact words."

"Well…I learned it from watchin *Blazing Saddles*, pardner. See. There's this part where The Waco Kid is tellin Bart about how he used to be the fastest gun, not in the west…" Candi paused, and then did her best Gene Wilder impression, "…in the world…"

"Anyways. The Waco Kid is braggin about how many men he killed. And then he says to Bart," she did her Gene Wilder voice again, "Yep. I must've killed more men than Cecille B. Demille." She laughed out loud and slapped her knees. "Course.

I didn't fucking get the joke at first. But later that same year at Thanksgiving. I was watchin that old flick *Ben Hur*. You know, with Charlton Heston. Cecille B. Demille did that flick too. Have you seen it?"

"Yeah"

"So you remember the chariot racin scene, then?"

"Yeah"

"Well. My Uncle Tom is watchin it with me. And *Blazing Saddles* is his favorite movie too. In fact! He's the one who introduced me to *Blazing Saddles*. Anyways. Uncle Tom explains it all to me. He tells me that The Waco Kid says he must have killed more men than Cecile B. Demille. Because in that chariot racin scene in *Ben Hur*. Like a dozen stuntmen got killed while filmin it." Candi laughed. "Uncle Tom fucking knew his flicks. That's for damn sure."

"I can honestly say, Candi. I spent three years of my life at Yale Divinity School studying philosophy and religion. And I never heard anyone offer theological commentary or textual criticism on the veracity of miracles in the Bible, using *Blazing Saddles*, *The Ten Commandments* or *Ben Hur*."

"And I'll bet they never did any of that fancy-schmancy shit you just said. In their best Gene Wilder voice, either?"

"No," Mike said, laughing, "No, they didn't"

"Well, pardner. If that's true. And you know I don't fucking judge. But if that's true. Then it sounds to me like you might've just fucking wasted three years of your fucking life up there. I mean. I'm just sayin."

"You know what, Candi? I think I'm beginning to feel that same way, more and more every fucking day."

"So. Like I was sayin before. If ol Cecile B. Demille can fucking part the waters in *The Ten Commandments*. Then I reckon God can too. And as for makin the sun stand still. It seems to me that since God created the sun. And he made it move in the first place. Then why can't he just make it stop for a little while?"

"You do realize, Candi. That the sun *doesn't* move? The sun always stands still. And it's the earth and everything else that moves around the sun. It's called heliocentrism. It's called science.'

"Huh. I reckon I never really thought about it that way. That's a good fucking point right there, pardner. So that means.

If the sun ain't movin in the first place. Then it's kinda impossible for God to make it stand still."

"Exactly," Mike said, recalling his Old Testament criticism class at Yale Divinity School, taught by John J. Collins.

"So. I reckon then. If that's true. Then God makin the sun stand still would be even more of an impressive miracle!"

"What?"

"I mean. If makin a thing that's *not* movin *stop* movin, is impossible. Then when God made the sun stand still, when it wasn't even movin. That means God fucking did the impossible. And when you do the impossible. You do a miracle…Am I right?"

"You lost me, Candi."

"I mean. If a thing is already standin still. Not movin. And then you make it stand still. You've done the fucking impossible. Am I right? And that means you've worked a fucking miracle! Am I right?"

"That's completely irrational, Candi. It just doesn't make any sense at all."

"Of course it doesn't make any sense. It's a fucking miracle. It's not supposed to make any sense. If it made any fucking sense. And you could explain it and understand it. Then it wouldn't be a fucking miracle now, would it?"

"I think you're missing the whole point here."

"Of what?"

"I think you're missing the whole point of skepticism. Of why certain people find the miracle stories in the Bible unbelievable."

"Oh yeah?"

"Yeah. If the Bible, or any book for that matter, suggests somebody is doing something impossible, then,"

"Like God makin the sun stand still when it's not even movin in the first place?"

"Yes, exactly. Like a story where God makes the sun stand still. Because we know through empirical science that the sun is not moving. When a rational person reads that story, she realizes there is an inherent contradiction based on empirical proof. And then she reasonably concludes that the story must therefore be false. That the story must be fiction"

"You know, pardner. You gotta real good point there. I mean. I reckon I never really thought about it much. Especially not the way you just explained it to me. I can really see why some people think that way."

"Really?"

"Yep"

"Just like that?"

"Yep"

"So," Mike said, "You mean I convinced you?"

"Yep. I'm fucking convinced. I mean I'm no dumbass." Candi crunched into the green blowpop, tearing the pink gum away with her teeth. "Course. Even though I agree with you. I can still see why other people believe the other way too."

"What's that supposed to mean?"

"All I mean is. It just seems to me that. It just makes sense for some people to believe God can do impossible things. Like makin the sun stand still when it doesn't even move. I mean that's just the way some people think about life."

"Course. In the other holster. It kinda makes sense for some other people, like you, to refuse to believe that impossible things can ever fucking happen. Because that's just the way they look at life. Nobody's right and nobody's wrong. And you're sure as hell not gonna fucking change their fucked up minds. I mean. It's just a way of lookin at things different, I reckon... Am I right?"

"Uh, no," Mike said, "You're wrong about that, Candi. It's about people being rational versus being irrational. Not about being right or wrong."

"But you just said that I was wrong?"

"Dammit," Mike said. "What I meant to say is. It's about being right or wrong *because* it's about being rational versus being irrational. It's one thing to believe that if God exists, God could part the waters of the Red Sea. Or even transform the molecules of water into wine. Or maybe even raise somebody from the dead. In fact. *If* God does exist then I'm sure God could do all those things."

"But," Mike said, "Making something stand still or stop moving, when it's already standing still and doesn't move in the first place, is just fucking irrational. And if anybody thinks that if God exists, God *actually* did that then they're a big fucking irrational dumbass."

"Yep," Candi said. "See there. It's just like I was tellin you before. We all just got different ways of lookin at things. And there's nothin anybody can do to change our fucked up minds about it."

"Oh, for Chrissakes"

"Yep. Just like nobody's ever gonna change my fucked up mind about the fact that there's no such thing as a Good Samaritan. Like I was sayin before. I can swallow pretty much anythin." Candi paused and then smiled. "And I'm talkin about miracle Bible stories right now." She laughed. "I mean I can believe just about any Bible story you wanna read me. But that fucking Good Samaritan story is a holy load of fucking horseshit if you ask me."

"But there's nothing miraculous about that story?"

"That's just fucking it, pardner. There's nothin miraculous about it. God's not even in that fucking story."

"True," Mike said. "In fact. I made this same point in my dissertation. If anything. The story of the Good Samaritan illustrates the absence of God in everyday life. That it is logically necessary for God *not* to intervene in human affairs and free will. Even when thieves attack and rob a helpless man along the road."

"That wasn't my fucking point at all," Candi said. "I already told you. I think your dumb luck theory is another holy load of-"

"*theodicy*...remember?"

"Whatever. Like I told you before. I think it's fucking fucked up bullshit."

"So tell me then," Mike said, "What was your point about the Good Samaritan story?"

"My point is. I think the Good Samaritan story is the most unbelievable story in the entire fucking Bible."

"Why?"

"Because there's no such thing as a Good Samaritan. They don't exist."

"What do you mean they don't exist?"

"Well I've never fucking met one."

"Yes you have"

"Nope, never"

"So what you're telling me. Is that no one has ever helped you out when you needed it?"

"Yep! That's exactly what I'm fucking sayin."

"What about your family? What about your daddy?"

"The whole point of the fucking Good Samaritan story is that the Good Samaritan was a fucking stranger. I mean. He didn't have any obligation to help the guy who'd been robbed. See. The whole point of the fucking fucked up story. Is that a complete fucking stranger saw somebody who needed help. And then fucking helped him. No strings attached. No gettin nothin out of it"

"I guess you're right about that," Mike said.

"You're goddamned right I'm right about that, pardner. We're all goddamned right I'm right about that!"

"Well. Just because you've never seen a Good Samaritan, doesn't mean he doesn't exist...Right?"

"I reckon I'm just the kinda person who needs proof. That's all."

Mike smiled and chuckled to himself. "Hey Candi. Do you realize? This entire conversation we're having came from you trying to tell me the real way you got the beer and blowpops earlier?"

"I reckon you're right"

"Well. Are you going to tell me or not?"

"Course I am, pardner. But first! I gotta finish tellin you why it's more believable that God answered my prayers when I was on my knees in the parking lot. You know. Than any of those other ways I mentioned before. So I already told you it couldn't have been panhandling. Because I never panhandle. Because I don't believe in Good Samaritans"

Mike smiled and said, "Good. I'm glad we're all caught up now."

"Anyways. It couldn't have been that I ran into an old friend who owed me money. Now I did fucking live here in Mexia, Texas. That part's true. But I don't have any old friends here. Because. By the time I got the hell outta Dodge. All my friends were enemies. And I owed all of them money!"

"But what about when you said that maybe somebody just thought you were fucking hot? And wanted to buy you beer and blowpops?"

"You mean because I'm such a good cock-teaser?"

"Exactly. I mean I'm just saying. I think you're fucking hot."

"So you think I'm a good cockteaser?"

"Yeah"

"Yeah what?"

"Yeah, Candi. I think you're a good cockteaser."

"And you really do think I'm a *good* cockteaser? Because let's fucking face it. All women are cockteasers. But not all women are *good* cockteasers."

"I think you're a *great* cockteaser," Mike said. "And that's way better than just good. I mean if I'd seen you at that store. I would've given you my entire fucking wallet. And my firstborn fucking child!"

They laughed together.

"You know what, pardner? I'll never call you a dumbass ever again. And I mean it too. I'll even shake on it. You know. The code of the Old West. Like back in the good old days. When a man's word was all he had. When a handshake really meant somethin." Candi turned in her seat to face Mike. She offered him a handshake and said, "Deal?"

"You really mean it, Candi?"

"Yep"

"You really mean it, this time?"

"Yep"

"You're not just joking?"

"Hey, pardner," Candi said. "I may be a fucking whore, it's true. But this is the fucking code of the Old West. You just don't go and break the fucking code of The Old West. I mean somethin's gotta mean somethin, right? Am I right?"

"Thanks, Candi." He shook her hand. It was warm and soft, and yet somehow strong also. Her hand felt good in his, and Mike realized he couldn't remember the last time he held a woman's hand. Or anybody's hand for that matter. He looked at Candi's hand in his and wondered how long it had been since she held a man's hand, or anybody's hand for that matter.

Mike wondered how many times this hand of Candi's which he now held in his own, had flagged down a car for a ride. Or unzipped a strange man's pants? Or how many times this hand of hers which he now held had stroked and pumped and flogged a stranger's dick? Or how many times this hand of hers had lifted a stranger's dick into her open mouth? Or how many times this hand had fought off an attacker, and lost…

Mike felt his hard-on returning.

"Well," Candi said. She let go of his hand and reached into the bag for another blowpop. "I sure am glad you think I'm a great enough cockteaser to get the whole fucking store given to me. But that's not how I did it either."

"Really?"

"Nope. I didn't really have time. I knew you might worry about me bein gone with the car and all. Course. I never thought for even one fucking second. That you'd think I'd smouched your fucking car and left you behind. You're a fucking asshole!"

"Like I said before, Candi. I'm really-"

"I mean talk about breakin the code of the Old West. They fucking hung people for smouchin horses back then. And I reckon they were right to do it too. I reckon there's just some things you should never ever fucking do. And one of em is smouch another man's ride."

"I don't know," Mike said. "Hanging just seems too harsh a punishment to me. If you really think about it. The death penalty is never rationally justified. In fact, it's downright barbaric."

"And that's exactly why you'd never have survived in the Old West, pardner. Because you fucking need other people to step up and protect your ass. You need real men to man up and stand up and fucking just do what's gotta be done. I mean let's face it. The only fucking reason you've survived this cattle drive is because of me. Am I right? I mean. You didn't fucking see me let the fact that I don't have a dick stop me from mannin up in the saddle."

"Listen, Candi. If you're still mad about earlier then I'm,"

"Like I was sayin before. I was in a hurry when I was at the store. And I knew you might worry about me bein gone with the car and all. So I didn't really have time to shift into full, great cock-teasin mode."

"Ok"

"So I go into the convenient store. And of course! There's this Arab behind the counter. And of course. It turns out this Arab fucking owns the store. Well right then and there I knew I was fucking golden. So I get the six-pack out of the cooler. And grab a bag of blowpops. Then I go right up to the counter. And then I wait until all the other customers leave. And then I say to him- I'll show you my tits if you give me this beer and candy. They're real beautiful. And they're real, too. So how about it?"

"Well of course. Like fucking clockwork. That Arab nods his towel head up and down. So I fucking flashed him my tits, just like this," Candi lifted her t-shirt and flashed her tits to Mike. "And fucking just like that. I was fucking outta there with beer and blowpops!"

"Wow"

Candi laughed and said, "Let me tell you. It's just like my daddy always said to me- Girl, be careful if you're ever over in that part of the world. Because there's nothin a raghead wouldn't do for a look at some homegrown American titties." Candi was still laughing. "Course. I don't think when Daddy gave me that advice. He was thinkin I'd take it and use it to get free beer and blowpops. But what can I fucking say? I'm a whore. Which means all I've got is my clit, my tits and my wits!"

"Did you just say- *raghead*?"

"What the fuck, pardner? You mean to tell me that I flash you my tits. And all you can do is complain about me bein a fucking racist? You're such a fag!"

"If it helps," Mike said, smiling, "The whole time I was saying it. I was thinking about your tits."

"Yeah," Candi said, smiling back at him, "It helps a little. And you're kinda right. That was a little bit racist of me, wasn't it?"

"Yeah it was"

"Well then. I reckon what my daddy should've said was- Girl, it don't matter what a man's wearin on his head, cause he'll do anythin for a look at your titties."

They laughed together- Mike with his hard-on and Candi with her clit, tits and wits.

Chapter 14

At the crossroads of LCR 254 and LCR 243;
How Mike and Candi dug for buried treasure;
And the horrible events and fearsome deeds that followed

"Well, pardner," Candi said. "You ready to go dig up some buried treasure?"

"You know, Candi. You don't have to stick to your story about buried treasure. You can just tell me the real reason why you needed a ride here to Mexia. Trust me. Whatever the reason. You can just tell me now. At this point I'll help you out any way that I can."

"What the fuck do you mean by, *at this point?*"

"I mean. After all we've been through together. I want to help you."

"I already fucking told you. I don't fucking need you're fucking help. You got it?"

"Ok. I got it."

"Then we're on this ride *together?* Am I right?"

"You're right, of course"

"And we're gonna dig up some buried treasure today? Am I right?"

"If you say so"

"And that means we all get what we want? Am I right?"

"Right"

"And both of us finally get what we deserve? Am I right?"

"Whatever you say, Candi"

"So tell me, pardner. What do you think you deserve to get out of our little odyssey?"

"Well, you know. Stories for my novel. New experiences and a little adventure. I must say. It's been anything but boring, Candi. You've definitely kept up your end of the deal."

"Funny...I didn't think that was *the end* you were interested in."

"What's that supposed to mean?"

"Pun fucking intended, pardner. What I fucking mean is. You didn't mention just now. That one of the things you wanna get out of our little odyssey is *more* than just get a blowjob. You wanna fuck me too. Am I right?"

"That's not what this trip is about, Candi. Or ever was about."

"Are you tellin me? That ever since I sucked you off on the Baytown Bridge. You haven't been thinkin about fucking me too?"

"All I'm saying is. That's not *all* I've been thinking about."

"But you do wanna fuck me, don't you?"

"Yes"

"Then I make you hard, huh?" She leaned over towards him and whispered, "I mean. I make it really hard for your dick, don't I?"

"Yeah you do"

"And I'll bet you've had a fucking hard-on this whole goddamned drive, haven't you?"

Mike nodded, feeling his hard-on swell up.

"And I'll bet you'd fucking trade all the stories and experiences and adventure. And all that other shit too. For just one chance to stick your dick in my pussy. Wouldn't you?"

"No, Candi. It's not like that at all. *I'm* not like that."

"Well then...Goddamn me to the bad place."

"Candi, I don't know what you want me to say. Just fucking tell me what you want me to say and-"

"I reckon, pardner. I was just hopin you'd say *yes* to that last question. I mean. Even if it wasn't really true. Even if you didn't really mean it. All I'm sayin is that it would've been nice to hear, at least. You know what I mean jelly bean?"

"Is it too late to change my answer then?"

'Yep, too fucking late. You fucking missed your chance, pardner."

"So what does this mean?"

"It means it's about fucking time for me and you to go dig up some buried treasure..."

Mike started the car and they drove down North Rosse Avenue.

"See that old railroad trestle down there?" Candi said. "All covered with graffiti? You know. I got fucking cherry popped under that trestle."

"How old were you?"

"None of your fucking business"

They passed under the old railroad trestle and then drove a little ways down the road.

"Right up here," Candi said, pointing ahead. "You're gonna see a rusty old beat up, green metal street sign. With white letters on it that says- LCR 254 and LCR 243. Pull on over to the side of the road and park near that fucking sign."

"What does the LCR stand for?"

"Who the fuck knows"

Ever mindful of his novel, Mike noted the surrounding landscape. It was a rural wooded area. Mostly scrub brush and oaks trees with an occasional run-down old frame house or dilapidated mobile home- very Southern gothic. Mike pulled over to the side of the road and parked near the sign. "Well," he said, "What now?"

"We're gonna walk it from here on out, pardner."

They walked for a bit, picking their way through yaupon bush and cacti. They climbed over a rusty, nearly fallen down barbed-wire fence until they reached a hoary old farm house.

"Are we trespassing?" Mike said.

"Nope. Don't worry about that. Nobody's lived here for a long fucking time."

"How can you be sure?"

"Because I grew up right here"

"You mean you lived here? In this house?"

"Yep. Born and raised"

"How long has it been since you were here?"

"None of your fucking business"

It was a white clap-board house with the front porch on the left side. The porch was crowded with aging furniture and overgrown with trees and brush. On the other side of the dirt driveway, over another barbed wire fence, the adjoining pasture was like a cemetery for old, rusty discarded outdoor propane tanks.

Mike and Candi walked around the house into the backyard.

"Over there is my granddaddy's tool shed," Candi said. She pointed to a small blue ramshackle shed. "After he got back from the war. Granddaddy fucking built that tool shed with his bare fucking hands. From nothin but junk wood and stolen nails."

There was an old rusty Master lock on the tool shed door. Candi looked around on the ground nearby and then picked up a big rock. She walked back over the tool shed and began smashing the rock against the lock.

"Hey!" Mike said, "Stop it! What do you think you're doing?"

"What the fuck does it look like I'm doin? I'm breakin this fucking lock."

"But that's breaking and entering, Candi. I don't want to go to jail."

"Well, pardner. You're right about it bein breakin. But it's not breakin and enterin until we actually enter. Am I right?" Candi laughed and continued to smash the rock against the lock, chipping away at the wooden door too. "Goddammit! They sure knew how to make a fucking lock back in the olden days."

"What do you need from the tool shed?"

"Oh I could tell you all about some of the fucked up things Granddaddy kept in this tool shed. But that's a whole other story right there. All we need right now is a fucking shovel. So we can dig up the buried treasure." Candi swung the rock again, finally smashing the lock. It fell into the dirt at her feet. "Fucking finally! Thank fucking God!" Candi said. She turned around to Mike, "And thanks for all your help too. You lazy sonuvvabitch!"

"Sorry"

Candi swung open the wide wooden door of the tool shed. It was dark and musty inside. It was full of cobwebs, lumber, coffee cans full of nails, cane poles for fishing and every single kind of tool ever fashioned by the hands of men. Candi stepped inside. She kicked a bucket of plumbing supplies and said, "You know what my daddy always used to say?"

"What?"

"In order to be a plumber. All a fella needs to know is that water runs downhill. And shit don't flush itself."

"Clever fellow," Mike said.

Mike spotted an old crumpled cowboy hat on the floor of the tool shed. It was a white Stetson cowboy hat and the black band was encircled by silver stars. He picked it up and put it on. "Well, pilgrim," Mike said in his best John Wayne swagger, "Do I look like a real cowboy now?"

Candi glanced back at him. She frowned and said, "Nope. Not even fucking close. Now take it off."

"What? No way! I think it's cool. In fact. I think I could actually get used to this look. Maybe I could ride off into the sunset right after I save the-"

"Hey!" Candi shouted at him. "You got cotton in your fucking ears? You stupid fucking faggot! I fucking said. Take off that fucking cowboy hat! Right fucking now!"

"Ok, ok," Mike said, "for Chrissakes." He grabbed the rim of the cowboy hat and began to take it off, but stopped. "You know what, Candi? I think I'm going to keep it on, actually. I'm going to wear it, for now. I actually like it."

"What?"

"You heard me"

"I said take it off, pardner"

"Or what?"

"Or else..."

"Or else what?"

"Fine! Fucking forget about it! If you wanna look like a stupid fucking faggot. Then that's your goddamned fucking business. Not mine."

Mike adjusted the cowboy hat. He smiled and said in his best John Wayne swagger, "You're goddamned right it's my business, little lady. I do what I want. When I want. And I don't take no lip from nobody."

"Unless you're takin lip wrapped around your dick. When some whore's suckin you off. Am I right?"

"Damn straight, pilgrim," Mike said, laughing, "Pun intended."

"There it fucking is," Candi said. "There's that fucking shovel." She climbed over an old John Deere riding mower. She reached into the corner of the shed and grabbed a shovel. "Here, pardner." She turned around and handed it to Mike. "Now let's get the fuck outta this tool shed and go dig up some fucking buried treasure."

Back behind the tool shed Mike watched Candi study the ground beneath an enormous live oak tree. There wasn't much grass. Mostly dirt, rocks and dried cow patties. Mike felt the Texas heat scorch the back of his neck. He noticed Candi was drenched in sweat. Her threadbare white t-shirt clung to her tits.

"You know what?" Candi said. "I don't remember exactly where he buried it. But I know it's fucking buried back here somewhere."

"Are you going tell me what exactly we're looking for?"

"Are you gonna shut the fuck up? While I try to fucking remember where this buried treasure is buried?"

"At least tell me *who* buried whatever is buried back here."

"I said," Candi yelled, gripping the wooden handle of the shovel, "Shut the fuck up!"

"For Chrissakes, Candi. It seems like ever since lunch. You've had a really short fuse. What's wrong?"

"Trust me, pardner. I've had a fucking short fuse my entire fucking life. And if you're just now figurin that shit out. Then if I were you. I'd get my fucking money back from Yale."

"Come on, Candi. Why are you all of a sudden being such a fucking bitch to me?"

"All of a sudden?" Candi said, laughing as she stared down into the dirt. "Come on! I mean this whole fucking ride. Have I ever been anythin else to you, pardner?"

"I guess," Mike said, "*I'd* like to think so..."

✳✳✳

About an hour later Candi was still digging in the dry Texas dirt underneath that big oak tree. There must have been a dozen holes by then. Mike sat on the ground nearby. He leaned against the tool shed, dandling the brim of his cowboy hat.

"Fuckers!" Candi shouted "Where did Granddaddy bury it? Fuckers! I don't even fucking know how deep he buried it. Fuck me with a chipped glass dildo!"

"So," Mike said, "It was your granddaddy who buried this *treasure*, huh?"

"Yep" Candi gripped the wooden handle of the shovel. Her hands were red and blistering. She whispered over and over and over under her breath, "Fuckers. Fuck me. Fuckers. Fuck me. Fuckers. Fuck me."

"Maybe it's a different tree," Mike said.

"Maybe you should just shut the fuck up."

"How long ago did your granddaddy bury this, *treasure?*"

"Why do you keep sayin it like that?"

"Like what?"

"Why the fuck do you keep sayin, *treasure*, like that? You still don't believe me? You still don't think there's any fucking treasure buried back here? Is that it?"

"Candi, all I know is. You're one of the most stubborn people I've ever met. And I wouldn't fucking put it past you. To tell me a tall tale about *buried treasure*. And then when we finally get to where it's supposed to be buried. You actually stick with your story. Even if it meant digging a bunch of holes for a whole fucking hour in the Texas heat"

"Listen here," Candi said. "My granddaddy told me he buried it back here behind the tool shed. He promised me I could have it. He left it to me."

"Left you what?"

"You're gonna find out soon enough, pardner." Candi took a deep breath and began digging a new hole.

"When does it start getting dark around here?" Mike said.

"Not until around 8:30. So we've got a few more hours yet."

"And you're seriously going to dig until it gets dark? Just so you can stick to your story? Wow, Candi. You are really fucking stubborn, you know that?"

"I'm gonna dig. Until I fucking find my granddaddy's buried treasure. And then, pardner. You're gonna eat some major fucking crow."

"Do you know what that saying means- *eat crow?*"

"Sure I do. You eat crow when somebody proves you wrong."

"Yeah, I know that. I meant. Do you know where that phrase comes from?"

"Nope. I don't fucking know," Candi said, still digging, "and I don't fucking give a shit!"

"My friend Sonny Quillan used to say that phrase too," Mike said. "He told me one time where it originated from, but I can't remember now exactly what he said. It seems like it had something to do with Rudyard Kipling. But I can't remember."

"All I know is. When I find my granddaddy's buried treasure. You're gonna eat so much fucking crow that you're gonna be shittin black feathers for a fucking week."

Mike laughed at her.

"That wasn't a fucking joke," Candi said.

* * *

About half an hour later, Candi was still digging.

"Fuckers!" Candi said. She leaned against the tree, cradling the hard shaft of the shovel between her tits, "Unfuckingbelievable!"

"For Chrissakes, Candi. Will you just give it up already? It's really fucking hot out here. And I'm hungry and thirsty. And this little charade of yours is really getting ridiculous."

"How many times do I have to tell you," Candi said, raising the blade of the shovel in the air, "to shut the fuck up?"

"How about this?" Mike said, wiping sweat from his face, "How about I go ahead and eat some crow right now? How about I admit to you that there really is buried treasure here. And that it's just dumb luck that you can't find it right now. And then we can go back into town. And get some Coors Light. How does that sound?"

"I told you I'm diggin til dark, pardner."

"How about we go back to the motel? Get some rest. And then tomorrow. We'll come back and dig some more? I'll even stop and buy a shovel and help you dig?"

"I don't fucking need your help. I already told you that."

"Come on, Candi. Work with me here. I'm trying to be reasonable."

"You know what, pardner? I think that's your whole fucking problem. You're always tryin so fucking hard to be so fucking reasonable."

"Well. Maybe I should try to be a little more like you then, huh? You're always trying so fucking hard to be such a fucking bitch." Mike paused. He thought for a moment, smiled and then said, "Or maybe I should've said- You're always trying so fucking hard to be such a fucking...cunt."

"Ooh! Congratufuckinglations there, pardner," Candi said. She kept digging. "Look who graduated up from sayin fucking bitch to fucking cunt. I mean to actually having the *cojones* to say fucking cunt! I'm proud of you, pardner. I really fucking am. Congratufuckinglations!"

"So," Mike said, "Does this mean you're going to take me up on my offer? For me to eat a little crow right now? So we can call it a day?"

"Nope"

"Dammit, Candi. If I don't get a drink of water pretty soon. I'll have a fucking heat stroke. I don't know how you do it."

"I'm one tough motherfucking *hombre*. That's how."

"I don't guess any of the water hoses still work around here?"

"Nope. Not for a long ass time. But there's a pond right down the road. Why don't you fucking mosey your little pansy ass down there and leave me the fuck alone."

"I know," Mike said, "How about I mosey my little pansy ass back to the fucking car? And then drive back to Houston without you? What do you think about that?"

"You'd never make it back without me, pardner."

"Really?"

"Yep"

"I think I could manage to find my way without you, Candi."

"Nope. No fucking way. Besides. Don't you wanna hear some more of my stories? I mean. Think about your fucking novel."

"I don't know. This whole *buried treasure* bullshit is beginning to make me think you're all out of stories. I mean all out of stories *worth hearing*, anyway."

Candi stopped shoveling. And with the blade of the shovel still in the dirt she looked up at Mike and said, "You're the goddamned whore, you know that? And you're gonna be a goddamned whore for the rest of your goddamned fucking life."

"*I'm* a whore?" Mike said. "You're calling *me* a whore?"

"Yep! And you know why?"

"Oh, please. Enlighten me. This I gotta hear!"

"You're a goddamned whore. Because you're gonna write your fucking novel usin all *my* stories. And then you're gonna pass them off as your own. And then you're probably gonna be famous. And make a million fucking dollars doin it. But! You'll still be nothin but a goddamned whore. Just like me!"

"Even if that were true about me. Which it's not. How would that make me a whore? That doesn't even make any fucking sense."

"Yep. You're a goddamned whore who can't write for shit. And if it weren't for me and our little odyssey, pardner. You wouldn't have any stories worth writin down."

"I still don't see how that makes me a whore. I mean it might make me a lot of things. It might make me a fucking thief. Or a fucking carpetbagger. Or a fucking plagiarist. Or even a fucking asshole. But it wouldn't make me a fucking whore. Not like you..."

"All I know is," Candi said. "I'd rather be a fucking whore like me than a goddamned whore like you. There's a difference."

Mike stood up and dusted off his pants. "You know what I realized just now?"

Candi turned her back on him and started shoveling a new hole.

"I just now realized. You are so completely full of fucking shit, it's not even funny."

Candi didn't turn around. She didn't react. She only kept digging into the dry Texas dirt.

"All this time," Mike said, "You've been telling me these fish tales of yours. Spinning all these outrageous stories. Just to keep me baited on your hook. Or should I say, *hooker*?" Mike chuckled and said, "Candi, you are so full of shit!"

"I am not"

"And you know the fishiest tale of them all? This! This right here! This bullshit story about digging up buried treasure! Wow! You are so full of shit!"

"I am not!"

"Well I'm fucking tired of humoring you. Even for the sake of my novel. I've had it!"

Candi drove the shovel into the dirt and it made the clinking sound of metal hitting metal.

"I'm really tired of playing pretend with you," Mike said.

Candi quickly shoveled more dirt away and then fell to her knees. She began digging with her hands.

"I'm tired of pretending we're on some kind of grandiose fucking odyssey. Or some Old West cattle drive. Or whatever other bullshit you happen to be-"

Mike watched Candi lean forward and reach down into the hole with both hands. He couldn't help but notice her blue thong again. She grabbed hold of something down in the hole. And then she leaned back, straining her arms as she tugged at something. Finally she drug out a rusty old metal box.

"Holy shit!" Mike said. "You actually fucking found something?"

"Granddaddy's old army surplus box," Candi whispered to herself. She dusted off the dirt and struggled with the rusty latch.

Mike stepped closer to her, trying to catch a glimpse over her shoulder.

Candi struggled with the rusty latch.

"I can't fucking believe you actually found the buried treasure."

Candi pulled open the latch and lifted the lid.

"What is it?"

Candi pulled something from the box and cradled it in her lap, close to her belly.

"Well," Mike said, chuckling, "I guess we both know now what I'm going to be eating plenty of." He stepped back as Candi scrambled to her feet.

Candi turned around to face Mike. She lifted a pistol into the air and pointed the long barrel at Mike's face. "You're goddamned right, pardner," Candi said, "You're gonna eat some serious fucking crow for supper."

* * *

"For Chrissakes, Candi," Mike said, leaning back away from the barrel of the pistol. "Be careful with that. It might be loaded, you know."

"Oh it's fucking loaded alright, pardner," Candi said. She shoved the pistol closer to Mike's face. "My granddaddy always kept his guns loaded. He used to tell me- Girl, there ain't no use in pointin an empty gun at a person. Less you plan to beat em to death with it."

Mike stepped backwards until his back was up against the tool shed. He raised his hands in front of him and said, "Ok, ok, very funny, Candi. You got me."

"Yep," she said, "I gotcha alright, pardner. Right where I fucking want you. Right where I've wanted you ever since I sucked your dick and fucking swallowed your cum on the Baytown Bridge."

Mike chuckled and said, "Ok, ok. The joke's on me. I get it."

"*Actually*," Candi said, "The joke's on both of us. But you're the only one who's gonna fucking get the punch line today."

"Come on, Candi. I know I said a bunch of mean shit to you a minute ago. But you're really making me nervous here. So maybe you should-"

"You really think I'm pissed off about what you fucking said to me a few minutes ago? Wow! Unfuckingbelievable! You really are a fucking *dumbass*. You know that?"

"What did you just call me?"

"You fucking heard me, pardner. I said you're the biggest fucking *dumbass* I ever met in my entire fucking life!"

"I can't believe you just fucking said that to me."

"Oh, fucking believe it, dumbass," Candi said. She glanced up into the sky at the approaching Texas sunset. "Well we're burnin daylight here, pardner." She kept the pistol aimed in his face as she kicked the shovel over in his direction. "Now pick up that shovel and let's fucking get to it. Your grave ain't gonna fucking dig itself."

✱✱✱

About half an hour later Mike stood in a shallow grave. He gripped the shovel handle with bloody and blistered hands. His clothes were soaked in dirt and sweat. His mouth was dry and he felt faint. He adjusted his cowboy hat. Regardless of what he said to her or how he pleaded with her, Candi would only say- "Keep diggin, *dumbass*."

Candi held the pistol steady, still aiming it right at Mike. Finally Candi said to him, "My daddy always used to tell me- Girl, there are two kinds of people in this old world. Them with loaded guns, and them that dig..."

Mike kept digging.

"In the Old West, you know. Back in the good old days. Texas Rangers would make the worst criminals in the territory dig their own fucking graves. And then they'd make them criminals stand right there in the grave they just finished diggin. And then they'd shoot them. Right then and there. And then they'd just fucking spread the dirt right over the top of em. And then they'd just ride off into the fucking sunset. And guess what, pardner? That's exactly what I'm gonna fucking do to you."

"*Please*, Candi, please. I'm fucking begging you here. Don't fucking do this!"

"Like I told you before, pardner. I fucking hate it when you say that word."

"Don't do this!"

"Take a wild fucking guess at what kinda gun this is."

Mike shook his head.

"It's an 1847 Walker Colt. Yep. That's right! Remember? The largest and most powerful black powder repeating handgun ever made? Yep! It's the exact same kinda pistol that Captain Augustus McCrae, Texas Ranger carried with him. You know. The pistol he smacked that uppity bartender with?" Candi stepped forward and leaned over the grave. She swung back and hit Mike in the face with the long barrel of the pistol, "Fucking just like that!"

Mike fell to his knees. He cradled his now bleeding upper lip and nose.

"Yep! The exact same pistol Gus killed that half-breed Indian outlaw Blue Duck with! And rescued Miss Lorena with too! And now. Well it's the exact same kinda pistol I'm gonna fucking end your miserable," she raised her free hand and made quotation marks with her fingers, "*existence*, with..."

Mike still gripped the shovel.

"In fact. I think I've decided I'm gonna gutshot you, pardner. You know what I mean? See. I'm gonna shoot you right in the middle of your fucking stomach. So that way it takes you longer to fucking die. My daddy always told me- Girl, a gutshot is the most painful way to die. I mean. It can take a body days to die from a gutshot. I always wanted to see it for myself."

"Remember in *Lonesome Dove*," Candi said. "When Gus rode off to rescue Miss Lorena? After she'd been raped and kidnapped by Blue Duck and those other outlaws? And along the way Gus gets chased by those buffalo hunters and Indians that Blue Duck sent to kill him? And their fucking chasin Gus on horseback. And Gus knows he can't get away. So Gus jumps right off his horse and pulls out that huge fucking knife. And then he kills his own fucking horse. So he'll have somethin to hide behind. And then he lays right behind his dead horse. And shoots at those outlaws who were chasin him. You remember that?"

Mike dropped the shovel.

"And then those outlaws fucking think Gus is too far away to actually hit them. So that one idiot buffalo hunter fucking gets up. And starts dancin like a fucking chicken. You know. To make fun of Gus and get him to waste his bullets shootin at them."

"But remember? Gus knows how to shoot from really long distances. So he adjusts his rifle. And then he fires off a single fucking shot. And then that bullet gutshots that fucking buffalo hunter. And it took that buffalo hunter like several days to fucking die. Remember that?"

"And remember how that buffalo hunter was in so much pain from that gutshot? That he was beggin his outlaw friends just to go ahead and fucking shoot him? And just fucking go ahead and put him out of his misery? But his fucking outlaw friends said they wouldn't waste a bullet on him. And then they stepped on his stomach with their boots and spurs. And then they even fucking scalped him too? And he still didn't fucking die! And then when Gus finally found their camp. He fucking killed every single motherfucking one of them outlaws. But even Gus wouldn't shoot that buffalo hunter. He just fucking left him there all gutshot to fucking suffer and die. Remember that shit?"

"Candi please!"

"Well. That's exactly what I'm gonna fucking do to you, pardner. Course. I'm not wearin boots or spurs. But I think these high heels will do just fine. Course. I can't leave you alive. But I can sit with you all night while you fucking suffer and die from bein gutshot."

"Why are you doing this to me?"

"You remember that flick I mentioned before? *Pat Garret and Billy the Kid*? I told you before. My granddaddy and my daddy fucking loved old Sam Peckinpah flicks. Anyways. In that flick Slim Pickens plays that sheriff who gets gutshot. You remember

Slim Pickens? He was in *Blazing Saddles* too. Remember when those racist asshole cowboys were dancin around singin the song *Camptown Races*? And makin fun of Bart and the other black guys? And then Slim Pickens rode up to them by the railroad and said-I hired you fellas to get a little track laid. Not jump around like a bunch of Kansas City faggots!" Candi laughed out loud. "You really gotta see that flick."

"Anyways. In *Pat Garret* ol Slim Pickens plays another sheriff. And he gets gutshot. And remember how he was buildin a fucking boat? Out in the middle of fucking nowhere? I mean there was just a little fucking creek or whatever right in the middle of the fucking desert! And he told Pat Garret that if he ever finished his boat. He was just gonna sail away. And then he fucking gets gutshot by those outlaws. And he crawls over near the water's edge. And just sits there cryin. And lookin out at the water. Wishin the whole time he woulda finished his boat and just sailed away. And remember how Bob Dylan's song, *Knocking on Heaven's Door* was playin for that whole scene? That was pretty fucking awesome."

"Why are you doing this to me?" Mike said.

"Too bad there's not gonna be any music playin when you get gutshot, pardner. Not that you fucking deserve any music."

"Why are you doing this to me, Candi?"

"Hey! Don't fucking blame me. You fucking did this shit to yourself."

"I don't understand"

"I reckon you shoulda been a Good fucking Samaritan when you had the chance, huh?"

"What?"

Candi screamed. "All I fucking needed was a ride over a fucking bridge! That's all I fucking needed! I mean. I was fucking stranded out there! And all I needed was a tiny fucking favor from some Good fucking Samaritan!"

"But you're the one who offered me the blowjob? It was your fucking idea!"

"You coulda just said to me- Ma'am, if all you need is a fucking ride over the Baytown Bridge. Then I'd be more than happy to just give you one. No blowjob necessary... You coulda just said that, pardner. Yep. You coulda just said that! But you didn't... Am I right?"

"I guess I thought that's just what you do. You know? For a living"

"That's just what we all do for a livin, pardner. We all fucking get down on our knees. And we all suck dick. And we all swallow cum. Every fucking day of our goddamned lives. It's like I said before. Life's all about dick."

"I'm truly sorry, Candi. You're right. I should've just helped you out."

"Well it's too fucking late for fucking apologies, pardner. What's done is fucking done. And now somebody's gotta step up and do somethin. So I reckon I'm just gonna have to fucking put you down."

"I made a mistake. Everybody makes mistakes, Candi."

"You're right about that, pardner. Everybody makes fucking mistakes. Me included. And God knows I don't judge. You fucking know that by now. But the trouble is. Almost nobody's gotta pay for their mistakes. You know? Really fucking pay for their mistakes. I mean whatever happened to fucking justice, right?"

"This isn't justice, Candi. This is murder."

"Hey, I know," Candi said, laughing. "Why don't you write a fucking philosophy paper about it? And then nobody could ever read it. Or ever give a fuck about what you think? Kinda like me."

"Please, Candi. I'll give you anything. Just let me go. I swear I'll give you anything you want, just-."

"All I fucking wanted was a ride across that bridge, pardner. That's *all* I ever fucking wanted…"

✳ ✳ ✳

A little later, Mike plunged the old shovel back down into the dry Texas dirt.

"Hey, pardner," Candi said, still wielding the pistol. "You never asked me about this 1847 Walker Colt. I mean. I know you got a lot on your fucking mind right now. But you just gotta be wonderin where my granddaddy got this fucking old antique gun from. Am I right?"

Mike kept digging.

"Well. During the Depression my granddaddy's family was camped along the Navasota River. So they could fish and hunt and make endsmeat. Anyways. One day my granddaddy is out huntin squirrels in the river bottom. And let me tell you. If you ever fucking think your life sucks the big one. Just be fucking glad you weren't my granddaddy. I mean he was the oldest of twelve kids. And his daddy was a fucking drunken loser. Who only showed up long enough to squeeze one out inside my great grandmother's pussy. And so my granddaddy had to basically play daddy to all those kiddos. Includin huntin every goddamn day to feed all of them."

"And they were sooo fucking poor. That my granddaddy didn't even have a gun. He had to fucking hunt squirrels with a goddamn slingshot! And if he didn't fucking kill any squirrels that day. Then the family didn't fucking eat supper. Can you fucking imagine the stress and pressure?"

"He told me once that he'd spend the mornin collectin smooth stones from the riverbed. And then he'd walk real quiet through the river bottom. With nothin but a fucking homemade slingshot and a handful of those stones. So. Whenever he'd spot a squirrel. Of course the squirrel would always scurry to the other side of a tree to hide. Well my granddaddy would stand real still. And then he'd just toss one of those stones to the other side of the tree. And that fucking squirrel would hear the stone rustle the leaves. And it would scurry back towards my granddaddy. And that's when he'd fucking get him one!"

"Anyways. One day my granddaddy was out huntin squirrels like usual. When he heard a man hollerin and screamin for help. So he made his way down through the brush to the river's edge. And there was a man right in the middle of the fucking river. He was caught up in a fucking treefall and drownin in the current. I think his horse had been spooked and thrown him into the river. I'm not sure. I don't remember. Anyways. The fucking point is. That stranger was a fucking gonner, for sure."

"Anyways. If you know anythin about the Navasota River. Then you know it's real muddy. And real deep and real dangerous. And full of fucking water moccasins. So what I'm sayin is. Any other man woulda probably chickened out. Maybe even rounded up that poor stranger's horse and just rode off into the fucking sunset. But not my granddaddy!"

"Nope. Granddaddy manned up and fucking did what had to be done. He fucking dove right into that river. And then he drug that stranger's ass all the way back to the fucking shore. And fucking saved that stranger's life."

"Well. Come to find out. That stranger was pretty well-off. In fact. It turned out he owned a big farm over near Peach Creek. So to repay my granddaddy for savin his life. That rich man gave him this 1847 Walker Colt."

"And right before he fucking died. Granddaddy told me he'd buried it back here behind the tool shed. In his old army surplus box for safekeeping. And he told me that he wanted me to have it someday. And that's why we're here, pardner! Because this fucking antique pistol right here is worth a whole fuckload of cash. It's a collector's item now, you know."

"So I'm gonna be rich as fuck. And you're gonna be dead as fuck. All because my granddaddy was out huntin squirrels one day. And saved some asshole's miserable fucking life. Quite a story, huh? How's that for a fucking fish tale?"

✱✱✱

A little bit later Candi announced, "That oughta be just about deep enough right there, pardner. Now just toss that fucking shovel right over here. Nice and slow like."

Mike's hands were bleeding now. And he was covered in dirt and sweat. He tossed the shovel near Candi's feet and collapsed down onto his knees.

"Now you got it," Candi said. "Now you know what it fucking feels like, huh?"

"I'm begging you, Candi," Mike hung his head, exhausted.

"Well. It's almost sundown, pardner. And you fucking know what that means, right?"

"Don't do this, Candi. You're better than this. I know you are."

"You don't know shit about me."

"I know you're not a cold blooded killer."

"Cold blooded killer? What the fuck? You still don't fucking get it, do you? I'm not a cold blooded fucking killer, pardner. Nope. I'm the judge, jury and fucking executioner here. I'm a

Texas Ranger. I'm the motherfucking justice in these here parts. *You're* the cold blooded killer, pardner. You're the outlaw. And now you're gonna fucking pay for what you done."

"I don't deserve this, Candi."

"None of us fucking deserve any of this, pardner. But guess what? We're all here in this roach trap. We're all fucked. And so we all better just make the best of it. Am I right? I mean we all gotta do what we gotta do. Am I right?"

"But that's just it, Candi. You don't have to do this. You have a choice here."

"You're goddamned right I have a fucking choice. And that's why I'm doin this. Because it's fucking gotta be done."

"Please, Candi"

"That's enough talk, pardner. We're fucking done talkin." She moved closer to the narrow grave. She tightened her grip around the pistol, aiming it at Mike's stomach. "Now stand up! And take off that fucking cowboy hat."

"What?"

"You got cotton in your ears? I fucking said- Stand the fuck up and take off that motherfucking, cocksucking, goddamned cowboy hat. Right fucking now!"

Mike's hands trembled as he got to his feet. He grabbed the brim of his cowboy hat, pulled it slowly from his head, and then tossed it over near the shovel.

Candi smiled and said, in her best John Wayne swagger, "You're not so fucking cocky now? Are ya, pilgrim? And I thought ya never took no lip from nobody?"

Mike moaned and shook his head.

"You know what's funny?" Candi said. "If you'd refused to take off that cowboy hat just now. Like you did earlier in the tool shed. I think I mighta done you a fucking favor. And given you a fucking bullet right between the eyes. Instead of a gutshot"

"What?"

"Yep! I reckon I woulda. But you fucked that up too, dumbass. So anyways. You're goin the hard way, pardner. You know. Like I said before. The kickin and screamin and pissin yourself way."

"You can't do this, Candi."

"By the way. I just gotta ask. Have you pissed yourself yet?"

"What?"

"Because I want you to," she raised her hands and made quotation marks with her fingers, "piss yourself, *before* I shoot you, pardner."

"What the hell?"

"Yep. Honestly I kinda thought you'd do it on your own. You know. When I shoved this fucking gun in your face. But it turns out you might have more spunk than I thought. God knows I swallowed enough of it."

"You're fucking crazy"

"Nope. I'm not fucking crazy, pardner. And I'm not fucking full of shit either. I'm just fucking doin what needs to be done. Now. Are you gonna use your dick hole and piss yourself? Or am I gonna have to shoot you in the fucking dick and then watch it leak out through a bullet hole?"

"For Chrissakes, stop it! Please! I'm begging you! I can't take it anymore!"

"Well," Candi said, "What's it gonna be, pardner? Your dick hole or a bullet hole?"

✳ ✳ ✳

About ten minutes later Mike was back down on his knees in the grave. His pants were soaken wet with piss.

"You know somethin, pardner," Candi said, smiling. "You oughta consider yourself kinda fucky. In fact. You oughta fucking thank me. I mean. I'm givin you a chance to die just like the outlaws in the Old West did. Course. It's kinda," she made her quotation marks again, "*ironic*, huh? You're not a real man. But you kinda get to die like one. Even though you fucking pussyed out and pissed yourself. I mean. I don't think any of those outlaws. Even though they were fucking outlaws. Ever would've let a two bit fucking whore with a gun scare them into pissin themselves. But you're such a fucking fag."

"Please, Candi. I'll do anything."

"You already made a deal with me, pardner. And that didn't turn out too well now, did it?"

"I mean it. I'll do fucking anything." Mike buried his face in the dirt, "Anything!"

Candi raised the ten inch barrel of the pistol to her mouth. She puckered up her lips and kissed it. "You'll do anything? You really mean that? Any fucking thing I say?"

Mike lifted his head and looked up at Candi. His face was smudged with sweat and dirt. "I mean it. I'll do anything you tell me."

"Anything?"

"Yes"

"Are you fucking serious?"

"Yes, I am."

"You better not be fucking with me. Anything? Right?"

"For Chrissakes, Candi. I'll do anything!"

"Well. My granddaddy always said- Girl, an eye for an eye and a tooth for a tooth. I mean the punishment should fit the fucking crime. Am I right?"

"Right"

"Then I reckon that means an eye for an eye and a tooth for a tooth. And a cumwad for a cumwad..."

"What?"

"Ok, pardner. Here's the deal. You made me suck your dick and swallow your cum. Well. I don't have a dick you can suck. And you can't suck your own dick. I mean let's face it. If you could suck your own dick. Then neither one of us would be in this fucked up situation. Am I right?"

Mike sighed.

"Right?"

"Yeah, right"

"So. I can't fucking make you suck my dick. Because I don't fucking have a dick to suck. And I can't fucking make you suck your own dick either. But you know what I can fucking do? I can make *you* swallow your own cum. Just like you made me do on the goddamned fucking Baytown Bridge."

"What?"

"Yep! Here's the way I figure it, pardner. An eye for an eye and a tooth for a tooth. And a mouthful of your cum for a mouthful of your cum."

"I don't understand"

"Here's the deal, dumbass. You're gonna jerk off into your hand. And then you're gonna lick up all your cum off your hand.

And then you're gonna swallow it. Now if that ain't fucking justice I don't know what is."

"Candi, please. Don't do this to me."

"You ever wonder what a whore is thinkin when she's about to suck a strange dick? Or what she's thinkin when some stranger is about to shove his dick in her pussy? Or in her asshole? She's thinkin exactly what you just said to me, pardner. Now you know how it fucking feels. That's fucking justice right there. Don't you think?"

"I don't know"

"Well you better fucking figure that shit out pretty fucking quick. I mean that's the deal, pardner. You gotta choice you gotta make."

"So," Mike said, "If I do it? Then you won't,"

"Go ahead. Just say it dumbass."

"Kill me?"

"Yep! That's the fucking deal, pardner. And it's a hell of a fucking deal if you ask me!"

✳✳✳

Mike whimpered and his hands trembled. He reached down and unzipped his green corduroy pants. His crotch was still wet and stinking of piss. He reached into his underwear and pulled out his flaccid dick.

"You better get to aidin and abettin that little felon of yours," Candi said. "He don't look too good." She laughed out loud.

Mike started stroking his dick but it didn't respond.

"What's wrong, pardner? You didn't seem to have any trouble gettin it up on the Baytown Bridge?"

Mike patted his dick lengthwise but still nothing happened. He whined and then choked the shaft of his debilitated dick harder than before.

"Come on!" Candi shouted, waving the pistol. "Pun intended!"

Mike jerked his dick with an as yet undiscovered rage...

"And, as for me, if, by any possibility, there be any as yet undiscovered prime thing in me; if I shall ever deserve any real repute in that small but high hushed world which I might not be unreasonably ambitious of; if hereafter I shall do anything that, upon the whole, a man might rather have done than to have left undone..."

***

"Are you gonna butter that corn cob sometime today?" Candi said. "Well. I reckon the fucking thought of swallowin *your own* cum. Doesn't turn you on as much as the thought of *me* swallowin your cum, huh? Why is that you think?"

Mike ignored her. He stared down his flaccid dick, still flagellating himself.

"You know," Candi said. "I always heard it was like impossible for a woman to rape a man. And I mean really rape a man. You know. Like really rape him when he doesn't want it. I mean I always heard it was like impossible for a man to get a hard-on when he's afraid. Maybe that's what's wrong with you, huh?"

Mike fell over on his side in the narrow grave. He closed his eyes and resumed wrenching on his dick.

"What the fuck are you thinkin about, pardner?"

Mike rolled over on his back, jerking harder and harder and harder, his eyes still closed.

"Or maybe I should say- *Who* the fuck are you thinkin about?"

Mike groaned. He beat his head against the fresh dirt.

"Maybe you oughta think about me suckin your dick on the bridge? I mean that seemed to work before...Am I right?"

Mike stopped flogging his dick. He lay back in his grave and then opened his eyes, looking up, staring down Candi.

Candi smiled, still pointing the pistol down at him. "You know somethin, pardner. And don't get me wrong here. But I don't think you're an all-around bad guy. You just fucked up real bad, you know? I mean we all fuck up sometimes. You know me. I don't fucking judge. But I reckon you just fucked up the wrong person this time, you know?"

Mike took a deep breath and started tugging on his dick again.

"So," Candi said, "If it'll help you out at all here. And let me tell you. I'm only willin to do this because like I said. You're not an all-around bad guy. I'd be willin to show you a tit. I mean just to help you out."

Mike raised his head a little and stared Candi down.

"Course. I'm only showin you one now." So with her free hand, Candi grabbed the hem of her white t-shirt. And then, with that picture of Hank Williams Jr. smiling down on Mike, she lifted it and exposed one of her tits to him.

Mike stared down Candi's tit. There it was in all its perfection. Her stiff nipple encircled by that enormous brown areolae. He pulled harder on his dick, with a renewed resolve and rage.

"There you go, pardner. Looks like you might be able to man up and save your sorry skin after all."

Mike's dick got harder and harder and harder.

"That's it, pardner! Holy fucking shit! Well! It looks like you might be able to choke the sheriff before the posse gets here, after all."

Mike stared down her tit. And then stared down his dick. And then stared down her tit again. And then stared down his dick again.

"Well, I'll be damned, pardner. Looks like you might just get a dishonorable discharge, after all!"

Mike leaned into the dirt wall of his shallow grave. His sweaty sunburned face was upturned towards Candi. He rubbed his hard-on.

"And you better not spill a fucking drop of that precious spooge either! God knows I swallowed it all. So you're gonna fucking swallow it all too!"

Mike jerked and jerked and jerked his dick.

"Well?"

Mike yanked his dick faster and faster and faster, moaning.

"Come on, pardner! You can do it! I fucking know you can!"

Mike tugged on his dick one final, furious time. And then he let it go. He groaned as his body drooped down in repose. His stiff dick dug into the dry dirt wall of the grave.

"Oh my fucking God," Candi said, "Not one fucking drop?"

Mike closed his eyes. He covered them with his trembling hands, panting desperately.

"Come on, pardner! Keep goin! You can fucking do it! I know you can! You can do it!"

"I can't do it, Candi," Mike whispered. His hard-on began to slacken.

"Come on, goddammit!" Candi shouted, "You're losin it, pardner!"

"I can't!" Mike shouted as he gasped for breath. "I can't fucking do it!"

"Yes you can!"

"No," Mike said, and then began to cry, "I can't!"

✳✳✳

About ten minutes later, Mike still lay on his back in the narrow grave. He looked up at Candi with tears in his eyes and dribbling down his cheeks.

"I gotta tell you, pardner," Candi said, frowning, "I didn't think you'd pussy out on me like this. I mean I even showed you my tit. You were sooo fucking close too! I mean. I really seriously thought you'd be able to man up and save yourself. Shit!"

Mike sat up slowly. He stared her down again and said, "Please, Candi. Please don't do this to me! I'm sorry for everything! I never should've,"

"Well. I fucking hate to do it, pardner. I mean I really fucking hate that our little odyssey has to end this way. But a deal's a deal. Am I right?"

"Please, Candi. I'm sorry!"

"You know what I'm wonderin right about now, pardner? I wonder. If I'd fucking refused to finish you off when we were half-way across that goddamned fucking bridge. You know? Not held up my end of the deal? I wonder if you woulda kept your end of our deal and dropped me off on the other side. Or if you woulda turned that fucking ride of yours around. And dropped me right back off at that God forsaken truck stop? That's what I'm wonderin…"

Mike clambered to his knees in the grave. His green corduroy pants were filthy and still unzipped, damp with piss and sweat. His flaccid dick dangled from his fly.

"I wish I fucking knew," Candi said. "I really, really wish I knew the fucking answer to that, you know?"

"I should've just helped you," Mike said, "I know that now."

"Well pardner. You learned that," she made quotation marks with her free hand, "*fucking lesson*, a little too late. All I know is. I kept up my part of our little deal on that goddamned fucking bridge. I swallowed your cum. And because I did. I lived to whore another day. But you? You didn't keep up your end of our little deal. I mean you couldn't even cum, much less swallow your cum! So you know what? You're gonna fucking get what you fucking deserve. Justice. Old West style." She raised the pistol with renewed enthusiasm.

Mike raised his hands into the air and began to cry again.

"Oh, for fuck's sake. Don't start cryin like a little goddamned fucking faggoty pussy. I fucking hate that! Let me tell you. There's nothin a woman hates more in this world than a man who cries. Trust me. Women don't want to see that shit. No matter how much they may say they do. So do me a fucking favor, pardner. And stop your cryin. At least man up right before you fucking die."

Mike didn't stop crying.

"Ok. I'll tell you what," Candi said. "Because you at least *tried* to cum in your hand. I mean because you got sooo fucking close to creamin. Even though you didn't. I've decided I'm not gonna gutshot you. I think you deserve better. Don't get me wrong now. I'm still gonna shoot you. But it's gonna be right between your fucking eyes. Quick and painless. Not like a gutshot. I figure it's the least I can do for you, pardner. How's that sound?"

"I don't wanna die, Candi. I don't wanna die!"

"Think of it this way, pardner. When you picked me up. You were fucking miserable. And for some fucked up reason I still can't figure out. You're still fucking miserable. So I figure I'm just doin you a fucking favor. Actually. I mean I'm just puttin you out of your fucking misery."

"Please, Candi"

"Look on the bright side, pardner. At least this way you won't have to worry about finishin that really, really long research paper for college. Am I right? What did you call it, again?"

Mike didn't respond.

"I said," Candi shouted, "What did you fucking call it?"

"Dissertation"

"Oh yeah, right. Dissertation. And what did you say you were? Because you hadn't fucking finished that?"

Mike wiped his eyes with trembling hands. The dirt from his fingers smudged into muddy sweat on his cheeks.

"I asked you a fucking question, dumbass!"

"What?"

"You know? Remember right after you picked me up? When you said you were somethin or other because you hadn't finished that fucking paper? And I thought you had a fucking STD?"

"ABD," Mike said.

"And what does that mean again?"

"All But Dissertation"

"Oh yeah, right. Well. Like I said before, pardner. The bright side is that you're not gonna have to be fucking miserable about bein All But Dissertation anymore. But! The not-so-bright-side is that you're ABF now- All But Fucked." Candi laughed out loud and said, "Get it?"

✳ ✳ ✳

"Well," Candi said, "I don't know how they do it in novels. But in the flicks somebody usually says a fucking prayer before an execution. Or at least some final words. Remember in *Lonesome Dove*? When Gus and Call have to hang Jake Spoon because he fell in with those outlaws? Because Jake rode along with those outlaws while they murdered farmers and stole horses. And it was real hard for Gus and Call to hang Jake. Because he'd been their friend. And he'd even been a Texas Ranger like them? And Jake and those outlaws are all sittin on their horses with their hands tied. And with nooses around their fucking necks?"

Mike said nothing. His lips were parched and his throat was dry.

"And remember when Gus mans up like usual? And he steps right up to his old buddy Jake and stares him down. And then he asks him if he has any final words?"

Mike's face was covered in dry dirt and sweat as he looked up at Candi.

"And remember what Jake said to all of them? Jake said- I never meant no harm boys. I was just tryin to get through the territory, that's all. Just tryin to get through the territory..." Candi smiled and said, "Remember that?"

Mike hung his head.

"Well, pardner," Candi said, "You got any final words?"

Mike shook his head.

"I reckon normally. I'd ask you if you wanted to say a fucking prayer. But I think we both fucking know. Even if you did pray. *Your* God's not gonna do shit. Am I right?"

"Please, Candi"

"Well, pardner. If you think about it. Our little odyssey started when I blew your fucking brains out on the Baytown Bridge. So I reckon it's only right that it ends with me blowin your fucking brains out again. Am I right?"

"And that," Candi said, "fucking reminds me of a joke. Wanna hear it?"

Mike kneeled in the narrow grave before her.

"What does a whore have in common with a pistol? One cock, and they're both ready to blow!" Candi laughed.

Mike stretched out his arms. His hands were still trembling. He stared up at her and said, "I'm sorry, Candi. Please believe me?"

"I know you are, pardner." She said, frowning. "That's what makes this so fucking hard." She pointed the pistol right at his face.

"I'm sorry!" Mike said, "Please! Believe me!"

"I do, pardner," Candi said, and then she pulled the trigger.

Chapter 15

In defense of whoring

As my pardner and me are now fairly embarked in this business of whoring, and as this business of whoring has somehow come to be regarded among most as a rather unpoetical and disreputable pursuit; therefore, I am all anxiety to convince you, of the injustice hereby done to us whores.

In the first place, it may be deemed almost superfluous to establish the fact, that among people at large, the business of whoring is not accounted on a level with what are called the liberal professions. If a stranger were introduced into any miscellaneous metropolitan society, it would but slightly advance the general opinion of her merits, were she presented to the company as a whore.

Doubtless one leading reason why the world declines honoring us whores, is this; they think that, at best, our vocation amounts to a sort of fucking business; and that when actively engaged therein, we are surrounded by all manner of defilements. Fuckers we are, that is true. But fuckers, also, and fuckers of the bloodiest badge have been all whom the world invariably delights to honor.

And as for the matter of the alleged uncleanliness of our business, you shall soon be initiated into certain facts hitherto pretty generally unknown, and which, upon the whole, will triumphantly plant the sperm at least among the cleanliest things of this tidy earth.

But even granting the discharge in question to be true, what disordered slippery whore's pussy is comparable to the unspeakable carrion of those battlefields from which so many soldiers return to drink in all ladies' plaudits? And if the idea of peril so much enhances the popular conceit of the soldier's profession, let me assure you that many a veteran who has freely marched up to a battery, would quickly recoil at the apparition of sperm, fannies into eddies the air over his head. For what are the comprehensible terrors of man compared with the interlinked terrors and wonders of a whore!

But, though the world scouts at us whores, yet does it unwittingly pay us the profoundest homage; yes, an all-abounding — adoration! For almost all the tapers, lamps, and candles that burn round the globe, burn, as before so many shrines, to our glory!

But look at this matter in other streetlights; weigh it in all sorts of scales; see what we whores are, and have been.

I freely assert, that the cosmopolite philosopher cannot, for his life, point out one single peaceful influence, which within the whole of human history has operated more potentially upon the whole broad world, taken in one aggregate, than the high and mighty business of whoring. One way and another, it has begotten events so remarkable in themselves, and so continuously momentous in their sequential issues, that whoring may be regarded as that Egyptian mother, who bore offspring themselves pregnant from her wanton womb. It would be a hopeless, endless task to catalogue all these things...

Chapter 16

A joke and then the punch line

"Bang!" Candi said. She frowned as she shook the pistol. "Well shit. I reckon you're not dead yet, pardner. And it doesn't fucking look like it's gonna be today!"

When Candi had pulled the trigger, Mike plunged his body down into the grave where he now laid cringing and mumbling to himself.

"Oh come on! I'm just fucking with you, pardner. This is all just a big fucked up joke!"

Mike huddled over in the grave, cringing. He glanced up at Candi.

"Holy fucking shit! You mean to tell me? You *really* believed this old fucking antique gun from 1847 still had fucking bullets in it? Oh my fucking God! You are the ultimate fucking dumbass!" She laughed out loud.

Mike whispered, "What?"

Candi smiled and pointed the pistol at his face again. "Holy fuck, pardner. You shoulda seen your fucking face. I mean you really fucking thought I was gonna shoot you. You really fucking thought you were gonna bite the bullet didn't you?"

"I don't understand," Mike said, "What do you mean?"

"I mean. This fucking antique six-shooter right here. It doesn't have any goddamned bullets in it." She pointed the pistol at his face again, cocked back the hammer, and then pulled the trigger a second time.

Mike winced backwards as he heard the hammer click.

"See, pardner. Nothin"

Mike got to his knees and said, "You mean,"

"Yep. I was never gonna fucking kill you, pardner. I just wanted to teach you a fucking lesson that's all. I mean after all this fucked up shit I just put you through just now. God fucking knows and I'll fucking bet. That from now on you're gonna be the *goodest* goddamned Samaritan on this fucking planet. Am I right?"

"For Chrissakes, Candi"

"And! I'll bet the next time you see some whore stranded at a fucking shithole truckstop in Baytown, Texas. You'll offer to give her a fucking ride. No strings attached. Am I right?"

"I can't fucking believe you did this to me," Mike said. "I can't fucking believe it!"

"Really?" Candi said. "Cause I think it sounds exactly like some fucked up thing I'd do."

Mike grabbed his flaccid dick and stuffed it back into his pants, snapping the elastic of his underwear.

"Come on, pardner. You know you had that shit comin, right? I mean you fucking got what was comin to you, right?"

Mike zipped up his green corduroy pants with his bloody, blistered, dirty fingers.

"Let's face it. You gotta admit. I was totally in the right. I mean you can't really hold this shit against me now, can you?"

Mike shuffled on his knees nearer to the edge of the grave. He rested his hands in the dirt near Candi's feet.

"In fact," Candi said. "How's about we call it even-fucking-Steven?" She held the pistol by her side. "I mean the way I figure it, pardner. You forced me to do somethin I didn't wanna do. And then I forced you to do somethin,"

Mike scrambled out of the grave and grabbed Candi's ankle, tripping her to the ground. He climbed on top of her and punched her in the face. He screamed, "You fucking cunt!" He punched her in the face again. "You goddamned stupid fucking cunt, bitch, whore!"

Mike wrestled with Candi's squirming arms and hands. He finally grabbed the pistol away from her. He sat up on top of her. He aimed the pistol down into her face and said, "Let's see how you like having a fucking pistol in your fucking face! You fucking whore!"

Candi stopped struggling. She just lay there looking up at Mike, staring him down. Her lip was busted and her eyebrow was bloody.

Mike dug his filthy fingers into her mouth and then pried her lips apart. He stuck the barrel of the pistol into her mouth and down her throat. "Let's see how you fucking like it now!" He screamed, "Let's see how you like eating fucking crow! You goddamn fucking whore!" He cocked back the hammer of the pistol and then pulled the trigger for a third time.

Candi winced and shuddered as the pistol dry fired.

Mike shouted, "Fuck you, you fucking whore! I'm gonna blow your fucking brains out!" He cocked the pistol again and pulled the trigger a fourth time.

Candi jerked her head back against the dirt as Mike crammed the pistol harder down her throat.

"You fucking cunt! Fuck you!" Mike yelled. "You fucking fucking whore! You fucking fucked-up bitch! Fuck you! You goddamned, fucking,"

Candi began to choke on the barrel of the pistol. She gargled for breath as a little bit of blood trickled out the side of her mouth.

Mike screamed, "Fuck!" He jerked the pistol out of her mouth. He threw himself off of her and onto his back in the dirt beside her. "Fuck me!" he said, "Fuck me! Fuck me! Fuck me! Fuck me!"

Candi coughed up some blood and spit as she gasped for breath. She rolled over on her side to face Mike. She wiped the dirt, sweat and blood from her mouth and face, and then smiled.

"Oh, fuck me," Mike said, "for Chrissakes- fuck me."

"Hey," Candi said to him, still coughing up a little blood into the palm of her hand, "If all you wanted me to do was fuck you, pardner. You could've just asked me nicely, you know." She laughed out loud.

"Fuck me all the way to hell," Mike said, dropping the pistol into the dirt.

"Well, pardner," Candi said. "Looks to me like you might just enter your house justified, after all."

Mike and Candi ended up lying there in the dirt together, side by side, next to that fresh narrow grave, under that old oak tree behind her granddaddy's tool shed, until dawn. And then finally, as the Texas sun rose over the surrounding cow pastures Candi said, "Well, pardner. What do you say? Are you ready to ride?"

Chapter 17

*The Ballad of the Four Whores with Stripper-Names;
Amends*

"I gotta tell you, pardner," Candi said, holding her copy of
Moby Dick. "You're lookin pretty fucking hot right about now. I
mean. I really, really fucking hated those faggoty green pants of
yours."

Mike and Candi were headed back to Houston. They'd left
Mexia around mid-morning, and were now driving southwards
along Texas Highway 14.

"Aren't you glad I insisted on picking out your new duds?"
Candi said. "And let me tell you. Nothin looks better on a man
than cowboy-cut, Wrangler blue-jeans. The tighter the better!"

Mike still felt awkward about everything that had happened. He was quieter than before and he knew Candi could tell.

"Yep. Like I always say. The tighter the Wrangler jeans, the
better!" Candi stared down at his crotch, "See, pardner. Now that
you're wearin those jeans. Whenever you get a hard-on from now
on. All the ladies are gonna be able to see it. And they'll know
what kind of pistol you're packin."

Mike actually felt his hard-on swell a little under her gaze
but he still refused to speak.

"I knew this stripper once," Candi said, "her name was Lyla.
And her stripper-name was Pocahontas. She claimed she was half
Indian. But I never fucking believed her. Anyways. She worked at
Treasures over near the Galleria. And whenever a man came into
the club and flashed her more than a twenty dollar bill. She always
used to turn to me and say- That fella can poca-my-hontas any
fucking day of the week!" Candi laughed out loud. "I think she
musta chosen that name just so she could make that fucking joke!"

Mike smiled, but didn't laugh.

"Ok," Candi said, "How about this for a good fucking joke? I mean. This one is a real fucking knee-slapper. And you'll probably like it too. Because it's kinda like a play on words or whatever. So it sounds really smart when you tell it. So here it goes. Are you ready for this for fucking joke?"

Mike shrugged.

"And let me tell you. This is not an easy fucking joke to tell either. It takes a lot of fucking practice to tell it just right. So are you ready, pardner?'

Mike shrugged and then nodded.

"This joke is a little story," Candi said, "not a bedtime story. But just a regular old story about four whores. Now these four whores worked the four street corners of the intersection of Scott Street and Old Spanish Trail in Houston. And these four whores had stripper-names too. Just like my friend Pocahontas."

"So the first whore's stripper-name was Everycunt. The second whore's stripper-name was Someothercunt. The third whore's stripper-name was Anycunt. And the fourth whore's stripper-name was Nocunt. Well. One day this man named Dick rides up. And he needs a job done. You know what I mean, right?" Candi nudged Mike's shoulder with her elbow, and winked at him. "Dick needs a job done...Get it?"

As a kind of knee-jerk reaction to her touch, Mike pulled away from her.

Candi frowned and then continued. "Anyways. Dick needs a job done. And so Dick asked Someothercunt to do it. Well. Everycunt was damn sure that Someothercunt would do it for Dick. But Nocunt ended up doing it instead. And then. Everycunt got angry because it was supposed to be Someothercunt's job. But it turned out that Nocunt never realized that Anycunt could have done it. So of course. Everycunt blamed Someothercunt and Nocunt for doing what Anycunt could have done in the first place!" Candi laughed out loud, and then paused to contemplate. "I think I told that the right way," she said, and then laughed again anyway. "Pretty good joke, huh?"

Mike remained silent, unable or unwilling to laugh.

"Ok. Listen up, pardner," Candi said, placing her hand gently on his shoulder this time. "I'm really, really, really, really fucking tryin here. You know? I mean it's not easy havin to fucking break the ice all over again. Help me out here, will you?"

"I don't know what to tell you, Candi"

"Are you still mad at me for doin all that shit to you with the pistol? Cause if you are. Then you can just fucking tell me."

"No. Actually, I don't think I am."

"So then. You've forgiven me, right?"

"I don't know if I can ever forgive you, Candi. And, actually, honestly. I don't even know what that kind of forgiveness would even look like. I just don't..."

"Well you're never gonna fucking know what it looks like until you fucking try it, right?"

"I guess so"

What Mike had been wondering ever since he crawled out of that narrow grave, what Mike really wanted to ask Candi was-Did you really know that gun was unloaded? He wondered if Candi knew all along that the gun was unloaded, which meant she was really just play-acting the whole time, and just pretending to kill him. Or did Candi really believe the gun was loaded the whole time? And she was really ready and willing to execute him? Maybe when the gun didn't fire, Mike thought, Candi did some fast thinking and just acted like she knew it was unloaded all along?

"Well, pardner," Candi said, "I just want you to know. Just for the fucking record. That whatever happens from here on in. I fucking forgive you for everything. And I mean fucking everything."

"Listen, Candi. I'm going to give you a ride back to Houston. I can promise you I'll do that much. But honestly," he said, pausing for an awkward moment, leaning his shoulder softly against the palm of her open hand, "that's really all I can promise you at this point."

"Well, pardner. You know I really appreciate the ride. I mean. I gotta tell you. It's been shits and giggles ridin shotgun with you on this little odyssey of ours. And if it makes you feel any better. I fucking promise to fucking behave myself until we get back to Houston."

"You promise?" Mike said.

"Yep. I promise, pardner. I promise."

"Thanks, Candi."

"And speakin of promises," Candi said, "I owe you a fucking apology. I really, really need to say I'm sorry for somethin."

"Let's just let bygones be bygones, Candi. We both did shit we're not,"

"No fucking way, pardner. You got me all wrong. I'm not gonna fucking apologize for any of that shit with the gun back there. I mean let's face it. We both fucking got what was comin to us back there. But! I do owe you an apology for somethin else. Somethin really shitty I did to you *before* all of that shit with the gun and the grave."

"Something else, huh?"

"Yep"

"But I thought you always hated it when I said- I'm sorry?"

"I do fucking hate it. And I still fucking hate it. In fact! I fucking hate apologies from anybody. But. The way I figure it is this. When you owe somebody an apology. Especially somebody you've ridden such a long way with. You better fucking apologize to em before it's too fucking late. And you miss your fucking chance. You know what I mean, jelly bean?"

"I think so," Mike said, "But what do you owe me an apology for?"

"For breaking a fucking promise I made to you. For fucking breaking the code of the Old West, pardner. I reckon you remember how I promised never to call you *that word*, ever again? Remember?"

"Yes"

"And then you started sayin all that mean shit to me. When I was diggin for Granddaddy's buried treasure? Remember? You started sayin how all my stories are just a bunch of bullshit? Remember that?"

Mike nodded.

"Well, pardner. That was some straight-up, fucked up shit you said to me back there. And there's no fucking excuse for how mean you were to me. No fucking excuse. But! As mean as you were to me. I shoulda not lost my fucking temper and called you *that word*, again. I mean. What I'm tryin to say is. I promised you. I gave you my word. And then I went and fucking broke my word. And breakin your word is some fucked up shit, pardner. And I'm really fucking sorry about that, ok?"

"Ok"

"It's like my daddy always said to me- Girl, back in the good old days, all a man had was his word. And if a man was good for his word then he was a good man. I've always tried to live by that shit, you know? I figure that no matter what fucking happens to us in life. That's the best any of us can fucking do. So how's that for a fucking philosophy of life, Mr. Yale Philosopher?"

"Thanks, Candi"

"Well?"

"Well, what?"

"I asked you a fucking question. How's that for a fucking philosophy of life? What do you think? I mean I really wanna know."

"Well. Let me think about it for a while," Mike said. "Can I get back to you on that?"

"You promise?"

"Sure, I promise."

"Ok, pardner," Candi said. She spit in her palm and offered him a handshake, "It's a deal, then? You'll get back to me on that one, right?"

Mike smiled and shook her hand. He savored the warmth and strength of her familiar grasp. He wondered if because of his new jeans, Candi would notice his hard-on swelling once again.

✳✳✳

A few miles down the road, Mike broke their silence and said, "By the way, Candi. That was actually a really clever joke you told back there. In fact. I think it's the best joke you've told me this whole trip. Uh I mean, this whole odyssey."

"You mean the joke about the four whores with stripper names?"

"Yeah. And just so you know. You told it exactly right. Perfect, actually."

"Well thanks, pardner. I'm glad you liked it. And if you can remember it right. Feel free to put it in your fucking novel, I mean. If you wanna"

"Thanks. I think I will."

"And if you can't remember exactly how it goes. All you gotta do is just drive down to the intersection of Scott Street and Old Spanish Trail in Houston, Texas."

Mike and Candi laughed together.

"So, Candi. Can I ask you something?"

"Shoot, pardner."

"You kept talking about stripper-names back there."

"Yep"

"So I guess you've known a lot of strippers, then?"

"Yep"

"So...have *you* ever been a stripper?"

"Well. I never worked in a strip club. If that's what you mean."

"Oh, ok. I was just curious."

"Just curious, huh? What? Do I seem like the kinda girl who would be a stripper?"

"No. Of course not. That's not what I was implying at all."

"Hey. Don't get me wrong here, pardner! I appreciate the fucking compliment! I mean. I gotta agree with you. I've definitely got the tits and the body for it. Am I right?"

"Definitely"

"So why'd you ask me that?"

"It's just that, when you said you knew a lot of strippers. And then you mentioned their different stripper-names. I just wondered if your,"

"You just wondered what, pardner?"

Mike recalled what Leonard Wallace had said to Candi back in Bremond, Texas. "Well I was just wondering if your-"

"If my what?"

"Never mind"

"Oh for fuck's sake, pardner! Why don't you just go ahead and just fucking say it, already? I mean. I already fucking know what you were gonna fucking ask me. Come on! Don't sweat it there, pardner. You're not gonna hurt my fucking feelings. You already know that. So go ahead and just fucking ask me whatever you wanna fucking ask me."

"Never mind, Candi. Come to think of it. It's not really that important."

***

A few miles down the road, Candi stuffed her copy of *Moby Dick* under her seat. She reached back under her seat and pulled out the pistol.

"What the hell are you doing?" Mike said.

"Don't worry, pardner. I promised I'd behave myself. Remember?" She pointed the pistol at the floorboard near her feet and took aim. "You ever wonder?" She pulled back the hammer slowly and said, "Why they call it, *cocking* a gun? I mean. That shit just can't be a fucking coincidence, right? *Cocking* a gun?"

"You're right. It's not a coincidence."

"See? I told you everythin was all about dick. Didn't I?"

"Yes, you did."

Candi smiled. She gently let the hammer back down on the pistol and said, "You know somethin? Everything's about to fucking change for me, pardner. And I do mean everything! I mean everything's about to get a whole lot fucking better for me. You just wait and see."

"What do you mean?"

"Yep! I'm about to have it made in the fucking shade. Cause when I get back to Houston. I'm never gonna have to suck or fuck another strange dick ever again."

"Oh yeah?"

"Yep! Cause I've got this buried treasure right here. And it's worth a fuckload of cash."

"How much do you think it's worth?"

"I already fucking know how much it's worth. Not too long ago. I asked around a few places in Houston. You know. About how much a gun like this was worth. And are you fucking ready for this? I had three different pawn shops tell me that an 1847 Walker Colt. Even in shitty shape. Is worth like a hundred grand."

"Are you fucking serious, Candi? You mean to tell me. That pistol is worth a hundred thousand dollars?"

"Yep. Sure as shit is. And this one's in pretty good goddamn condition too. And so I'm gonna be a hundred thousand fucking dollars richer when I get back to Houston. And nothin's gonna be the same for me. Ever again! I guaran-goddamn-tee you that, pardner!"

"Wow," Mike said, "That is a fuckload of cash."

"Yep. God fucking bless my dear old granddaddy. For divin into that muddy Navasota River that day. I mean can you fucking believe it? I am one fucking lucky whore."

"You're a *fucky* whore alright!"

They laughed together.

"So," Mike said, "what are you going to do with that much money?"

"Well. I'm not exactly sure yet. But! I'm sure as shit not sharin any of it with your sorry fucking ass!"

They laughed together again.

* * *

"Dammit," Mike said, "I really need to go to the bathroom." He noticed a green sign along the highway that read: GENTRY CREEK. "Let's pull over at this roadside park up here on the left," he said. "I'll make it a quick stop over in the bushes. And then we'll be right back on our way."

"Can't you fucking hold it until we get to the next town?" Candi said.

"No, I really can't. I really need to piss. Right now"

"Come on, pardner. The next town's not too far. I mean this roadside park's in the middle of fucking nowhere."

"Oh for Chrissakes, Candi. It'll take like five minutes."

"Hey!" Candi said. "Whatever fucking happened to- Always go forwards, always go downwards, and never go to the left or the right?"

"Don't worry," Mike said as he pulled off the highway into the roadside park. "I promised you I'd get you back to Houston. And these days. I'm a man of my word."

"Ok," Candi said, "As long as you promise me that while you're gone. You won't get lost in the fucking labyrinth. And you won't get killed by the fucking Minotaur."

"Well. If I do get lost. Or I do get killed. I think it's actually going to be your fault."

"And how do you fucking figure that shit?"

"Well you never got me a sword. Or any red yarn."

"Yeah. I reckon you're fucking right about that. But I did get you some Wrangler blue jeans."

"True"

"And let me tell you somethin, pardner. Ever since you been wearin em. I've been noticin you packin some serious fucking heat down there." She leaned over and patted his bulge.

"Cut it out," Mike said, pushing her hand away. "I've really gotta piss. And you're not helping anything."

Candi laughed and said, "I'll bet you don't even really have to piss. I'll bet you're just making up this whole, I-need-to-go-to-the-bathroom shit. As a fucking excuse to go out in them bushes over there. And bust you a nut. Is that it?"

"Very funny," Mike said. He parked the car and killed the engine.

"You know, cowboy," Candi said. She eased one hand up his leg, towards his crotch, "If you really need to bust a nut that fucking bad..." She stuck her other hand in her shorts. "I've gotta bush right here you can use if you want." She laughed and winked at him. "Whatta you say, pardner?"

"Not funny, Candi. I told you already. I've really, really gotta piss."

"I'm not tryin to be funny, pardner. I'm tryin to get lucky. *Actually*," she said, "I'm tryin to get *fucky*."

"Seriously. Cut it out," Mike said. He opened the car door.

"Ok, pardner. But this is your last fucking chance. I mean. Here's your one chance to fuck me in my pussy with your dick. Come on. I know that's what you wanna do. I mean. Don't you wanna feel me cum all over your dick? Don't you wanna make me cum? And make me fucking scream your name?"

"I mean it, Candi. I'm not falling for this one. I know you're just joking with me. I know you're just fucking with me because you know I've really gotta piss. And you like to make me suffer."

"But I'm *not* jokin this time," Candi said, groping his crotch. "And this time I'm not just fucking *with* you. I really just wanna fuck you."

"Nope, sorry. No way. This little joke's not gonna work." He shoved her hand away. "I'm smarter than that. And I've really, really gotta piss."

"But I want your dick inside me right now. I wanna unzip those Wrangler jeans. Whip out your hard dick. Climb on your lap. Slide down on your dick. And finally feel you fuck my hot, wet pussy with it. I really, really, really, really, really need your dick. And I really need it right now!"

"Nope! Not gonna work," Mike said. He got out of the car. He leaned down with the car door still open. "How about this? When I get back from slaying the Minotaur in the labyrinth. And by that I mean pissing in the bushes. When I get back. If you're still into this little joke of yours. *Then* I'll fuck your fucking brains out."

"And will you slap me around a little bit before you do?"

"Of course"

"And then tell me to go make you a sandwich after?"

"You betcha, little lady," Mike said, feigning his best John Wayne voice, "I'm gonna ride your pussy like I was in a fucking rodeo."

"And then you'll ride off into the sunset?"

"You betcha, little lady"

"Then it's a fucking deal, pardner."

Mike started to shut the car door, but Candi stopped it with her foot. "Only if you promise to take me with you," Candi said. "You know. When you ride off into that sunset of yours..."

"Deal," Mike said. "But where do you want to ride off to? Besides of course, the sunset?"

"Nowhere special...pardner"

"Nowhere special, huh?"

"Yep," Candi said. "Nowhere special... I always wanted to go there..."

"You got it, little lady," Mike said, still feigning John Wayne. "But first. I really, really gotta take a piss. So I'll be right back."

Candi removed her foot from the door, smiled and said, "And they fucking say," she made quotations marks with her hands, "*romance*, is dead."

They laughed together.

Mike smiled at her. He slammed the car door and then hurried off towards a nearby wooded area. As he entered the bushes, Mike glanced back at Candi over his shoulder. He saw her face. He saw her smile at him with a smile he had never seen before. And then he saw her mouth the words, nowhere special...

Chapter 18

Some dumb luck near Gentry Creek

In his overzealous attempt to make sure that nobody driving by the roadside park could see him pissing, Mike had walked quite a ways into the bushes. Despite his hard-on, he had managed to piss for what seemed like half an hour, and now felt much better.

Mike thought about the way Candi had grabbed his crotch before he got out of the car. How she'd put her hand down in her shorts and massaged her pussy. He could still hear her voice as she described sitting on his lap and fucking his dick. He recalled the moment when he glanced back and spotted that beguiling smile on her face. That smile that made him suddenly forget the oak tree behind the tool shed, the shovel, the gun and the grave. That smile that suddenly forced him to somehow forgive her for everything. That smile that made him hope against hope that this time, Candi was not just fucking with him about fucking him. And that her nowhere special comment was not just a joke.

As he trekked back through the live oaks and yaupon bush, Mike heard the car begin honking over and over and over again. "What a fucking cockteaser!" he said to himself, chuckling. Candi would be proud of him for using the word cockteaser so naturally, he mused. "I'll give it to you, Candi," he whispered to himself, "You never fucking give up."

Mike neared the edge of the bushes and approached the clearing where the car was parked. The horn still honked desperately.

Mike wondered if the car windows were rolled down. If Candi hadn't started the car for the sake of the air conditioning, Mike thought, then she probably would have rolled down the windows to keep cool. If so, then if he yelled she would hear him. Mike decided to make her proud of him and yelled, "Hey, Candi! You are such a fucking cockteaser! You know that?" He smiled to himself and chuckled again. He stepped from the bushes and yelled, "We sure got," he raised his hands up in a wide, triumphant gesture, making Candi's familiar quotation marks with his fingers, "*fucky*, that this roadside park was,"

Mike stopped and stood perfectly still. He dropped his arms and stared forward. The car finally stopped honking. Mike could see Candi sitting in the passenger's seat, riding shotgun, where she always sat, staring him down.

Mike saw a rusty old ramshackle tow truck parked right up behind his car, trapping it where it was parked. The bumpers were almost touching. The tow truck was spray painted a tacky yellowish-gold, almost like an ancient chariot. Hand-painted black letters scrawled along the side of the tow truck read:

JOHNNY REV TOWING
"For the Good Lord so loved the world…"
JOHN 3:16

Mike watched four filthy men circle his ride like buzzards. Candi sat inside, still riding shotgun as always. Mike noticed the men ogling Candi. Each of them circling the car and staring her down like she was a stinking, rotting piece of roadside carrion. A man wearing a red bandana tugged on the handle of the driver's side door, but with no success.

One of the other men, wearing a green tractor t-shirt, kneeled at the passenger's side window and tapped on the glass. He puckered up and then kissed and licked the glass, feigning fellatio only inches from Candi's face inside.

Another man with a scraggly bushy beard, beer-gut belly, and wearing a straw hat lined with chicken feathers, looked up and spotted Mike. He brought his fingers to his lips and whistled, and then yelled to the other men, "Looks like we got us some company, fellas!" They all turned their attention to Mike, and then strutted slowly towards the front end of the car. Mike noticed that all of them were nursing cans of beer and staggering a little.

Mike took a deep breath. He walked slowly towards them, just past the concrete picnic table, and then stood his ground alongside the metal trash can.

The man with bushy beard walked up to Mike, grinned and said, "Howdy there, stranger. We spotted yer ride from the road. And we figured ya was broke down. Ya'll need any help?"

"We're not broken down," Mike said, trying to keep his voice from cracking. "I just pulled over for a second to go to the bathroom. Thanks, though. I appreciate you stopping to-"

"So ya ain't broken down then?"

"No"

The other men didn't smile as they slowly surrounded Mike. "Where ya'll headed to, stranger?"

"We're on our way back to Houston."

"Houston? The big city, huh?" He scratched his beard with gnarled, greasy fingers. "Well. I reckon it ain't The Good Lord's country. But a man's gotta hang his hat somewheres..."

Mike didn't know what to say.

"Well. Ya'll drive careful now," he said, but just stood there, grinning at Mike.

After a few minutes of awkward silence, Mike said, "Um, excuse me. Would you mind moving your truck so we can get back on the road?" He pointed gently, politely at their tow truck. "It's the way you parked. You have us trapped in right there."

The man in the red bandana did a drunken shuffle forward a few steps. He said to Mike, "Are ya fuckin tellin us what to do, stranger?"

"Uh, no I'm not."

"Well it sure fuckin sounds to me like ya are."

"I'm really sorry"

"I reckon it's still a free fuckin country. And we'll park wherever the fuck we want to."

Mike noticed him slurring his words. He swallowed hard and took another deep breath. He smiled at them again and said, "I really didn't mean to be rude. It's just that you have us trapped there with your truck." Mike hoped, or desperately wanted to believe, that these men did not really understand the parking situation. "So. If you wouldn't mind just moving your truck really quick. Then we'll just get out of your way."

Mike glanced over at Candi, still sitting motionless in the car. The sunshine of that Texas afternoon glared down on the windshield, and Mike was unable to discern the exact expression on her face.

"How bout this, stranger?" The man in the red bandanna said. He stepped even closer to Mike. "I reckon yer the one who's trapped here. So how bout ya just step right up. And take them keys away from us. And then ya can move the *goddamned* truck yerself?"

"How many times I gotta tell ya, Dub," the man in the beard said. He stepped over and placed his hand against Dub's chest, pushing him back. "Guard yer tongue, Dub. Guard yer tongue against the blasphemy."

"I'm real sorry, Rev," Dub said, backing up. "It's just that this here stranger's got me all riled up, that's all."

"Well, Dub. That still ain't no excuse for the blasphemy. And that sure as shit ain't no excuse for bein rude to this here stranger neither. See, Dub. Some of us round here was raised up right. Just cuz yer mama was a Jezebel. And she never teached ya right from wrong. Don't mean we all got brought up like that." A grim smile was nailed to his sunburned face in the shade of that straw brimmed hat. Mike noticed this man didn't seem as drunk as the others, and that he was the leader of the bunch.

"Hey, Rev," Dub said, "Ya ain't always gotta talk so much fuckin shit about my mama, ya know."

"I gotta speak the gospel truth, Dub. I just gotta. And ya know good and well. Just like everbody else round these parts. That yer mama was a Jezebel if there ever was one. And there ain't nothin The Good Lord hates more in a woman than her bein a Jezebel. See here, Dub. I'll testify. There ain't a man in Limestone County that ain't poked his pecker into yer mama's mark of the beast. And that's The Good Lord's honest truth of it too! And that's why The Good Lord put me on this here earth." He turned to face Dub, pointing his finger at him. "Look at me, Dub. Look right at me right square in the eyes, Dub."

Dub kicked the dust and then looked up at him.

"Have I testified *anythin*? And I do mean *anythin* bout yer mama? That ain't The Good Lord's honest to gospel truth?"

"Nope. I reckon ya ain't."

"That's right. I ain't." Rev turned back to face Mike, "See, stranger. The Good Book reads thissa way- Thou shalt *not*! And I do mean *not* bear false witness against thy neighbor. And not you, stranger," he pointed right at Mike, "and not Dub here," he pointed back at Dub, "and not even Dub's filthy Jezebellin mama. Nope! Not nobody is ever gonna make me do different. See?"

Mike suddenly felt his stomach turn and sicken.

"Yeah, I reckon yer right, Rev," Dub said, staring back down into the dirt. "But. Well. Goddammit, Rev! I know it's fuckin true. I just don't fuckin see why ya always gotta be fuckin remindin me of it. That's all."

"Ya done done it again, Dub. Ya better guard yer tongue against the blasphemy," Rev said. He gazed more intensely at Mike and then said in a sermonic tone, "See, stranger. The Good Book reads thissa way- Thou shalt *not*! And I do mean *not* take The Good Lord's name in vain. See. Folks who talk that way are headed *straight*! And I do mean *straight* for perdition."

"I'm real sorry, Rev," Dub mumbled.

"Don't apologize to me, Dub. When ya git down on your knees and ya say your prayers tonight. Ya better do yer apologizin to The Good Lord. See. It's *his* forgiveness! And I do mean *his* forgiveness yer a gonna be needin. Not mine."

"Hey, Rev," one of the other men said, "What's a Jezebel anyway?"

"What's a Jezebel? Good Lord! Don't nobody read The Good Book no more?"

Dub said, "I read it, Rev. Just like ya told me. And I remember what ya said a Jezebel is."

"Guard yer tongue, Dub." Rev said. "I'll tell it. See. The Good Book reads thissa way- Once upon a time... Way back in the olden days. There was this woman named Jezebel. Now. She didn't believe in The Good Lord. And she didn't never read The Good Book neither. Nor even try to live her life by it neither. And Jezebel was what they used to call, back in the olden days, a painted woman..."

"What's that, Rev?"

"It means, fellas. She didn't hardly wear no clothes."

"Sounds like a damned cock-teaser to me," Dub said.

"Jezebel was a slut and a whore," Rev said. "And she used her filthy mark of the beast to get ol King Ahab to up and marry her. See. The Good Lord had chose Ahab to be the king over his chosen people. But Ahab went and got himself led astray by Jezebel. And ya know what Jezebel got Ahab to do, fellas?"

"Preach it, Rev," Dub said.

"Jezebel used her filthy mark of the beast to git King Ahab to turn his back on The Good Lord. She even got him to start worshippin them pagan gods."

"Pagan gods? What the fuck is that?"

"Yep, fellas. They had them these pagan gods way back when. See. Them folks who never did listen to The Good Lord. Well they'd up and worship just about anythin. And I do mean anythin and everythin. They'd up and worship mountains. And flowers and rocks. And even trees!"

"Holy shit," Dub said, "Who'd worship a fuckin tree? I mean it just stands there and don't do nothin. Right?"

"They even worshipped animals," Rev said. "And they even gave em names too! See. Jezebel she worshipped a bull. And they named that bull, Bale."

"She worshipped a fuckin bull? Holy shit, fellas. Did you fuckin hear that shit?"

"And that ain't the worse of it, neither. Ya fellas know how a bull's got a big ol huge pecker. And how when ya get a bull excited. His pecker will get damn near three feet long."

Dub said, "I sure do wish I was a bull! Huh, fellas?" He and the others laughed.

"It ain't funny, fellas," Rev said. "It ain't funny, cuz The Good Lord don't think it's funny."

The men stopped laughing.

"See. Folks like Jezebel worshipped a bull. And they worshipped it's pecker. Because it was sooo big. And ya know what else they done? They'd build up mounds of dirt. And then they'd put up a big pole right near the top of the mound. Kinda like a fence post or a flagpole, ya know. And then they'd get right down on their knees. Bow right down and they'd worship that pecker-pole."

"Holy shit," Dub said, "Them folks musta been bat-shit crazy!"

"Nope, Dub," Rev said, "They wasn't crazy. Them folks knew exactly what they was doin."

"Well shit! Worshippin a pecker-pole sure sounds fuckin crazy to me."

"Nope! Them folks wasn't crazy. They was just *apostate*."

"What the fuck does that mean?"

"How's bout we ask this here stranger what it means," Rev said, turning to Mike. "After all. I seen all his fancy books there in the back of his ride. So I reckon he's got him lots of fancy book learnin. So I'll bet he knows the difference between an *apostle* and an *apostate.*"

"Well, stranger? What's the fuckin difference, huh?"

Mike didn't answer him.

"Then I'll tell it to ya, fellas," Rev said. "I learnt it in my Bible classes in Huntsville. See. An *apostle* is a sinner who knows he done wrong. But then repents for his sins. Kinda like me. But an *apostate* person is a sinner who knows he done wrong. But he just refuses to repent for his sins."

"So," Dub said, "it's kinda like bein real, real stubborn, huh?"

"See. Them folks way back when. They wasn't crazy. They knew damn well what they was doin was wrong. And The Good Lord. He can always tell bout what folks are really thinkin. In their hearts, ya know? See. The Good Lord can always tell bout whether a man really knows what he's doin is wrong. Or bout whether a man's crazy and just don't know no better."

"Kinda like with Lil Neezer, huh?" Dub said.

Rev shot him a glare, and Dub looked at the ground.

Rev turned back to face Mike. He pressed his hands together, palm against palm, like he was preparing to bless a meal. "Well now. Looky at what we got here, fellas. See. I done told ya'll a thousand times before. The Good Lord don't never let ya down. And The Good Book don't never lead ya wrong. It reads thissa way- Ask and ye shall *receive!* And I do mean *receive.*"

"Please, sir," Mike said, still hoping that a rational appeal might somehow work. "We really don't want to bother you and your friends. We really just want to be on our way."

"But we ain't been properly introduced yet, stranger," Rev said. "See. I don't reckon I know how they do it in the big city. And I don't reckon I wanna know neither. But where I come from. When ya meet a man. It's just good manners to shake his hand and introduce yerself."

Mike wondered if they noticed his hand tremble as he raised it for a handshake. "My name is Mike."

"Well pleased to meet ya," Rev said, taking his hand and pumping it up and down gently. "I'm the *right*! And I do mean the *right* Reverend Jehu Armstrong."

Mike forced a nervous smile. He tried to let go of the handshake but Rev held on and continued to pump it gently.

"Ya know why folks call me the *right* reverend, stranger?"

Mike shook his head.

"It's cuz I was baptized right up yonder, down the road over there. In the swimmin hole at the Confederate Reunion Grounds. I was just thirteen years old. And ever since I was sixteen. I been preachin The Good Lord's word. Yep. I been preachin it *word for word*! And I do mean *word for word*. Right straight from the King James Bible. And then. See. I was ordained into the gospel ministry by the Southern Baptist Church. When I was just seventeen. And that's what makes me a reverend. See?"

"Nice to meet you," Mike said.

"But that ain't what makes me a *right* reverend, see?"

Mike felt his mouth go dry.

"Ya know what makes me a *right* reverend, stranger?"

Mike just shook his head again.

"Well, stranger," Rev said, grinning. "It didn't take me long to figure out. I liked raisin Hell a lot better than preachin about it!" He turned to the other men, laughed, and then turned back to face Mike. "Well, stranger. The Good Lord don't take kindly to folks turnin their back on him. So he made damn sure I got caught for all my sins. And that's when The Good Lord up and sent me off to Huntsville for a spell."

Mike tried to pull his hand away from their lingering handshake, but Rev held on, pumping and squeezing even tighter than before.

"And that's when The Good Lord gotta hold of me again. And he reminded me why he put me on this here earth. See. I repented *all* my sins! And I do mean *all* my sins. And then I got baptized again. And then I sat down and read The Good Book. All the way through. From front to back. Genesis all the way to Revelation. See. I read it over and over and over again."

"And then I took me some Bible classes too. They offered em there where I was. And I studied The Good Book all day long. I memorized it too. I done memorized the whole thing. Ever blessed word. See. The Good Lord saw fit to give me seven long years in that place. And he sure knew what he was doin too. Cuz I sure had me lots of time to study The Good Book. And get myself right again."

"And while I was there. I started preachin The Good Lord's gospel again. Ever Sunday and ever Wednesday in the chapel there. And ya know what happened, stranger? Ever man in that place would show up ever Sunday. Just to hear me preach. It was a real life miracle! See. I was like Abraham. Or like Moses or Isaiah. Or John the Baptist. I was like one of them prophets. See. Ever man in that place would come ever Sunday. Just to hear me preachin."

Mike realized that rationality was not going to work here.

"See, stranger. The Good Book reads thissa way- Even though yer sins be as red as scarlet...they shall be *as* white! And I do mean *as* white as snow."

Mike tried to get a better look at Candi. He tried to discern her mood, movement or even her facial expressions. But the sun still glared off the windshield. He didn't want to lift his hand to shade his eyes for a better view of her, because he didn't want to draw needless attention to her. Mike was glad Candi was safe inside the car, for now. But then again, part of him desperately wished that she was by his side.

"See, stranger," Rev said. "I started off *right* with the Good Lord. And then I went and walked on the wide and crooked path for a spell. Ya know. The path that leads *right* to perdition. But! The Good Lord gotta hold of me. And set me *right* again. And that's why folks call me the *right* Reverend Jehu Armstrong."

Rev finally released Mike's hand.

"Well," Mike said, kneading his throbbing hand, "It's been really, really nice to meet you, *right* reverend. But me and my friend really do need to be going. So please. If you don't mind-"

"So stranger. Yer from Houston?"

"I'm sorry. We're already really late. And we really need to be going, so,"

"I asked ya a question, stranger. Now ya don't wanna be rude like Dub over there, do ya?"

"We drove here from Houston," Mike said, deciding to try a new strategy of humoring him. "But I'm not originally *from* Houston."

"But ya was in Houston, right?"

"Yes"

"Ya ain't one of them Sodomites, are ya?"

"What?"

"Ya ain't one of them Sodomites, are ya? Ya know. Queer?"

"Uh, no. I'm not."

"Ya sure bout that, stranger?"

"Yes, I'm sure."

"Well, ok then. A man never can be too careful, ya know. See. They got *lots*! And I do mean *lots* of them Sodomites down there in Houston."

"You're right, uh...they really do have, uh...lots of them"

"So ya ain't *from* Houston, huh? Well that don't surprise me none. In fact. I'll testify right now. Yer from up north, ain't ya?"

"Yes"

"See there, fellas. I could just tell it."

The other men smiled and nodded in agreement.

"So, stranger. Whereabouts up north are ya from? Hold on. Wait just a second. Don't tell me. Let me testify to it."

Mike watched Rev's bloodshot eyes roll back and his chubby chapped lips quiver.

"I reckon its way, way up north. Is it up farther north than Dallas?"

"Yes"

"See there, fellas! I could just tell that too!"

The other men nodded in agreement.

Dub said, "See there fellas! Rev's never wrong when he testifies."

"Well, stranger," Rev said, "how far up north?"

"I was living in Connecticut."

"Connecticut? All the way up in Connecticut? But ya ain't from *there*, are ya?"

"No"

"See, fellas. I could tell that too. So what was ya doin all the way up there in Yankee-land?"

"Going to school"

"Ya mean like college, school?"

"Yes"

"Sounds like a waste of time if ya ask me."

"It was, actually," Mike said, as a kind of kneejerk reaction.

"Ya better not be *tryin*! And I do mean *tryin,* to be smart with me, stranger!"

"No, sir. I'm not trying to be smart."

"So ya really think your schoolin was a waste of time then?"

"Yes, I do actually."

"I could tell it. Yep. I could tell it. See. The Good Book is the *only* book! And I mean the *only* book worth readin. My daddy and mama always said- There ain't nothin a man needs to know that ya can't find right there in The Good Book."

"You're right," Mike said, "I agree with you. Now. Would you mind, please, moving your pickup? So me and my-"

"So, stranger. Where'd ya meet yer woman over there? I mean she don't look to me like she's from up north."

"Please," Mike said, "We just want to go, ok."

"I said- Where'd ya meet yer woman over there?"

"Houston"

"See. I could just tell. See. That there woman don't look like a Yankee to me." Rev turned around and stared at Candi in the car. He winced in the afternoon sunshine, so he put his hand to his forehead, shielding his eyes. He took another long look at Candi and then smiled over at her. "Ma'am," he said to her, tipping his straw hat.

But when Rev turned back around to face Mike again, his courteous smile melted into a crooked, broken frown couched in his sunburned cheeks. "Ya know what else I can tell, stranger? I can tell that yer woman is a Jezebel. Just like Dub's mama."

"Please, Reverend," Mike said, "We don't want-"

"That's the *right* reverend to you, stranger!"

"Sorry," Mike said, "I'm sorry. I mean. Please *right* reverend. We just don't want any trouble here."

"See, stranger. When I testify. I'm never wrong. Just ask these fellas here. I'm never wrong. Cuz like I told ya already. The Good Lord himself set me back on the right path. And when The Good Lord sets a man back on the right path. The Good Lord himself is a gonna make damn sure that when that man testifies. That man's gonna speak the gospel truth. And that's why. See. I'm always gonna speak the truth when I testify."

"Please," Mike said, "I don't understand why you're-"

"And ya know what that means? Don't ya, stranger?"

Mike made no reply.

"It means I was speakin the truth a couple of minutes ago too. Ya know, stranger. When I first testified about *you*! And I do mean *you*. And the truth about what *you* are."

"I don't understand. Please, can't we just go and-"

"I could just tell it about ya. Ya know? See. That's why The Good Lord himself put me on this here earth. To testify the truth. And the truth is... Yer woman over there is a Jezebel. I mean Good Lord, fellas! Can't ya smell that Jezebel? It don't matter none whether a man is righteous or unrighteous. A man can always smell a Jezebel! See. I can smell her wicked, filthy mark of the beast all the way over here. And it *stinks*! And I do mean *stinks* like perdition!"

Mike began to tremble.

Dub said, "I smell it, too, Rev! Yer right!"

"And you, stranger," Rev said, stepping even closer to Mike. He pointed his finger right in his face, "You *are* a Sodomite. Yep. Yer nothin but a damned Sodomite. See. I knowd it all along, fellas. Right from the start."

Dub said, "Ya mean he's a fuckin queer?"

"I mean," Rev said, "This here stranger likes to have him unnatural relations with other men. I mean. He likes to lay down with other men. And know them. I mean he likes to have another man's pecker in his mouth. Suckin on it. And he even likes to have another man's pecker stuck all the way up inside his butthole."

Dub bent forward, choked a little, and said, "Holy fuckin shit, Rev! Stop it! That's some nasty-ass fucked up shit right there!"

"See, stranger," Rev said. "The Good Book reads thissa way- And likewise also the men, leavin the natural use of the woman, burned in their lust one toward another. Men with other men! Men workin that which is *unseemly*! And I do mean *unseemly*! And they shall receive unto themselves that recompense for their error."

Rev gestured to the other men, and they all moved in closer to Mike. "See, stranger," Rev said, "Ya know what we do to Sodomites round these parts?"

"Please," Mike said, "I've got money. It's all yours! Just take it and go!"

"Oh, don't ya worry none bout that," Rev said. "Me and the fellas are gonna take all yer money, right as rain. And everythin else ya got too. But first. We gotta rough ya up. On account a ya bein a Sodomite and all."

"And then. After we're all through roughin ya up real good. We're gonna help ourselves to that Jezebel of yers over there." Rev turned, pointed right at Candi, raised his nose to the wind, and smelled long and deep. "Good Lord, fellas! Can ya smell that? That's what the mark of the beast smells like, right there!"

"Holy shit," Dub said, "Ol Rev is gettin fired up for another sermon!"

"I'm a gonna testify, fellas," Rev said. "See. The way I figure it is. If a woman's already done ruined herself by bein a Jezebel. Then I don't think The Good Lord would hold it against us. If we got our peckers wet in her muddy little pond."

"Oh hell yeah!" Dub yelled. "Preach that shit, Rev!"

"See, fellas. The Good Book reads thissa way- The spirit is willin but the flesh is weak." Rev grabbed his crotch, stomped his foot and said, "And my flesh is feelin awful *weak*! And I do mean awful *weak* today, fellas!"

"Holy shit, Rev," Dub said, "I sure am glad you decided on that! I mean look at that bitch! The Good Lord, he sure knew what he was doin the day he put her together!"

"Please, guys," Mike said, "I'll give you all my money. And we won't tell anybody about any of this. I promise we won't tell the police. I promise! We just want to get back on the road."

"Ain't nobody gotta worry bout the law round these parts, stranger," Rev said, pointing to his truck. He cupped his ear, listening and said, "Ya hear that, stranger? That right there in my pickup. Right there on my dashboard. That's a police radio scanner. Ya know what that is?"

"See. There ain't but two sheriff's deputies on patrol in all Limestone County tonight. See. One of em is my second cousin. And right now his patrol car is parked twenty miles over yonder. He's gettin ready for an all-night stake out. So he can catch him some poachers."

"And the other deputy. Well. His patrol car's gonna be parked all afternoon in Mexia at The Holiday Inn. Or as I like to call it, The Holiday Sin." Rev chuckled and slapped his knee. "See, stranger. That deputy parks his patrol car there every other day. Just like clockwork."

"Hell yeah he does," Dub said. "Everbody knows he's fuckin that slant-eyed, oriental bitch who works the counter there. Yep. I hear it's the only goddamn Chinese food in town worth eatin!" Dub laughed. "That's a good one, huh, fellas? Ain't that a good one?"

"I warned ya Dub. Ya better guard your tongue," Rev said. "That ain't very funny to me. See. This world don't make no sense to me. This world just ain't right no more. And it plum makes me wanna vomit. See, fellas. This world has got to where there ain't a motel or gas station left. That ain't owned by some raghead or some gook."

"Ya sure are right bout that, Rev," Dub said.

"See, fellas. I'm testifyin to ya right now. This world just ain't right no more. See! Looky right here, fellas! This is what I'm talkin bout! How does this damned Sodomite end up ridin round with that Jezebel over there? It just don't seem right to me. And it just don't make no sense to me at all. Nope. See. The world just ain't right no more. It just don't make no sense…"

"Please," Mike said, "Why won't you just let us go? I don't understand, please!"

"See, fellas," Rev said. "This world don't make sense to nobody. Not even this stranger here."

"Please…I'm begging you. Please!"

"So that takes care of the deputies, see," Rev said, turning his attention back to Mike. "Now the sheriff. He don't live too far from here. Just over yonder on the other side of Gentry Creek. But! It's his day off, see. And there ain't no way he's gonna git off his lazy white ass. Less somebody radios him. Or he hears somethin."

"So ya see, stranger. All we gotta do is listen real careful to that there police scanner there. And as long as we're real quiet like," he pressed his finger to his lips and made a hushing sound, "me and the fellas can do whatever we wanna do." Rev turned back towards the car again, staring Candi down and licking his lips, "Whatever we wanna do, see? Includin your Jezebel's filthy mark of the beast over there."

"Please," Mike said. "Just leave us alone. Please!" In desperation, he cupped his hand over his eyes, hoping to catch a glance at Candi's face. He needed her next to him.

"Put your hand down, stranger," Rev said. "There's a gonna be plenty of time for ya to watch your woman. *After* we rough ya up"

"Yeah," Dub said, laughing, "Plenty of time for ya to watch us fuck the shit outta her!"

The men eased towards Mike, surrounding him.

"Hold up there fellas," Rev said, "I almost forgot. I want Lil Neezer to watch us rough up this stranger here."

"Holy shit," Dub said, "Lil Neezer loves this kinda shit."

"Yep," Rev said, chuckling, "Daddy always used to say- Lil Neezer could sleep through a snowstorm. If there was such a thing in Limestone County!" Rev brought his fingers to his lips and whistled like he was calling a dog. He yelled, "Neezer! Neezer! Wake up, Neezer! Git your fat butt up outta that pickup and get on over here! Pronto!"

Mike watched an obese young man struggle to sit up in the bed of the truck. He wore baggy black cargo-style pants, unlaced combat boots, and a threadbare wife-beater spotted with bright red stains. He dripped with sweat. Pieces of hay and paint chips stuck in his hair and on the side of his face where he had been sleeping.

"Neezer! Neezer!" Rev yelled. "I said- Git your fat butt over here, pronto! Pronto!"

After a desperate clumsy struggle, Lil Neezer finally lumbered out of the pickup. He just stood there in dumb silence for a moment, leaning against the tailgate and staring back down into the bed of the pickup.

"Neezer!" Rev yelled, "Neezer! Git your fat butt over here, pronto! Pronto, ya hear me! I know what you want, Neezer! And you can have some more strawberry soda. *After* we rough up this here stranger, ok? Now move it! Pronto, Neezer. Pronto!"

Lil Neezer licked his chapped, bovine lips, still gazing into the bed of the pickup.

"Strawberry soda, Neezer. That's right! Now if I have to tell ya to git your fat butt over here one more time. I'm gonna git out Daddy's chain. Tie your ass to the bumper there. And you can ride all the way back home like that!"

"Holy shit!" Dub said. "I ain't watched Rev here git all Jasper Texas on anybody's ass in a long goddamned fucking time!"

"And if you don't start guardin your tongue like I told ya, Dub," Rev said, "You're gonna be watchin me Jasper Texas from the wrong end of my daddy's chain!" Rev yelled louder than before, "Move it, Neezer! Pronto! Pronto!"

Lil Neezer let out a big sigh, wobbled over and joined the other men surrounding Mike. He stood next to Rev.

Rev patted Lil Neezer on the head like he was a dog. "Well, stranger. This here's my younger brother, Ebenezer. See. After our mama died. The Good Lord rest her soul. Everbody just started callin him Lil Neezer, for short."

Lil Neezer smiled a gargantuan, gaping smile, revealing his grimy, blackened teeth. He stared down Mike with his bulging, bloodshot eyes. Mike noticed Lil Neezer breathing heavily, almost panting, while spit drooled down from his lips onto his chins, jowls, neck and chest.

"What ya think, Lil Neezer?" Rev said, "Ya gonna like this little treat I found for ya? Ain't ya?"

Mike watched Lil Neezer slide his swollen hand down along his enormous belly, and then stick his fat fingers down into the front of his pants.

"See, stranger," Rev said. "Our daddy was a preacher. Just like me. The Good Lord rest his soul. And Daddy gave both me and Neezer here, good King James Bible names. See, stranger. In The Good Book. The name Ebenezer means, stone of help. And that's because in The Good Book. One of The Good Lord's prophets. Well he set him up a stone, and-"

"What kinda stone was it, Rev?" Dub said, "Was it like a gravestone?"

"No, Dub! It wasn't nothin like a gravestone! Now shut up! See, stranger. That prophet wanted to remind everbody bout how The Good Lord helped his chosen people beat them Philistines that day."

"What prophet was it, Rev?" Dub said. "I think I mighta heard this story at vacation bible school."

"It was the prophet, Ezekiel. Now shut up!"

Mike watched Lil Neezer fumble into his underwear, and then start to jerk and tug on his dick.

The men chuckled.

"Holy shit, fellas!" Dub said, pointing down and laughing, "Looks like Lil Neezer flesh is feelin weak today too!"

"Lil Neezer's flesh is always feelin weak," Rev said, slapping Lil Neezer's arm. He slapped his face. "Not yet, Neezer! Not yet! Now git your fat hand outta your pants, pronto! It ain't time for that yet! We gotta rough this here stranger up first."

"Yeah, Neezer," Dub said. "We gotta rough him up first. That a way he won't move around any when you go and cornhole him in the ass!"

"Hey!" Rev yelled, kicking dirt at Dub. "My little brother ain't never cornholed nobody. Ya got that? Do all of ya'll got that? Cornholin is for Sodomites! And Lil Neezer ain't no damned Sodomite. No way. No how! Ya'll got that?"

"Sorry, Rev," Dub said, "I never meant it like that. I just meant that,"

"I know what ya meant!" Rev said, slapping Lil Neezer's face again, even harder than before. "Neezer! Ya wait your turn like everbody else. Now stop it! Pronto!"

Lil Neezer tugged his hand out of his pants and frowned. Lil Neezer lift his hand up to his own blistered, bloated veiny nose. He crammed his fat fingers into his nostrils, sniffed deeply, and then licked them.

"See, stranger. Our daddy always hoped both us boys would turn out to be preachers. Just like him. And he prayed to The Good Lord on his knees *every day* of his life for it, too. And I do mean *every day*! But like I said before. This world just don't make no sense no more."

"Ya think it made any sense to my daddy? How I got baptized, and then I got ordained? And how I was doin The Good Lord's work? And then one day I up and git sent off to Huntsville for all my sins? Ya think that made sense to Daddy?"

"And ya think it made sense to my Daddy? When Lil Neezer here was born dumb? See, stranger. Lil Neezer here ain't never been right in the head. Not since the day he was born. Yep. He's as dumb as a fence post. And Lil Neezer ain't never spoken a blessed word neither. Ya think any of that made sense to my daddy?"

"Mama always said to me- Even though The Good Lord didn't see it fit to give yer little brother any brains. The Good Lord put him here on earth. So I could name him Ebenezer. So ya could always remember that The Good Lord always helps ya out whenever ya need him. I reckon that was her way of makin sense of it...."

"Now. When Mama wasn't around, Daddy always said to me- Yer little brother Neezer is as dumb as the day is long. But he ain't never bit the hand that fed him. And that's more than I can say for most folks. I reckon that was Daddy's way of making sense of it..."

"Never made no sense to me though. And it still don't. But I reckon it ain't supposed to. See, stranger. The Good Book reads thissa way- The Good Lord works in mysterious ways."

"He's at it again, Rev," Dub said, pointing down at Lil Neezer's crotch.

Rev slapped Lil Neezer in the face, busting open his chapped bottom lip. "Stop it, Neezer! Stop it, pronto!"

Lil Neezer tugged his hand from his pants. He moaned and whined and then rubbed his bloody lip.

"And I reckon that's somethin else that never made no sense to Daddy and Mama. See, stranger. Lil Neezer here. Well. He'll poke just about anythin that moves. And I mean it too. Lil Neezer here will stick his fat pecker in *anything*! And I do mean *anything*!"

"It's true," Dub said, "I seen him do it, too!"

"Dogs, cats, pigs, horses, cows. It don't matter none. Ya name it. And Lil Neezer here will stick his fat pecker right in it. And it really don't matter what it is neither. It could be a mark of the beast. Or a mouth. Or even a butthole. And it could be a man or a woman. It really don't matter none to Lil Neezer here. Just so long as he can stick his fat pecker in it, he's happy. Ain't that right, Lil Neezer?"

Lil Neezer nodded and reached back into his pants. Rev slapped his arm again and said, "Not yet, Neezer! I done told ya already. We gotta rough up this here stranger first. And then ya can put your pecker in his butthole."

"Oh hell yeah!" Dub said, "I seen him do it. There ain't nothin Lil Neezer likes better than a butthole!" He looked over at Rev, grimaced and said, "Course. That don't mean Neezer likes to cornhole. Or that he's a queer. That ain't what it means at all."

"He just don't know what he's doin. That's all, fellas," Rev said. He gently patted Lil Neezer's head, and then carefully wiped away the blood and drool from his lip. "See. The Good Lord saw fit to make Lil Neezer here dumb. And so I reckon. If Neezer's so dumb he don't even know the difference between a man and woman's butthole. Or even a pig or cow. Then The Good Lord's gotta understand that."

"I'll testify to ya, fellas. Lil Neezer ain't no queer. And he ain't no cornholer neither. And it don't matter how many buttholes my little brother puts his pecker in. The Good Lord knows better. You got it?"

"We got it, Rev," Dub said, "Ain't we got it, fellas?"

The other two men nodded in agreement.

"And! Lil Neezer here," Rev said, "He sure ain't no damned Sodomite neither. Not like this here stranger."

"Hey, Rev," Dub said, "What's The Good Book say bout fuckin a woman in the ass? That's ok, right?"

"Nope. The Good Lord don't like that neither. See. The Good Lord didn't create buttholes for folks to go and put peckers in. It's as plain and simple as that."

Dub looked puzzled and said, "But it ain't the same as fuckin another man's asshole? Right? I mean. It ain't *as bad*, right?"

"You right, Dub," Rev said, "It ain't the same at all. You right, it ain't *as bad*. But it still ain't right."

"Good thing," Dub said.

"Please," Mike said, "Just let us go. Please! I'm begging you!"

"See, stranger," Rev said, grinning. "Here's how it's goin down. First. Me and the fellas here are gonna rough ya up *real bad*! And I do mean, *real bad*. But we ain't gonna kill ya. Don't ya worry none bout that."

"See. When me and the fellas are done roughin ya up real bad. I'm gonna let Lil Neezer here stick his pecker in your butthole. I reckon we ougta give that poor old cow we got in the barn back home a night off. And then. After Lil Neezer's done with ya. Me and the fellas are gonna get to know your woman over there *real well*! And I do mean, *real well*. And you're gonna watch us do her too. So, stranger. How's that sound to ya?"

Mike's hands and legs trembled.

"I said- How's that sound to ya, stranger?"

"Please," Mike said, "Please don't do this."

"Grab hold of him, fellas," Rev said. "I reckon it's time for some good old fashioned recompense."

Two men grabbed Mike by the arms and Dub punched him in the gut. Mike doubled over, gasping for breath, but the two men held him upright.

As Rev moved in for his turn at a punch, everybody heard the car door open and turned around.

"How does this sound?" Candi screamed at them, "You bunch of stupid inbred goddamned fucking sons of bitches! I'm gonna fucking blow your fucking brains out!" Candi stalked towards them with her pistol raised in the air.

Rev and Dub threw their hands up. The other two men held on to Mike. Lil Neezer cowered down on his knees like he was praying.

"And you know what?" Candi said to Rev, aiming her gun in his face with a smile, "I think I'm gonna fucking start with you, preacher-man!" As she moved forward, Rev backed up. He stopped when his back bumped up against a big post oak tree. "Now," Candi said to him, "How does *that* fucking sound to ya?"

Rev raised his hands up even higher and his voice trembled. "Hold on there now. Good Lord, woman! There ain't no need to be gettin all bent outta shape. Me and the fellas was just havin us a little fun. That's all." Rev gestured carefully with his trembling hand, and the two men let go of Mike and stepped back. Mike slumped onto the ground, cradling his ribs and coughing.

"Now! You fucking listen to me, preacher-man," Candi said. "It's *this* fucking Jezebel right here. Who's gonna fucking tell you stupid hicks how it's fucking goin down! You got it?" She stared them all down.

"First!" Candi said, "You're gonna fucking throw the keys to your piece of shit truck to my friend there! And then! When he's all done movin your fucking truck outta the way. I'm gonna slash your fucking tires! That way you're not goin anywhere!"

"And then! My friend's gonna get his ass back in our fucking car. And once he's got our ride pointed in the right direction. With the fucking engine runnin. And the fucking air conditioning goin. And maybe even some Lynyrd Skynard on the fucking radio. I'm gonna jump in shotgun like. And me and him are gonna ride off into the fucking sunset. Now! How does *that* fucking sound to ya, preacher-man?"

"Listen here, woman," Rev said, "Me and the fellas was just horsin around. See, here. Ya don't have to get all,"

"I fucking said," Candi screamed in his face, pressing the pistol closer, "How does *that* fucking sound to you? I asked you a fucking question! Answer me, goddamn you!"

"Good Lord, woman! It sounds fine. Just fine," Rev said, his voice trembling even more now. "Just settle down there. Good Lord, woman! I ain't figurin on gittin shot today. Or any other day neither."

"Get up, pardner," Candi said to Mike.

Mike gasped for air but didn't stand up.

"Come on, pardner!" Candi yelled at him. "We don't have all fucking day! Get your ass up! I mean we gotta get the fuck outta here. Before I fucking lose it! And shoot every last one of these sorry motherfucking, cock-sucking son of fucking cunt-bitches!"

Still on his knees, Mike gasped for air and said, "I'm ready, Candi."

"Somebody!" Candi screamed, "Somebody better hurry the fuck up! And fucking give my friend those motherfucking keys! Before I fucking start shootin! I fucking mean it!" She stared in Rev's eyes, "Pronto!" she screamed, "Pronto! Fucking pronto!" Candi moved a little closer to Rev and said, "I already told you, preacher-man. I'm gonna fucking start with *you*!"

"Ya heard her, fellas!" Rev yelled to them, "Come on now! Give him my keys!"

"You know what, shithead?" Candi said to Rev. "I oughta fucking shoot you. Just for the fucking fun of it. You know that? Those goddamn chicken feathers in your silly little fucking hat would fucking fly all over the place!"

"She's crazy, fellas!" Rev screamed. "Give em the damn keys! Quick! I mean now! She's gonna kill me, fellas!"

"Give her the goddamn keys!" Dub shouted.

"I can see it in her eyes!" Rev yelled, "She's gonna kill me, fellas!"

"No she ain't," the man in the green tractor t-shirt said. He stepped forward towards Candi. He pulled the truck keys out of his pocket and dangled them in front of him. "This bitch ain't killin nobody. I think she's fuckin bluffin."

"What are you doin, Bric?" Rev screamed. "She's crazy! She's gonna kill me! She's gonna kill us all!"

Dub moved back slowly behind Bric to stand closer to the other man.

"Hey, dickhead," Candi said, calmly turning to face Bric, "You got fucking cotton in your goddamn ears or what? I fucking said-Give my friend those goddamn fucking keys. Right fucking now!"

"Fuck you…bitch. I ain't gonna give him shit."

Rev screamed and banged his head backwards against the tree trunk. "Bric! Give em them keys, Bric! Good Lord! Do what I tell ya! She's crazy! I seen a bunch of pill bottles in their car when we was lookin in there. Look at her eyes, Bric! She's outta her mind!"

"You better fucking listen to the preacher-man here, Bric," Candi said. "Look out, fellas! The fucking *right* fucking reverend is fucking testifyin again! And guess what? This time! He's fucking right! Trust me, boys. You got *no* fucking clue. And I mean *no* fucking clue who you're fucking dealin with here!"

"Calm the fuck down, Rev!" Bric said, "This bitch is fuckin bluffin. She ain't crazy on pills. And she sure as shit ain't gonna shoot nobody."

"Hey preacher-man," Candi said, "You better tell your shit for brains buddy over there. He better guard his fucking tongue. Before I fucking lose it and blow *your* goddamn fucking head off."

"Guard your tongue, Bric! Good Lord! Ya better guard your tongue against blasphemy. Else we're all goin to the Pearly Gates today!"

"She's fuckin bluffin," Bric said again. "This fuckin bitch ain't gonna shoot shit. Especially not with that ol fuckin six-shooter of hers. I know me somethin bout guns, fellas. Hell! Look at that ol six-shooter would ya! It's a goddamned antique! She ain't shootin shit!"

"I said- Guard your tongue, Bric!"

"Hell!" Bric said. "I'll bet that ol six-shooter ain't even loaded. I mean. Where the fuck would anybody even git any bullets for an old six-shooter like that? I'm tellin ya, Rev. This fuckin bitch is bluffin! I just know it!"

Bric smiled back at Candi, and then put the keys back in his jeans pocket. "Go ahead then, bitch," he said. "Go ahead and shoot me then. Go right ahead…bitch. That's right. I'm callin your fuckin bluff…bitch."

"Good Lord, Bric. Just give em the keys."

"I swear to fucking God," Candi screamed. "If you don't give him those fucking keys right fucking now! I'm gonna fucking blow your motherfucking brains out!"

"I think *you're* the one got cotton in her ears…bitch," Bric said. "You go right ahead and fuckin shoot. If you're gonna shoot.

I'm callin your fuckin bluff…bitch. And you better fuckin hope. For you and your friend's fucking sake. That you *ain't* bluffin." Bric smiled and started to take a step forward towards Candi.

Mike watched Candi turn the gun away from Rev onto Bric. And then he heard Candi speak in a familiar tone of voice. She didn't scream this time. And Mike recognized the over exaggerated country-bumpkin voice Candi had used with him many times before. "Listen up here. Ya two-bit, redneck peckerwood. If ya think I'm fuckin bluffin ya," she cocked back the hammer on the pistol, "then ya just go ahead and fuckin try me! Come on then, country fucker! What are ya fuckin waitin for? Why don't ya wipe the cow-shit off your boots? Man-up! And just fucking try me then?"

Bric hesitated in mid-step.

Candi shot Mike a wild-eyed glare, and then she started panting like a wild animal. "Well, pardner? Ya want me to kill em all now?" She was still using her country bumpkin voice. "Huh, pardner? Ya want me to kill em all? Or what? I mean. What do ya want me to do, pardner?"

Mike watched everyone's confusion quickly turn to fear.

"I told ya she was crazy!" Rev yelled. "Now give her the keys!"

Mike noticed that Bric's face was now pale.

Candi still stared only at Mike, refusing to acknowledge Bric or the others as any real threat to her. "I'll fuckin do it right now!" she said to Mike. "And ya know I will too, pardner. Ya fucking know I will! I'll kill em all! Ya know me, pardner! I can fuckin hold these turkeys til the bad place freezes over. Or til you say different!"

Mike slowly got to his feet and stood behind Bric.

"There ya go, pardner! There ya fuckin go!"

Bric glanced over his shoulder at Mike, and then stared back at Candi.

"Now come on, pardner!" Candi said, still using her country bumpkin voice. "All ya gotta do is say the fuckin word here! Ain't that what we talked about before, pardner? Ya know. If they move…kill em all? Remember? Ain't that fucking right, pardner? If they move…just kill em fuckin all!"

"Hey, stranger," Rev said, "Tell her not to kill me or my brother neither, will ya? Tell her for me! Please! See. I'm beggin ya, stranger!"

Bric turned his head slowly and stared Mike down.

Mike glanced over Bric's shoulder into Candi's baby blue eyes. And then, for just a brief moment, Candi suspended her mock insanity by winking at him. Mike felt his strength return. He took a single deliberate step forward towards Bric and said, "Hand over those keys."

Bric didn't move, didn't flinch. He only stared Mike up and down, his face a little paler than before.

"I'm beggin ya, stranger," Rev said "Tell her not to kill me!"

Bric looked back at Candi, and then shuffled his boots a little in the dirt.

"If they move..." Candi said, and then shifted her eyes deliberately down at Bric's boots, "kill em all...ain't that right pardner?"

Bric swallowed hard and then looked back at Mike once again.

"How's about we all sing a fuckin church hymn together?" Candi shouted. She began to sing. "Shall we gather at the river? The beautiful, the beautiful river? Shall we gather at the river? That flows from the throne of God!"

Lil Neezer curled up in a fetal position near the trash can and started to whine and moan.

Bric shot a startled glance back at Candi.

"Shall we gather at the river?" Candi sang, stomping her feet and marching in time, still aiming the pistol at him, "The beautiful, the beautiful river? Come on you sorry pieces of shit! Sing it with me!"

Dub and the other man backed away slowly, as if preparing to make a run for it.

"Shall we gather at the river? The beautiful, the beautiful river?" Candi sang louder and louder, "Shall we gather at the river? The beautiful, the beautiful river? Come on, preacher-man! I know ya know this fuckin song! Sing it with me, goddamn ya! The beautiful, the beautiful river! That flows from the throne of God!"

"Tell her to stop!" Rev screamed at Mike, "Tell her to stop!"

"Shall we gather at the river? The beautiful, the beautiful river?"

Lil Neezer started howling like a dog.

"Shall we gather at the river? Come on, goddammit! I mean looky! Even the fucktard knows this fucking song!" Candi laughed and kept singing, "Shall we gather at the river? The beautiful, the beautiful river? The beautiful, the beautiful river?"

Bric turned to face Mike once again.

Mike shouted over Candi's singing, "I said- Hand over those fucking keys, shithead!"

"Shall we gather at the river? The beautiful, the beautiful river?"

Bric stared Mike down. He shifted his body weight, finally resting both boots firmly on the ground. "Ok, goddammit, ok!" Bric yelled over Candi's singing. "I fuckin give up! Ya'll fuckin win!"

Candi stopped singing. Dub and the other man froze. Lil Neezer stopped howling and Rev opened his eyes.

Bric moved his hand slowly into his jeans pocket and then pulled out the keys. He held them up and dangled them in the air. "Here," he said to Mike, "Just take em and git the fuck outta here, will ya?"

Mike smiled at Candi, exhaled deeply, and reached for the keys.

"Oops," Bric said, and then tossed the keys into the metal trashcan nearby. He grinned at Mike and then turned back to face down Candi. "I fuckin warned you…bitch. Now," he said, taking a small step towards Candi, "I'm callin your fuckin bluff."

"Not another fucking step," Candi said, "or I'll blow your fuckin brains out!"

"Oh you're gonna be blowin somethin alright…bitch," Bric said, adjusting his hard-on, "but it ain't gonna be my fuckin brains."

Dub and the other man stepped in closer towards Mike.

Rev took a few steps away from the tree towards Candi. Lil Neezer struggled to his knees and then crouched behind her.

"Ya see, fellas," Bric said. "What did I fuckin tell ya?" He took another step towards Candi. "This fuckin bitch has been fuckin bluffin the whole goddamn time! I done told ya! She ain't gonna shoot shit with that ol antique six-shooter."

"I'll fucking do it, motherfucker!" Candi yelled.

Bric laughed. He took another step towards her and said, "You'll fuckin do what…bitch? You'll fuckin sing us another crazy-ass hymn? Come on, bitch! Just fuckin give it up, already!"

Mike glanced back over his shoulder where Dub and the other man waited to grab him.

"Come on…bitch!" Bric said, "Hand over that ol six-shooter, will ya? Hell! You're gonna have to fuckin give it up sometime."

Candi kept the pistol aimed right at Bric's face.

Bric stood poised in mid-step, only inches from Candi. He smiled at her, staring with a condescending confidence down the barrel of her antique pistol.

Mike took a deep breath as he watched Candi stare down Bric. Mike watched her steady, confident hand take deadly aim. He watched her unflinching eyes convince these men she was a capable and willing killer. He heard a kind of desperate abandon in her voice as she screamed threats. But most of all, Mike noticed Candi's steadfast finger, gently squeezing the trigger of an antique pistol they both knew would never fire…

"Well…bitch," Bric said, "Ya gonna give it up, or what?"

Candi looked over at Mike and winked at him. And then she stared down Bric again. Candi stepped forward and quickly pressed the long barrel of her pistol flush against Bric's forehead.

Candi smiled and then pulled the trigger a fifth time. "Bang!" she said, and then laughed out loud. Bric's face went pale white and he recoiled back a few steps.

"Holy shit, fellas," Dub yelled, "that bitch *is* fuckin crazy!" Dub and the other man backed up.

Rev darted back up against the tree.

Once Bric regained his footing, his face went flush-red with anger. He said to Candi, "You are the craziest, cock-suckin, bluff-inest bitch I ever fuckin seen! You ain't never gonna give it up, are ya?"

"You're right, shithead," Candi said. "I'm the whorest fuck-inest whore you ever did see!" Candi hurled herself forward at Bric with wild abandon. She swung her pistol with both hands, like a baseball bat, and hit Bric square in the jaw with the barrel. Blood spurt from Bric's lips and he crumpled to the ground like a butchered ox. Candi yelled to Mike, "Let's ride, pardner!"

Mike started to move but felt his legs and feet freeze up. He felt his stomach churn and then lurch with sudden nausea.

Candi spun around to where Lil Neezer was crouched behind her. He whimpered up at her and started crying hysterically. Candi backed up a few steps and then kicked off her heels. Lil Neezer raised up his fat hands and made like he was praying. "Goddamned fucktard!" Candi yelled. She charged forward and kicked Lil Neezer dead in the throat. Lil Neezer yelped. He reeled backwards, rolled in the dirt and then hit his head on the metal trash can.

"Neezer!" Rev yelled, still cowering against the oak tree. "Good Lord! Lil Neezer!"

Candi ran over and kicked Lil Neezer in the mouth. She yelled, "You goddamned!" she kicked him in the throat again, "fucking!" she kicked him in the mouth again, "fucktard!" She kicked Lil Neezer in the mouth again, lost her balance and then fell over backwards. Lil Neezer choked up blood and spittle. Lil Neezer coughed and spit out a few chipped and broken teeth into the dirt. He moaned like a wounded animal.

Mike still just stood there, frozen. He glanced over his shoulder and saw Dub and the other man backing up even farther away, frightened by this spectacle, looking like they were going to make a run for it again.

"Come on, pardner!" Candi yelled to Mike, "Let's ride!" She got up and scurried back over to Bric. She stood over him.

"Help me! Somebody help me!" Bric screamed, shielding his bloodied face with his filthy hands, writhing and moaning in the dirt.

Candi raised her pistol into the air with both hands again. Bric screamed, rolled over, and then curled up his body. Candi swung her pistol down full-force, like an axe. She hit Bric in the back of his head, slashing off bits of hair, flesh and bone from his skull. She collapsed to her knees next to his body, panting for breath.

Mike just stood there. He winced at the sound of Bric screaming. He cringed when he spotted Bric's open scalp in the dirt. There was a large flap of severed skin, like a slice of ham, peppered with bits of nappy black hair, bone chips, and blood hanging down. Mike grabbed his stomach, wilted forward, and then puked a little in his mouth. He swallowed immediately and it burned his dry throat.

"Come on, pardner!" Candi said between breaths, "We're almost there!"

Mike looked up, just in time to spot Rev charging Candi from behind. "Candi!" Mike yelled to her, "Candi watch out!"

Candi scrambled to her feet and spun around. But Rev was already there. He kicked the pistol from Candi's hand and it tumbled away into the dirt underneath the car.

"Getta hold a that stranger, fellas!" Rev yelled. He towered over Candi, grinning down at her, and said, "This here Jezebel is all mine!"

Dub and the other man obeyed and moved cautiously towards Mike.

Mike turned around to face the men, remaining perfectly still. And then, as a kind of unintelligible kneejerk reaction, Mike raised-up his fists for a fight.

Dub and the other man halted.

"Ya ain't so tough without yer gun, are ya?" Rev said to Candi.

Candi flung herself forward, tackling him. Rev toppled over to the ground on his back with Candi squirming on top of him. She lunged down with open hands, scratching his face and breaking off some of her fake fingernails into his cheeks. Rev screamed and struggled but was trapped beneath her.

Still, Mike stood perfectly still, standing his ground. He stood tall now with his body erect, his arms and shoulders taut, and his fists up. Dub and the other man still stared him down. They were confused. And yet, even though his fists were up, Mike could not keep them from trembling. Mike watched his own hands, capable of clenching into fists; and yet, incapable against fear and trembling.

Dub stared Mike up and down and then a malefic grin cut across his ignorant face. Dub nudged the other man with his elbow and said, "We ain't gotta worry. He ain't gonna do shit."

Mike flinched under those words.

Dub and the other man looked at each other, nodded one to the other, and then stampeded forward in tandem. Mike stood still and they tackled him. They wrestled him down into the dirt.

Candi punched Rev in the nose, over and over and over again. He screamed and gargled to breathe. Candi's fists dripped with hot blood, snot and spit. Rev reached up and yanked Candi's hair, tugging her head down, trying to buck her off.

Mike quickly relinquished his struggle.

"We almost fucking got em, pardner!" Candi yelled to Mike, with her back to him.

Mike felt his body slacken beneath the aggressive, brutal weight of his attackers, until finally, he lay perfectly still... trapped.

"See! I done told ya," Dub said to the other man, "He didn't do shit!"

Mike's head was pressed into the dirt. He watched Candi still struggling against Rev.

"Don't ya think we oughta go over there and help out Rev? I mean. Before that crazy bitch up and kills him?"

"Hold yer fuckin horses there," Dub whispered to the other man. "Not yet, we ain't gonna."

"Huh?"

"Well, I reckon," Dub said, "Rev is a doin a hell of a lotta prayin right about now. Don't ya reckon?"

"Yep"

"Well, I reckon," Dub said. "Me and you can just wait right here. And thatta way. Rev can just see for his own damn self. Whether The Good Lord's gonna answer his fuckin prayers."

"Goddammit, Dub," the other man said, "I reckon Rev shouldn't a talked so much Jezebel shit about your mama, huh?"

Dub just laughed and said, "Yeah, I reckon not."

"Be we ain't really gonna just let that bitch kill him, are we?"

"Nah," Dub said, "Don't ya worry none bout that. If Rev really needs us. Me and you will fuckin step up."

Mike watched Rev jerk down Candi's head by her hair. But Mike never heard Candi scream out in pain. In a frantic blind scramble, Candi's stubborn hands found Rev's face. She groped her fingers along his cheeks, feeling for his eyes. And then, in a sudden fierce thrust of her body, Candi dug her remaining fingernail deep into Rev's eyeball.

Rev screamed and let go of Candi's hair.

"Holy fuckin shit!" Dub yelled.

Candi leaned down into Rev's face, nose to nose with him and yelled, "Good Lord, preacher-man! How's that for some fuckin recompense?"

"Candi, look out!" Mike yelled, but Dub and the other man pushed his face back down into the dirt.

Candi sat up and spun around, just in time for Bric to punch her in the face.

Chapter 19

"Goddammit! I reckon that's gotta be the bluffinest bitch I ever fuckin seen," Bric said to the others. He kneaded his aching jaw. "Hey, Dub. Hand over that bandana of yers. I gotta have me somethin to wrap up my fuckin head with."

"Holy shit. No, Bric," Dub said, "That's my favorite fuckin bandana!"

"I said- Fuckin hand it over. Now!"

Dub kicked the dirt, took off his bandana, and then handed it to Bric. He stared at Bric's scalp and said, "Wow! She sure fucked ya up pretty good."

"Goddamn right she did! That fuckin bitch right there almost broke my fuckin jaw too!"

"And with that ol antique six-shooter of hers too!" Dub said, laughing.

Bric tied the bandana over his wounded head. He licked his bleeding lip, kicked the trash can, and then turned to stare down Candi. "Yer gonna pay for this ya fuckin bitch! I done told ya. Back when I called yer bluff. Ya better shoot me...or else!"

"Hey, shithead," Candi said to Bric, "How'd you like to kiss my sister's black cat's ass?" She laughed out loud. She nudged Mike with her elbow and said to him, "Hey, pardner. I bet this shit-kicker here would just love that."

Mike and Candi sat next to each other on the concrete bench, alongside the picnic table.

Lil Neezer sat in the back of the tow truck drinking a strawberry soda.

"I swear to fuckin God," Bric said, "I'm gonna kill this fuckin bitch, right now!"

"Guard yer tongue, Bric," Rev said calmly, walking back over from the truck. He pressed a wad of greasy napkins against his bloody eye. "See. The Good Lord answered our prayers. He saw fit to help us out today. We oughta all be thankful we ain't dead as doornails."

"Thankful? Hell!" Bric said. "Where the hell was The Good Lord? When this crazy-ass fuckin bitch was singin her hymns? And wavin that old fuckin six-shooter in our faces? Where was The Good Lord then?"

"See, fellas. The Good Lord he works in *mysterious* ways! And I do mean, *mysterious* ways. The Good Lord is a gonna teach me a lesson today, fellas. Remember. The Good Book reads thissa way- All things work together for the good. For them that love The Good Lord and for them what's been called accordin to his purpose."

"Oh, horse-shit, Rev," Bric said. "I'll tell ya what. Since ya like to testify so goddamn much. Why don't ya tell me and the fellas here. Just what kinda fuckin lesson was The Good Lord plannin on teachin ya? I mean when this crazy-ass bitch was crammin her fuckin fingernail down in yer eyeball? Huh? Tell us that!"

"Holy shit, Bric," Dub said, "Calm the fuck down, will ya?"

"I done already told ya once, Bric," Rev said, pressing the greasy wad of napkins harder against his eye, "Guard yer tongue against blasphemy. And git down on yer knees. And thank The Good Lord for helpin us out today."

"Oh, come on, Rev," Bric said, "Ain't ya gonna testify no more today?'

"Leave him the fuck alone, Bric!" Dub said.

"That's right, Rev," Bric said. "Ya ain't got shit to testify bout now? Do ya? And I reckon The Good Lord ain't got shit to teach nobody, huh?"

Rev stood up suddenly and grabbed Bric by the throat with his free hand. "So! Ya wanna hear me testify, Bric? Ya wanna hear the right reverend Jehu testify, today? Well then! I'll testify!"

"Looky here fellas! Looky real close right here, fellas!" Rev shouted, gripping Bric's throat even tighter. "The Good Lord he worked a miracle today! For once... I was blind!" Rev peeled the greasy, bloody napkins away from his eye. "But now... I see!" He smeared the wad of napkins on Bric's eyes and then crammed them into his gaping mouth. Rev released Bric and laughed out loud.

Bric staggered away, spitting and wiping his face.

"I reckon, Bric," Rev said, rolling both his eyes around and laughing, "Ya been washed in the blood of the Lamb now, huh? I'll bet ya believe in miracles now, huh?"

"Holy shit, Rev," Dub said, "Ya sure gotta way of makin a sermon!"

"No hard feelins, right Bric?" Rev said, offering him a handshake. "See. I'm already askin for yer forgiveness. I'm a man who knows how to repent of his sins."

Bric spit a few more times and wiped his face. He glared at Rev and then looked at the other men.

"We all wanna be forgiven for our sins, Bric," Rev said. "See. The Good Book reads thissa way- If ya wanna be forgiven then *first*! And I do mean *first*, ya gotta forgive others."

"I reckon," Bric said, accepting his handshake, "I reckon I'm gonna need forgivin someday. Just like everbody else..."

"And you're gonna guard your tongue against blasphemy from now on? Right?"

"Yeah, I reckon."

"I done told ya, fellas," Rev said, "and I'm a gonna keep on tellin ya til the cows come home. The Good Lord he works in mysterious ways."

✳ ✳ ✳

"Well, fellas," Rev said, "I reckon we gotta make us a new plan." He clapped his hands and rubbed them together.

"What do ya mean, Rev?"

"See. It's gittin awful late in the day already, fellas. It'll be dark soon," Rev said. He walked over to the car and opened the door. "See. That Jezebel over there. She done wasted all our time. We shoulda done already been through roughin up that stranger by now. And now it done got late already. So we gotta git us a new plan."

Rev pulled Mike's typewriter out of the backseat and then tossed it to Dub. "Put that there in the pickup. We can pawn it." Mike watched him lift the box of books and papers from the car, and then set it on the trunk. "Hey there, stranger. These yer books and yer papers from school?"

Mike glanced over at Candi but she didn't respond to him. "It's probably a bunch of queer porn," Dub said.

"I don't reckon there's a copy of The Good Book in here, Dub. If that's what ya mean."

"Yep, Rev. That's what I meant alright!"

"Hey, preacher-man," Candi said, "Fuck you! And you know what esle? Fuck your Good Book. And fuck your Good Lord too while you're at it!"

Rev dropped one of the books, hung his head, and said, "What did ya just say?"

"You fucking heard me," Candi said. "You don't even fucking know who JC is. Motherfucker! And so I say. Fuck you! And fuck your Good Book! And fuck your Good Lord too!"

Rev yelled, "Somebody tell that Jezebel to guard her tongue."

Bric stepped over and slapped Candi, "Shut up, bitch! Ya shut yer fuckin bitch mouth right now!"

Mike put his arm around Candi to steady her but she leaned away from him.

Candi laughed even louder and yelled, "Hey, preacher-man! I got a great goddamned idea! How about you get down on your fucking knees. And *you* suck your Good Lord's dick?"

Bric reached back to hit Candi again but Rev yelled, "Cut it out, Bric! Let that Jezebel alone... for now."

Bric lowered his hand and stepped back.

"Hey, shithead," Candi said to Bric. "Maybe while preacher-man over there is suckin off his Good Lord's dick. You can be his little bitch and let him cornhole you in the ass? What do you think of that, huh?"

Bric leaned forward but Rev yelled, "I mean it, Bric! Let her alone for now!"

Candi smiled and then blew Bric a kiss.

"Put this here box in the pickup too," Rev said. He packed all the papers and books back inside. He handed it to Dub. "Well, fellas. I reckon that bout does it. There ain't much here."

Rev walked back over to the picnic table and the men gathered around him like a small congregation. "See, fellas. We got us a Sodomite and a Jezebel right here. And I reckon The Good Book is crystal clear on what we oughta do with both of em."

Candi stood up off the bench.

Mike tugged at her arm and said, "Candi, please. Don't!"

Candi jerked her arm away from him. "Listen here, preacherman," she said, standing on her tip-toes, "Goddamn your two-bit, redneck peckerwood all the way to the bad place!"

"Just sit down," Mike said to her.

"And! Goddamn your fucking Good Book to the bad place too!"

"Candi, please stop!" Mike said, 'I'm begging you." Mike felt nauseated again and hung his head down in his hands.

"Ya'll ever heard such blasphemies, fellas?" Rev said.

"Holy shit, no," Dub said, "I ain't never heard nobody talk like that."

"Me neither," Rev said. "Not in all my life."

Mike slid off the bench and fell to his knees. "Please, guys! Please just let us go!"

Candi bent down and grabbed Mike by the neck, choking him a little. "You shut the fuck up, pardner! Just shut the fuck up!" She pulled him back up onto the bench by his neck.

"Please! Please!" Mike said, shaking his head. "We promise we won't tell anybody! Just let us go. It's not too late!"

Candi slapped him hard across the face and yelled, "*Mike*! You gotta listen to me now!"

Mike froze. He stopped yelling. He opened his eyes and looked calmly at Candi.

"Listen up, pardner," Candi said, "We don't have much time left here."

"Candi," Mike whispered to her, "What did you just call me?"

"Listen up, pardner," Candi placed her hand gently on his face this time, in the exact same spot where she'd slapped him. "You gotta bite the fucking bullet here, pardner. I mean you gotta man up real fucking quick. Alright?"

"I can't do it, Candi," Mike said, "I just can't do it."

"Sure you can, pardner," Candi said.

"No, I can't."

"You can! You fucking can, pardner! I fucking believe in your ass. You hear me? I fucking believe in you," She held his face close to hers and whispered, "And I always fucking will..."

"But how?"

She patted his cheek, winked at him and said, "Watch this shit, pardner."

Candi stood up and whirled around to face down Rev and the other men. "And you know what else, preacher-man?" Candi said. "While you're at it. You go right on ahead and goddamn your fucking Good Lord to the bad place too. Right along fucking with you! And you can tell him I fucking said so too!"

"I'm gonna testify to ya right now, fellas," Rev said. "Ain't *nobody*! And I mean *nobody*, is gonna git away with talkin like that bout me. Or The Good Book. Or The Good Lord neither."

"Well guess what, shit for brains?" Candi said, grinning, "I just fucking did get away with it just now. Didn't I?" She laughed.

"Holy shit, Rev," Dub said, "What in the hell we gonna do with this crazy bitch?"

"My flesh is feelin awful weak," Rev said. "I reckon I'm gonna need The Good Lord to forgive me for my sins again."

"Holy shit, fellas," Dub said, "It's our lucky day, ain't it?"

✳✳✳

A few minutes later Rev helped Lil Neezer up out of the pickup. He herded him over to the car. "Come on, Lil Neezer, pronto! Move it! I want ya to watch this here. Then maybe ya can learn a thing or two."

Bric and Dub had dragged Candi over to the car. They were holding her down in the backseat. Candi had kicked and struggled and cussed them the whole way.

The other man stood between Mike and the car. He held a small pocket-knife in his hand. "Don't ya move, stranger," he said to Mike. "Don't ya move. Or holler. Or do any fuckin thing. Ya hear me?"

Mike just stood there, motionless, watching the car.

"I'm gonna fucking bite your goddamn dicks off," Candi yelled. "And then! I'm gonna shove em up your motherfucking asses!"

"Goddammit," Bric said, "Don't ya ever give up...bitch?"

Rev and Lil Neezer walked up and stood on either side of the car.

"Holy shit, Rev," Dub said, "What stinks?"

"Goddamn, yer right, Dub," Bric said, "It smells like fuckin shit!"

"Settle down there, fellas," Rev said. "See. I reckon when this here Jezebel went and kicked him. Lil Neezer here went to the bathroom all in his pants."

"Ya mean Lil Neezer went and pissed and shit himself?"

"He don't know no better," Rev said, "Ya'll know that."

"Hell, Bric!" Dub said, laughing. "Ya ain't one to talk neither! Seems to me like ya almost shit yourself. When this here bitch put that six-shooter to yer head. And then she pulled that fucking trigger!"

"Ya shut the fuck up, Dub!"

Candi yelled, but her voice was weak and raspy, "You're all fucked! You better fucking kill me you sons of fucking bitches! You hear me! I'm gonna fuck every last one of you!"

"Keep her quiet, will ya, fellas?" Rev said. "Neither me nor The Good Lord himself is a gonna abide her blaspemin tongue much longer!"

"I'm gonna fuck all of you!" Candi yelled. "I'm gonna fuck you! I'm gonna fuck *you*!"

"What the hell is this crazy bitch talkin about, Rev?" Dub said. "What's she mean? *She's* gonna fuck *us*?"

"I done told ya. Keep her ass quiet!"

Bric pulled the filthy red bandana off his head. He balled it up and then stuffed it down into Candi's mouth. "There! That oughta shut this bitch up, huh?"

Candi made muffled sounds, choking on the bandana.

"Holy shit, Bric," Dub said, struggling to hold Candi down. "Look at her go! I gotta tell ya! This here bitch really scares the shit outta me!"

Candi wriggled one arm free and managed to tug the bandanna out of her mouth. She screamed, *"Mike*! Help me! *Mike*!"

They forced her back down again and crammed the bandanna back into her mouth.

"She don't ever fuckin give up, do she?" Bric said. "That's for damn sure!"

"Goddammit, Rev," Bric said, "Lil Neezer stinks all to fuckin hell! Can't he wait in the fuckin truck?"

"Shut that door, Lil Neezer," Rev said. Lil Neezer fumbled with the back door and then finally shut it. "Now, Lil Neezer. I want ya to watch me real careful now, ya hear? Ya need to learn yeself how to do with yer pecker. What The Good Lord himself intended a *real man* to do."

Lil Neezer leaned down with his face against the glass, slobbering and panting.

"Goddammit, Rev," Bric said, "Ya mean I gotta do it with Lil Neezer watchin me!"

"Don't worry, man," Dub said, laughing, "You'll git used to it! We all do."

Over near the picnic table, the other man glanced back and forth between Mike and the car. "Fuck me," he said, fixing his gaze on the car, "I sure do wish I could go over there and watch em!" He turned back and stared down Mike. "I bet ya even wish you could watch em too, huh?"

Mike noticed the afternoon sunshine glimmer off the tiny blade of the small pocket knife. The afternoon sunshine seemed to shoot off the tiny piece of steel. And its scorching blade seemed to reach up and stab at Mike's face, slicing into his skin.

"Ya like my knife, stranger?" the other man said to him.

Mike glanced up at the other man's face. And maybe it was just the shadows, but it seemed to Mike like the other man was laughing.

"Well," the other man said, "I like it too. It's an Old Timer. My granddaddy left it to me when he got kilt. And when it's my turn over there," he said, winking at Mike, "I'm gonna use it too."

Dub and Bric wedged Candi down in the backseat where she could barely move.

Candi made desperate muffled sounds through the bloody greasy bandana.

Lil Neezer just stood there. He looked down on them with a dumb crooked smile.

Candi still struggled.

"I'll testify to ya, fellas," Rev said. "See. This here's a Jezebel right here. If I ever did see me one..." Rev reached down and grabbed Candi's shorts. She writhed and wriggled and struggled. But Rev finally pulled them off her. "And that right there fellas," Rev said, pointing down and taking a long, deep breath, "that's a mark of the beast. If I ever did smell me one..."

∗∗∗

"I done told ya, fellas!" Dub said, "And I was right as the rain too. I done told ya that stranger wasn't gonna do shit. And that's exactly what he done."

Mike was surrounded again. He glanced back over at the car where the men had left Candi's body laying in the dirt. Mike noticed she still wasn't moving.

"You was right!" Bric said. "Hell! He just fuckin stood right here. And didn't do shit!"

The other man laughed and said, "And all I had on me was this little ol pocket knife too. That's all! And this fuckin pussy here he just stood there and fuckin watched."

"Holy shit, fellas," Dub said, slapping his knee, "This *was* our lucky day."

Mike glanced back over at the car but Candi still wasn't moving.

"Hey, stranger. Ya ain't even gotta worry bout her no more," Bric said. "She ain't gonna do shit now."

"Nope," Dub said, adjusting the big silver buckle on his belt, "Not now she ain't."

"That's enough of that kinda talk, fellas," Rev said. "Remember. The Good Book reads thissa way- Pride goes before a fall."

"Sorry, Rev," Dub said. "I reckon me and the fellas are just excited. Ya know. Bout finally gettin to rough up this here stranger. That's all."

"Well we ain't gonna rough him up, fellas," Rev said. "He ain't worth it."

"What the fuck, Rev?"

"Nope," Rev said, "I don't reckon we even need to rough him up."

"Whatta ya mean, Rev?"

"See, fellas. I reckon this here stranger is a gonna do... whatever I tell him to do."

"He will! If he knows what's good for him."

"See, fellas. If I tell him he's gonna git down on his knees," Rev said, and then pointed down to the ground, "I reckon he's just gonna git right down on his knees."

Mike ignored them. He stared back over at the car again.

"Well I'll be damned, fellas!" Bric said. "I reckon this here stranger mighta went and grew a pair when we wasn't lookin. Ya think?"

Mike scrutinized Candi's spent, spiritless body as it lay there in the dirt. He studied her arms, legs, feet, hands and fingers for the slightest movement. He couldn't see her face. But he examined her head for even the smallest gesture of life. Maybe she was faking it, he thought. Maybe she was calculating a plan. Mike watched for any sign of life to reassure him. But just like before he saw nothing.

"I don't think he's gonna do it, Rev," Bric said.

"Are we gonna git to rough him up then, Rev?" Dub said. "Cuz me and the fellas will get him on his knees. That's for damn sure."

"Nobody's roughin up nobody!" Rev said. "Don't ya worry none, fellas. I reckon he'll do what I say."

Mike looked back at the men, and then into Rev's face.

"She *ain't* gonna help ya, stranger," Rev said, staring down into Mike's eyes. "See. She *can't* help ya. I done already seen to that."

Mike glanced over at Candi and realized that she didn't look like she was breathing.

"That's right, stranger," Rev said. "I done seen to that myself. See. When I was done with her. I made sure she wasn't gonna do nothin. Then I just went and dumped her body right out that there car window. See. I'm gonna go back to Huntsville where The Good Lord needs me. Yep. Them fellas came every Sunday. And I do mean every Sunday. Just to hear me preach from The Good Book. See. That's why The Good Lord put me on this here earth. And that's why I just gotta get on back to Huntsville, quick as I can."

"Holy shit, fellas," Dub said. "Looks like Rev ain't done breakin his probation just yet!"

"Now. See here, stranger," Rev said. "Ya best just do like I tell ya. And if ya do. Maybe. And just maybe now. You'll git lucky today too."

Mike stared for one final moment at Candi's inert, broken body.

"Now. Like I done told ya before," Rev said. "Get right down on yer knees there."

Mike hung his head and got down on his knees. He glanced back at the car but couldn't see Candi anymore.

"See there, fellas," Rev said. "I done testified this here stranger would do what I said. Didn't I?"

"Ya sure did, Rev"

Rev brought his fingers up to his lips and whistled.

"Holy shit, fellas!" Dub said, clapping his hands. "It's Lil Neezer's turn now!"

Lil Neezer shuffled up and stood next to Rev, right in front of Mike.

"Ya wanna put yer pecker in this stranger's mouth, Lil Neezer?" Rev said, pointing down at Mike. "Or ya wanna put yer pecker in his butthole? Which one's it gonna be?"

An idiotic smirk washed over Lil Neezer's bloated sweaty face. He nodded, squealed like a pig, and then reached into his pants.

"Look at him go there, fellas!" Dub said. "Hey, Bric! Ya ain't never seen Lil Neezer's dick have ya? Holy shit! Lil Neezer's got the biggest fuckin dick ya ever seen! I reckon what The Good Lord didn't give him up here," Dub said, pointing to his head, "he done made up for down there!"

"Guard yer tongue, Dub!"

Lil Neezer fumbled with his pants and finally unbuckled them. He dropped them down around his ankles. He tugged his underwear down around his knees.

Mike's face was just about level with Lil Neezer's crotch. And the warm stench of piss, shit and sweat burned Mike's eyes and nostrils and saturated his mouth.

"Hey, Bric! Ain't that just the biggest dick ya ever seen in yer whole fuckin life? I was right about it, huh? I was right?"

"I'll be damned all to hell," Bric said. "You *was* right! No wonder that old cow hollers when Lil Neezer goes out to the barn!"

"Guard yer tongues, fellas!" Rev said. He rested his hand on Neezer's shoulder and whispered, "See there, Lil Neezer. Ya can do whatever ya want with this here fella. See. Ya can put yer pecker in his mouth right there. See. Ya like that, don't ya? Or ya can stick yer pecker in his butthole. See. And I know ya really like that."

Lil Neezer licked the palm of his hand and all his fingers too. He slobbered all over them. He reached down, grabbed his dick and started jerking on it.

Mike watched Lil Neezer's gargantuan dick swell and harden only inches from his face. He watched Lil Neezer's hand pumping up and down. Sweat mingled with piss. Spit and crusted flakes of shit oozed in between his puffy fingers.

Mike dry-heaved and choked, but couldn't puke.

"Not just yet, stranger," Dub said, laughing, "Not just fucking yet..."

The other men laughed.

Lil Neezer jerked his dick in a kind of moronic reverie, seeming to forget all about Mike.

"Lil Neezer!" Rev said, slapping him on the back of the head, "Don't git carried away there."

Lil Neezer let go of his dick, panting heavily. He turned to Rev with a dumbfounded look on his face. Rev pointed down at Mike. Lil Neezer looked down at Mike too, and then smiled his dumb, crooked smile.

"Open your mouth, stranger," Rev said.

Mike closed his eyes and opened his mouth.

"And you better keep it open, too!"

Mike took a deep breath but all he could smell was Lil Neezer. All he could hear was Lil Neezer's panting and the laughter of the other men.

"Now go right on ahead, Lil Neezer," Mike heard Rev say, "and put your pecker in this stranger's mouth. See there. He's gonna suck it for ya."

Neezer grunted. He grabbed hold of his hard dick and hoisted it towards Mike's mouth.

And then... Mike heard the gunshot.

"Holy shit, fellas," Dub yelled, "That crazy bitch got that fuckin six-shooter to work!"

The men frantically ducked in every direction, seeking cover.

Lil Neezer howled and spun around. But his underwear were still around his knees, so he tripped and fell into the dirt.

Mike opened his eyes. He saw Candi lying on her belly in the dust next to the car. She was aiming her pistol at them, the barrel still smoking from the single gunshot.

"We got lucky fellas!" Dub yelled. He crouched with the other man behind the picnic table. "That crazy bitch sure as shit ain't no kinda good shot!"

"Goddammit!" Bric said from behind the oak tree. "She don't never give up, do she?"

Lil Neezer brayed like an ass. He rolled around in the dirt.

"Good Lord, fellas!" Rev yelled from behind the trash can. "We gotta git her before she up and shoots Lil Neezer!"

Through the dust Mike noticed Candi's head wobbling, like she was dizzy. He saw Candi's arm falter a few times as she struggled to keep the pistol up and aimed true. And then Candi's arm finally wavered. And Mike watched her drop the pistol into the dirt.

"Holy shit, fellas!" Dub yelled, "I think she done dropped her six-shooter!"

Mike knelt there in the dust and watched Candi crumple like a rag doll onto the ground.

"She dropped it, fellas!" Bric yelled. "She's down for the fuckin count! Let's git her"

Mike scrambled up onto his feet and ran towards the car.

"Get him, fellas!" Rev yelled. All the men rushed after Mike.

Mike dove down into the dirt next to Candi's lifeless body. He fumbled for the pistol. He felt the handle and raised it up. He spun around on his knees and cocked back the hammer. Mike took aim through the dust, just as Bric kicked the pistol from his hands.

"Holy fuckin shit!" Dub said, "That was a fuckin close one, huh fellas?"

"You're goddamn right it was," Bric said, dandling the pistol.

Mike was kneeling down next to Candi's body.

"We was just lucky that crazy bitch was such a bad shot, huh?"

Rev and the other man were helping Lil Neezer get to his feet.

"Looky here, Dub," Bric said. "I'll be damned all to hell. This here six-shooter. It only had one fuckin bullet in it! Only one fuckin bullet!"

"Holy shit! How many times ya think she pulled that god-damned trigger? Before she figured that out?"

"Well, fellas," Dub said, "That ain't the first time *we* got lucky today."

"I'm startin to think," Bric said, "that The Good Lord does answer prayers."

"He answers me," Rev said, walking over to the tow truck. "The Good Lord answers me ever time I pray to him." He reached behind the seat and grabbed a tire iron. He walked back over to where Mike was kneeling. "Ya know why The Good Lord answers me when I pray, stranger?"

Mike placed his hand on Candi's back but didn't feel her breathing. He patted her gently on the back, but she didn't move. It was like knocking softly two times on the door of unhappiness. Mike looked up at Rev.

"He answers me cuz ever time I sin. I always repent of my sins. And ever time I repent of my sins, I git forgiven. See?"

"Preach on, Rev," Dub said.

"See, stranger," Rev said. He swung the tire iron up and then down into his open palm. "The Good Lord done made for-giveness possible. Cuz he knowd we was all gonna sin. So ya see. Sin is just as big a part of The Good Lord's plan as forgiveness is. Course. In order to go to Heaven. Ya gotta be forgiven. And in order to be forgiven. Ya gotta repent. And in order for ya to repent. Well. Ya gotta sin. So in order for ya to go to Heaven, ya gotta sin. That's logic, see. I mean that's just usin the good common sense that The Good Lord gave ya."

"Yer right, Rev," Dub said, "that's just logic."

Mike turned Candi's body over onto her back but she still didn't move. He leaned down and put his ear to her mouth, but didn't feel any breath.

"See. I done told ya she can't help ya," Rev said. "See there. I told ya I was goin back to Huntsville." He gripped the tire iron with both hands, like a baseball bat. "And when I git through with ya, stranger. They're gonna make damn sure I stay in Huntsville for a long time."

Mike watched the rusty, greasy end of the tire iron dangling in the air above his head. And yet. All Mike could think about was Candi's smile. He'd come to love her smile so much. And he'd spotted that familiar smile on her face, right after she'd fired that final shot from the pistol. Right before she lost her aim and her body crumpled into the dirt.

In this moment Mike should've been thinking about death. But instead. All he could think about was Candi's smile. And all Mike could hear was Candi's laughter, echoing across a vast darkening chasm.

"Goddammit fellas!" the other man yelled. He jumped out of the cab of the tow truck and ran over to them. "Hold up there! I just heard on the police scanner. Somebody round here musta heard that fuckin gunshot a minute ago! And they done called it in to the fuckin sheriff!"

"Holy shit, Rev," Dub said. "We better split."

Rev squeezed the tire iron. His face was full of wrath. He raised it up over Mike's head, and then lowered it slowly back down. "Dub's right, fellas," Rev said. "We better git. Before the sheriff gits here."

"But, Rev," Bric said, "I thought ya wanted to go back to Huntsville?"

"I do," Rev said, grinning down at Mike now. "But I got me a couple more sins I need to commit first. I mean I gotta whole lot more repentin to do, fellas. Before this night's over!" Rev turned and ran for the truck, "Let's go!"

Bric shoved Candi's pistol down into his jeans and clambered into the bed of the tow truck. Lil Neezer was already there, sipping on strawberry soda and nursing his broken teeth and busted lips. Dub and the other man joined them. And then that tow truck just sped off down that lonesome Texas highway.

The sheriff never showed up that day...

So Mike just sat right there in the dust. He leaned back against the spare tire that he'd watched Candi change. Every once in a while a car would drive by. Each car would slow down just a little to rubberneck and watch Mike just sitting there next to Candi's lifeless body. But nobody ever bothered to stop. This bizarre parade of ambivalence gave Mike the nauseating sensation of being watched by himself.

So Mike just sat right there next to his ride. He just sat right there next to Candi, who in his mind, was somehow still riding shotgun... Yep. Mike just sat right there. Sat right there until damn near sunset.

Chapter 20

Of Funerals, Fucked-Up Shit and Famous Last Words

In the few hours that he just there in the dust, Mike couldn't stop thinking about Candi, and how she never gave up…

OPTIMISM - noun/ˈɒptəˌmɪzəm

1. a tendency to look on the more favorable side of events, and to expect the most favorable outcome.

2. the belief that good will ultimately triumph over evil in the world.

3. the belief that goodness pervades reality.

4. the philosophical doctrine that the existing world is the best of all possible worlds.

✱✱✱

Mike recounted their little odyssey. Every mile and every town. Every word and every argument. Every story and every lie. Every touch and every tease. Every smile. And every promise…spoken and unspoken. Mike recalled a particular conversation of theirs, on their way going to Mexia, somewhere around Groesbeck, Texas.

"Hey pardner," Candi had said. "You remember that part in *Tom Sawyer*? When Huck and Tom get to see their own funeral? When everybody thinks they're dead. But they're not really dead?"

"Sure, I remember that"

"Wouldn't that be cool? I mean. To see your own funeral?"

"I don't know," Mike said. "It would definitely be morose. That's for sure."

"Hey! I got an idea. Let's play the- Plan Your Own Funeral Game."

"The what?"

"You got cotton in your ears? I fucking said- Let's play the, Plan Your Own Funeral Game."

"Where did you learn a game like that?"

"I didn't. I just made it up. Just now"

"Ok"

"So here goes," Candi said. "If you could plan your own funeral. What would it be like?"

"Actually, I wouldn't even care," Mike said. "I'm not going to be alive for it anyway."

"Oh come on! That's not the fucking point. This isn't philosophy class."

"Well," Mike said, "How about you go first. What would you want your funeral to be like?"

"Only if you promise to play along after me"

"Sure"

"You promise?"

"Yeah, I promise."

"Ok, then," Candi said. "I reckon I'd want a small funeral. You know. With just my fam and my close friends there. In a little country church, of course. Kinda like Union Grove. But nothin special. Nothin too fancy. And maybe a potluck dinner after. And my fam could all talk about me. And share stories about me."

"Does your family know where you are?"

"Nope"

"So if something happened to you. How would your family know?"

"Huh. I reckon I never really thought about it."

"Does your family know what you do for a living?"

"You mean. Do they know I'm a whore?"

"Yeah"

"You mean. Do they know I suck and fuck strange dick for cash?"

"Yeah," Mike said, chuckling.

"You mean. Do they know I give blowjobs to assholes? For a rides over bridges?"

Mike frowned and said, "Cut it out, Candi."

"No!" Candi said, "My fam. They don't know shit about me. I reckon nobody fucking does. I mean if you really think about it."

"Don't they care about you?"

"Of course they fucking care about me! They're my fucking fam, aren't they?"

"Sorry, Candi. I didn't mean to,"

"Don't fucking apologize, pardner. You know I fucking hate it when you apologize. And don't you dare fucking say you're sorry for that either!"

Mike hesitated, smiled, and then said, "Sorry"

They laughed together.

✳ ✳ ✳

"So, pardner," Candi said, "What about you? What would you want your funeral to be like?"

"Actually. I think I'd like to be buried way out in west Texas. Out in the Big Bend country. In a simple pine box. In a lonely graveyard in Terlingua."

"Why the fuck do you wanna be buried way the fuck out there? I mean it's in the middle of fucking nowhere. Don't get me wrong. It's fucking beautiful. But it's still out in the middle of fucking nowhere."

"If I was buried way out there. Then only the people who really gave a shit about me. Would be willing to make that long drive to be at my funeral. And I'll bet there wouldn't be many of them either."

"That's weird," Candi said.

"What's weird?"

"Well. I reckon I just imagined your funeral really different from that."

"Oh yeah?"

"Yep. I kinda figured that you'd have this huge fucking funeral. You know? Like with hundreds of fucking people. I mean standin room only. And all your friends and fam. And all your fancy-schmancy college friends too. And all your students would be there. You know? Everybody who's life you fucking influenced by bein a philosophy teacher. And makin them fucking think about the meaning of life and all"

"I guess never thought about it that way," Mike said.

"Hey! Wait a second. How the fuck does a Yankee like you? Even fucking know about a place like Terlingua, Texas? Way the fuck out in the Big Bend country?"

"A friend of mine went out there recently," Mike said, thinking of Sonny Quillan.

"Oh yeah? And how does he like it?"

"Well. He's never coming back. That's for sure."

"Wow. He musta really liked it out there then? Course. I reckon after livin in fucking Connecticut like ya'll did. When he went out there. He musta thought he fucking died and went to heaven."

"Something like that..." Mike said. "I got an invitation in the mail to visit him out there."

"Oh yeah? Did you go?"

"No," Mike said, "I didn't go. I mean I should've gone. But I just didn't..."

✷✷✷

"So," Candi said, "What song would you want played at your funeral?"

"Can we stop talking about funerals, please? It's depressing, for Chrissakes."

"It's part of the fucking game. And you fucking promised you'd play along."

"Ok"

"So. What song would you want played at your funeral? You know. A song to sum up your whole life. And give everybody at your funeral a chance to think back on you."

"Well," Mike said, "maybe *Dust in the Wind*."

Candi pinched her nose. She made the sound a buzzer makes when you get the wrong answer on a gameshow and pointed her thumb down. "What the fuck? *Dust in the Wind*? Come on, pardner! That's a horrible God-awful fucking song. You just gotta fucking pick another song. That one just ain't gonna cut it. Sorry!"

"What? Wait a minute! You don't get to decide whether the song *I picked* for *my funeral* is not going to work. Ok? My funeral. My decision"

"Normally you'd be right. But that's the abso-fucking-lutely worse fucking song for a funeral. Ever! I mean I just can't let you pick it. Sorry"

"I think it's a great song."

"Why?"

"It will make people at my funeral think about the absurdity of human existence. And the futility of life. It will make people feel like I've felt. My entire fucking life. If only for a few minutes"

"Now why would you wanna go and fucking do that to people? Especially people who drove thousands of miles for your funeral? Way out into the west Texas desert. All the way to Terlingua. All because they actually gave two shits about you. You know what, pardner?" Candi said, chuckling. "I'm gonna have to blow a fuck-ton of strange dick to get all the way out there for your funeral."

Mike chuckled.

"But seriously, pardner. Makin everybody even more depressed about the," she raised her hands and made quotation marks with her fingers, *"absurdity of human existence,* at your funeral. That's just the last act of a desperate asshole, if you ask me."

"Ok, fine," Mike said, "Let's hear your perfect choice for a song at your funeral."

"Well. I don't know if I could pick just one song. I mean there's gotta be a fucking Baptist hymn. That's for damn sure. Maybe that hymn, *Gather at the River.* You know? The one that crazy young guy sings at the beginnin of *The Wild Bunch.* When he's holdin that gun on those people and actin all crazy? I fucking love that fucking scene!"

"Every time I visited my grandmother," Mike said, "she would tell me which Baptist hymn she wanted played at her funeral. Every time I saw her she would always remind me. Every time she would remind me that I was the only one she'd ever told. And that she was counting on me to remember."

"That's really sweet, pardner. So what hymn was it?"

"That's just it," Mike said, "When she finally died. I couldn't remember."

"What the fuck?"

"I know. I just couldn't remember. I still can't believe it."

"So what song did you decide on for her funeral?"

"I just opened up a hymnbook and randomly picked one."

"And which one was it?"

"I don't remember."

"Goddammit, pardner. That's some seriously fucked up shit right there."

"I know."

"Hey," Candi said. "Can we please forget about how you fucked over your own grandma? And basically shit all over her memory. By forgettin her favorite fucking hymn. And just get back to me choosin my funeral song?"

"Sure"

"Ok. So there's gonna be a Baptist hymn. And of course. Two or three of my birthday songs. And maybe even,"

"Hey, wait a minute," Mike said, "You only get *one* song. That's the game. I played along. And all you did was give me shit about my one song. So you only get one song. Got it?"

Candi smiled at him and caressed his shoulder with her trigger finger. "I fucking love it when you tell me how it's gonna be. You know that? My clit is sooo hard for you right now, pardner."

"Cut it out. And just pick one fucking song already."

"You think you could pull over right up here? Maybe slap me around a little? Shove your dick in my pussy. And then talk that way to me some more? I mean. You're makin me really really fucking wet."

"I'm serious, Candi," Mike said, pushing her hand away. "Stop it."

"Hey! I can't fucking help it if I'm a woman. And," she made quotation marks, "*ergo*, a cock-teasin, dick-lovin, cum-catchin whore. I mean. That's just the way God fucking made us. And don't act like you don't like it either."

"Will you just pick a funeral song and tell me already?"

"What for? You won't fucking remember it if I do? And then! You'll probably just end up pickin some random fucking song. Or even worse! You'll play Dust in the fucking Wind at my funeral! Listen up, pardner. If you play *Dust in the Wind* at my fucking funeral. I'll come back and haunt your fucking ass for all fucking eternity! You got it?"

"Got it"

"Hey," Candi said, "I think I almost got my song! I narrowed it down to two songs. Both of em are my birthday songs. The first one is a little-known classic by Mr. Jimmy Buffet. And it's called *Stories We could Tell*. And the other is my birthday song from last year. It's a country song called, *I Ain't Here for a Long Time, I'm Here for a Good Time* by King George."

"Who?"

"George Strait"

"So which one are you going to pick?"

"It's gonna have to be... Well, uh...Dammit. Umm... Well. Uh, fuck me...Well,"

"Tell you what, Candi. Since both of those songs sound to me. Like they're both perfect for you. If I have anything to do with it. I'll make sure they play *both* of them at your funeral."

"Wow, pardner. I'm really a fucky girl! You really mean it?"

"I do"

"And you'll remember?"

"Yes," Mike said, smiling, "I'll try to remember this time."

"You promise?"

"Yeah, I promise."

✳ ✳ ✳

"So. Since your first pick *Dust in the Wind*, fucking sucked the big sweaty one,' Candi said, "What's it gonna be, pardner? What's your funeral song gonna be?"

"Ok, fine," Mike said. "How about, *Still Crazy After All These Years* by Paul Simon?"

"Never heard it. But it's gotta cool title. That's a start, I reckon."

"Have you ever heard of Simon and Garfunkel?"

"Yeah, sure. I heard of em. But I couldn't tell you anythin they sung."

"Never mind then"

"So give me a line from that song."

"Why?"

"I mean. If it's gonna fucking be the song they play at your funeral. Then give me a line from it. So I can imagine what people are gonna hear. And what they're gonna think when it's playin. After all. It's my fucking job to decide whether or not it's a shitty funeral song. Since you obviously can't be fucking trusted to do it right."

Mike thought to himself. He smiled and then said, "Well. There's this great line in that song. And it seems like the older I get. The more that line makes sense to me. It goes, *and I would not be convicted by a jury of my peers, still crazy after all these years...'*"

"Huh," Candi said.

"Well?"

"Wait for it, cowboy," Candi scratched her chin dramatically.

"Well?"

"I think that's the perfect fucking song for you, pardner."

"Thanks"

✳ ✳ ✳

"Ok," Candi said, "Here's the final question in the, Plan Your Own Funeral Game. Are you fucking ready for this shit?"

"Yes"

"What would your famous last words be?"

"Wow," Mike said, "That's a really tough one."

"I know, I know," Candi said, beaming with pride, "I just made that shit up. Just now"

"Famous last words, huh?"

"Yep"

"Remember before?" Mike said, "When I told you about Socrates?"

"Sure," Candi said. "He was that Greek dude who asked waaay too many fucking questions. So they made him drink that fucking poisoned wine? Right?"

"Yeah, *that dude*," Mike said.

"What did you say that poison was called again?"

"Hemlock. They mixed it with wine."

"Let me tell you somethin. They'd have to mix that shit with somethin a whole lot fucking stronger than Boone's Farm to get me to fucking drink it! That's for damn sure!"

"Whenever I think about famous last words," Mike said, "I think about Socrates. Before he drank the hemlock. He said to his disciples- Do not be afraid of death. For when you die. One of two things will happen. And neither of them is cause for fear. When you die. Either death is like a dreamless sleep. Which means you feel no pain and there's no suffering. Or! The soul lives on after the body. To have many more adventures. Either way. Socrates said- Death is not something to be feared."

"Wow," Candi said, "That's pretty fucking cool."

"I know. There's a reason Socrates is considered the father of philosophy."

"Yep. Pretty fucking cool. But pretty fucking dumb too. I mean, if you ask me."

"What?"

"I mean. What if after you die? Your soul fucking goes to the bad place?"

"What do you mean?"

"I mean. Soc said your soul might live on after you die. And have adventures. Am I right?"

"Right"

"But Soc made it sound like. Anywhere your soul went after you die. Would be a fun adventure. But what if your soul went to the bad place? I mean. There's no way in hell that's gonna be a fucking fun adventure." She chuckled and said, "Pun fucking intended, pardner...Get it?"

"But, Candi. Socrates didn't believe in hell."

"Who gives a shit whether Soc believed in the bad place or not. That's not my fucking point here. My fucking point is. That there *might be* a bad place. And if there might be. *Just might be* a bad place. Then you got every fucking reason to be afraid of dyin and goin there. That's all I'm sayin."

"I guess I never thought of it that way."

"Sorry, pardner. Don't get me wrong here. Soc is still a cool dude in my book. I mean. When he fucking stepped up and drank that hemlock shit. He fucking manned up and checked out on his own terms. And you know how I feel about that. But those last words of his. Nothin but a bunch of warm fuzzy philosophy bullshit. If you ask me"

"Thank you very much, Candi."

"For what?"

"For knocking my hero off his pedestal. I really really appreciate that."

"Anytime, pardner," Candi said, unwrapping a blowpop and shoving into her mouth, "Any fucking time."

* * *

"You wanna hear some fucking sweet famous last words?" Candi said.

"Sure"

"Well. If you want some awesome fucking kick-ass famous last words. Then there's only one man for the fucking job. That's right! You gotta go to my main man. The man himself. The man of the fucking hour. Yep! The man of the fucking hour for like two thousand years now. Drum roll please!" She drummed her hands on the dashboard. "JC!"

"Oh, for Chrissakes," Mike said, "not this Jesus shit again."

"You remember JC's famous last words? Don't you, pardner? After all those assholes beat the shit out of him. And then nailed his fucking ass to that fucking cross. JC said- Father, forgive them, for they know not what they do. You remember that?"

"Yeah, Candi. I remember."

"I mean not only did JC stand up for people who couldn't stand up for themselves. But JC fucking forgave people who didn't even want to be forgiven. And didn't even fucking deserve to be forgiven either. Now those are some bad-ass famous last words. Yep! JC totally kicks Socrates' lily ass!"

"Hey, wait a minute," Mike said. "I just remembered something. Actually. Those weren't Jesus' last words."

"Uh, yeah they fucking were too."

"No, no," Mike said. "I'm serious." He thought back to Harold Attridge's New Testament class at Yale Divinity School.

"I'm fucking serious too," Candi said. "And you better think twice before you go and fuck with JC's famous last words."

"Yeah. I remember now," Mike said. "*After* Jesus asked God to forgive the people who crucified him. Right before he actually died. Jesus said- Father, into your hands I commit my spirit. And that's actually when Jesus breathed his *last* breath. And *those* were actually Jesus' famous last words."

"Holy shit, pardner," Candi said, frowning. "I think you're right. No wait. You *are* fucking right. Well, goddammit. You mean to tell me I've been wrong this whole fucking time? Well fuck me all the way to the bad place."

"But think about it this way," Mike said. "Jesus did say to forgive them while he was actually hanging on the cross. I mean *while* he was dying. So technically. They could still count as his famous last words."

"Nope. No fucking way, pardner," Candi said, frowning. "You're right. I was wrong."

"Hey, Candi. There's no need to take it so hard. Ok?"

"I'm ok, pardner. I mean I reckon…Well I reckon it's just… Now I kinda fucking know how I made you feel a minute ago. I mean. I went and knocked *your* hero off his pedestal. So then you went and knocked *mine* off his cross. I reckon it's only fair…"

✳✳✳

"Well, pardner," Candi said, "Now that me and you are all alone. With no more heroes, I mean. I reckon me and you are gonna have to come up with some famous last words of our own. Am I right?"

"I guess so"

"So… What are yours gonna be then?"

"Well, whatever they end up being," Mike said, chuckling. "After our little conversation about pedestals and crosses. Whenever I end up saying them. I'm going to be worried when I do."

They laughed together.

"You know what, pardner? When I first *blew* you…Uh, I mean. When I first *met* you," Candi smiled and winked. "I reckon. Not only had you fucking forgotten how to *take* a joke. You'd fucking forgotten how to *tell* a joke too."

"I hadn't forgotten, Candi. I just didn't remember… remember?"

✳ ✳ ✳

Mike just sat there now. The sunset melted over the big Texas sky like a heap of red white and blue candle wax. Mike tried to remember whether Candi had been smiling when she raised that pistol and fired that final shot. That final shot, he thought, which had saved his life. And right then he decided to decide that Candi had been smiling, even though he couldn't remember for sure. And all because that's the way Mike wanted to remember her...

"My fucking pussy hurts like the goddamned bad place," Candi said.

Mike gasped and turned to face her. Candi was lying there on her side in the dust. She kneaded her abdomen with both hands. And of course, she was smiling.

"Candi!" Mike said.

"God fucking dammit," Candi said. Her voice was hoarse. Dried sweat and blood were cached in globs of dirt all over her face. "Holy shit, pardner. Let me tell you. My fucking pussy hasn't hurt this fucking bad. Since that night in Rock Ridge after the Number 6 Dance later on."

"Candi!" Mike said. He turned to face her and bent over to hug her.

Candi pushed him away. "Hey, asshole! What part of- I'm in fucking pain because I just got the shit raped outta me? Do you not fucking understand?"

"Sorry, Candi. Sorry"

"Goddammit, pardner! How many fucking times am I gonna have to fucking tell you? You know I fucking hate it when you fucking apologize!" She moaned and then rolled over on her back. "Fuck me."

"You're alive."

"Yep. I'm alive alright. I reckon the whole checkin out on your own terms thing ain't as easy as I fucking thought it was, huh?"

"I can't believe it."

"And speakin of not bein dead, pardner. How the fuck did *you* survive? I mean I figured you for a gonner for sure."

Mike just shrugged.

"Well. Let me tell you, pardner. We both got real fucky today. I mean. It just don't get any fuckier than this shit right here. Am I right?"

"I still can't believe you're alive."

"You know what? I musta come to about an hour ago. I mean it took me awhile to come back to my senses and all. So I've just been layin here watchin you all that time. And you were in like a fucking trance or somethin. It was weird. What in the fuck were you thinkin about?"

"Nothing"

"Oh come on, pardner. Just fucking tell me. What were you thinkin about?"

"Nothing, Candi"

"Were you thinkin about fucking my dead body?"

"What?"

"You were! I fucking knew it! You were thinkin about fucking my dead body! Weren't you?"

"What the hell?"

"You're fucking sick, pardner! You know that?" Candi laughed. She coughed up some blood and let it ooze down from her bottom lip into the dust. "You're a fucking sick, dead-whore rapin pervert!" She laughed some more.

"You're the sick one," Mike said.

"I just call em like I see em," Candi said. She glanced down her body. "Hey, pardner. Where the fuck are my shorts?"

"They must still be in the car."

"See! I was fucking right about you!" Candi laughed again, "Yep. So when you thought I was dead. You took off my fucking shorts. So you could fuck my dead pussy. I mean how else would you know where my shorts were? It all fucking makes sense now!"

"Oh for Chrissakes, Candi. Let me get them for you."

"Don't fucking sweat it, pardner. I'll get up and get em in a minute. Besides. After what my poor pussy's been through," she waved her hand back and forth over her crotch, fanning it, "She probably needs the fresh air. Know what I mean, jelly bean?"

Mike didn't laugh and he didn't smile.

"You know what I always wondered, pardner? And maybe since you're a philosopher. Maybe you'll fucking know the answer to this one. I always wondered. If you rape a whore? Does it really count as rape? Or is it just more like shopliftin?"

Mike hung his head and still didn't laugh.

Candi did laugh, even louder than before. "Oh come on, pardner! That's some funny fucked up shit, right there."

✱✱✱

Mike watched Candi slide her hand slowly down her belly. She finally rested her open palm on a neatly trimmed patch of hair. He watched her gently slip her trembling fingers all the way down into her pussy. Candi closed her eyes and grimaced as she maneuvered her fingers around inside. "Good thing I broke all my nails off in that preacher-man's face, huh? Makes this shit a whole lot fucking easier. Let me tell you."

When Candi finally pulled her fingers out of her pussy, they were covered with black bloody ooze. "If you're gettin turned on right now, pardner. Then I'm gettin me another fucking ride back to Houston."

Mike looked away quickly.

"Not too fucking bad," Candi said. "Let me tell you. I've seen fucking better. And I've seen fucking worse too. I reckon I was just real fucky all those assholes had teensy-weensy little dicks." She wiped her fingers in the dirt. "Not like you, of course, pardner." She turned her head and winked at him.

Mike grimaced.

"So you really thought I was dead, huh?"

"Yeah"

"Just like Tom and Huck?"

"Yeah," Mike said, smiling, "Just like Tom and Huck."

"Well, pardner. Don't get me wrong here. I'm glad I made it. But! I reckon this means I'm not gonna get to see my own funeral either. And that kinda sucks the big strange sweaty one."

"I guess so"

"Dammit!" Candi said.

"You know, Candi. I would have played your funeral songs for you."

"Wow, pardner. You mean you didn't forget?"

"No. I remembered...remember?" Mike hoped that Candi would acknowledge his gesture, but she ignored him.

Candi looked back up at the sky and then closed her eyes again. She gritted her teeth. She raised her knees slowly and painfully up to her belly and then farted. She laughed out loud and said, "Oops! Look out there, pardner. Trust me! That's gonna be one smelly fucking fart. Better keep your fucking distance. That was a, my asshole just got raped kinda fart, right there!"

Mike couldn't help but wrinkle up his nose and face as he smelled the stench of Candi's fart on the warm breeze.

"I fucking warned you! Didn't I? Let me tell you. Those kinda farts. They fucking stink like the fucking bad place."

Candi grunted and groaned as she turned over on her side to face Mike. She reached around behind her, and Mike could tell she was digging with her finger into her asshole. "Let me tell you. As long as you can really squeeze out a good fart. Kinda like I just did. Then this part's a lot fucking easier. Trust me."

Mike watched her suddenly wince with pain. "Holy fuck!" she said. Candi jerked her hand back around and planted it in the dirt. She buckled into a fetal position. Mike noticed that her hand was covered in blackish blood and runny brown shit.

"Candi. We really need to get you to a hospital. And we need to call the police."

"No fucking way, pardner. I'm not goin to any fucking hospital. And we sure as shit ain't callin the fucking cops."

"But, Candi. I really think,"

"Listen up, pardner. You gotta promise me somethin. Promise me you won't take me to any fucking hospital. And you gotta promise me you won't call the fucking cops either. No matter what"

"But why?"

"I'll tell you later." Candi sat up slowly and painfully. "You promise, right?"

"Ok," Mike said, "I promise."

Candi raised her bloodied shitty hand up to her face and spit into her palm. And then she offered Mike a handshake. "You promise me, right?"

Mike took a deep breath and then took her hand. He nodded as he savored the warmth and strength of her grasp.

"Thanks, pardner"

"You promise you'll tell me why, later?"

"Yeah. I promise. But in the meanwhile. We better get the fuck outta Dodge. I mean before the cops or anybody else shows up here. I wouldn't bet on us gettin this fucky twice in one day." She struggled to get to her feet.

Mike jumped up. He bent down to take her arm and said, "Here, let me help you."

Candi was on her knees in front of him now. She looked up at him, frowned and said, "I don't need any help, pardner."

"You're hurt, Candi." Mike grabbed her arm. "Let me help you."

"I don't fucking need any help." She jerked her arm away and lost her balance. She fell back down into the dirt. "Keep your goddamned fucking hands off me."

"Ok," Mike said, backing away.

Candi struggled back up to her feet. She leaned against the car, breathing heavily and wincing in pain. "Well, pardner. Since you're sooo fucking good at rememberin these days. Do you remember where you said you'd take me?"

"No," Mike said, "where?"

"You're close," Candi said, "you're awful close..."

Mike was puzzled.

Candi frowned and said, "You don't fucking remember, do you?"

"Uh, just give me a minute. Ok?"

"Don't you remember, pardner? Right before you went off into the bushes to take a piss? You promised we were gonna ride off into the sunset together. And we were gonna go..."

"Oh yeah!" Mike said, "Nowhere special"

"Yep," Candi said, still frowning. She stared down at the dirt, sighed and said, "Yep. Nowhere *fucking* special..."

"See," Mike said, "I actually didn't forget..."

"Yep"

"I didn't forget..."

"Yep"

"Candi, I didn't forget... I just didn't remember...remember?"

"Yep"

"Candi? Are you sure you're ok?"

"Sure, pardner," Candi said, perking up with a sudden smile, "Let's ride!"

Chapter 21

How Mike and Candi laughed together;
Back to Houston, Texas;
A date at Miller Outdoor Theatre;
One more bridge to cross;
And what became of Mike and Candi afterwards

"You wanna hear a great fucking joke, pardner?" Candi said.

Mike and Candi drove down 610 East on the south side of Houston.

For the last few hours, Candi had talked almost non-stop. And Mike had just listened. Candi had been telling him "whorror" stories. About what it was like for her in the backseats of cop cars. And about her long nights in the Harris, Grimes and Brazos county jails. And about the beds with arm and leg straps in the hospitals and half-way houses of Houston, Huntsville and Galveston.

Candi told Mike how much fun she'd had kicking in the crooked teeth of that fucktard. She told him how Bric couldn't stay hard and didn't cum when he was raping her. She told him how she damn near came when Dub was raping her. Though not because he had a big dick, but probably because he punched her during it. She told him how that preacher-man had raped her in the asshole- "I fucking knew he was a fucking faggot," she'd said to Mike.

Candi told Mike how she wished she'd been a better shot with her granddaddy's pistol. She told him how she thought it was really fucked up that those goddamned fucking assholes were gonna get to pawn her granddaddy's pistol and get rich, instead of her. She told him how she wished she'd bought the more expensive fake fingernails at Walgreens. So she could've fucking ripped that preacher-man's eyeball right out of his goddamned fucking skull- "Wouldn't that have been somethin to see, huh? Pun fucking intended," she'd said to Mike.

And then Candi told Mike, in way more excruciating detail than he would've preferred, how she always maneuvered and manipulated her body, especially her pussy muscles, during a rape. "It really fucking helps your pussy not get torn up so goddamn much," she'd said to Mike. "And it also helps that I'm sooo fucking good at it by now. You know the old sayin- Fucking practice makes fucking perfect."

Mike was now sick to his stomach.

"Well, pardner?" Candi said, "Do you wanna hear this fucking joke or not?"

Mike shrugged.

"Ok, then. Here goes. What has eight legs and makes a woman scream?"

Mike shrugged again.

"Gang rape..."

Mike swerved the car over two lanes of traffic and exited Kirby near Reliant Stadium.

"Hey," Candi shouted, "What the fuck are you doin?"

Mike sped down the exit ramp and then pulled their ride into an empty parking lot. He stopped the car, killed the engine and then shouted, "I can't fucking take it anymore, Candi! I just can't take it!"

"What the fuck are you talkin about, pardner?"

"I just can't take it anymore!"

"What do you mean *you* can't fucking take it anymore?"

"You know what I mean, dammit! I mean. What happened *back there*."

"You mean what happened back there? At that goddamned roadside park?"

"Yeah, back there"

"You mean back there? Where I got fucking raped in my pussy? And in my fucking goddamned asshole?"

"Stop it"

"You mean back there? Where I called out for you to fucking help me?"

"Please, Candi, don't..."

"You mean back there? Where I called out your name, pardner? Back there where I called out your fucking name? So you could help me? So you could fucking save me? You mean back there? Where all you fucking did was just stand there? And fucking do nothin? Is that what you fucking mean? You sorry ass piece of fucking shit! Answer me! Is that what you mean?"

Mike broke down and cried. He beat his forehead against the steering wheel.

"That's right! You sorry fucking sonuvvabitch! I called you by your fucking name! And you still didn't do shit to help me! You better tell me right now that you didn't hear me! I mean. If you didn't hear me...that would at least be somethin, right?"

"Please, Candi"

"I fucking said- You better tell me you *didn't* hear me! Say it, goddammit! You *didn't* fucking hear me when I called out your name! Say it!"

"I *did* hear you!" Mike yelled. "I heard you. I heard you. I heard you..."

Candi drew back into silence and fell back against her seat. "What the fuck?"

"I fucking heard you," Mike said. He cried and snot dripped from his nostrils. "I heard you call my name. And I still didn't fucking do anything. I just stood there..."

"Oh my fucking God," Candi said, "Oh my fucking God."

"I can't take it anymore," Mike said, "I just can't take it anymore."

Candi grinned and said, "*You* can't take it anymore? *You?* Well! Well that's just too fucking bad, pardner!" She leaned in towards him and whispered, "Because you're gonna fucking take it...Just like I fucking took it back there in that goddamned roadside park. Just like everybody in this goddamned fucking roach motel! Fucking takes it every fucking day! You hear me?"

Mike buried his face in his hands and cried.

✳✳✳

They sat there in that parking lot for a long while. Candi stared out her window at the radiant, sparkling lights of Reliant Stadium, juxtaposed against the darkened, once glorious facade of the Astrodome nearby. Mike had finally stopped crying. He rested his head on the steering wheel.

"I'll bet you thought I was gonna say, spider..." Candi whispered, breaking their silence.

"What?" Mike said, sniffling.

"I'll bet you thought I was gonna say, spider..."

"What do you mean?"

"You know. The punch line to that joke I told you before. Remember? What has eight legs and makes a woman scream? I'll bet you thought I was gonna say, spider... Didn't you?" Candi laughed out loud. "But then I went and said- gang rape, instead. You shoulda seen your fucking face, pardner. That shit was fucking priceless..."

Mike didn't laugh.

"Oh, come on, pardner," Candi said, "That's still some funny fucked up shit right there!"

But Mike still didn't laugh.

There are two kinds of laughter in the world. There is a despairing laughter at the joke which is human life, which bubbles up from a sudden and acute sensation of feeling trapped in the world, with nowhere to go and the awareness of being hunted down like a wounded animal. And then there is all other laughter...

Mike wondered- Is it worse to be the one who got raped by four men in a roadside park? Or to be the one who just stood there watching, and did nothing to help, while somebody else got raped by four men in a roadside park? And at that moment, inexplicably, Mike finally burst out laughing.

"That's it, pardner," Candi said. "See! I told you that was a funny fucking joke!"

Mike laughed harder than he'd ever laughed before.

"There you go, pardner. Now you fucking get it." Candi slapped her knees and laughed. "I told you that was some funny fucked up shit..."

✳ ✳ ✳

A little later that night, Mike and Candi drove down Main Street towards downtown.

"Hey, pardner," Candi said, "There's somethin under my fucking seat. I just kicked it."

"What is it?"

Candi leaned forward and reached under her seat. "Holy fucking shit!" She lifted up her copy of *Moby Dick*. "Wow! Can you fucking believe this shit?" She hugged the book. She thumbed through its dog-eared pages and then read aloud, "But in pursuit of those far mysteries we dream of, or in tormented chase of that demon phantom that, some time or other, swims before all human hearts; while chasin such over this round globe, they either lead us on in barren mazes or midway leave us whelmed..."

Candi looked puzzled for a moment, but she smiled and said, "Ain't that fucking beautiful, pardner?"

"Yes," Mike said, looking over at Candi, "Yes, it is..."

"I don't know what the fuck it means," Candi said. "But it's fucking beautiful anyways!" She cradled *Moby Dick* in her arms like a baby doll. "So what *does* it mean, pardner?"

Mike watched her cradling the book. He smiled and said, "It means...no matter how fucked up things get...they'll always get better."

Candi smiled and said, "I knew there was a reason I liked this fucking book. More than any other fucking book in the whole wide fucking world."

"Hey, wait a minute," Mike said playfully. "How can *this* be your favorite book? It doesn't start with- Once upon a time... And there's not even a happy ending."

"Hey, motherfucker," Candi said, "Don't fucking ruin the end for me!"

"But I thought you said before that you'd already read it?"

"I did, I did," Candi said. "I reckon I was just hopin against fucking hope. You know? That this time..." she held up the book like it was a sacred relic. "That this time it might have a different ending. You know? A happy ending. Or at least a *happier* ending... You know what I mean, jelly bean?"

"I've heard of a story with a happy ending," Mike said. "But I've never heard of a story with a- *at least* happier ending."

"Well, pardner. Let me tell you. If life is fresh out of happy endings. Then I'll fucking settle for a- *at least a happier ending*... any fucking day of the week."

Mike chuckled.

"You think that's too much to ask for, pardner?"

"You mean, for a - *at least a happier ending*?"

Candi nodded.

"Well. I guess that all depends on who you're asking."

"Yep," Candi said, frowning, "I reckon you're right. I figured as fucking much..."

✳ ✳ ✳

Mike and Candi dropped off their ride at the rental place downtown. Mike had wanted to pick up some limes, club soda, and Tanqueray, and then get a room at The Magnolia Hotel.

"But you promised me," Candi had said to him. "You promised that after our little odyssey was over. That you'd fucking take me out on a date to Miller Theatre."

"I didn't think you were serious."

"Fuck yeah, I was serious."

"You really want to go tonight? I mean after everything that's happened?"

"Fuck yeah, I really wanna go tonight. *Especially* after everythin that's fucking happened!"

"Not tonight, Candi"

"Listen up, pardner. Don't make me play the- I just got raped while you just fucking stood there and did nothin card, ok?"

And so with that having been said, Mike and Candi rode the rail from downtown Houston to Hermann Park.

They got to Miller Outdoor Theatre and found a spot on the grassy hill overlooking the stage. "Goddamn," Candi announced, still holding her copy of *Moby Dick*, "It's a beautiful fucking night. Huh, pardner? I mean. Looky at all those fucking stars! And looky at that beautiful Houston skyline!"

Mike noticed a couple with two kids on a nearby blanket. They began to pack up their picnic.

"I think this just might be the most beautiful fucking goddamned night ever!"

Mike and Candi sat down on the grass facing the stage, where several actors in colorful costumes were singing.

The couple finished packing their picnic and walked away, heading towards the other side of the hill.

"You're fucking right, Candi," Mike said loudly, almost shouting. He watched the family. "This is the most fucking, cocksucking, motherfucking beautiful night I've ever fucking seen!" He chuckled as the family fled.

Candi turned to him and whispered, "Hey, pardner. Shut the fuck up, will you? I mean some of us are tryin to watch the fucking show here."

Mike grinned and turned his attention to the stage.

"So what the fuck do they call this shit?" Candi said.

"They call this shit, opera."

"I know it's fucking opera, dammit. I mean. What do they call this particular show?"

"It's called, *Madame Butterfly*"

"And what language is that fucking bitch singin in?"

"Italian"

"But she's fucking Oriental?"

"What?"

"But she's Oriental?" Candi whispered, leaning into Mike. "So why the fuck is a fucking Oriental bitch singin in Italian?"

"Because," Mike said, sighing, "Puccini. The man who wrote the opera. He was Italian."

"But why the fuck did some Italian dude? Write a fucking opera about some Oriental bitch?"

"Hey, Candi," Mike said, smiling, "Shut the fuck up, will you? Some of us are trying to watch the fucking show here."

Candi grinned and said, "You're on your way to bein a real fucking dickhead. You know that?"

"Oh yeah?" Mike said, "Well you're *already* a real fucking cunt. Did you know that?"

She leaned in closer to him. She rested her hand on his thigh and said, "Did you just call me a fucking cunt?"

"You heard me...cunt."

"Yep, I sure did," Candi said, sliding her hand up his thigh. "And you know what?"

"What?"

She gripped his crotch, squeezed and said, "*I'm* the cuntenest cunt that ever did cunt." She let go and winked at him. "And *you're* the dickenest dick that ever did dick."

"I guess I am."

"Goddamn right we are. And I reckon that means we were kinda meant to be together. Am I right?"

"Goddamn right," Mike said, leaning into Candi's shoulder, "goddamn right."

* * *

After the show Mike and Candi strolled down the grassy hill towards a wooded path. "There's a lake over there, pardner. Let's go see it."

It was getting late and everyone was leaving Hermann Park. Mike and Candi walked alone down a gravel path adjacent to a cove in McGovern Lake where the paddleboats were docked. Ducks congregated along the bank near the trunks of trees. Mike noticed Candi stagger a little sometimes. Occasionally she'd place her trembling hand discreetly on her belly, but only for a brief moment.

"What the hell is that?" Mike said. He pointed to a large rat-like animal diving into the dark waters of the lake.

"It's a nutria," Candi said. "It's like a cross between a fucking beaver and a rat." Candi chuckled to herself. "Hey, pardner. I just said- fucking beaver."

"That thing was huge," Mike said, ignoring her comment. He stopped by the bank and knelt down to watch it swim away.

"Yep," Candi said, grinning. "But not nearly as fucking huge as a jackelope!"

Mike laughed. He turned around to face her and said, "Shut the fuck up. You dumb fucking cunt."

"I gotta say it, pardner. When we first fucking met. You were such a goddamned fucking dumbass."

Mike stepped forward and said, "And now?"

"Well. At least now I don't have to punch you in the fucking nuts. Just to get you to call me a cunt. I mean that's somethin, right?"

They meandered down the path towards the lake. They stopped at the base of a small footbridge that arched over the part of the cove that opened up into the lake. At the foot of the bridge there was slab in the sidewalk that read:

The
Tiffany & Co
Foundation
Bridge

"Well looky what we got here, pardner," Candi said, "another fucking bridge…"

Mike winced a little as those all too familiar words escaped Candi's lips.

"I shoulda figured as fucking much," Candi said. "It's kinda ironic. I mean if you really fucking think about it. Am I right?"

"I don't know if *ironic* is the right word," Mike said, choking on his words a little.

"Yep. One more bridge to fucking cross…"

"I wish," Mike said, "I could forget about the whole goddamned thing. You know?"

"No, pardner," Candi said. "You wish *I* could forget about the whole goddamned thing. There's a fucking difference, you know."

Mike stared down into the dirt, and then off over the serene surface of the lake. He felt an apology swelling up in his throat but choked it back.

"Don't you fucking dare," Candi said, staring him down. "I swear to fucking God."

Mike pressed his lips together tightly. He made a zipper motion across his mouth and then smiled at her.

"Let's face it, pardner. There's always gonna be just one more bridge to cross. If you know what I mean."

"Yeah, goddammit," Mike said, "I think I know exactly what you mean…"

Candi shrugged and then started walking up the bridge. She turned to Mike and said, "How about this fucking view, huh? It just doesn't get any better than-" Suddenly, Candi tripped. She stumbled backwards and fell down the bridge, rolling into the gravel.

"Candi!" Mike said. He rushed over to her side. He knelt beside her and tried to cradle her. "Are you ok?"

"Yeah, pardner. I'm fucking fine." She chuckled to herself. "Fucking *fine*…But you already fucking knew that, right?"

Mike nodded and smiled.

"Really, I'm fine. I hope you don't think a little trip and fall like that. Is gonna keep me from takin in that view of the lake from this bridge."

"I don't think that's such a good idea, Candi."

"Well I don't give a rat's fucking ass what you think, pardner."

"At least let me help you up."

"I can help myself."

"Candi, let me help you up, ok?"

"Get your goddamned fucking hands off me," Candi said. She jerked her body away from him and tumbled back down into the gravel. "I fucking said- I can fucking help myself. Got it?"

Mike stood up slowly and backed away a few steps. He watched Candi roll over and then struggle to her knees. She pressed her hands into the gravel and pushed her body up, but fell back down again.

Mike just stood there. Candi repeated her struggle. She took a deep breath and then finally hoisted herself up onto her feet. She wobbled for a moment, dizzy from the effort.

"Well, pardner," Candi said, trying to steady her body. "What do you fucking think about that, huh? I fucking told you. I don't need any of your fucking help."

"You know what, Candi," Mike said, shaking his head, "I think you're the stubbornest fucking cunt I've ever met."

Candi bowed as gracefully as she could possibly manage. She said in her best demur, Southern belle voice, "Why thank ya kindly, good sir."

They both laughed.

"Ok," Candi announced, "Let's fucking try this shit again." She bent down and snatched up her copy of *Moby Dick*. She walked slowly towards the bridge with careful, deliberate, and obviously painful steps.

As Candi finally reached the foot of the bridge, Mike moved forward towards her.

"Don't you fucking dare, pardner. I swear to fucking God."

Mike watched her take that first step onto the bridge. She was cringing as she climbed forward. He noticed a fresh, red bloodstain on her shorts in between her legs. She stopped suddenly, breathing heavily and gripping her abdomen.

Mike moved forward towards her.

"I said- Don't you fucking dare!"

"Shut the fuck up!" Mike said, marching towards her. "Just shut the fuck up. You stupid stubborn fucking cunt!" He bent down and swept her up into his arms. She struggled at first but he held her tightly against his body. Finally she relaxed into his embrace. "Now," Mike said, "I'm going to carry you over this fucking bridge. I'm going to carry you over this fucking bridge. If it's the last goddamned thing I ever fucking do! You got it?"

"Yep. I got it, pardner."

"I said- You fucking got it?"

"Yeah," Candi said, smiling now, "I fucking got it, alright."

"Good," Mike said, "and don't you ever fucking forget it."

"Whatever you say, pardner. After all. You're the man round these parts."

Mike hoisted her up. He tightened his grasp around her and then started trudging slowly up the footbridge. As he ascended the small footbridge, he leaned forward into each slow difficult step, steadying the weight of both their bodies. He felt the tense muscles of Candi's bruised and battered body find repose in his strained embrace. He felt her arms tighten around his taut neck and shoulders, and then melt again into a gentle hug. He felt her copy of *Moby Dick* pressing into his chest. He felt her fingers softly caress the nape of his neck, like a lover might do in quiet moments after making love.

"If you think about it, pardner," Candi whispered to him. "This is the second time you've picked me up and carried me over a fucking bridge."

"Yeah," Mike said, "I guess it is."

"Does this mean I owe you another blowjob?"

Mike chuckled and said, "I thought I told you to shut the fuck up?"

"Oh yeah, sorry"

"Did you just apologize to me?"

'What?"

"Candi? Did you just apologize to me?"

"No"

"I think you did"

"Oh yeah, pardner? Well you know what I think?"

'What?"

"I think it's your turn to shut the fuck up."

"It's a deal."

Mike finally reached the apex of the bridge. He stopped and turned them towards the lake. He took a few steps forward and then leaned over, propping up Candi's body between him and the wooden railing of the bridge. "How's this for a view?" Mike said to her.

"I'd say I got the best seat in the fucking house."

"It really is a beautiful night."

"It's the most beautiful fucking night...fucking ever."

Mike smiled and leaned into her, savoring the faint hint of raspberry mingled with sweat, dirt and blood.

"There's usually a big ass fucking fountain in the middle of this lake," Candi said. "It shoots water up like a thousand feet in the fucking air. I wish it was goin."

Mike gently dusted gravel off Candi's bruised knees.

"See those buildings all lit up over there," Candi said. She pointed across the lake. "That's the fucking Texas Medical Center over there. See the top of that building? The one that's glowin all red? It changes colors, you know. I mean. It's all different colors all the time. Sometimes it's blue, green, red or whatever. It sure is beautiful, ain't it?"

"Yes"

"That's what the Las Vegas strip looks like, you know? All fucking lit up and beautiful like that."

"When did you go to Vegas?"

"Never been," Candi said. "But I imagine that's what the Las Vegas fucking strip looks like. I mean. I'll bet it's fucking beautiful."

"It is beautiful..." Mike said, looking at Candi, "But not nearly as beautiful as this..."

Candi didn't notice him looking at her. She just stared up at the big bright colorful lights of the Texas Medical Center. "Well I sure am glad you like it, pardner. And I sure am glad I brought you here."

"I'm glad too"

All of sudden the fountain in the middle of the lake bubbled. A giant water spout shot up high into the air, splashing down over the surface of the dark water.

"Holy fucking shit!" Candi said. She pointed at the towering column of water. "Looks like it's our fucky night, pardner!"

Mike and Candi both felt a clean, cool mist blow across their faces, carried over the bridge by the midnight breeze.

Candi grunted and groaned as she shifted her body to turn and face Mike. She smiled and said, "Guess what, pardner?"

"What?"

"I finally thought up my famous last words."

"Just now?"

"Yep, just now"

"Wow"

"You wanna hear em?"

"Sure"

Candi leaned into Mike and pulled him closer. She softly kissed his cheek and then said, "Remember me, to whoever rides by…"

Mike smiled and said, "I will, Candi. I promise." He leaned in for another kiss.

Candi drew her head back. She frowned and said, "That ain't how it works, pardner. The whole fucking point of somebody's," she made her quotation marks in the air with her fingers, "*famous last words*, is that they're the *last* fucking words that get said."

"Oh, so that's how it works, huh?"

"Goddamn right! Now, let's try this shit again. Ok? I'm gonna say my famous last words. And you're just gonna stand there smilin at me. Gazin into my fucking baby blue eyes. Just like the hero always does when he finally gets the girl. The music's gonna play. Probably another George Strait song. One with lots of good fiddle in it. And then the fucking flick is gonna be over. Roll the fucking credits! The fucking end!"

"The *fucking* end?"

"Yep! The *fucking* end…Trust me, pardner. That's the only kinda end there is these days. So you think you got it?"

"Yeah, sure. I got it"

"So you're not gonna fuck up my famous last words this time?"

"No way," Mike said, "I know how it works now."

"You sure bout that?"

"Let's see," Mike said. He scratched his chin in mock contemplation. "You're going to say your famous last words to me. And then I'm going to look into your eyes and,"

"No goddammit! You're gonna *gaze* into my fucking eyes. *Gaze!* You gotta fucking *gaze!* I mean. The hero always gazes when he gets the fucking girl. You got the fucking girl, pardner. So be sure to fucking gaze."

"Ok, ok. I'm going to *gaze* into your, fucking eyes. Because I'm the hero and I got the girl."

"Yep"

"And then the music will play. And then it's the end."

"It's the what?"

"Oh yeah. It's the *fucking* end. I almost forgot."

"You didn't forget, pardner," Candi said, grinning, "You just didn't remember... remember?"

"You know," Mike said, smiling back at her. He cradled her in his arms. "Those would actually make for some pretty memorable famous last words."

"What?"

"You know. What we've been saying back and forth to each other. About forgetting and not really forgetting. And remembering..."

"No fucking way," Candi said. "My famous last words are waaaaaay fucking better."

"I don't know, Candi. I think those other words are pretty damn good too."

"Well then. If you think they're sooo fucking great. Then why don't you just fucking go and put them in your fucking book then?"

"Actually, I think I just might do that."

Candi frowned and said, "So, pardner. Does that mean you're not gonna put *my* famous last words in your book?"

"I'll have to think about it. Sorry..."

"You don't sound very fucking sorry."

"That's because I'm not."

Candi smiled at him.

"After all," Mike said. "*I am* the man. And I'm also the hero around these parts. And I did get the girl, right? So that means I don't have to be sorry about shit. Right?"

Candi smiled. She leaned into Mike, pulling him closer. She softly kissed his cheek and said, "Remember me, to whoever rides by..."

***

Candi swore to Mike that she felt better...

So after carrying her the rest of the way over the small footbridge, Mike put Candi back down and let her walk alongside him.

"See, pardner," Candi said, grunting. She limped with each painful step. "I told you I was okay. It's like I told you before-Sometimes you just gotta walk it off."

"Let me call us a cab?" Mike said.

"No fucking way, pardner." Candi gripped her copy of *Moby Dick*. "Let me tell you. If I can't ride shotgun with you, then I'm not ridin at all... You got that?

"Got it"

Mike and Candi walked slowly south down Hermann Park Drive. They took a right on Cambridge Street and then walked down past the gates of The Houston Zoo. As they continued to walk down Cambridge, across the street from the Texas Medical Center, Mike noticed a bum sleeping on nearly every park bench. They walked all the way around to the RICE/HERMANN PARK railway platform.

Mike and Candi sat on a bench on the platform, waiting for the next rail to arrive. It was past midnight now and they were all alone.

'So, Candi," Mike said. "Are we still headed for, nowhere special?"

"Fuck yeah, we are. Where the fuck else would we be fucking goin?"

Mike smiled and said, "I don't know about you. But I could use a long hot shower. And a few cocktails"

"You said it, pardner. Oh! And you better fucking be takin me back to The Magnificent Magnolia Hotel tonight."

"Of course"

"And you better fucking be makin me gin and tonics in the bathroom again! With lots and lots and lots of Tanqueray!"

"How'd you guess?"

"And this time! You better fucking be gettin us a king size bed."

"Whatever you say"

"And this time, pardner," Candi said, resting her hand on his knee. "You better fucking stay sober long enough to fuck my fucking brains out."

Mike smiled. He placed his hand on top of hers and said, "I wouldn't miss it for the whole world."

"Holy fucking shit!" Candi said, pulling her hand away. "I can't fucking wait to have me another bubble bath. Goddammit that's gonna feel fucking great! Let me tell you, pardner. I'm pretty fucking goddamn sure. The Magnificent Magnolia Hotel is the greatest fucking place in the whole wide world!"

"You know what I love about you, Candi?"

"Listen up, pardner. You can fucking tell me what you *like* about me anytime you wanna. But you better not ever fucking say that you *love* anythin about me. You got that?"

"Yeah, sure..."

"Well?"

"Well what?"

"Are you gonna fucking tell me what you *like* about me or not?"

"Ok, then. I *like* it that you think everywhere you go is the best place in the whole wide world."

"Maybe that's because I've never been nowhere special... You ever fucking think about that?"

"No, Candi. I don't think that's it at all. I think it's more than that, actually."

"Hey. Whatever you fucking say, pardner. I mean. After all. These days you're the fucking man round these parts. Am I right?"

"And don't forget, hero?"

"Yeah, yeah, yeah. You're the fucking man. *And* the fucking hero."

"So if I'm the man *and* the hero? Then that means in the end? I get the girl. Right?"

"You mean to tell me? You wanna be the fucking man? *And* be the fucking hero? *And* you wanna get the fucking girl in the fucking end?"

"Why not?"

"So I reckon this means that now. You wanna try and wear a fucking cowboy hat too?"

"Yeah, actually. I definitely want to get one before we leave Houston."

"Whatever you say, pardner"

"You're going to have to help me pick one out, you know?"

"Whatever you say, pardner. You're the man"

"So you really think I can pull off wearing a cowboy hat?"

"You're gonna pull it off," Candi said, "or you're gonna fucking die tryin. That's for damn sure."

"Well then. That's exactly what I'm going to do."

"You know what, pardner?" Candi said, gazing at Mike. "I believe you fucking will…"

✳ ✳ ✳

"Hey, pardner. The rail's gonna be here soon," Candi said. "And that means my fucking appointment with Dr. John better be pretty damn quick." She whimpered in pain as she got up from her seat.

Mike chuckled and said, "You're not going to abort another one of my babies are you?"

Candi laughed and said, "Hey! Fuck you, pardner! It's not my fucking fault I keep havin to flush these little fucking bastards down the john. It's your goddamned fault, you know?"

"How is it my fault?"

"I already fucking told you like a thousand fucking times!" Candi said, still laughing. "I mean. It's you're fucking fault. Because you're the fucking dick who came in my mouth on The Baytown Bridge!"

"Yeah…you're right…Yeah, I am," Mike said. He laughed along with her. Mike sat up straight. He raised his chin into the air enacting a kind of royal proclamation. "Yeah! I am!" he said loudly. "*I'm* the fucking dick who came in your mouth on The Baytown Bridge!"

"And *me!*" Candi proclaimed, mimicking his proud gestures, "That makes me the fucking cunt-whore who swallowed all your cum on The Baytown Bridge!"

"Yes!" Mike said, "Yes, it does indeed!"

They laughed together.

***

Mike waited on the bench while Candi went to the bathroom. Mike watched down the darkened tracks for an approaching rail. He glanced over and spotted Candi's copy of *Moby Dick* on her empty seat. He reached over and grabbed the book. He thumbed through its dog-eared, dirty, blood-stained and crinkled pages. He read over some passages he'd highlighted in college. He even noticed where Candi had written down some of her own remarks, and drawn smiley faces next to them. Mike smiled. He lifted the open book to his nose and then took a deep breath. He could smell Candi all over the battered pages of the venerable tome.

Mike heard the sound of the rail approaching. Candi was still gone to the bathroom. Mike lowered the book and thumbed through it sacred pages again. Mike spotted the rail approaching. Candi was still gone to the bathroom. And then... On the front page of the book. In the blank space between the title MOBY DICK and the name HERMAN MELLVILLE. Mike noticed that Candi had written down in her childish scrawl- *Remember me, to whoever rides by...*

THE FUCKING END

Candi's List of Flicks You Just Gotta Fucking See

Lonesome Dove (1989)
The Man Who Shot Liberty Valance (1962)
The Wild Bunch (1969)
Rio Bravo (1959)
Time Bandits (1981)
The Muppet Movie (1979)
Bring Me the Head of Alfredo Garcia (1974)
Blazing Saddles (1974)
Pat Garret and Billy the Kid (1973)
Ride the High Country (1962)
Sky Scraper (1996)

Mike and Candi's "little odyssey" Playlist

or, the unofficial SOUNDTRACK for
Candi, or the optimist

Whenever Kindness Fails, Robert Earl Keen
(beginning credits rolling)
Baby Blue, George Strait
Key Largo, Bertie Higgins
Walking in Memphis, Mark Cohn
If the South Had Won, Hank Williams Jr.
Long Line of Losers, Kevin Fowler
The Perfect Country and Western Song, David Allen Coe
Earthbound, Rodney Crowell
Sweet Home Alabama, Lynyrd Skynyrd
Knockin on Heaven's Door, Bob Dylan
Shall We Gather at the River, Andy Griffith
Here for a Good Time, George Strait
Stories We Could Tell, Jimmy Buffet
Dust in the Wind, Kansas
Still Crazy After All These Years, Paul Simon
The Cowboy Rides Away, George Strait (ending credits rolling)